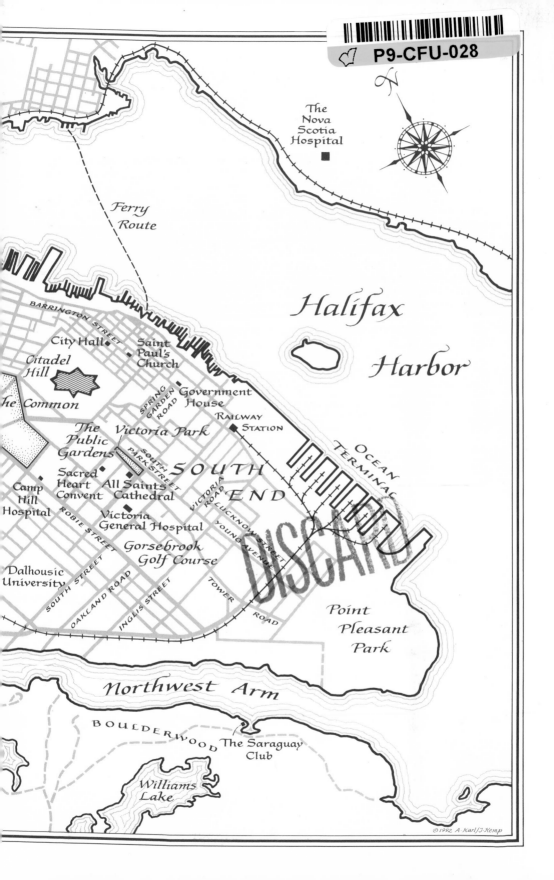

The Nova Scotia Hospital

Ferry Route

Halifax Harbor

BARRINGTON STREET

City Hall

Saint Paul's Church

Citadel Hill

The Common

Spring Garden Road

Government House

RAILWAY STATION

The Public Gardens

Victoria Park

SOUTH PARK STREET

OCEAN TERMINAL

Sacred Heart Convent

All Saints Cathedral

SOUTH END

VICTORIA ROAD

LUCKNOW STREET

Camp Hill Hospital

DISCARD

Dalhousie University

Victoria General Hospital

ROBIE STREET

Gorsebrook Golf Course

YOUNG AVENUE

SOUTH STREET

OAKLAND ROAD

INGLIS STREET

TOWER ROAD

Point Pleasant Park

Northwest Arm

BOULDERWOOD

The Saraguay Club

Williams Lake

© 1992 A. Karl/J. Kemp

BURDEN OF DESIRE

NAN A. TALESE

# D O U B L E D A Y

*NEW YORK*
*LONDON*
*TORONTO*
*SYDNEY*
*AUCKLAND*

# *BURDEN*
# *OF*
# *DESIRE*

## Robert
## MacNeil

PUBLISHED BY DOUBLEDAY
a division of Bantam Doubleday Dell Publishing Group, Inc.
666 Fifth Avenue, New York, New York 10103

First published in Canada by Doubleday Canada Limited
105 Bond Street, Toronto, Ontario M5B 1Y3

DOUBLEDAY and the portrayal of an anchor
with a dolphin are trademarks of Doubleday,
a division of Bantam Doubleday Dell Publishing Group, Inc.

Library of Congress Cataloging-in-Publication Data

MacNeil, Robert
Burden of desire/Robert MacNeil.—1st ed.
p. cm.
1. World War, 1914–1918—Nova Scotia—Halifax—Fiction.
2. Halifax (N.S.)—History—Fiction. I. Title.
PS3563.A323435B87   1992
813'.54—dc20   91-28919

Canadian Cataloguing in Publication Data
MacNeil, Robert 1931–
Burden of Desire
ISBN 0-385-42019-6
I. Title.
PS3563.A3187B8   1992   813'.54   C91-095455-0

ISBN 0-385-42019-6

**CENTRAL**

To Donna, for everything

At the start, they tried to evoke an idea of the scale and impact of the weapon they were devising. They began by studying the effects of past explosions, like that of the fully loaded ammunition ship which had gone up in the harbor of Halifax, Nova Scotia, in 1917 . . . The new weapon could be expected to produce several times the blast, so, using scale laws, they multiplied up the effect of the Halifax accident. These calculations were to enable Oppenheimer and his colleagues to visualize in much greater detail the devastating potential of the new weapon.

—PETER GOODCHILD, *J. Robert Oppenheimer: Shatterer of Worlds*

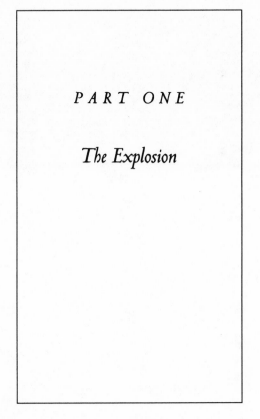

PART ONE

*The Explosion*

IN HER SLEEP Julia Robertson must have felt the change in the weather, for she pushed the blankets aside and brushed the thick blond hair away from her face.

Occasionally Halifax has a winter day so mild that you could imagine the Gulf Stream, leaving North America for Europe, losing its way and creeping in closer to the coast of Nova Scotia. Then this severe northern province, like a hard-bitten spinster dreaming, receives an unexpected caress: hints of warmth borne north from the tropics, and false premonitions of spring.

Uncomfortable in the overheated bedroom, Julia awoke before dawn. She thought, In a few days it will be two years. Two years since Charles had sailed for France. December fifteenth was nine days away. She lay in the dark and silent bedroom considering. They had actually been apart longer than two years, because after he had joined up, there was all the training that took him away. Really, since the wedding in September 1914, they had lived together less than a year . . . and now it was nearly two years since she had seen him.

This waking too early happened more often now; it was not yet light, and Mollie the maid was still asleep. She heard a horse's quiet clopping sounds and the clink of milk bottles as the Farmer's Dairy wagon stopped outside. There was no snow, so they had not yet replaced the wheels with sleigh runners. Julia got out of bed and parted the heavy curtains that were part of the effort to make the city a less inviting target in case a German zeppelin came three thousand miles to bomb it.

Outside the light was dim and gray. Through the bare trees in Victoria Park she could see the form of All Saints Cathedral softened by mist. Too early to go out. Julia turned off the hissing radiator and settled back into bed.

All over Canada, all over the British Empire, women would be waking like this, the little pain in their hearts familiar from three years of war: some younger than Julia's twenty-six years, many older—wives, sweethearts, mothers, sisters—in this moment before rising, before putting on the public face of duty, in the privacy of their beds cursing the war that had taken their men away and was destroying them in such appalling numbers. French women, and German, and Russian, and American women (because they were now in the war), waking with this knot of anxiety that had to be tidied away for the day when they put up their hair and buttoned their boots. Thousands more, of course, poor souls, awoke with a different emptiness; women who knew that their men were not coming back. Each day's casualty list increased their numbers and heightened the anxiety of women like Julia who had men still alive on the Western Front.

Yet that was only one part of the aching loneliness, and she could talk about it with the others. Another part could not be discussed. She took the pillow from Charles's side of the bed and hugged it against her, pressing her breasts into it. The physical longing would recede for weeks or a few days, then come back as fiercely as now. It frightened her, because in moments when she felt it strongly she couldn't confine it to Charles. It was so long, he had faded in her sensual memory . . .

She mustn't lie here and think like this. She threw back the covers and dressed hastily, impatient with hooks and small buttons. At the dressing table she quickly brushed her long hair and pinned it up loosely. The pretty bedroom was stifling; the lamp she had lit made it seem like night. When she pulled the curtains aside, it was bright out and the dawn gave a rosy tinge to the gray stone of the cathedral.

She had to get out to breathe. She crept down the stairs, slipped into an old tweed coat; couldn't be bothered to adjust a hat, instead wrapping a long scarf around her hair and neck. It didn't matter. No one she knew would be out so early; to go out later in the morning she would have to put herself together more carefully.

Anyone seeing her striding vigorously up South Park Street and across Spring Garden Road would have noted the energy in her slim figure, her legs thrusting impatiently against the long skirts of her dress and coat. Any passerby who met the gray eyes in the pale face framed by golden hair would have thought, What a beautiful woman.

Craving space and air, Julia headed for the road leading up Citadel Hill, which dominated the city, its old fortifications as obsolete now in 1917 as the enemies it had been built to confound.

At the top Julia was out of breath and so warm that she had to remove her scarf. She stood enthralled at the beauty of the morning and the breathtaking view over the city and out to sea. She saw it with a painter's eye, automatically organizing and balancing the scene and, noticing herself doing it, felt the familiar twinge of regret for her own abandoned efforts. As usual she rationalized. A thousand painters would do it better. Jim Morrice would. In her mind she could see his Impressionist treatment of the scene, the subtle drawing, the translucent effect he got by diluting the pigments with varnish. Morrice had been her mentor in Paris.

The harbor water was still, covered with a thin film of mist made luminous by the sun newly risen over Eastern Passage. Only far outside the harbor mouth could she see any sign of the restless Atlantic. The sunlight caught a white spill of foam as a wave curled onto the shoal beyond McNabs Island. A lone cargo ship was heading into the harbor. All else was peaceful.

Below her the prosperous streets of the South End where she lived were empty. The old town clock on the harbor slope showed a few minutes before eight. A ferry crossed to the town of Dartmouth, furrowing the still water. All the other ships, berthed in the miles of docks or anchored in midstream, looked asleep.

She turned briskly to continue her walk around the star-shaped moat bordering the stone redoubts of the fortress. This side of the Citadel overlooked the smoking chimneys of the city's North End, which grew out of the commercial streets along the harbor. It was filled with small factories and machine shops and the thousand trades of a busy military port, housing the people who performed them and the servants of people like Julia in the South End. In brief visits to Mollie's family Julia had found it mean and squalid. A few fine buildings lingered from earlier days, but many streets above the harbor had been packed with cheap wooden houses and sagging tenements. Sanitation was poor and the sidewalks were unpaved. The teeming North End of Halifax and the gracious South End, separated by the imposing bulk of Citadel Hill, might have been two different cities.

Julia completed her circuit of the Citadel and walked quickly home, knowing that Mollie would have made coffee. She was eager to get out Morrice's painting of her—and the Matisse. It suddenly came to her that it was silly to go on keeping them in her bedroom cupboard because Charles didn't like them. She wanted to see them and be reminded of her freedom in Paris.

The lone cargo ship Julia had seen entering the harbor was the S.S. *Mont Blanc,* a French freighter of 3121 tons, owned by the Compagnie Générale Transatlantique but under orders from the French navy. She was en route from New York to Bordeaux. Fearful of German submarines, the thirty-eight-year-old captain, Aimé le Medec, had stayed close to the New England coast on the four-day voyage from New York. He had anchored for the night just outside Halifax, awaiting clearance through its submarine defenses. By 8 A.M., with a Halifax pilot on the bridge, the *Mont Blanc* entered the harbor.

She had been loaded in Brooklyn, New York, the steel of her holds carefully lined with wood, fastened with copper nails, which produce no sparks when struck. The crew of the *Mont Blanc* were forbidden to smoke, even to carry matches on deck. No liquor was permitted on board.

Her cargo was high explosives. In her holds were 2300 tons of picric acid, 225 tons of TNT, and 62 tons of gun cotton. Loaded as deck cargo in metal drums were 35 tons of benzol, the highly volatile aviation fuel. She was not flying the customary red warning flag for a ship carrying explosives. The naval authorities controlling Halifax Harbor knew the nature of her cargo, but no one else.

For a century and a half Halifax had occupied a strategic point on the sea route from America to Europe. In the days of sail, prevailing winds and the Gulf Stream current made it advantageous to run past the coast of Nova Scotia. The French realized it first and built a formidable fortress at Louisbourg, on Cape Breton Island. Belatedly, in 1749, the British founded Halifax and fortified its superb harbor.

The great ships that made the British Empire were abominable sailers: sluggish, difficult to maneuver, incapable of sailing close to the wind. God made Halifax for them. As they entered on a north-to-northwesterly course, at an easy angle to the prevailing southwesterly winds, one broad reach would carry them ten miles inland, away from gales and enemies. There, the harbor was pinched like the waist of an hourglass, but opened again miraculously into Bedford Basin, a vast inner bay four miles long and two broad. It was big enough to accommodate the whole British navy, deep enough for the largest vessel, with a mud bottom that would hold any anchor in a blow.

Bedford Basin was the immediate destination of the *Mont Blanc*. She had orders to anchor and await the protection of the next convoy across the Atlantic. It would take her about forty-five minutes' steaming to reach the entrance to the Narrows.

Born to oppose the French, Halifax had soon become a bastion against American Revolutionaries, the forward base against George Washington's forces, and protection for the largest middle-class migration in history—thirty-five thousand Loyalists who fled the Revolution. When Britain fought America in the War of 1812, Halifax was again a vital base for the Royal Navy. It was easy to defend and was ice-free in winter. Lush virgin forests of the king's timber awaited the shipwrights' tools. The waters teemed with fish and the forests with game. All Halifax lacked for the British navy were whores and grog shops, and it soon provided them.

With heavy commerce in merchantmen, fishermen, privateers, smugglers, and passenger vessels, as well as armies and navies, Halifax learned to service, entertain, and exploit all whom the oceans delivered to its door. Its merchants prospered and their wives and daughters blossomed in the glittering or raffish society that came by sea.

To the west lay another inviting finger of ocean, the Northwest Arm, making Halifax almost an island. Halifax society boated there for pleasure, held snowshoe and sleighing parties in winter, and played the first games of hockey.

On the peninsula between the Arm and the harbor, Halifax rose as a small Georgian town of dressed local granite and expanded into a Victorian city of ornate wooden architecture.

Its class structure echoed British society, with colonial abbreviations and the military castes of a garrison town. It had the added spice of royal dukes as governors and young princes as serving officers. They founded a Royal Yacht Squadron, no mere yacht club. Such morsels nourished a self-esteem that outsiders considered intolerably smug, while prosperous Haligonians thought that God had arranged things quite nicely. Everyone knew his place: officers, gentlemen, and the middle class lived south of Citadel Hill; other ranks and the working class lived to the north.

All was fine when war and danger brought ships and regiments.

In the unfortunate intervals of peace the city wilted like an un-watered flower. The 1914 war had providentially ended such a drought. Suddenly the languishing docks, shipyards, ship chandlers, rail terminals, telegraph offices, rooming houses and hotels, broth-els and blind pigs, oil and sugar refineries, textile and clothing factories were all humming. Through the funnel of Halifax, Can-ada poured its human and material wealth across the Atlantic to save the empire.

By 1917 the German submarine menace was destroying the nerve of the Allied forces. The land war in France was a ghastly stalemate. The battle of the Somme had ended in November 1916, leaving 1,265,000 dead: 650,000 German, 195,000 French, and 420,000 from Britain and the empire. In four months the Allies had advanced eight miles. Every foot gained had cost two hundred lives.

Germany called for peace talks, but the Allies refused. Early in 1917, Germany announced unlimited submarine warfare against all shipping. In the first three weeks of February, 134 ships of non-combatants, including American, were sunk. On March 18 alone, German submarines sank three American ships. On April 2, the United States declared war.

Because of the submarine menace, British and American ships now steamed in convoy, and Bedford Basin inside Halifax Harbor became the point where they assembled for their escorts of war-ships.

This morning, as the *Mont Blanc* approached the Narrows, an-other vessel weighed anchor in Bedford Basin and headed for the Narrows at the other end. She was the S.S. *Imo*, six thousand tons, owned by the Norwegian South Pacific Trading Company. She was en route to New York to load up with relief supplies for Belgium. To deter German submarines, the words BELGIAN RELIEF were painted in huge white letters on her sides. Captain Haakon From was on the bridge with another Halifax pilot.

Sea traffic normally keeps to the right, but as the *Imo* entered the Narrows from the west, the captain and pilot saw an American tramp steamer approaching and moved to the left of the channel to avoid it. Then they spotted a tugboat towing barges and altered course again.

Now the *Mont Blanc* entered the Narrows from the east. Seeing the *Imo* occupying the right side of the channel, the French ship blew her whistle and moved farther to the right, closer to the Dartmouth shore. But the *Imo* gave two blasts, indicating she would turn left, putting the two ships even more obviously on a collision course. The *Mont Blanc* stopped her engines and began turning to her left. The *Imo* was drawing dangerously close and gave two more blasts of her whistle. The *Mont Blanc* pilot desperately increased her turn to the left. The *Imo* gave three blasts, signaling engines going astern, but momentum kept the ship moving forward. The *Mont Blanc* could not move out of the way, and a collision was inevitable. The bows of the larger *Imo* tore into the *Mont Blanc,* bursting drums of benzol on deck and cutting into the hold, packed with high explosives. Then the *Imo*'s reversing propellor began pulling her astern, her steel scraping against the *Mont Blanc*'s torn plates and showering sparks over the spilled aviation fuel. There was an instant flash of flame, and the whole foredeck was ablaze.

Captain le Medec watched in horror. The *Mont Blanc* was drifting toward the Halifax shore. He couldn't anchor in midstream, because the anchor mechanism was behind the roaring flames on the foredeck. He had no equipment to fight such a fire. He couldn't scuttle the ship, because it would take hours to open the rusty seacocks. The flames were creeping into the forward hold. The freighter was a giant bomb likely to explode at any second. All he could do was to save his crew. He gave the order to abandon ship. Two lifeboats had already been lowered. The forty men aboard dropped into them and rowed desperately for the Dartmouth shore.

On the Halifax side hundreds of people had gathered at their windows to watch the spectacular fire. The captain of the tug *Stella Maris* anchored the barges he was towing and raced for the blazing freighter to do what he could. The *Mont Blanc* drifted into a wooden pier, setting it alight. The Halifax Fire Department was called and sent its one motor fire engine to the scene. The Canadian cruiser H.M.C.S. *Niobe* sent a boat to the *Mont Blanc.* The British cruiser H.M.S. *Highflyer* dispatched another. Their sailors tried to rig a towline to haul the burning ship out to midstream. The plates of her sides were already too hot to touch. None of the British or Canadian sailors knew that she was full of explosives.

The men who knew, the French crew, beached their lifeboats on the Dartmouth side and ran for the nearby forest. They passed a woman holding a baby and shouted at her to run. She didn't understand. One of the French sailors snatched her baby and ran for the trees, with the hysterical mother chasing him.

Peter Wentworth was alone that early morning at the high altar in All Saints Cathedral. The young clergyman was trying to dispel a surge of anger that curdled his stomach and brought the taste of bile to his mouth.

Leaving his house, he had found an envelope bearing his name but no postage. He opened it as he walked up Tower Road toward the cathedral.

"Read this and be ashamed, you slimy, cringing weakling." The printed note was signed, "A loyal Canadian."

It made Peter sick with anger that anyone should think him a coward. Three times he had asked to go overseas as a chaplain with one of the Nova Scotia regiments, only to be told, "God needs you here."

The new conscription act had produced hysteria. Editorials demanded that able-bodied Canadian clergymen join up as five thousand ministers in England had done. In the streets he had seen women handing white feathers to men as symbols of cowardice.

It calmed him a little to enter the quiet orderliness of the empty cathedral. Soft December sunshine warmed the transept, and the small Gothic windows of the nave scattered splashes of ruby and Prussian blue over the floor and pews.

Peter stopped at the chancel steps to bow and cross himself, his private High Church gesture. It expressed his longing for deeper meaning, a stronger religious emotion, a sense of God's presence, all disappointingly elusive in the daily rites of the Anglican Church.

He walked reverently up the chancel to inspect the change of altar cloths for an afternoon funeral. A woman from the Altar Guild was bringing flowers to replace the gold and russet chrysanthemums left from the First Sunday in Advent. He opened the carved altar rail and closed it behind him, then knelt, his hands on the altar, to pray for serenity and patience. *Oh, Heavenly Father, vouchsafe to me the wisdom to see my own frailties, but grant me also the patience to bear the frailties of others.*

Yet pushing aside his fury at being thought a coward only made room for the return of his anger at Margery.

Peter owned two surplices, the white garments worn over the

cassock during services. He should have had three, but there were always too many other demands on the household's income. He had taken one surplice home to be washed and ironed a week before. Last night he took the second, only to find the first was still in the wash.

The children, Abigail and Michael, both had runny colds and fevers. Margery looked on the verge of a cold herself, her hair lifeless, dark circles underscoring her wide-set eyes. When she saw the second unwashed surplice, she leaned against the kitchen table and began to cry. "Peter, I'm sorry, I'm sorry, I'm sorry!" her voice rising in despair.

The children looked up at her and went on with their supper. They were used to her crying. So was Peter. She had never recovered her spirits from having Abigail and finding herself pregnant with Michael a few months afterward. That was when Peter's careful world had begun to fall apart.

"I just forgot. There's been too much to do."

It had gone on for four years. Their doctor said her blood had been depleted by childbirth, and prescribed tonics.

Peter had prayed for Margery and prayed with her. But he had responsibilities in the cathedral. The dean had chosen him over many young deacons. He could not afford to shirk his duties; indeed, he had to perform them with extra zeal. The more chaotic his home became, the more he needed the certainty that his zealousness would be rewarded.

"But I must have a clean one for tomorrow. There's a special service."

"All right, all right. You'll have your precious surplice!"

Still crying, she struck a match to light the Ruud hot-water heater and went to the washtubs in the scullery off the kitchen. It was typical that she would overreact and throw herself into the task instantly. The gas roared up around the coils. She rolled up the sleeves of her dress, a dress too good to be worn at the washtubs. Clothes were the way her mother spoiled her.

As the hot water poured into the deep tub, she thrashed the wire soap basket back and forth to make suds. The motion disturbed him—too vehement, faintly irrational. She put in the two surplices but snatched her hands back with a cry.

"Oh, it's scalding! I forgot to run in the cold." And with both reddened hands against her lips, she broke down and wept.

Peter was overcome with pity, but anger licked at the kinder emotion. Fighting down an urge to handle her roughly, he put his arms gently around her.

"Now, now it's all right. It's all right." He kissed her cheek, covered with tears.

"It's not all right." She sobbed, her body collapsing against his. "I'm useless. I can't do anything. Everything is too much for me. I'm no good to you. I'm no good to anyone!"

"That's not true." But it was largely true. This was an old conversation. "Go and lie down. I can do these."

She sobbed afresh. "You shouldn't have to do them. It's not your job."

"It doesn't matter whose job it is." Peter used his most reasonable voice. "Go upstairs and lie down. I'll rinse them out and bring you a cup of tea."

Listlessly, she obeyed. As she passed the children, Abigail said, "What's for dessert, Mummy?"

"Tapioca," Margery said. "Ask Daddy. It's in the bowl in the pantry." Her voice was colorless.

"Tapioca, ugh! May we have strawberry jam on it?"

Margery didn't respond. He heard her feet dragging slowly upstairs.

"Daddy, may we have strawberry jam on our tapioca?"

"Please! Please!" they both shouted.

"Have you been good children?" Peter asked.

"Yes," they both said, smiling. Their fevers gave them very pink cheeks.

"Well, you are good children in the eyes of God."

He got out the strawberry jam and plopped a spoonful on Abigail's tapioca.

"Ladies first," he said.

"A bigger spoonful on mine!" Michael said, holding his bowl ready. When he got his jam, Abigail said, "Mine's bigger."

"No, it isn't!"

"Yes, it is!"

"No, it isn't! Daddy, Abbie says hers is bigger."

Their quarreling touched him. It suggested the companionship he had missed as the only child left after the death of his brother.

"They're both the same," Peter said firmly, putting the jampot in the cupboard. "Be thankful for what you've got."

In the scullery, he took off his black jacket. He undid the gold cufflinks, which had been Margery's engagement present, and rolled up his shirtsleeves. He looked down at his black trousers and the dickey front under his clerical collar; he couldn't afford to soil them. He fastened a long apron around his neck and waist, and plunged his hands into the soapy water. He had washed a lot of clothes in the years of Margery's unhappiness. Hundreds of foul diapers to be soaked, washed, boiled (or the babies got rashes), rinsed, wrung out and hung out to dry, gathered in, folded, and put away in time to wash another set. The smell never quite left the house.

Peter wrung out the surplices with an angry test of his strength. If he hung them near the kitchen stove, they should be dry in the morning. Possibly Margery would feel better and could iron them before he had to leave.

Sometimes after one of her really bad days, the act of comforting her, treating her like a sick child, made Peter feel better himself and convinced him that this time Margery would turn the corner and see things more brightly.

After lighting the gas and putting the kettle on for her tea, he ate several large spoonfuls of the tapioca. It tasted like childhood.

He took the tea up to Margery, who was lying fully clothed on the bed. She said weakly, "Could you see them to bed, Peter? I'm afraid I can't manage it."

"Don't worry." The sight of her helplessness aroused him.

Putting the children to bed involved bathing both of them in the big bathtub. It was important to Peter to perform the evening ritual with them precisely as if it were a normal house. But Margery's stockinged ankles were at the back of his mind.

He read to them for fifteen minutes, then got them both out of bed to kneel on the floor to say their prayers: "Now I lay me down to sleep, I pray the Lord my soul to keep."

Margery had not moved on the bed. He closed the bedroom door and lay down beside her, putting an arm around her. She sighed, sleepily, and whispered, "I'm sorry."

"It's all right."

His body still carried the little current of excitement caused by the glimpse of her stockinged feet and ankles disappearing under her skirt. Because her mother bought them, Margery wore expensive silk stockings even around the house, when cotton would have been more practical. It irritated him that she was extravagant, even if he didn't pay for the stockings, but the thought of the silk on her legs aroused him. Her lack of energy, her passiveness also excited him. He leaned closer and kissed her cheek. She did not respond. He moved his hand and caressed her hip through her clothes. She did not move. Gently he touched her breast. She murmured faintly and he took it as a little encouragement. He moved his free hand down and caressed her leg. He could feel the material move against the silk underneath.

"I don't want to, Peter. I'm too tired."

He sighed and continued to stroke her until finally she said, in a voice half-asleep, "Oh, do it if you want to. I don't care."

She made no resistance when he removed her stockings and underclothes. He was not sure whether she was asleep or awake. She seemed like a person chloroformed. His gust of desire shook the bed, but she did not move.

But it was what had happened later that sickened him to remember now, kneeling at the altar.

Very quietly he had undressed, turned out the light, and slipped into bed. He settled himself comfortably and began to breathe evenly.

Suddenly in a clear, cold voice Margery had said, "If you've started another child, if you've made me pregnant again, I'll kill myself. I couldn't stand it."

He was startled. He had thought her fast asleep, and he had not thought of pregnancy.

STEWART MacPHERSON was at Camp Hill Hospital because Lieutenant David Hart, an army psychiatrist, wanted his support in a difficult meeting.

Heavy casualties from the recent battle of Passchendaele had flooded military hospitals in Britain, accelerating the return of convalescents to Canada. The hospital ships unloaded stretcher and ambulatory cases directly onto special trains at the docks, but many men were too ill to stand days of jolting rail travel and were held in Halifax until they grew stronger. Camp Hill, with 240 beds, had just been built to handle the rising numbers.

The latest shipload of wounded had included seven shell-shock cases, but the Camp Hill administrator, Colonel Bell, did not want mental cases in the wards with wounded soldiers. He had hidden them at the end of one ward behind a row of white bed screens. Hoping to get rid of them, he had called in Dr. Hattie, superintendent of the Nova Scotia Hospital—the insane asylum, as everyone called it.

The elderly colonel was not alone in his aversion. As he moved a screen to admit the visitors, a double amputee in a nearby bed called out, "Going to see the nut cases, Doctor?" and the raucous laughter of men with physical wounds carried easily into the closed-off section. Young Dr. Hart shot an embarrassed glance at Stewart, but the psychiatric patients appeared not to have heard; they looked vacant or absent, except one, who was leaning on crutches, staring out the window.

Dr. Hart told Dr. Hattie, the silver-haired asylum superintendent, "Two of them are deaf—and one mute. I'll give you complete histories in Dr. Bell's office."

Hart, who had a thin face and large black eyes that looked ready to weep, was one of the newly qualified psychiatrists the army had recruited to control the epidemic of what the Canadian army now called "psychogenetic disorders." The popular term "shell shock" had been officially banned. Dr. Hart was responsible for all such patients in Halifax military hospitals. He had called Stewart in several months earlier when he needed a psychologist to administer whatever tests could reveal more about these men. Their problems had become so fascinating to him that Stewart was beginning to regret abandoning psychiatry for the safer career in academic psychology. Dr. Hart knew that and wanted him this morning as an ally.

As Colonel Bell replaced the screen he had moved to admit them, Stewart and the other two doctors looked at the seven men lying or sitting on their beds and the one on crutches, who remained standing with his back turned.

Although it was now familiar, the contrast still moved him. These men, who had no physical wounds, looked far more ill than the men beyond the screens, missing arms or legs or eyes, facing a lifetime of crutches or wheelchairs. Nothing made it clearer that wounds of the mind created serious illness, but the effort to deny it still dominated most military thinking. Stewart could see it in the fleshy face of Dr. Bell, the self-important administrator, who observed with distaste as Dr. Hattie went from patient to patient with

Dr. Hart, describing the symptoms. They turned to the man on crutches, who appeared not to notice them.

"Total functional paralysis of right leg . . . hemiplegia left leg . . . no lesions but very marked vasomotor changes . . . loss of sensibility to pinprick . . . badly oriented as to time and place . . ."

Next was a thin young man sitting on the edge of his bed, continually throwing his hands forward, like someone trying to shake off water after washing.

"Severe persistent convulsive twitchings . . . myoclonic or pseudoclonus . . ."

The patient stopped to rub his eyes, then began shaking his hands again.

The next man stared past them to the window, tears running down his face, his lips moving in an urgent but silent conversation.

Dr. Hattie's years of experience with severely disturbed people was apparent. He looked intently at each anguished face, held a hand, patted a shoulder, as though by reading the faces and touching the men, he could understand the condition.

In the adjoining bed a man with red hair held his bony hands clamped over his ears.

"Totally deaf to external sounds, but he hears frightening noises all the time, explosions, shells whistling, guns firing . . . That gives him night terror . . . When he screams, the nurse finds him with everything—even the rubber sheet—pulled over his head."

"He's deaf but he screams?"

"Yes."

In the last bed an anxious man asked Dr. Hattie, "Has my friend come back yet?"

"I haven't seen him, Corporal Wood."

"He was here last night, but is he coming back?"

Dr. Hart said, "He's been asking the same question for months, apparently. He still has convulsive seizures . . . not genuine epilepsy but psychogenic. In between he asks for his friend . . . possibly a friend killed at the front. Evidently he can't think of anything else."

Stewart listened, but his mind kept flitting from the immediate present to images that created a different, simultaneous present. Still hearing the doctors and observing the patients, he could hear and see Christine laughing in bed, the warning from the college chancellor. When he tried to focus his attention, the problem snapped back with a fresh little punch of anxiety. He must settle it. After this meeting he would drive out to the college and think it through quietly.

"Well, there you are," Dr. Bell said briskly to the superintendent. "They are all quite tractable and not a scratch on 'em. No wounds to dress . . . in fact, no medical treatment required, just simple nursing—and no discipline problem." He talked as though the seven patients were not present. "We'll go back to my office and discuss it."

The patients, like caged animals, watched them leave.

In his office Colonel Bell offered them cigarettes from a silver box inscribed with a regimental crest and the date 1908. There were years of mess dinners in the large stomach straining under the Sam Browne belt.

"I'm not going to beat about the bush with you, gentlemen. I think it is utterly wrong to dump these cowards and malingerers in my wards with men who bear the honorable wounds of battle. Up to now they've found room for the nervous cases at Cogswell Street or somewhere else, and I think it should stay that way."

Young Dr. Hart had clearly been expecting this. "With great respect, sir, that is not in line with the new Medical Corps policy. Cowards and malingerers, as you put it, have been weeded out long before this. They've been cured and sent back to the front, or discharged, or disciplined."

"As they bloody well deserve. What kind of an army can you run if any chap who gets the wind up can say he's paralyzed and get sent off for a nice rest cure? Soldiers have always tried it on. It's the first thing I looked for as a medical officer. I think it's preposterous to mollycoddle these fellows. You'll turn us into an army of weepy women."

"Colonel, these men have been through months of treatment. Everything that can be done has been tried. They're chronically ill."

"Just my point. If they're incurable, they're going to end up in insane asylums like Dr. Hattie's anyway. It is not good medicine to throw them in with men who need every ounce of grit and spirit to pull through their wounds. It depresses them."

"They didn't look very depressed to me." Dr. Hattie laughed.

Dr. Hart said earnestly, "They don't carry the same guilt as the nervous cases. Their physical wounds get them treated with honor. These other men have been treated with dishonor or suspicion from the moment they became incapacitated. It just adds to their guilt for letting down their fellow soldiers."

"Well, they should feel guilty," said the colonel. "And the best proof I know of is that you never see a wounded man with shell shock. Do you?"

"No," said Dr. Hart.

"Well, there you are! What do you psychiatrists make of that?" He said "psychiatrists" sarcastically.

"Wounded men know they're excused from further fighting."

"Honorably excused, you mean!"

"Yes, of course."

"But these cowards can't get honorably excused, so they fake it. And it amazes me that the army falls for it and hires doctors like you to make excuses for them." The fat colonel's neck was turning dark red and his voice was rising.

"I didn't say they were incurable," Dr. Hart came back. "They haven't been cured yet. Everything is very rushed in England. They have hundreds of cases at a time. The emphasis is on quick cures to get men back to the front. About two thirds of the time it works. We're getting the ones who didn't respond."

Stewart knew about the "quick cures." Soldiers diagnosed with hysteria were locked in isolation rooms to think about duty, family, responsibility. They got stern lectures from doctors talking like disciplinary officers. Some underwent hypnosis or chloroform anesthesia. Many received extremely painful faradization, strong electric current applied to a paralyzed leg or larynx to demonstrate that the muscle could move. To Stewart, these practices put medicine in an ambiguous role.

It was time he helped Dr. Hart. He said, "Colonel Bell, why couldn't you put them in one of your empty wards for the time being? Just to reduce the friction with the other wounded?"

The colonel snapped, "Mr. MacPherson, since you are not a doctor, I would thank you to keep your opinions to yourself. I don't know what this has to do with psychological testing anyway, so I don't know why you're here this morning."

"I asked him," Dr. Hart said. "MacPherson has a very good understanding of these cases. He has seen scores of them now. And he has a background in psychiatry. He studied Freudian methods with Ernest Jones in Toronto."

"I might have known." Colonel Bell snorted. "The sex doctor! The next thing you'll be telling me is all these men ran away—" The angry colonel did not finish.

The last sight on earth for hundreds of people was a flash of light, brighter, greater, more dazzling than the sun. An instant later they were dead or blind.

When a rifle is fired, an ounce of explosive powder in the shell burns rapidly, fomenting hot gases, which quickly expand and force the bullet out of the shell. When the *Mont Blanc* exploded, her cargo was the equivalent of eighty-three million ounces of explosive doing collectively what one rifle shell does.

At 9:04:45 the seismograph in the physics building at Dalhousie University, a mile and a half way, registered the event. The stylus flew to one edge of the paper and jammed.

Seconds later came the shock wave through the air, driven by a bubble of burning gases expanding at astronomical velocity far in excess of the speed of sound.

The most violent and destructive tornadoes may have maximum winds of three hundred miles an hour. The air wave from the *Mont Blanc* burst outward at seven times that speed, twenty-one hundred miles an hour. No structure could withstand it. Within one second it flattened every building on the near slope of Halifax, obliterating two and a half square miles of the North End, crushing wooden houses into kindling, bursting open brick schools and churches, punching out walls and floors in concrete factories, twisting roads, and snarling railroad tracks. For miles all windows shattered, lacerating the eyes of hundreds of people who had been watching the fire.

One mile from the explosion, Fort Needham hill deflected the shock wave upward and laterally, diminishing its velocity. Thence, at seven hundred miles an hour it sped south and west over Halifax and east across the harbor to the city of Dartmouth, blowing in doors and windows, cracking walls, shifting foundations. A second after Fort Needham it struck Citadel Hill and was again deflected, saving the South End from the devastation to the north.

The steel hull of the *Mont Blanc* exploded like a monstrous fragmentation grenade. It burst into thousands of jagged pieces of shrapnel hurled outward, knifing into buildings and human flesh. All the sailors trying to make fast a towline were vaporized except one, Able Seaman William Becker of H.M.S. *Highflyer,* who was thrown across the harbor and swam to the Dartmouth shore. The exploding fragments riddled the *Imo,* killing the captain and pilot. The shaft of the *Mont Blanc*'s anchor, weighing half a ton, flew two miles to the head of the Northwest Arm. A cannon was found an equal distance at Albro Lake in Dartmouth.

The shock went downward, displacing harbor waters, creating a mammoth tidal wave that engulfed the nearby streets, drowning pedestrians, and flooding buildings sixty feet above sea level. The tugboat *Stella Maris* was carried up on a nearby dock. The stricken *Imo* was blown across the harbor and beached on the Dartmouth side. The force gouged huge boulders out of the harbor bottom and flung them high into the air. One rock weighing a ton landed on the freighter *Picton,* three hundred yards from the explosion, killing seventy of the eighty stevedores who were unloading her cargo.

As the dazed survivors looked about, a black oily rain began falling from the huge dark cloud over the town. It fell for ten minutes, like liquid tar, blackening faces and penetrating clothing so that rescuers thought many white people were from Africville, the Negro shantytown by Bedford Basin.

One third of the homes and businesses of the city of fifty thousand people were obliterated in a flash, and the wreckage immediately began to burn. In thousands of crushed houses, coal and wood cooking stoves were overturned, setting the splintered wood on fire. Ruptured gas lines instantly ignited. Many who survived the explosion now faced a more terrible death, trapped in houses that were on fire.

In the cathedral, Peter Wentworth felt a wall of air smack into him, almost knocking him over. Then a deafening sound, like a train roaring by, suddenly filled the church.

He turned to see the entire cathedral space alive with flying glass, spiraling, twisting, falling—for a frozen instant, beautiful—autumn leaves in a whirlwind, brilliant pieces of glass flying into the center of the nave, glittering and iridescent. An eerie, still moment, then tinkling splintering, almost individual notes, almost a collective crash, as the pieces struck pews, pulpit, brass lectern, choir stalls, and floor. When it had apparently stopped, a few more pieces slid off the angled sills of the Gothic windows. Then silence, and he could hear shouts from outdoors through windows left gaping to the winter day, lead banding in shreds between stone and wooden frames.

Everywhere—on top of the altar, on the carpet in the chancel, in the choir stalls, down the entire length of the nave—were pieces of broken glass. The heavy east door had been blown open but was still on its hinges.

Peter ran down the center aisle over the shards of glass, through the arched oak door. People were running out of their houses to look at the sky. A woman was holding a towel to her face. He saw blood. A vast column of black smoke was rising north of Citadel Hill. He began running down Tower Road toward home. Windows were broken in many of the houses; people were looking out, bewildered. He heard screams in the distance and saw a horse galloping in terror, a milk wagon swaying crazily behind, the driver gone.

He had two more blocks to go and was gasping for breath.

Remorse played into the fear of what he would find at home. He had behaved cruelly to her last night—selfishly, thoughtlessly— and this morning.

The surplices had been still slightly damp and it took a long time to heat the iron on top of the stove. Margery was weepy and anxious to please. She finished one surplice and Peter said impatiently, "I'll take that. I can get the other tomorrow."

"It's not very good," Margery said. "I couldn't get the creases out by the yoke."

Peter had noticed. Around the neck opening was a band, and the fullness of the garment was gathered into the seam. Properly pressed, the gathers should look full; carelessly ironed, they were flat, like pleats, which was how Margery had pressed them.

His front windows and the front door were intact. He ran up the steps.

"Margery?"

"Peter?" she called from the kitchen. "Oh, I'm so glad you came. What was it? There was a terrible noise and the back windows came crashing in."

"Are you all right? Are the children all right?"

"Yes. But what was it? I've never heard anything like it. It was incredibly loud."

Peter hugged her in relief.

"I think it's in the North End. That's where the smoke is. Look, if you're all right, I've got to get back. The cathedral's a wreck. All the windows are shattered. It's devastation. I've got to get back. I'll telephone later."

"I don't think you can. I tried to ring Mother but the phone is out. The electric light too."

"I'll be back later."

"What'll I do about the windows that are broken?"

"Cover them with anything you can for now. I've got to go."

"Peter? Wait!" She came back into the front hall, carrying the other surplice. She looked like a child eager to be praised. "I have this ready for you."

"Thanks, I don't need it now."

At precisely the same instant, he felt a rush of gratitude and a flash of irritation because on that surplice too she had ironed all the gathers flat.

In the park in front of the cathedral, he met a large throng. Some of the people had cuts that were bleeding, and a woman was tearing up a petticoat to make bandages.

In the dean's house all the front windows were missing, and Margaret Creighton was beckoning excitedly. "There seem to be many people hurt. Are you all right? Donald's in here." Peter found the dean, his avuncular but shrewd superior, hanging up the telephone. "Doesn't work. I'm trying to tell the undertaker we certainly can't manage a funeral today."

Peter told him of the flying glass in the cathedral.

"It's a miracle you weren't badly cut."

Mrs. Creighton said, "Peter, is Margery all right?"

"She's fine. Just some windows were broken." He wasn't sure how much the dean and his wife knew. He didn't want the reputation of a man with a wife who couldn't manage. A bright, efficient wife was part of the job.

"Well, there's nothing we can do here. Peter, at least go and find out what's happened. Please God, if the navy has blown something up, it's over and that's the end of it."

Following the rising smoke, Peter climbed the near side of Citadel Hill. Only when the North End came into view did he grasp the immensity of the disaster. He saw an unbelievable panorama of devastation, half of the North End enveloped in smoke and flame. It was like looking down into hell. Along both sides of the harbor large ships had been thrown ashore, some on their sides. Warships riding at anchor were burning.

Hundreds of people were fleeing, across the Common to the west, south into the Wanderers Ground, up the slopes of the Citadel toward him. The slopes were covered with people, many badly hurt and unable to run any farther, who collapsed on the grass and turned back to stare at the destruction. Some were on their knees praying. There were many with bleeding cuts; others looked unharmed; most of them were covered with black, oily dirt. A young woman was whimpering near him, shivering in her dress.

"What happened?" Peter asked.

"I don't know. An explosion." The girl began to sob.

"Are you hurt?" Peter asked.

"No, I'm frightened. The soldiers say there's going to be another explosion. They told us to get out."

Peter looked down the hill. People were still running. All the streets away from the North End were filled with wagons, cars, and trucks, with people on foot running alongside faster than the vehicles.

"You'd better find somewhere warm," Peter said. "You'll get a chill."

He left her and marched down the rough grass on the north slope and into the streets leading to the devastation. A few blocks to the north almost every house had been ground into splinters, or crushed in, or torn open, or squashed flat, or rolled over. Trees and telephone poles were snapped off. Many of the houses were on fire.

There were wooden houses and tenements built close together with churches, schools, shops, factories. People were crawling out. Children dragged out adults. People with ghastly wounds pulled themselves out. Searchers were carrying bodies from the wreckage and laying them in front of the houses. Wounded people were sitting or lying by the dead.

A man digging at fallen bricks with his bare hands was crying out, "Dottie? Dottie? Can you hear me?" Behind another flattened house an old woman wrapped in a shawl emerged from the rubble clutching a silver teapot to her bosom.

A sailor in uniform sat on the curbstone, his face in his hands, sobbing. Beside him on the ground were the bodies of three small children. Peter thought, How cold it must be for them, until he realized they could not feel the cold. A little girl was standing there with her hand on the man's shoulder, saying, "Never you mind, Mr. Snow. They'll wake up. You wait and see. They're just asleep. They'll wake up. Never you mind." Like a little mother.

A motor truck came, already piled with bodies, and soldiers began lifting the three little bodies onto the pile. A corporal asked the sailor the name of each dead child and the address. It took him a long time to remember, as if he had to come back from a great distance to tell each name. A tag was tied to each child's wrist and the soldiers placed each body as reverently as they could on top of the awful pile.

"Where are you taking them?"

"Chebucto Road School. It's where they're putting the dead."

The truck moved away. Peter was shaking. As much for his benefit as the sailor's, he knelt and said a prayer. The sailor appeared not to hear.

Peter didn't know the name of the street—somewhere off Agricola; he had never been up there. The houses were very poor, pathetic when you saw them ripped open, the mean furnishings revealed.

He had often tried to imagine what it would be like in France, how he would act on witnessing the carnage. This was worse than anything he had read about, mutilations he could not have imagined, leaving the people still alive. A woman's face was ripped off but was attached on one side, and somehow she had the presence of mind to hold the bloody flap in place, like a mask. His stomach rose when he saw an eye hanging out of its socket on thin, silvery sinews. And it was all strangely quiet. There was little moaning or shrieking, only a few screams above the crackling and roar of the flames.

Peter fell in with a mixed group of soldiers and civilians trying to rescue people before fire swept all the houses. They were looking down at a woman actually cut in two at the waist. Her eyes were blinking, her fingers twitching. Shuddering, he turned away and closed his eyes. When he turned back, the woman was still and her eyes were closed.

A heavyset man with sergeant's stripes on his greatcoat watched Peter saying a prayer over her.

"That's not going to do her any good."

Peter ignored him, but he went on, "I said that to a chaplain in France. He was praying away over a bunch of bodies. I shouted to him to forget the praying and get out of it, but he didn't. Then a shell landed with a big flash. Concussion knocked us all down. When I looked back, he'd gone. Blown to hell!"

"Perhaps he was blown to heaven," Peter said.

"Come on! You been over there, Padre?" he asked with smirk. He had a coarse face and oily hair, which kept falling down from his uniform cap, when he'd swipe it up again. Peter hated explaining why he was not in France.

"No, the bishop ordered me to stay and work here." It always sounded lame.

The sergeant came back, with a nasty grin, "Wish I'd had a bishop to say that to me. But bishops don't come out our way very often."

Peter knew he was sneering, but it made him want to work even harder.

"What's your name, Padre?"

"Peter Wentworth."

"You belong to a church?"

"All Saints Cathedral."

"Oh, lah-di-dah! All Saints Cathedral. You're a long ways from the South End up here."

They were lifting a man with crushed legs carefully into a horse-drawn milk wagon, when another soldier shouted, "For Christ's sake! It's all women in here."

They crawled under a stairway still standing into the parlor of a larger house. The upper floors had collapsed, but the stone chimney and the stairs were holding the rest up at an angle. On a velvet sofa, on the floor, beside a piano, seven youngish women were scattered. They were covered with bricks, plaster dust, pieces of lath. But through it their faces and pale limbs could be seen. They were wearing only underclothes and stockings, the colors garish against their pale skin and the dust. On the dead faces were bright patches of rouge and lipstick.

Peter knew before the sergeant shouted, with a coarse laugh, "It's a goddamned whorehouse!"

The men looked down at the dead women, digesting that information. Peter had read about police raids on such houses and about trials for prostitution. There were said to be thousands of such women in Halifax. He was unwilling to look at the half-clothed bodies, yet unable not to look. The sight was more sobering than many more gruesome things he had seen. He could avert his eyes but not his thoughts from the silk-stockinged legs, from the thighs —from his treatment of Margery.

"What do you think of that, Padre?" asked the sergeant.

Peter's mouth was dry with plaster dust and with disgust at his own prurience. He could not think of anything to say.

"They couldn't have been open for business at nine in the morning," one man said. "They work at night, don't they?"

"Come on!" said the sergeant. "There's a war on! There's always someone who wants it bad, coming off a ship or a shift in the dockyard. They're always open for business. Isn't that right, Padre? Like a church—always open for business." He laughed.

"Poor things," one of the younger soldiers said. "Never knew what hit them."

"Well, we got to get 'em out before they fry," the sergeant said. "You're excused, Padre. Probably you don't want to touch flesh that's sinned like theirs. You probably think they got what they deserved, don't you? God struck them dead, eh?"

"They are God's creatures like us," Peter said.

He swallowed his squeamishness and helped to lift the dead women out. His hands closed around the ankles of one girl, feeling the strange coldness of her skin through the silk. He fought but could not stop his eyes from straying over her as he and the other men stumbled over broken plaster and a swaying section of shingled wall. There had never been any uncertainty about this girl's availability to men. Her profession demonstrated her willingness. Margery had not been willing, and he had forced her. His trembling did not show, but he was appalled to discover morsels of sexual curiosity alive for a dead girl whose attractions when she was living must have been meager. But he had never seen another woman undressed.

The other men treated the women respectfully, even tenderly, laying them out by the curb with a strange dignity, wrenching a dusty tablecloth from under piles of bricks to cover them. Peter was moved by their tenderness, but it did not wash away his self-disgust.

Only the sergeant persisted. Pushing his hair back under his hat, he said to Peter, "Where do you suppose they're going, Padre, heaven or hell?"

"God will decide," Peter said firmly.

"Do you really believe all that stuff?"

"Yes, I do."

He saw the sergeant smirk.

Stewart MacPherson felt Camp Hill Hospital shudder as though slapped by a giant hand. A gust of air blew in the window with astonishing force, hurling glass into the opposite wall in a thousand fragments, embedding some like daggers in the woodwork. When Stewart looked, the cigarette had vanished from his fingers. All the papers on Colonel Bell's desk and the medical files in Dr. Hart's hand had been snatched away and pasted against the wall. Some papers were just now fluttering to the floor.

"What was that?"

"I don't know."

They heard shouts from the corridor. Stewart crossed the floor of broken glass and opened the door. A man was running by with blood on his face. People were shouting.

"The Germans?"

"A bombardment?"

"Maybe the furnace blew up."

"A zeppelin raid maybe."

"Or the naval magazine going up."

A nurse ran by holding her face, with blood dripping garishly onto her white apron.

"Help me, please."

Dr. Hart took her arm. "This way, in the first ward. I'll bandage it."

"All you all right? Everyone all right?"

"Doctor! They need help in Ward Three."

"Out of the building. Better get out of the building."

"No, wait, it's too cold outside for the patients."

"Tell the matron and head nurse to come down here."

"All the windows have been blown out, sir. There's glass all over the beds."

Nurses hurried by in outdoor cloaks.

"How many patients are hurt? Do a systematic check and report to me. Tell all doctors to report to me at once."

As the colonel, panting for breath, shouted orders, the bustle and confusion mounted.

Stewart went out the front door of the hospital and saw black smoke rising to the north. A car was pulling in fast. The driver stopped and helped a man with a bloody face get down and walk inside. He called to Stewart, "They need more help up there."

"Where?"

"Up there. North End. It's unbelievable. There's hundreds hurt up there."

Stewart ran back into Bell's office and grabbed his overcoat. He was climbing into his car outside when an officer limped over.

"Where you going?"

"I was just going to see if I could help. A man said there are hundreds hurt."

"I'll come with you." Painfully but briskly the officer dragged his bad leg around the car and got in.

"John Coleman. Major." His clipped speech was like a parody of a British officer's, as was his thin gray mustache, but he had a CANADA patch on his greatcoat.

"Stewart MacPherson. How do you do?" They shook hands.

The major took charge. "The doctors say there are damned few ambulances, but we'll find them some customers."

They drove up Robie Street but had to keep detouring until they found a way by driving over the debris into streets in which every building had collapsed and many were burning.

When they saw the first bodies, the major said briskly, "Never mind the dead ones. Can't help them. Thought I'd left all this behind over there."

"You've been in France?"

"Wounded. I just got back a week ago."

"Are you a patient at Camp Hill?"

"Never mind that. Look, quick!" the major barked. "Some bad ones coming out there."

Stewart saw a little girl, her dress soaked with blood, carrying a baby who looked too heavy for her, and pulling her mother by the skirt. The mother's face was covered with blood, and she was holding both hands over her eyes. Stewart and the major got them all into the car. The woman was moaning. The little girl was silent. The noise of crackling fires was very close. Tarry smoke stung their eyes and was choking in the throat. A woman was screaming in the distance.

Immediately workers came out from behind a shattered wall, carrying another woman. "Take her, quick! Bad shape." They carefully placed her in the back seat. She had a triangle of glass protruding from her chest. Coleman said, "For Christ's sake, don't need that!" He pulled the jagged glass out and dropped it in the road. The wound was running fresh blood, and he put his gloved hand flat on her chest to stop it. His quick practicality amazed Stewart.

The woman's moaning made a gurgling sound.

"Hurry up, man! Fast as you can!"

Stewart drove wildly back to Camp Hill, but there was a long line waiting for treatment.

"Christ!" said the major. "Better find another hospital."

"I'll go to the Victoria General. It's the biggest."

"Hurry. She's bleeding a lot."

As fast as he could, Stewart drove down South Park Street. The major hobbled rapidly past the crowd outside the hospital, shouting, "Emergency, emergency! Stretcher bearer!"

The little girl, still holding the baby, suddenly spoke for the first time: "Mister, are we all going to die?" He turned to look at a white face and startling dark blue eyes, framed in black hair.

"No. You're going to be all right," Stewart said.

"Is that lady going to die? She doesn't say nothing."

"No," he said to reassure her, but when he turned to look, he saw that the woman with the wound in her chest had fallen back, her white face twisted unnaturally.

"She's dead, ain't she?" the child said.

Her mother suddenly groaned and asked, "Betty, is the baby all right?" Her voice was faint.

"He's asleep," the little girl said. "But he's some cold."

"Cold?" The mother took one red hand away from an eye. The socket was a bloody pulp with slivers of glass sticking out. She touched the baby and screamed, "No, no, not the baby!" She ran her hand frantically over the baby, reaching inside his clothing, until she felt that he was dead. Her hand left bloodstains on the baby's clean clothes.

"I'm sorry, Mama. I tried to look after him. But he just went cold." Her mother was sobbing. Stewart had to turn away. She was weeping blood and tears together.

With difficulty Stewart and the major half-dragged, half-carried the dead woman out of the back seat and laid her on the grass. Coleman led the blinded mother to the line of people waiting for treatment, and Stewart took the baby from the little girl, conscious that he had never held a baby before. He carried it awkwardly, then reluctantly laid it on the grass. He heard the mother wail, "No one's with the baby. I can't see where they put him!"

"It's all right, Mama. I'll sit with him."

The little girl sat down where Stewart had placed the dead baby beside the corpse of the other woman. She acted as though her mother asked her to do that every day. But she was shivering in her bloodstained dress. Stewart remembered a traveling rug in the trunk and got it out.

"Stand up and put this on." The child let him wrap her in the black-and-white MacPherson tartan; then she bent over the baby. "We have to wrap him up too."

"I think you'd better stay with your mother. I'll take him inside. What's your name?"

"Betty O'Shaughnessy."

"And what street was your house on?"

"Roome Street."

"I'll tell them. You go and stay with your mother, Betty."

In the crowded corridor he found an orderly to take the dead baby and record its identity.

"Worse than France. Bloody sight worse," the major said. "Never see women and little kiddies hacked about like this. Just men. Makes it worse."

It was the first human thing the major had said.

They repeated the loading and delivery. Stewart grew numb. Any one of the scores of injuries he saw might individually have made him sick: a child's severed head in one street by the curb; limbs and parts of limbs sticking out of the wreckage; face wounds too ghastly to look at. A woman walked past them with part of her face carved off as if by a sharp knife, leaving an edge like newly butchered raw beef.

But many had died with no sign of injury.

"Their faces look better, somehow. Fairly peaceful. Weren't

expecting anything. Chaps killed in France have been fearing it for months. They die with faces tensed up and hands clenched. These people never knew what hit 'em."

Some of the dead laid out on the sidewalks were naked except for their shoes or boots. The major limped by them and looked down.

"I've seen that," he said. "Force of the blast can strip 'em just like that."

A minute later, on Agricola Street, a young woman walked toward them quite naked except for her boots. As they drew near, a soldier jumped off a truck and helped her to put on his greatcoat. The woman walked on as though she hadn't noticed.

They made so many runs to and from the hospital that Stewart lost count.

There were lulls. Streets they patrolled looked empty; then, around the corner would be another batch.

"What do you do when you're not lugging mangled bodies around?"

"I'm a psychologist. I'm an associate professor at Dalhousie University, and I'm doing some work for the Medical Corps on shell shock. That's why I was at Camp Hill when you stopped me."

"I've seen a lot of that. Some poor buggers never come out of it."

"A lot of army people won't take it seriously as an illness."

"Didn't at first myself. Not something you see much in the regular army, with the discipline, esprit de corps, and all that. But this war's different, and most of the troops are civilians. Some of them just can't take it. Regular soldier would die of shame before he'd show his fear to the others, or let them down."

"I'm told that one senior officer called it childishness and effeminacy."

"Well, you can't blame them for taking a hard line. One chap sees his mate get out of the trenches because he's shell-shocked. Soon you've got dozens claiming they're shell-shocked. You can't stop it. You've got to nip it in the bud."

"How do you do that?"

"Get the first man who shows it back behind the lines to the field hospital fast. I don't know what they do to them, but a lot come back better soldiers. Some of them go balmy again, right round the twist. And some get what they deserve—the ones who run away, the deserters."

"What happens to them?"

"They're court-martialed. Some are shot."

Stewart paused, wondering whether his voice would betray his revulsion. "How can they tell the difference between a deserter who should be punished and a man whose mind is disturbed, who is ill?"

"At first they didn't bother. If a man deserted, or showed cowardice in the face of the enemy, he was punished. Now they realize the army picked up a lot of men it should never have recruited—misfits, nervous types, degenerates—and it's better to weed 'em out. Bad apples."

They had just returned from the hospital, empty, when soldiers led up a pregnant young woman they had dug out of a basement. She was not visibly hurt but was screaming.

"She's in labor. Quickly!" They pushed her into the back seat. The major, wincing as he bent his bad leg, climbed in beside her.

"It can't be now." She panted. "It can't be now. It's too soon. I've months to go. It's too soon. Please don't let it come now."

"There, there, darling," the major said. "You'll be all right. Just hold on to me." His voice was softer and his accent had changed.

In the rear mirror Stewart could see him holding the thin girl in his arms. He noticed her Newfoundland accent and her poor clothing. She looked undernourished and too young to be having a baby. She must have been bent over a washtub when the basement caved in. Her sleeves were rolled up above the elbows, and she had an apron over her swollen belly. She was panting and saying, "Oh! Oh! Oh!" And then a very loud scream: "Noooo!"

"I think we've got a baby," the major said. "Hurry up, man. She's had a baby."

Stewart drove frantically to the Victoria General. In the cold he was sweating. It was quiet behind him. He glanced back, but both heads were below the seat. "How is it?"

"Not good." The major straightened up and whispered over the seat. "Baby's dead. Very tiny. Little boy. Born dead. But haven't anything to cut the damned cord with." The girl was crying hysterically—shuddering, high-pitched sobs.

She got out of the car and carried her dead baby into the hospital with its umbilical cord still attached.

. . . .

Peter heard a voice shouting, "Any wounded?" and he saw Stewart MacPherson, leaning out a car window.

"Peter, my God, what are you doing?"

"Trying to dig people out."

"We're taking wounded people to hospital. Any here?"

"I don't think so."

"Ghastly, isn't it?"

"Yes."

"Is Margery all right? And the children?"

"Yes."

"I'll see you later."

Peter recognized the MacPhersons' large black Paige as it lurched over a heap of bricks. He remembered it driven by a chauffeur.

The sergeant noticed it. "Big car. One of your rich friends from the South End, eh?"

"I've known him since we were children," Peter said stiffly.

"What is he, a banker?"

Seeing Stewart MacPherson made Peter notice how filthy he was. His black clerical overcoat had turned grayish white from plaster and dust. His face was smudged with soot and dirt on top of the oily mist that had fallen from the sky. His blackened, bloody hands felt swollen and numb from wrenching up boards and throwing bricks. The fingernails were broken and rimmed with dirt.

He was following the soldiers past a house blazing so fiercely that they had to make a wide detour to escape the heat. They pushed into the next house, almost totally collapsed but with a wall still standing, an upright piano smashed into tiny fragments by the collapsing chimney. As they picked their way over the mounds of broken lath and plaster, a woman's voice quite near him said distinctly, "Oh, Father, thank God you've come!"

In a corner obscured by rising dust and smoke was a handsome middle-aged woman, pinned across her hips by a large beam and, above it, the edge of the roof.

"We got to lift it. Get it off her," the youngest soldier said.

"Are you crazy?" the sergeant said. "We'd never get that beam up if there was fifty of us. We'd need a crane to lift that."

"Then what do we do?" The fire was coming closer. "We can't leave her like that, for God's sake!"

Peter could barely hear the woman above the roaring and crackling of the fire. She must have been so crushed below the hips that it was a miracle she could draw breath to talk.

"Father, I haven't much time. Absolve me. Give me the last rites."

Peter said, "I'm not a Catholic priest. I am an Anglican minister. Church of England. I can't absolve you."

"Holy Jesus," she said, "absolve me anyway."

"But I don't think—"

"I don't care what you are, Father. For the love of God and the Blessed Virgin, give me the last rites."

The sergeant saw Peter hesitating, wanting to help but holding back. He said roughly, "Absolve her, you bastard! Absolve her, or I'll kill you!"

He shoved Peter down by the shoulder and turned away, muttering, "Fucking parson!"

Peter fell painfully onto his knees in the rubble of lath and broken glass. "But I don't know how," he said.

The woman smiled. "You say it like this, Father. You make a cross on my forehead. I saw them when my mother was dying. You make a cross on my forehead."

Peter had never seen anyone dying in agony. The only dead he had prayed over had been serenely dead. He was choked; he could scarcely talk. He made a small cross in the plaster dust on her forehead and said, "In the name of the Father, the Son, and the Holy Ghost—"

"—and the Virgin Mary," the woman said.

"—and the Virgin Mary, I grant you absolution—"

"Say, '*Ego te absolvo,*' " she said weakly.

And Peter said, *"Ego te absolvo"* and then from somewhere in the past remembered, *"in nomine patris, et filii, et spiritus sancti."*

Behind him a man shouted, "Get out! Get out! The wall's falling!"

The woman looked at Peter for a moment and closed her eyes. Hands grabbed him and dragged him over the rubble into the street. The wall crashed, and the fire rushed in with a roar. The crackling was very loud, and he could feel the frightening heat.

For a second behind the roar, Peter thought he could hear the woman screaming. He ran forward, but as the heat began to burn his face, ten feet from the flames, he stopped. The men grabbed him and pulled him back. One was the sergeant, who had pushed him down. His voice was kinder. "You can't help her. There's a lot of them went that way. Nobody could get her out. You did what you could."

The raging flames engulfed the building. Peter knelt in the street but felt an immediate and overpowering conviction that it was pointless to pray.

On seeing Peter Wentworth, Stewart MacPherson snapped back to reality. He had been feeling out of his body, a spectator, not a participant. The shock must have been playing tricks with his mind. Suddenly his senses seemed to turn on: he could smell the acrid smoke, feel his eyes smart, hear the crackling of the dry wood.

"I've known that fellow all my life," he said. "He's a minister at the cathedral. We practically grew up together."

"He looked a little crazed to me," the major said.

"He's always been rather intense."

And he had known the officer beside him for only two hours. Yet the stranger had become familiar, and Peter Wentworth, a stranger. If shock did that to a professional psychologist, what was it doing to all the poor creatures they had been helping?

All afternoon, he and the major filled the Paige with mutilated people. Dried blood darkened the fabric of the seat. They now drove to any hospital or first-aid station that would accept patients. The lines got longer, swollen by desperate crowds searching for missing relatives. Fluttering in the rising wind outside each first-aid station was a handwritten list of people treated there. Private doctors set up emergency clinics, and their living and dining rooms quickly filled with people waiting to be treated.

The explosion had not closed the harbor. Providentially an American hospital ship, U.S.S. *Old Colony,* steamed in and was immediately filled with severely wounded civilians. By late afternoon American marines were sent ashore to help Canadian and British sentries police the miles of devastation. Looters were rumored to be robbing houses, taking jewelry and money from the dead. The sentries had orders to shoot looters on sight.

The army took over the search for survivors and bodies, moving street by street to miss no one. They found frightened people still hiding in cellars or garden sheds.

As the afternoon light faded, doctors operated by candlelight and kerosene lamps in Camp Hill Hospital. Badly wounded people were laid two to a bed, on the floor between beds, and in the corridors. The gaping windows had been covered and the radiators were working, but the constant opening and closing of doors to the winter night chilled the corridors. Patients shivering on the floor were given hot-water bottles, and when they ran out, orderlies heated bricks in the kitchen ovens, wrapped them in towels, and put them by the patients.

In Camp Hill it was noticeably quiet. No one was screaming or whimpering. People showed remarkable acceptance of what had happened to them. Some waited for hours, their wounds not washed, head lacerations matted with blood, hair, and dirt. Many died waiting. The hospital dining room floor was covered with mattresses. Dead and wounded lay side by side.

Every few minutes a doctor or nurse stepped over the rows of bodies, refining the triage. The sufferers were patient and altruistic. Stewart saw a sick man point to the woman beside him and say, "No, no, take her first. She needs it more."

A doctor gave a hypodermic syringe and a box of morphine capsules to a woman medical student. "Find those in the most extreme pain and inject them. Use it sparingly. We're nearly out."

On the next journey Stewart and the major were told to take the wounded into the hospital kitchens. A surgeon was operating while cooks were preparing food. A doctor with bloody rubber gloves saw the two men straightening up from laying a small boy on the floor.

"Can you give me a hand in here?"

In the next room, there was a woman on the table, her eye sockets pools of blood. The doctor was wearing a stained rubber apron over his vest and tie. His shirtsleeves were rolled above the rubber gloves.

"No anesthetic. We've run out. I've given her a shot of morphine. Have to remove both eyes. Hold her for me. You hold her legs. You hold the arms, like this."

Trembling, Stewart held the woman's arms down but could not refrain from watching as the doctor expertly removed one eyeball and then the other. The woman scarcely twitched, until he bathed the empty sockets with antiseptic; then she groaned and tried to lift her arms.

"Next patient," the surgeon snapped. Orderlies put another beside her on the table before lifting her onto the stretcher they had just brought in.

"Hundreds of eyes," the surgeon said, "filled with glass."

They held patients for several more quick eye removals until nurses took their places.

By the door, Major Coleman said, "I'd like to go to the lavatory and get something in my room. Back in a jiffy."

Stewart hurried down the dark corridor to the ward with the shell-shock patients. The corridor floor was crowded with bodies, leaving little space for walking. The hospital had lost its antiseptic odor and now smelled of unwashed bodies, smoke from their clothing, kerosene from the lamps, and candle wax.

He found the ward but it too was crowded with wounded civilians; the shell-shocked men he had seen that morning had gone. The harried nurse didn't know where they had been moved.

He pushed his way back through the congested corridors to the hospital office, where he found Colonel Bell, a white coat over his uniform, his balding head running with sweat.

"Dr. Hart? Oh, the lieutenant. We sent him off to the first-aid post on the Common. They needed a doctor more than we needed a psychiatrist today."

"What happened to the shell-shock cases?"

"I packed them off with Dr. Hattie to the insane asylum. I needed the beds. We've got more than a thousand casualties—maybe fifteen hundred; no one's had time to count—in a hospital built for two-fifty. So I can't worry about a few men who are physically fit."

The administrator looked pleased that he had had his way.

When Stewart returned to the car, Major Coleman was climbing stiffly into his seat.

"Three children in my bed, and two on the floor; but they need it more than I do."

"How bad is your leg now?"

"Not so good. Still a lot of the kaiser's hardware in it. Got to come out someday. Just not used to spending much time on it yet. So I got this." He held up a bottle of whiskey nearly full. "Emergency rations. Thought we deserved it. After you." He offered the bottle to Stewart, who gratefully took a large swig. Then the major drank and gave a loud sigh of satisfaction.

"That'll keep us going. It's getting colder."

The light from a few burning houses made it possible to search for the wounded and to pull out the dead.

By nine o'clock, the Victoria General had stopped accepting victims. All of its corridors and stairways were full of huddled people. Others were taken to the nearby School for the Blind, which was opened as a shelter and emergency hospital. The wounded were carried across a floor covered with broken glass; no one had had time to sweep it up. Patients were being comforted by women and girls from homes in the neighborhood, who were washing wounds, filling hot-water bottles, making tea and Bovril. The Army Supply Depot had brought a truckload of mattresses and blankets, which covered the upstairs floor space. Doctors, nurses, and volunteers had to step around a perpetual stream of worried relatives looking for loved ones.

They delivered several bodies to the makeshift mortuary at Chebucto Road School. Soldiers had boarded up the basement windows. For now, they piled the bodies anywhere on the floor.

The night advanced and the scenes of horror receded. Most of the fires were out or burning under control, which was fortunate, because the wind was blowing up. As they crossed the Common, they saw it billowing into hundreds of tents the army had erected there.

Coleman grew chattier. "Know what the bloody colonel said? The fat man who runs Camp Hill? I forget his name. You know him?"

"Colonel Bell."

"Officious bastard. When I went past his office, he was bustling around full of himself, tossing off orders right and left, loving every minute of it. I heard him tell some civilians: 'At last the war has come to us. I'm glad. People will know that we're in it.' How much of the bloody war has he seen, I wonder?"

"He's left over from the old Hospitals Commission they just replaced with the Army Medical Corps. Medically, he's out of the Stone Age." Stewart felt the need to explain his own civilian status. "I couldn't go myself. Bad eyes."

"I assumed that," said the major, "looking at your glasses.

You're a good worker, though. Cool head today when a lot of chaps couldn't have stood it. And a strong stomach."

"Thanks." Stewart felt uncommonly pleased with the praise.

They stared through the windshield until Coleman took another swig of whiskey and said, "Imagine being glad something like this has happened? Bloody hell! When I think what the chaps are going through in France for self-important twits like that! Enough to make you vomit!"

But Stewart was thinking that, assuming this explosion was accidental, no one intended that all these people should have had the precious envelope of their humanity torn open like this, their bowels ripped out, their eyes lacerated, their brains spilled. Yet every day in France, for three and a half years, men had done this intentionally. The Canadian government was ordering men to do it. Major Coleman, so gentle with the girl giving birth in the back seat, had been doing this professionally: eviscerating, lacerating, decapitating, amputating, disemboweling. Every day in France more people than all they had seen today, thousands more, were put into the abattoir by design. Was it any wonder that minds crumpled?

Late that night Peter dragged himself home. The wind was cold. His face and hands were frozen. The house was warm; Margery must have covered the broken windows and put coal in the furnace. He heard nothing. She and the children must be asleep.

Feeling his way in the dark, Peter fell into a kitchen chair and sat in a daze. He kept telling himself, I'll get up and make a cup of tea. A cup of tea—and something to eat. But all thought dissolved in hypnotic images of the day, and the same words, like a locked phrase of music, revolved in his head: . . . *"in nomine patris, et filii, et spiritus sancti."* He felt utterly exhausted and could not get warm, although he was close to the stove. After a while he rose painfully to light a candle and find the sherry decanter. Ignoring the delicate glasses, he poured the fortified wine into a kitchen tumbler. From the pantry he took a tin of Scottish oatcakes his mother had made and ate them methodically as he drank the sherry.

From another part of his brain, like someone talking in the next room, he kept hearing, *"in nomine patris, et filii . . ."* In the name of the Father, and of the Son, and of the Holy Ghost.

From childhood Peter had believed that behind everything was God, hidden but present, in the deepest blue in the sky, the darkest pool, beyond the hills, past the line where the sky touched the sea. God was there, but out of sight, just beyond the senses. That childish feeling had accompanied him into adult life and into his divinity studies.

Then he began to expect some contact, a personal epiphany. He imagined childish things: a light so dazzling that it blinded him; a voice like thunder when the clouds, the sky, the curtains of the universe would part—some revelation of the divine presence as his personal reward for faith and discipline.

Knowing it would come, he had tried harder to earn it, to be worthy of it, to cause it to happen. He had found deep pleasure in all the observances: in prayer, in self-denial, in cold chapel on winter mornings, in chastity until marriage, always expecting the deeper meaning to come.

But in that instant today, sobbing and shuddering from the death of the trapped woman, kneeling to pray, he had felt a flash of certainty: the revelation was negative. The God he had imagined would not have killed that woman—and all the others. To think of those people mangled, torn, crushed, eviscerated, burned; those who were alive tonight suffering all the tortures imaginable— some, God save them, still trapped in burning houses or freezing basements.

Why? That woman he had tried to solace—how fumblingly, how hesitatingly—what indescribable agony had she experienced in those last moments, knowing with absolute certainty that she would die by fire? Die by fire! It was too much to contemplate.

And the ferocious face of the sergeant, moved enough to kill him if he refused to help her: "Absolve her, or I'll kill you. Fuck-ing parson!"

The Psalm said, *But he that trusteth in the Lord, mercy shall compass him about.*

What mercy? He had heard her scream as the flames engulfed her.

He had winced when she asked for absolution, recoiled a little to think she had mistaken him for a Catholic priest. To be Catholic in Halifax meant to be lower class. The people who ran the law firms and trust companies, the banks, the shipping companies, the of-ficers and gentlemen, the people who belonged, were Anglican or

Presbyterian—or at least Protestant. The social reflex had caused him to shrink back; for a few seconds it took primacy over his Christian compassion for a soul in mortal terror.

Peter trembled. For the first time in his life, he was not certain what he believed.

Just before eleven o'clock Stewart and the major were told the search crews had stopped for the night. Stewart took Coleman back to the big house on Victoria Road, where they found most of the front windows broken. Stewart closed the tall inside shutters and drew the heavy curtains. He lit a fire in the study, and they huddled close to it, still in their coats, eating cold meat and cheese and drinking whiskey.

Major Coleman said, "I can't understand anything as stupid as governments banning drink in wartime. Best part of being over there. Never lacked for a drink."

"All part of making us a purer, better Canada," Stewart said. "Borden's sales pitch for the Unionist Government. Have you been following all that?"

"Oh, yes. But I've been two weeks in a hospital ship before landing here and a bit groggy before that. They told the troops a vote for the Liberals is a vote for the kaiser."

"Do the troops believe that?"

"The troops will vote for anything that sounds likely to get them out of there. They don't care if you give women the vote: they'd give horses the bloody vote, if it meant getting it over with. If you're wounded now, they patch you up and send you back to the front. Chaps know they've got to get killed or crippled to get out."

Coleman looked around at the antique desk, the walls of bookshelves, and the two leather sofas. "You have a wife and children?"

"No, I'm not married. A woman who worked for my parents comes twice a week, and she leaves me food."

"Well, I landed on my feet when I stopped you. Don't know where I would have laid my head tonight, or got a bite to eat. This is quite a mansion."

"It was my parents' house," Stewart said. "They died at the beginning of the war. It was in my father's family for three generations."

Coleman laughed. "Can't imagine anything like that in Medicine Hat, where I come from. Almost everyone in town moved there in this generation."

"What do you do in civilian life?"

"History teacher in a high school. They filled me full of English history in the Old Country, so when the war came, like most Englishmen out west, I jumped up and went back to fight for them. Henry the Fifth and all that. Seems a load of old codswallop now."

"Why?"

"Well, reckon myself a Canadian now. Don't sound it much, I know. But serving with the Canadians over there, you get another view of the Old Country. I didn't grow up a gentleman. Came from ordinary people—small shopkeepers and clerks in Barnet, north London. My father had a small men's haberdashery. Wasn't for me. I joined the army for adventure, Soldiers of the Queen, and all that. Saw a bit of the world, Egypt, India. Through the Boer War."

He pointed to several ribbons on his jacket.

"Kept my nose clean and kept getting promoted—sergeant, sergeant major, regimental sergeant major—top of the line. I began to get itchy feet in South Africa. Bloody marvelous country, Kaffirs, Boers, and all. Do you mind if I put my leg up?"

Coleman put down his whiskey glass and used both hands to lift his wounded leg onto his sofa.

"There!"

Stewart could guess the pain from the great sigh and the perspiration on Coleman's forehead. The major picked up his glass. "After South Africa I got posted to Gibraltar, then Canada, and I didn't go home. Got out and settled down. Mad for all that empty space out west. Became a schoolmaster, and there I was, as good as anyone else. Of course when the war came I had to enlist, and with my background they made me an officer right off. So I went overseas as a gentleman. Only I wasn't. The minute I stepped ashore in England, I knew my place again. It was a shambles at first and they shoved us into British regiments to make up their losses from the Marne."

His speech had relaxed, as though he had forgotten the part he was playing.

"The moment I found myself in the British officers' mess, all my old feelings came out. And they could sense it. In my mind I was still an NCO. The way I said 'sir' to anyone a notch above me gave it away. I was terrified I would run into my old regiment and they'd see my pips and call me out for impersonating an officer.

"Then when Ottawa raised hell and we got the first Canadian division, I was fine again. They gave us some of the worst places to fight—Arras, Vimy, now Passchendaele. We were shock troops. But the bloody British officers! The senior, regular army officers, I mean, not the chaps they pulled out of university. Talking high up in their noses about *our brave colonials*. I could have shot some of the buggers myself."

"Are you sorry you went?"

"No. Made me free of all that. Went over there still feeling British but came back Canadian. Just thank God I came back more or less in one piece. There's a lady I'm planning to marry. She teaches in the same school. Ever been out west?"

"No."

"You should go. A different country. Canada feels a lot different out there. Here in Nova Scotia, it could still be part of England."

"How long were you in France?"

"About two years—minus a few leaves in England."

Stewart said, "Before today, I had seen only two people dead. My mother and father. Natural deaths, of course. My father died right here, in fact. A stroke. I don't know what I felt today."

"I expect it'll catch up with you later. It seems unreal the first time you see it." He poured himself more Scotch and looked at the fire. "One thing makes this better than France, you know. At least it's over. In the trenches the poor buggers survive one attack that turns their guts to jelly, then it's quiet. But they never know when the next lot's coming. Anyone can be brave if he knows this is the worst of it. It's hard to be brave when you're never sure it's finished. Today was like one big shelling in France—and brief at that. At least we don't have to face another one in a few hours, or tomorrow. And more the day after that. And so on."

They were both quiet.

Coleman said, "What made you take up psychology? I've never met anyone who had anything to do with it."

"I suppose I wanted to understand more about myself, how my mind worked, and therefore how other minds worked. What causes us to do the things we do. To be honest about it, sex had a lot to do with it."

Stewart was astonished to hear himself say that. He had never told anyone that before.

"Sex?" An embarrassed inflection, then more relaxed. "Well, you can't just leave a bloody remark like that hanging in the air without explaining it, can you?"

Stewart was at ease; Coleman's candor made him talkative.

"I don't know about you, but I came through my boyhood with a lot of anguish about sex, guilt about masturbation, a feeling that I was different from everyone else and should be ashamed. Do you know what I mean?"

"Well, yes. But I mean"—Coleman looked away and smoothed his mustache with the edge of his glass—"one doesn't usually talk about that sort of thing."

"That's right. But it's unhealthy to keep it a secret, that Victorian silence about anything that happens below the belt."

"But it disturbs people to talk about—bodily functions—all that."

"That's the point. The theory is that by pushing it out of our minds, burying a lot of fear and anxiety, we can make ourselves ill."

"Whose theory is that, then?" As he relaxed, Coleman sounded more like the working-class Londoner.

"Sigmund Freud."

"I've never heard of him."

"He's the Viennese doctor who invented psychoanalysis."

"Well, I've never heard of that either," Coleman said.

"With his own patients, Freud found that the chief source of much mental disturbance was sex."

"That's understandable, isn't it? I mean they're Europeans! Viennese, you said? Europeans are a lot more mixed up in things like that than we British are. That's what they say about the French and the others, isn't it?"

"Well, I don't think people are that different anywhere. But the moment Freud began publishing his ideas, he was reviled by many, called every foul name."

"Not too surprising. You get into that area and it makes decent people uncomfortable."

"But that's just the point. People are uncomfortable because they as individuals and the whole society share the same fears and guilt."

"But you wouldn't want your wife or sister reading ideas like that, would you?"

"Why shouldn't they read them? Women have sex, too—"

"Steady on, old chap!"

"Even Queen Victoria had sex, for heaven's sake!"

"Only to have heirs to the throne."

"How do you know that?"

Major Coleman laughed.

Stewart said, "You're thinking of her as an old woman, fat and sour from years of grieving. How do you know she wasn't a passionate little thing when she was young, as hot as anything you probably found as a soldier on your travels?"

"How do I know?" The major yawned. "Because she was the queen, mate."

"I studied in Toronto with a British doctor, Ernest Jones, who believed that sex has replaced religion as an outlet for human intolerance and prejudice. He said we used to persecute people for wrong religious beliefs—tortured them, burned them at the stake —but now sex is the devil, and people are persecuted for it. He said the *odium theologicum* has been replaced by an *odium sexicum*."

"Making a bit of a mountain of a molehill, isn't he?" The major yawned again and stretched. "I don't like to be rude, but I'm for a bit of kip. I can't keep my eyes open."

"I'm sorry. I'll get us some blankets. We'd better sleep here. It's the only room with any heat."

Stewart went upstairs with a candle, which guttered in the drafts coming through the shutters from the unglazed windows. His bedroom was freezing. He collected blankets and pillows and went back to the warmth of the study. Coleman was carefully lining up the crease in his trousers to hang them over a chair. In his long underwear, wincing as he moved his bad leg, he made himself comfortable on one of the sofas flanking the fireplace. Stewart banked the fire with coal and blew out the candles. The glow from the fire gave light enough to see by. He settled on the other sofa.

After a few minutes, he said, "I wonder whether anyone picked up that little child's head from the street. Did you see it?" Coleman didn't answer.

The wind was loud around the house, crying in the bare elms outside. Northeasterlies meant bad storms. Stewart listened to the howling, imagining what some people must be enduring. What had happened to the scores of people they had lifted and driven all day? People who had lived near him in the same city for years, but in reality another city. Once or twice in college years he had gone to bootleggers, up narrow stairways past steel fences and guard dogs. As distressing as their injuries was the poverty, the meanness of the houses eviscerated by the explosion. Even the sidewalks were not paved like those in the South End.

It grew warm near the fire and snug under the blankets; his head buzzed from the whiskey. But as he drifted toward sleep, Stewart began to feel strangely cold. He awoke, shivering violently. All his muscles seemed to be shaking at once. His teeth were chattering uncontrollably, yet the room was still warm, the fire was bright, and the blankets were close around him. He got up and crouched in front of the fire. The shivering gradually subsided and his muscles stopped their involuntary shuddering, but now he was sweating heavily. He had to open his shirt and then go up to his freezing bedroom for a towel and a fresh shirt. The major slept, undisturbed.

Dry and comfortable again, Stewart lay down, thinking he should make notes on this acute anxiety attack, delayed shock, sudden acceleration in pulse rate, and profuse sweating.

Only then did it strike him that he had totally forgotten about Christine. The anxiety that had nagged him all morning had been wiped out by the explosion. Like amnesia. How strange.

Christine Soames: her foreignness had intrigued him from the first days of the term. He had instantly noticed her dark eyes, and it was obvious from her accent and aura that she was not a local girl. Then he had been told she was the daughter of the American consul. In the first lecture she stood out: bright, eager, more aggressive than the Nova Scotian girls. Stewart had kept glancing at her, as though he were delivering the lecture just to her—and she noticed.

There was something urgent in her thin body, a quickness that made him unable to resist speculating about her physically. When he pushed her out of his mind, her aura came back, more insistently. And she was constantly there in his lectures.

She had knocked on his office door with a question. She wore a musky scent, not quite masking a faint sweatiness, odd in an American, a very European smell compared with that of the Canadian girls, who smelled of nothing sultrier than lily of the valley. It was a warm day in September, a tardy bee buzzing at the window. The sleeves of her dress were unbuttoned and rolled back. When she stretched to put a paper in front of him, the sunlight caught the fine hair on her forearm, and he wanted to put his lips on it to taste her skin. He imagined the taste quite explicitly. He was almost convinced that she expected an advance right there. Of course, it wouldn't do to be tempted into an indiscretion, particularly with the daughter of a foreign official. Yet it was precisely her foreignness that tempted him.

Their meetings began innocently enough. Christine came more frequently to his office, seeming to know when Professor Becker, who shared it, would be absent.

In a lecture he briefly discussed Freud's *The Interpretation of Dreams,* and Christine materialized the next day, saying the book was not in the library. She borrowed his copy and was quickly back, wanting to discuss it. Discussing it meant discussing her dreams, which meant discussing her libido, as charged with desire for Stewart as his for her. They began to come to this big, empty house to make love. Their unhesitant manner made it obvious that there had been a mutual intention from the start.

It lasted six weeks, until Christine unwarily mentioned the professor who had told her about Freud. Her father had a fit. He would not have his daughter taught such filth. He ordered her to withdraw from the course; when she refused, he said she must leave the university. When she protested more vehemently, he sent Christine and her mother to Boston, two weeks ahead of their planned Christmas vacation. Yesterday he had carried his outrage to the chancellor, who summoned Stewart.

"Professor MacPherson, this is a very grave matter. I have received a complaint from the American consul, Mr. Whittaker Soames, concerning his daughter, who is one of your students."

Panicked, Stewart instantly assumed total discovery: confession by Christine, hysteria, confrontations, accusations, legal charges, professional disgrace . . . but it was not so.

"Her father alleges that you have introduced the teaching of Sigmund Freud into your lectures. I am compelled to ask you whether that is so."

"I have mentioned him once or twice, yes."

"Freud, I believe, is not in the curriculum for the course you teach, introductory psychology, Professor MacPherson?"

"No, he is not."

"Then why would you even mention this man whose name decent people and respectable academic opinion have come to revile?"

"It seemed relevant at the time. There is also a body of contrary opinion regarding Freud—"

"Not at this university. And there is no justification for conduct that causes a distinguished foreign official to remove his daughter from our halls. That is inexcusable. He tells me he will now send the girl to another university. What do you think of that?"

"I think he is overreacting," Stewart said, but thought it impolitic to add that Soames's tirade suggested repressed fears. In his relief, he must have smiled.

"Your attitude is too casual, sir. You have offended a prominent person, you have offended the university, and by your flippant manner you offend me."

The chancellor retreated behind his desk for more dignity.

"I should dismiss you, but I knew your father and liked him. He was my banker for many years. We played golf together. So I am inclined to give you a chance to redeem yourself. I will put you on probation for one term. Your lectures will be monitored; your conduct will be watched. If it is satisfactory, if there are no further lapses, you will be reinstated with full standing. If you do not wish to accept such terms, you may, of course, resign. I hope you will be good enough to consider the matter and give me your answer tomorrow."

On probation for mentioning Freud? The anger and fear the name provoked continued to astonish Stewart. It was what had driven Ernest Jones out of Toronto in 1913, although Jones had encouraged the anger by playing the Freudian bull in the china shop of their sensibilities.

But this was not just Freud. The punishment was for alienating the American consul. Luckily no one knew the whole truth about Christine; all Stewart had heard from her was a brief and anguished telephone call, very apologetic, sweetly solicitous of him.

Something else had just reminded him of Ernest Jones—what was it? His height! The little Welsh doctor was only five feet, five. Stewart towered over him, and Jones quite obviously bristled at it. Yet Jones had taken a liking to Stewart. Passionate acolytes for the teachings of Freud were rare, and few other students dared to brave all the controversy surrounding Jones. But for Stewart, the new convert, to be in almost living contact with Freud and Jung, whose work was also beginning to excite him, was irresistible. Jones was in constant touch with Freud's circle, writing letters, spending months with them in Europe at congresses, attending conferences in the United States, writing, lecturing, publishing, treating patients, all with feverish intensity. And in intervals of this hyperactive life, he urged Stewart to make psychoanalysis his career.

"You have the right sensibility, good sympathy, a clear mind, wide cultural curiosity."

Stewart was immensely flattered. Jones could be as charming as he could be biting and condescending. "Of course, with your rudimentary Canadian education, you have a long way to go, and you haven't even begun your medical studies . . ."

He might have been persuaded, but when Jones suddenly left Toronto, Stewart was convinced that the only promising career for him was in academic psychology.

He lay on the sofa considering. To accept the chancellor's probation would be to admit guilt, in effect joining the hysterical campaign against Freud's efforts to lift the veils of ignorance and fear. But there was little choice. Yesterday Stewart had hovered between the proud gesture of resignation and acceptance of his punishment. It was clearer tonight. The proud gesture would leave him with nothing. The Scots had a talent for proud gestures, magnificent moments that led to greater humiliations.

His body already missed Christine's innocent carnality. How must she be feeling? As ambivalent as he? Relieved to be out of a dangerous situation but longing for it back? Sex and guilt playing indispensably into the complicated strands of feeling, the phrase he had picked up as an undergraduate, "the end of desire is the beginning of wisdom." But desire ended was desire renewed, and merely thinking about Christine renewed desire.

Stewart was wide awake. The major was snoring quietly.

Until the encounter in the North End, Peter Wentworth hadn't entered Stewart's thoughts for a month or two.

When they were small children, Peter had come to all the large birthday and Christmas parties in this house.

Peter's own house was plainer but cozier than Stewart's, where a cook and a housemaid ran things. Peter's mother did her own housework. She was a brisk little woman, born in Scotland, who wore her hair in a bun and never talked down to them.

They would sit in her kitchen on a rainy or snowy day, watching Dorothy Wentworth making a pie or a cake, while she talked to them about something else. It always gave him pleasure to remember her competent hands cutting butter into flour, rolling out dough, peeling and coring apples, sprinkling them with sugar and cinnamon. She let the boys use the small nutmeg grater.

Her kitchen smelled of tea frequently made and gas from the stove. Near the back door was the wooden icebox. The ice man came puffing in without knocking, carrying a large block in his tongs. He brought in with him the odor from the horse that pulled his cart and the peaty smell from the sawdust that came from the ice houses. Traces of sawdust often clung to the blocks.

When the boys went on small expeditions, Mrs. Wentworth made sandwiches. She buttered the cut end of the loaf, cut off the slice, buttered the end again, then cut another slice.

"Why don't you cut off the slice and then butter it?" Stewart asked. "That's the way our cook does it."

"Why do you think?" she asked without stopping her work.

"I know!" said Peter. "Because it doesn't get crumbly and make holes in the bread."

"Now, now," said Mrs. Wentworth. Her musical accent made it sound a little like *noo, noo.* "Stewart is your guest. You should let him answer first."

"But I knew!" said Peter.

Peter's mother was the kind of woman boys find agreeable and even fun to obey. She began every instruction with a phrase like "Shall we?" Or "How would you like to . . . ?" "Now, boys, why don't we just get these things tidied up and then we'll be ready for a wee snack of something."

It was strange to Stewart that Dorothy Wentworth and his mother were friends. Frances MacPherson was fussy, dithery, someone who expects to be disobeyed. She would sigh and say, "I don't know how Dorothy Wentworth does it. She has almost no help in that house, and no money, yet her garden is a marvel."

Stewart had since observed that some women used the same techniques on their children as they did on their husbands, and he presumed that that was what so exasperated his father. He saw Frances fluttering ineffectually but possessively around their only child, despairing of this, terrified of that hurting him; fussing and petting and cosseting. Stewart could see that it infuriated him. The newspaper page would be turned with a more vehement snap, and he would say, "Oh, Frances, leave the boy alone! Stop fussing at him. You'll turn him into an old woman before he's ten years old."

"But he's eaten only half his porridge, and it's so cold and awful outside."

"Eat your porridge, Stewart, for God's sake, and stop your mother moaning about it."

"Andrew, I am not moaning and you hurt me to say that." She would sniff and pull a small handkerchief from her sleeve.

Stewart's father was an angry man behind the meek and obsequious banker's exterior. His anger came out in small puffs like leaks from a steam engine whose boiler pressure is too high. A day of solicitude for the money of prosperous Haligonians built the pressure up again. Invariably some of it escaped at mealtimes.

If Peter and Stewart asked their mothers for permission to do something, like go across the Arm for a picnic, it was as typical for Mrs. MacPherson to think of the grief they could come to as it was for Mrs. Wentworth to say, "Oh, what fun! I don't think that'll hurt them. And if it does, they'll learn a lesson, won't they?" She should have been the anxious one. She had lost an older boy to drowning.

Peter did not grow up with the nagging and whining that were part of the climate in Stewart's home, nor the endless harping on unimportant details. Stewart envied Peter his mother. Mrs. Wentworth always seemed the same, brisk and good-humored. She acted as though it was a pleasure, not a nuisance, to talk to small boys.

Stewart's mother wore flowery, flouncy clothes, with lace-fringed sleeves that caught on things. The boy liked Dorothy Wentworth's simpler, neater clothes, like a nicely dressed schoolteacher who wants to keep her sleeves out of the chalk.

"So," Jones had observed, "your mother was the more feminine of the two, more the coquette?"

"Yes."

"And that disturbed you, so that you liked Mrs. Wentworth's practical ways better?"

"Yes."

"Do you know why it disturbed you that your mother was fluttery and feminine?"

"It's a strong feeling. I can't explain it."

"I think you could if you worked at it. We'll come back to it."

But they never had. It was one of many ends left dangling.

Stewart also envied Peter's wiry, athletic body and hated the flabbier shape and slower reflexes that made him the object of other boys' laughter. The fact that he could think faster and read more was no consolation. He disliked most of the games by which boys rehearsed a manliness modern times had made largely irrelevant: running, jumping, climbing, throwing, hitting, wrestling. Yet when a snowball knocked Stewart's glasses off, when he panted stiff-kneed behind the pack, some instinct told him that his were the skills now favored by evolution—intelligence, language, and humor.

The knowledge gave him a mental refuge from ridicule. The boys called him "sissy" a lot. They said he ran like a girl, and he knew they were right. Pink with humiliation, owl-eyed without his glasses, Stewart was ashamed, yet, in a deeply private place, not ashamed. For a few adolescent years their scorn placed him pretty accurately as to sexual identity—somehow ambiguous—until nature ended the uncertainty.

Stewart's pain became acute when they went away to boarding school at thirteen. Sons of clergymen were accepted at reduced fees, which is how John Wentworth managed the cost. When Peter's plans were announced, Stewart's father seized the notion that boarding school would "make a man" of his son. When his mother protested, his father said it was just what Stewart needed and what good luck to have a fine chap like Peter, his close friend, as a companion. Stewart would emerge, he argued, hardened up, more confident, more of a man.

The expense, about $150 a year, was no deterrent. Mr. Mac-Pherson's bank thrived even before the war pumped millions into the depressed Halifax economy. With half a percentage here and a quarter there, enough of it stuck to his father, in the almost invisible way of monied people in Halifax, that Stewart had reason to be grateful after he died of a heart attack.

When Frances MacPherson almost as suddenly died of pneumonia a year into the war, he was very well off. That was how he could keep the house on what Dalhousie paid an associate professor.

Rothesay had looked delightful when he and Peter first climbed the hill from the village station in 1902, the school cart coming behind with Stewart's brand-new black metal trunk *(Stewart Henley MacPherson, Rothesay Collegiate School, Rothesay, New Brunswick,* neatly lettered on the lid) beside Peter's battered trunk, survivor of his father's many second-class journeys abroad.

The September day glowed. The clustered school buildings formed a small village under the bosky trees, the chestnuts about to drop, glimpses of misty countryside below the hill in the Kennebecasis valley. Even their dormitory, a peeling Victorian mansion, varnished and painted to a fair standard inside, gave an illusion of homeyness.

The glow quickly faded for Stewart. He loathed undressing in a room of eight boys, hated showing himself, because he thought his penis looked infantile in his plump thighs and stomach. He disliked the line of battered washbasins and toilet stalls with broken door latches. He flinched from the constant shouting and throwing of water, the wet towel ends snapped at bare buttocks. Fifteen years later, he still rejoiced that he had escaped those years. Nature had stamped him for an adult; childhood had to be endured.

Peter thrived on it. He laughed, pounded other boys with pillows, got pounded without caring. He took the harassment of senior boys lightly, and they soon picked on those who resented or feared it more, like Stewart. Peter even came honorably through the dreaded initiation, which left Stewart sick with fear and rage.

They were warned for weeks. Psychological torture preceded the physical. "Wait until you see what they do," said a veteran of the previous year. "One year, a boy nearly died."

They're exaggerating, Stewart thought. It can't be that bad when it happens. All this talk is just part of the fun. But it was far worse than he could have imagined.

It was raining that Saturday, a very cold rain. Rothesay had extensive forest lands. Away from the school, a path led into the woods to a swimming pond on a dammed-up stream. The path was guarded by older boys, each with a cane or stick, standing on both sides along the half-mile to the dam. Already soaked and cold, new boys had to run the gauntlet. The faster boys could dodge or nip by, getting a miss or a glancing blow. Stewart ran badly anywhere, but on this broken ground he stumbled and half-tripped every few steps. His glasses steamed up and slipped down his nose, so the way ahead became a blur. His lungs ached with panting. The hits with the canes stung unbearably. After a few blows, he was crying out, "No, please." To his shame he heard himself sobbing like a child, enormous *boo-hoo* sobs, but there was no stopping, because boys behind, terrified of the canes, kept pushing on. He tripped on a root and fell. His glasses dropped off, and the nearest persecutors, delighted to have a stationary target, began hitting him on the ground. He curled up to protect himself. Then he heard Peter shouting, "Stop. It isn't fair! I know him. He can't run well. It's not fair." At first no one paid any attention. They lashed out at him as well, shouting, "New Boy, move on. New Boy, move on!" But then an older boy said, "He's right! It's not fair! Let Fatty get up!"

And they did. Peter picked up Stewart's glasses and pulled him along the track, and no one struck them after that. They came to the pond and a big crowd of cheering, jeering boys lining the wooden dam. They had dug up the earth and wetted it to make a large mud hole. It looked like a pigsty with a white, naked boy slopping in it. It was Stewart's turn next.

"Take off your clothes, Fatty!" someone called. It took him a moment to understand.

"Take off your clothes, New Boy," they all shouted. "Strip."

Stewart took off his clothes. His bare feet hurt on the stony ground. Someone pushed, and he fell violently into the mud, which oozed and slimed all over him. It was very cold. In a chorus they shouted, "Screw the mud, Fatty! Screw the mud!" When he did not understand, someone smacked his bare buttocks with a cane, and as he arched away from the pain, they cheered so that he realized what they meant. Humiliated, but more afraid to disobey, he pumped at the mud until someone shouted, "Stop!"

In the silence, the torturer said, "New Boy, I name thee Fatty. Forevermore, that is your name, and you must always answer to it. Now, what is your name?"

"Fatty."

Everyone chanted, "Fatty! Fatty!" Stewart tried to climb out but had nothing solid to push against and kept sliding back. Finally, two boys grabbed his hands and pulled him out; two more grabbed his ankles, swung him several times, and flung him far out into the pond. He spluttered in water even colder than the mud and thrashed out for the bank, where they helped him ashore, now comrades, not tormenters.

Then it was Peter's turn. Having seen what to do, he jumped into the mud before they could push him, "screwed" the mud quickly, and was christened—why, Stewart never knew—Scruff.

"Scruff, Scruff," they all cried out and threw him into the pond. Shivering, Peter and Stewart pulled their clothes on their wet bodies and walked back to the school.

"Well," Peter said, "it wasn't so bad." He was ruddy and cheerful. Stewart could not say anything. He was shaking with the cold and pain and shock at such barbarity. But he felt something like love for Peter, who had rescued him from the fiends on the path. Peter seemed to have forgotten it.

"Come on," he said, starting to jog, "let's hurry up. I wonder what's for supper."

For the next few days Stewart never wanted to be apart from Peter, fearing that, without him, he would endure terrible things. It began to annoy Peter to have ungainly Stewart always placing himself next in line, never straying far during the breaks when boys committed endless cruelties on the weak, like punching one's upper arm with a knuckle projecting from the fist. Stewart's flaccid biceps were mottled with blue-and-green bruises changing color as they receded. Peter edged himself away, and gradually Stewart felt able to stand apart, although he was still nervous, flinching from an expected blow when someone passed near.

It seemed that very little bad happened to Peter because he wasn't afraid of it happening. But Stewart's vulnerability made him an irresistible target.

For almost the entire first year, they lived in terror of the call "New Boys to the sixth!" Quite arbitrarily, the sixth-formers decided to punish or harass or merely scare the New Boys. Outside the dining hall after supper a boy shouted, "New Boys to the sixth." The call made Stewart sick with fear; soon he could not come out of the dining hall without glancing to one side, fearing to see the messenger.

All the new boys would file in. Spaced around the walls were the sixth-formers, virtually grown men. Each had a cane. The new boys each faced a desk around the perimeter in a horseshoe of terror. The leader recited alleged crimes or misdemeanors: a boy had sauced a monitor who wanted his shoes shined or his bed made; boys had run away and hidden when a monitor called for a "fag." New boys had been late to their seats in chapel. The prosecution complete, he pronounced sentence: a general discipline. They were ordered to bend over the desks in front of them with their jackets pulled up over their heads. The monitors then paraded behind them, hitting each boy on the behind with his cane as he passed. There were about a dozen monitors. The thwacks were loud. With one round, a boy got a dozen thwacks. Sometimes the sentence was two rounds, sometimes three. It was unbearable. Some boys cried out. When Stewart thought of it now, a grown man, his stomach turned and his scrotum shrank in fear. It was indescribably painful, the agony of one blow still rising in intensity, as he tensed for the next, filled with fear and impotence. Yet when it was over most of the boys straightened up, pulled their jackets down, and marched out, looking flushed but cheerful. If they had any tears, they surreptitiously brushed them off with their sleeves; such was the cult of manliness, they did not dare look as though it bothered them.

Peter said the canes hurt but only one of the monitors was really cruel. "You can tell some of them are holding back. Better to bear it and be a good sport."

For exercise on weekends, teams of boys would go into the forest and cut wood for the school's many fireplaces. It was useful and pleasant work. New boys were seldom asked, so Peter and Stewart were surprised when Arthur Glass, who was a monitor, asked if they wanted to go. It was unusual for a monitor to *ask* anything. They said yes, and on a sunny Saturday afternoon collected axes, wedges, mauls, and two-man saws to head into the woods. Glass had also rounded up two boys a year or so older, Jeffreys and Wade.

Glass notched a large birch with his axe; then he and Wade felled it with the two-man saw, driving in a wedge to keep the cut open. Stewart's fumbling efforts with the axe produced small nicks, so they gave him the task of pulling the brush away. But Peter took turns in sawing the trunk and heavier branches into four-foot lengths, that were split with wedges and stacked in a cord. Even Stewart found the work pleasant. He liked the smell of the wood, the slippery feel of the papery white bark, the fat chips flying as the sharp axe bit into the juicy core.

It was hot, and Glass called a break. They sat on logs and stumps while he and Jeffreys and Wade pulled out packets of British Consuls cigarettes. When offered them, Peter and Stewart looked at each other shyly and accepted. They lighted up and puffed and coughed along with the others.

Afterward Stewart could never remember how Glass had the effrontery to give the signal, or even what his signal was, but it must have been something the other two were used to. To the new boys' amazement, Glass calmly took off all his clothes and lay back on the moss and the grass. Neither Peter nor Stewart yet had pubic hair, while Glass was astonishingly hairy between his legs and elsewhere. More astonishing was his penis. Stewart had never seen an adult penis, and this was not only adult but erect. It looked astonishingly big. He stared, wondering what happened next.

"Well, aren't you fellows going to give me a hand?" Glass said, in the manner of someone about to lift a table. Jeffreys and Wade, grinning sheepishly, threw away their cigarettes and squatted one on either side and began massaging Glass's penis. Glass lay back contentedly for a few moments, then raised his head and looked at the new boys.

"Don't you want to help?" he asked Peter.

Peter had turned white, and said quietly, "No."

"Why not? Be a good sport."

"No," said Peter, a little more forcefully.

"As you like. What about you, MacPherson?" Stewart was suddenly full of odd feelings: fear of Glass and echoes of the power of the monitors, some considerable disquiet at the sight of Glass's nakedness, and a little sick feeling.

"Well, come on!" Glass said impatiently.

As if pulled by a puppet master, Stewart's hand reached out and touched Glass. He was not circumcised, and the skin was brownish. After a few tentative pats, Stewart pulled his hand back, as if from a stove. His fingers tingled as though an electric current had gone through them.

"What's wrong with you, Wentworth?" Glass said.

"Nothing. I don't want to," Peter said defiantly.

"Too bad for you. Come on, fellows, we haven't got all day."

Wade and Jeffreys resumed stroking him more vigorously, obviously practiced hands, and in a minute Glass ejaculated. That, too, Peter and Stewart had never seen, and they stared, amazed.

On the way back, Glass said, "I wouldn't mention that to anyone if I were you. All right?"

"All right."

"All right."

As soon as they were alone, Peter said angrily to Stewart, "Why did you do that? Why did you touch him? It's disgusting."

"I thought I had to," Stewart said.

He saw a different look on Peter's face, as if the skin on his cheeks had shrunken. Stewart felt queasy, whether from the cigarettes or the spectacle of Glass, he didn't know. But again he admired Peter. Why could he say no, Stewart thought, when I couldn't? He worried afterward. They never discussed it again. When either of them saw Glass, they looked away.

Years later in the sessions with Ernest Jones, Stewart skimmed over the episode, but Jones kept bringing him back, insisting that he be honest in dredging his memories. When his resistance finally dissolved, so, miraculously, did the shame he had always felt, and thereafter he could remember it quite easily, with no embarrassment.

About two weeks later, Stewart heard the dreaded call, "New Boys to the sixth!" Terror swept through him, but he could not run away. Like Peter, he was drawn by the crowd to the place of execution. Trembling, he took his place facing one desk. The head monitor was distracted for a few moments. Arthur Glass was standing at the front and recognized Peter and Stewart. His eyes went quickly back and forth between them and then he said, commandingly, "Wentworth and MacPherson, you may leave." They went outside followed by scared, envious glances from the still condemned.

"Why did he do that?" Stewart asked.

"Because he's afraid," Peter said and broke into a run to race for the North House, leaving Stewart behind.

Stewart did what he could to survive, to find pockets of comfort, but he was limited in ways to shine. He did well at his studies, but that carried no prestige. Other boys' parents smiled indulgently at him on Prize Day, but it meant nothing to the boys.

Peter settled comfortably into the middle of the class, but he was effortlessly popular because he played everything with enthusiasm and grit—rugby, hockey, cross-country running, track and field events. He made the first rugby eleven in the fifth form, for his speed on the wings and his daring.

Stewart watched the matches, as was compulsory, muffled up in scarves and a raincoat. The play would come thundering by on the touch line; red-faced boys, panting, gasping, their breath visible in the chilly air, their bare knees smeared with grass stains, mud, and blood. A boy would have the ball crooked into his elbow and be running for the goal line when Peter would appear from an angle, swift as a hare, and throw himself perfectly horizontal, for an instant flying in the air a foot off the ground, his arms extended. His fingers would catch the runner's boots, and both boys would crash onto the turf, with a great *ooofff* as the wind went out of them. The Rothesay boys cheered their guts out. A few older girls from Netherwood, the sister school, squealed with delight. It looked like one of the illustrations in an English school story: "Thrilling Moment on the Touch Line." The younger Rothesay boys looked at Peter as though at a god; they stood close to him as he sat up, got his wind, and ambled back to the scrum quietly pleased. No one showed off so little.

Once Stewart overheard one of the masters say to another on the sidelines, "That's the sort of chap who wins medals for valor."

"That's the sort of chap who gets himself killed," the other said and laughed.

Peter appeared to care far less about scoring or winning than about the pleasure it gave him to play. Hockey gave him similar exhilaration: the much colder winter air, gasped into starved lungs, the flash and scrape of the blades on the ice, the quick stops with a spray of powdered ice, the sudden spurts to get past a defenseman, the thrill of skating at the edge of control, vulnerable to the slightest check, the joy of hip-checking an enemy to send him spinning off balance. Some joyful devil, some echo of an ancestor who thrilled to battle with a broadsword, or boarded a captured ship with a cutlass, must have lived on and leaped in Peter's veins. He was not afraid.

But Peter never paraded his ability and was quick to praise the teammates who needed it. The combination made him a hero at school.

Boys' schools offered plumpish, uncoordinated fellows like Stewart only two roles—victim and clown. He was immediately cast as a victim. The entire repertoire of practical and cruel jokes was revived for his benefit: apple-pie beds, missing clothes, salt in his tea. They did not invent anything new. He awoke one night to find his hand in a bucket of warm water and several boys sitting on the next bed, with their hands over their mouths, stifling giggles.

"What is it? What's going on?"

"Too bad! He didn't do it," they shouted.

"Do what?"

"Wet the bed! Wet the bed!" they screamed in delight. "When you put a sleeping person's hand in warm water, he wets the bed." They collapsed in a heap on the other bed, laughing uncontrollably.

At first, on such occasions, Stewart cried, feeling so desolate, so unhappy that they had all ganged up on him, including Peter. The more he cried, the more they enjoyed it.

The bell would ring for breakfast and his glasses would not be where he always put them at night. More and more frantic about being late, he searched, half-blind, feeling as much as looking, over the bedclothes, under the bed, on the night table. Then, precious minutes lost, he would find them mysteriously replaced where he had left them. Just as the master would come into the room, Stewart could finally bend down to put on his shoes and find the laces tied together, not with one but many knots, wetted and pulled very tight, taking ten minutes to pick out.

"You're late, MacPherson," the master would say unpityingly. The other boys would race out, jostling and pushing, and he would be left sitting on his bed, overheated, flushed, bent over his shoes trying to pick apart the devilish knots.

Stewart was not sure whether Peter ever committed the actual pranks, but he made no effort to stop them and laughed with all the rest. Stewart gradually came to understand that Peter spent his fund of compassion sparingly—only when it really mattered. He knew intuitively when it was vital. When it was not, he took on the protective coloring of being one with the tormentors, or was absent.

There was only one other occasion when Peter intervened.

The two boys from the woodcutting incident, Wade and Jeffreys, ignored them the rest of that term. Stewart saw them only when they hurried from building to building between classes, to chapel or to meals. It was the Rothesay fashion never to put on outer clothes when dashing between buildings. Even on the coldest winter days, with deep snow and temperatures well below zero, everyone walked from house to meals, from meals to chapel, in regular school clothes and shoes, collars turned up, hands in pockets, books crooked in the elbow. When it was cold, there was always a crush at the doors, boys still outside, blowing breath plumes in the frosty air, pushing against the boys already inside to get into the warmth.

In one of those jams, Stewart was shoved against Wade and Jeffreys, so close that he could smell tobacco on Wade's breath. He was very thin, with a prominent Adam's apple, half a head taller than Stewart, with curly dark hair and a pinched face. Slightly bucked front teeth pushed his upper lip into a little bow. His lips always looked red and wet. Wade was sallow, his skin gray. He wore his hair cut short and brushed up the wrong way like a hamster.

"There's Fatty MacPherson," Wade said. "It's Friday, Fatty. Coconut cream pie for dessert."

No one had ever made such a friendly conversational overture, and Stewart felt a rush of gratitude, mixed with the residue of uneasiness from the scene in the woods.

The crowd pushed farther into the dining hall. "Stop shoving back there!" an exasperated master shouted. Wade put his hand on Stewart's upper arm and felt the flesh through his jacket. "Nice and plump," he said. "A few more coconut pies and he'll be ready for market, I'd say."

Jeffreys laughed. "Roasted or broiled, would you say? Do you like your MacPherson roasted or broiled, sir?" Other boys listening began to laugh as they pushed in.

"A delicate, well-fleshed little capon, a veritable capon of a boy . . . tenderly roasted in its own juices. But what about stuffing, Jeffreys? We mustn't forget the stuffing."

"Ah, the stuffing," said Wade. "Of the greatest importance; makes all the difference *how* you stuff him." Again he touched Stewart, this time patting his behind.

Their friendliness warmed him. The little jokes seemed harmless, compared with the cruelties of his dorm mates.

After that, whenever he passed in the yard Wade would pinch

Stewart's arm like the witch in *Hansel and Gretel,* and say, with his glittering eyes and wet lips, "How's the little capon doing? Almost ready for market?" Their friendliness banished Stewart's uneasiness about them.

Afterward Stewart concluded that his reputation as the school sissy made them approach him for the annual play. Another boy disappointed them and they suddenly needed a convincing Katharina for *The Taming of the Shrew.*

Midway in the winter term, Wade stopped him outside the dining hall. "Mr. Watson wants to see you."

They went to a different house and opened a door into a precious island of civilization, the masters' common room. It was like being at home. The night was fiercely cold, and here a bright fire was burning. There were comfortable chairs, a thick carpet, curtains, a table with coffee and biscuits on a tray. There were older boys looking quite at home, drinking cocoa or coffee.

"Sir, this is MacPherson I told you about," Wade said, delivering Stewart to a white-faced man with a big nose and very pale hair brushed straight back and long at his neck.

"Aha!" he said in a deep, resonant voice, pulling his pince-nez up on its ribbon, "Let me look." He held the gold rim in extremely long fingers. Mr. Watson was the teacher of music and French, the master of the choir, and, as Stewart now discovered, the unquenchable spirit behind the school theatricals.

He scrutinized Stewart, reaching out one long hand to turn him around while holding his glasses with the other. Even his lips were pale. Except for the watery blue of his eyes, he looked like a blond cadaver. But his voice was very much alive, and he made the most of it. It sang deep in his chest as he rolled his *r*'s and prolonged his vowels.

"Have you ever acted, MacPherson? Ever been in a play? Been on the stage? Ever been to a *see* a play?"

"No, sir." His voice sounded like a little squeak next to the rolling thunder of Mr. Watson's.

"Well, let me see you walk—over there."

"To where, sir?"

"Walk over to the table and help yourself to a cookie."

"Thank you, sir." Stewart heard Mr. Watson say, "Well, the gait is nice, but can he speak lines? MacPherson, come back here. You can read, I suppose. They still teach boys your age to read?"

"Yes, sir."

"Let me have you read this, out loud, as well as you can." He gave Stewart an open book, with his finger marking a place in Katharina's speech at the end. " 'Thy husband is thy lord, thy life, thy keeper.' "

So began Stewart's metamorphosis. It was one of the simpler passages in Shakespeare, and he could read well.

Mr. Watson gave a little yelp of pleasure.

"Too, too perfect. What stunning good luck! Wade, you are a brilliant fellow to have found him. Gentlemen! Gentlemen! Your attention for a moment. I think we have found our Katharina. We are saved from disaster. I cannot believe our good fortune. My boy, you have come in the veritable nick of time. We have only five weeks and they will fly. We must work very hard, because I am determined—boys, over there, attention!—I am determined that this production of the Rothesay Players will make history. Now, everyone find somewhere to sit. On the floor will do for some but not for my aged bones. One of you pass the biscuits, and we will begin a first read-through. Does everyone have his copy of the play?"

"No, sir," Stewart said, now grasping that he was to be part of this exercise.

"Well, here you are, MacPherson. You'll have to go through and mark all the speeches Katharina has and all the cues."

"But, sir. I'm supposed to be in the study hall doing prep until bedtime."

"Oh, dear, yes. How the mundanities of life crowd in upon our art! You'd better go. I will read your part tonight. Tomorrow I'll speak to your house master to release you on Tuesday and Thursday evenings. We'll also rehearse on Sundays. As soon as you can, start to memorize your lines. You'll find some cuts I've made in the text. A few lines not quite suitable for tender ears. The sooner you are word perfect—gentlemen, this applies to everyone—the sooner you are word perfect, the sooner real acting can begin."

Stewart emerged into the sharp night air deliriously happy that two evenings a week he would be back in that cheerful room.

Thus was uncovered Stewart's not inconsiderable talent for "play acting," as his father derisively put it; performing, as some called it; entering sympathetically into the essence of another character, as Mr. Watson saw it; and dressing up and showing off, as Stewart then thought of it.

He did Katharina quite well. Everybody said so, including Mr. Watson, who said he was terrified that Stewart's voice would change before he could play another female part the next year. The unboyish way of moving, which had brought him so much ridicule, looked natural in this part. The applause and laughter that washed over him the two nights of the performance were so delicious—nourishment, nectar, honey—that he drank them up and never doubted for a moment that he deserved them. The success also had a strange effect on the school. Some boys ragged Stewart for a while about wearing a dress and wig. But he had become somebody. People began saying "Fatty," not cruelly, as before, but in a friendly tone. Peter treated Stewart less warily. He had heard the applause and the big laughs in the comedy parts.

"Stewart, you were really good," Peter told him the first night. "I almost forgot who you were at times. You really seemed like somebody else."

Mr. Watson gave a party after the final performance on Saturday night. With their costumes off but a rim of makeup still in their hairlines, they gathered again for cocoa, ice cream, and cookies.

Mr. Watson made a speech. "I think we can all agree, we have had a stunning success. (Cheers) Does anyone here not think it was a stunning success? (Boos) If so, let him cast the first stone. I had a brief moment with my friend Mr. Ramshaw from the village. Mr. Ramshaw is a widely traveled and very cultured man, a man who has witnessed countless theatrical performances in London and New York—all the great theaters. Mr. Ramshaw said to me, very confidentially, that this was the most professional performance he had ever seen at Rothesay. (Cheers) And Mr. Ramshaw is not a man who gives praise lightly.

"Of course, we could never have done it without Matron's and Nurse Gibbs's marvelous effort with the costumes. I toast you ladies from the bottom of my heart. Everyone, please, a toast and three cheers to Matron and Nurse Gibbs. (Three cheers) May their needles ever move as cleverly as now. And, Nurse Gibbs, for your splendid makeup. Wherever you got the wig for Katharina, I wouldn't like to ask. I hope some grand lady of the village doesn't catch cold. (Big laughs)

"The stage crew also performed brilliantly, and here I have to thank Mr. Grieves and his team of carpenters and painters and the lighting men. Good heavens, what wonders they performed! Oh, dear, Nurse Gibbs, it will be going to your head, but I must also commend you for the inspired collection of props. Absolutely splendid.

"Now the performance. I am almost at a loss for words—all right, all right, those who know me would never credit that—but I am without words adequate to tell the prodigies you have performed this year. You have made your director's heart glad. Now, those who have been with us in past years know that I think it invidious in a group effort like ours to single out individual players for notice. We are a collective effort, we happy few, we band of brothers, and everyone contributes his best. But I know you will all agree if this year I break my rule. We are all, I think, quite astonished by the performance of young MacPherson as Katharina. Quite astonished at the delicacy of feeling, the wit, the extraordinary definition he gave the part. So a toast to young MacPherson—a fine and a difficult job, young sir. If you were a real girl I would not hesitate to kiss you in the manner of theatrical folk (roars from the boys) but, in the circumstances, it might be misconstrued (louder roars) and we want no scandals, eh? I shall content myself with shaking hands and saying 'Well done.' "

Blushing, deliriously happy, Stewart said nothing. No one had ever praised him like this.

Stewart became as much a personage as Peter for his heroics on the playing field, and the boys in the dorm stopped torturing him. People even began to say, "Hello, MacPherson."

However, and inevitably perhaps, there was a darker consequence and one of the episodes in the abbreviated analysis that had most interested Dr. Jones.

Wade had a smaller part in the play. After a Sunday afternoon rehearsal he invited Stewart back to his room in the South House, where, he said he had some cake sent by his mother. Indeed, he produced a fruitcake from a tin in the tuck box at the head of his bed. He got out some other treasures, cards and pictures, and when Stewart said, "I'd better be going," he said, "Well, don't you want to play a little?" and put his hand on Stewart's thigh. Stewart felt panicked. Wade did not take his hand away but took Stewart's hand in a strong grip and put it on his own trousers. Stewart could feel him very hard inside. Stewart's own body, still awaiting puberty, made no response. He felt unable to do anything except follow Wade's orders. Wade undid his trousers and put Stewart's hand on his erection and guided it until he had an orgasm.

Stewart left quickly after that, going back to the North House in the twilight, washing his hands obsessively, feeling ashamed, in particular fearing that Peter would somehow know what he had done.

Although the sense of shame remained, he felt compelled to return to Wade's shadowy room for several Sunday afternoons to do as he wished. Stewart had no sexual response; he had a sort of premonitory thrill, mixed with disgust.

It must have been the fourth such Sunday. The snow had turned to rain and they were on Wade's bed when Stewart heard boys running upstairs. He stopped and stood up.

"I've got to go. People are coming," he whispered.

"You've got to finish," Wade said.

"No."

He grabbed Stewart and yanked him down just as the door burst open and several boys tumbled in.

Wade instantly snatched up a book and said, "See, it's right here: Mafeking. Hello, this is Fatty MacPherson. We're looking at my Boer War stuff."

Stewart left in a hurry, and the next time Wade suggested going to his room, Stewart refused. He felt shame and fear at having come so close to being caught. Wade persisted, but Stewart found ways of avoiding him. As they passed in corridors, he sometimes made a grab at Stewart. Once, backstage during a rehearsal, he pushed Stewart into a corner and rubbed against him until someone came by and he leaped back.

Stewart avoided him after the play until one Sunday, coming out of the dining hall after lunch, Wade and Jeffreys were together. Wade pulled Stewart to one side, letting the stream of other boys go by.

"Want to come with us down to the village?"

"I'm not supposed to," Stewart said.

"No one will know. Come on. There's a new ice-cream shop."

Stewart hung back, suspicious. Wade looked around then, suddenly, grabbed Stewart's wrist, and pulled sharply, toppling him off balance and forcing him to walk with him.

"I really don't want to go. I've got work to do to catch up."

"Come on." Jeffreys and Wade both took his wrists and, as they were much stronger, forced Stewart along.

They took a shortcut off the village road, down a grassy hill. Beyond the trees Stewart could see the spire of the Rothesay village church. They pushed through bushes into a little clearing.

"I told you," said Wade, "how he's been avoiding me. I thought we should teach him a little lesson."

"The plump little capon is ready for a lesson, I think," said Jeffreys, the literary one. "A lesson in stuffing."

Stewart did not realize what they intended even as they pushed him to the ground. Jeffreys sat on his chest and held his arms while Wade undid his trousers and took them off. Stewart kicked his legs to stop him, but the two rolled him over on his face, Jeffreys holding him down while Wade tried to push his legs apart. With his face in the pine needles, Stewart could not see what was happening but felt hands pulling at his legs. Then he heard Peter's voice: "Stop it! Stop! Stop! Stop!"

Stewart was released and rolled over to see Peter in the clearing, his fists hitting Wade, who was stumbling as he tried to pull his trousers up from his knees. Jeffreys dived through the bushes and disappeared. Wade got his trousers up and ran too. Stewart, humiliated, sat on the ground, sobbing.

"You'd better get up and come back," Peter said. "I saw them pull you away from the dining hall. I thought I'd better come after you to see what they were up to."

Stewart got up and straightened his clothes. Peter helped him brush the pine needles off. "They're perverts, you know. Sick people. My father told me about such people."

"Your father told you?" was all Stewart could think of to say. He could not imagine gray, remote Canon Wentworth knowing or saying anything about such earthy matters.

"You should have known from the day in the woods with Glass. They're all perverts. When they're men, they put them in jail. That's where Wade and Jeffreys belong—in jail."

In Stewart's memory, Peter stood there that day, uttering the simple convictions, looking noble, like the ink drawings of the young heroes in boys' adventure stories. With his straight jaw, his hair a little tousled, he needed a caption like "With Peter's Nice Hook to the Jaw, the Bully Lay Sprawling in the Dust."

Stewart had no sense of irony about it then: he was too ashamed and too grateful.

On the way up to the school, Peter said, "I think I should tell the Bishop about them." The Bishop was the house master's nickname.

"Why would you tell?" Stewart asked.

"Because perverts like that should be expelled. That was disgusting, what they were doing just because you're—just because you're soft and not strong enough to fight them off."

"But if you tell, what if they tell on us?"

"What do you mean?"

"Tell about us and Glass in the woods?"

"We've got nothing to be ashamed of. They made us go into the woods."

"But I touched him," Stewart said, fearing that if Wade were exposed, he would reveal the Sunday afternoons.

"Yes," Peter said, "I'll have to think about that." He was silent as they climbed the hill. Then he stopped and looked at Stewart in the face. "Stewart, you're not a pervert yourself, are you? You don't like what they do, do you?"

"No, of course not."

Jones had later asked, "And secretly did you like it?"

And Stewart had said, "It's difficult to be completely honest about it."

"Which means you did enjoy it to some extent?"

"It made me feel disgusted, but it was in a small way thrilling."

A day or so later, Peter said, "I've been thinking about Wade and Jeffreys. I don't think I should tell on them. I hate to be a squealer. And they must be awfully scared right now that we'll tell. Perhaps that will make them see the error of their ways."

Peter could say "make them see the error of their ways" soberly, without self-consciousness, when Stewart was not sure that he could ever have said it. But, then, he was not a clergyman's son. For a long time, however, Stewart thought about the error of his own ways.

Watching the fire settling down in the grate, Stewart realized that Peter looked at life much as Major Coleman did.

Ernest Jones had told him, "You are the product of a society that believes sex shameful, dirty, slimy, to be hidden, as guilt-inducing to the adult as masturbation is to a boy. It believes that women have no enjoyment in sex, and sex in marriage should be for procreation only, with continence in between. That is the fantasy that sustains the Edwardian hypocrisy: sex is better not mentioned, because if you don't talk about it or think about it, it won't happen."

If Stewart wanted to continue at Dalhousie, he would have to conform publicly. If the university withdrew its backing, the Army Medical Corps would probably drop him. All the work on motivational behavior and personality types, the new tests he was just beginning to use—essential to his doctoral ambitions—would be thrown away. It was an interesting time in psychology. The Americans were giving hundreds of thousands of recruits the new Stanford-Binet and the Woodworth Personal Data Sheet. For the first time in human history there would be an comprehensive baseline of information.

His ambition to study further in Germany, where all the ferment in experimental psychology had been taking place, was out of the question until the war ended. Without his associate professorship, he would have nothing to do. There was no choice. He had to admit he had been foolish—but lucky. The consequences could have been far graver. Discovery of his affair with Christine would have meant instant dismissal, no probation. He had to accept. There was no choice.

He would give the chancellor a note in the morning.

IT WAS SNOWING HARD when Peter got up and lit the wood range. Margery seemed more cheerful. Since milk and bread deliveries had stopped, she made a list and went out with the children for groceries and more candles. She had swept up the broken glass and tacked blankets and old curtains over the windows, but the wind was forcing snow in at the edges. Peter watched her, wondering how someone so easily made frantic by domestic routine could behave so normally in such chaos. His own mind was in turmoil, but he could not dwell on that.

Stoking the furnace, he noticed the stack of storm windows he had been meaning to put up. It was one of the economies that irritated him: even his parents had a man who came to do the storm windows. He got a ladder and, with difficulty, his hands freezing in the driving snow, attached the storms outside the windows that had blown in.

Then he walked to the cathedral in winter boots, a rough old coat, and warm hat.

Dean Creighton was there, standing in the devastation. It was a strange sight. Snow was blowing in through the windows and swirling in the interior, which was brighter than Peter had ever seen it. Snow had already dusted the pews and the broken glass. As he stood there, telling the dean of his experiences with the victims, the snow continued to powder the heads of the carved angels and saints ornamenting the pulpit and choir stalls. Several women were collecting armloads of prayer books and hymnals.

Dean Creighton had a self-satisfied face with a large nose on which a gold pince-nez perched theatrically. When short of something to say, he would take off the glasses and reflectively rub the indentations on his nose; he did so now.

"There is little we can do, Peter, but pray the weather improves. It might have been a lot worse. Compared with what you've seen, we have been fortunate to escape so lightly. Some of the churches, I'm told, were completely destroyed. Even so, this is going to be a massive job, a Herculean effort."

"Don't worry, sir." Peter said. "I'll get it organized."

"I'm sure you will. I have volunteers picking up the prayer books so that they don't get ruined. I've taken the vestments off the altar. We can be of more use helping people today. I went to City Hall. It looked terribly confused to me. But they said the desperate need is clothing. Thousands of poor wretches have lost everything. Perhaps that is what we should do for today: organize clothing for them."

Peter said. "I know people with a horse and a large sleigh. I could go around collecting clothing."

"That's a very good idea, Peter. You always have the practical answer. I'll leave it to you. Take it to City Hall. That's where they're distributing everything."

Peter was relieved to be spared another day of pulling bodies from wrecked buildings. He had looked at his hands this morning, unable to believe what they had touched the day before, what his eyes had witnessed.

He was turning to go when the dean said, more confidentially,

"Some people are saying it was German sabotage. What do you think of that?"

"It wouldn't surprise me, with all they've done to the world the last few years."

"They say they don't know how many dead yet. It could be thousands. And the injured—thousands and thousands."

It was already heavy going in the snow as Peter walked down Tower Road to his boyhood home, a small house just before Inglis Street. The familiar sights looked strange, because many houses had windows boarded up and in others snow was blowing into dark interiors. But the neighborhood felt different because Peter himself felt out of place, an altered person.

His parents' house had scarcely been touched. His father was dressed, as usual at home, in a clerical collar and a cardigan sweater. He had been made a canon of the cathedral in recognition of the history of the Church of England in Canada he had long been compiling. The title was honorary and carried no duties. Dorothy Wentworth, a diminutive, practical Scotswoman, gave Peter a cup of tea and asked carefully about Margery. Peter knew she understood the condition of his household but almost never discussed it.

His parents were in their seventies. Their first son had drowned at fourteen, before Peter was born. Outsiders thought the tragedy gave the household an air of quiet sadness but that the Wentworths had borne it all admirably. Peter knew he had never quite replaced his brother.

The neighbor helped to harness the sleigh to the old horse and Peter set off. He turned up South Park Street, thinking to try one side against the wind and come down the west side with the blowing snow at his back.

The horse waited while he went from door to door. People were eager to help, thankful that their part of town had escaped so lightly. In some houses people made homeless were taking shelter, and they had been given the spare clothing. But he soon began to collect a pile of blankets, overcoats, sweaters, trousers, dressing gowns, mittens, hats, and scarves.

People he knew from childhood or through the cathedral invited him to come in from the snowstorm while housewives or maids went through closets and trunks. In several houses, it was obvious from the emotion of the donors that the clothing had belonged to men killed overseas. It was handed to him wistfully, reverently.

Much of the clothing was in good condition. It made him think of the secondhand clothes he had worn as a boy. In the thrifty ways of Halifax, other people passed on things their boys had outgrown, covering the kindness with a remark like "They grow so fast, there's no point spending good money on a new coat every year. He'd just be out of it the next."

Often such things did not fit Peter perfectly; he would tighten his belt and try to push the extra fullness out of sight under his jacket or sweater.

Once Peter pointed out to his mother that Stewart was wearing a new jacket. With no self-consciousness, Dorothy Wentworth said, "Now, Peter, the MacPhersons are very well-to-do people and we are not. Stewart's daddy is a banker, and bankers are rich. Your daddy is a clergyman, and clergymen are never rich. But we are rich in the things of the spirit and the things of the heart. We have to get along as best we can. But remember, both of you: clothes do not make the man. It is the man who makes the man."

Peter never mentioned Stewart's clothes after that, although he noticed them. It became an article of his loyalty to his parents. Sometimes he was envious of Stewart's clothes and sometimes proud of himself for not being envious, but it did not occur to him to be bitter toward his parents. Economies like that, and the recognition of their necessity, were part the bond that tied them together. He was even proud of the knowledge that his family did not "waste" money on unnecessary new clothing. His father's income dictated it, but so did his devotion to a less material life, a life of service to others, a holy and Christian life. In the right mood, as he grew older, it could give Peter deep satisfaction to remember that he was here to

renounce the devil and all his works, the vain pomp and glory of the world, with all covetous desires of the same, and the sinful lusts of the flesh,

as his godparents had promised at his baptism.

But he also longed to have clothes bought that fitted him, and on the rare occasions that happened, the astute Mrs. Wentworth noticed his happiness. She covered the moment by saying, "You look very nice, laddie, but always remember, it's not the clothes that make the man." Peter never believed that as genuinely as he thought he should.

Well before he reached Spring Garden Road, the sleigh was full. The horse trotted down to City Hall, where volunteers helped to help carry in armloads of the clothing. Then Peter pointed the horse back to South Park Street for another load.

By noon the snowstorm was a full blizzard and the wind was cutting his face. When he pulled out of the traveled center of the road to let someone pass, the horse labored through the drifts.

Stewart awoke thinking, to his surprise, of Margery Tobin, before her marriage to Peter Wentworth, and then he remembered Major Coleman and his conversation the previous evening. He turned stiffly to look at the other sofa. There was just light enough to see the major still asleep. The room was cold. It must be very early.

Margery had been part of Stewart's adolescent fantasy when they were growing up. He had just passed the pubertal frontier and entered that long period of torture the modern age put young people through, pretending that they were not fully sexed and, when evidence could not be denied, pretending that their behavior was unhealthy or sinful. He went through lectures from the school chaplain, with liberal quotations from Baden-Powell about the dangers of "self-abuse," about taking cold baths or going for a run when they felt certain desires. Stewart's desires would not be so quickly put down. They needed urgent attention, even while he was standing in the cold shower intended to erase them. But the lectures, the boys' secretiveness, and Stewart's shame over the encounters with Wade half-convinced him that his desires were unnatural.

He was sure Peter did not have such carnal thoughts. He never gave any sign of them. Perhaps it was all the sports he played; they gave him a healthful, manly outlet for all that energy. That is what the books said. But he remembered the feel of Wade's penis and longed for someone to touch his. Several times a day, the urgent need would sweep over him, a dizzying, burning, almost stinging feeling until it could be relieved, anywhere he was, sometimes taking awful risks, but the need being too great for him to care. And the whole world carried on as though this did not happen, encouraging Stewart to think he was the only boy with such sick and unwholesome needs.

It is absurd, Stewart thought now, that the conspiracy still exists —in the age of Freud and Havelock Ellis—they still condemn young boys, particularly, because their autoeroticism appears to be stronger, to an age of guilt. We give them *Romeo and Juliet* and pretend that the smutty conversation and Juliet's betrothal at fourteen is an anachronism, put down to earlier patterns of living and lusty Italian blood; implying some biological retardation of the species between then and now; when the evidence of freedom from disease, better sanitation, and improved nutrition would suggest the opposite—even earlier sexuality.

He remembered the whole school parading once a month down to the Rothesay village church and filling the pews on one side while girls from Netherwood filled the other. There were some very beautiful girls, but Stewart could not imagine any lusts of the flesh beneath their brown tweeds.

He was further burdened by his appearance. While his looks improved—the Spartan Rothesay life *did* toughen his body, and he got taller—he still had more flesh than he needed. When girls looked, they looked past him. They looked at Peter, who grew more handsome each year. At Christmas dances, the girls listened to Stewart's jokes, they laughed with him, but they preferred dancing with Peter, who appeared indifferent to them.

Stewart had agonies on those sparkling nights in some of the bigger houses in Halifax. He was excited by the atmosphere of many candles burning, a huge Christmas tree with lighted candles, a small orchestra playing, and the intoxicating mélange of scents of the many girls in the hot room: their soaps, their powders, their perfumes, their gardenia and camellia corsages. But he dreaded the difficulty of filling his dance card; many girls would quickly say, when he approached them, "Oh, Stewart, it's terrible, but I think I'm just this minute full," but not quite cleverly or quickly enough to disguise the glance past him for another invitation. So he got the wallflowers and girls they called "chums," jolly girls he had known since childhood, not the willowy, thistledown, feather-light creatures he longed for. Such unsuccess fed the creeping anxiety that he was destined to be what the boys in school called scornfully a "fruit." Why, if he were normal, Stewart had wondered, lying awake with a burning erection, would he be thinking of another boy's body, not a girl's?

Then he had a dream that made everything clear. In the dream, as sensually vivid as real life, Stewart found himself having intercourse with a woman, as if it were the most natural thing in the world. At first she was not identifiable, but he had the convincing experience of being between her legs in a full sexual embrace and climax. He awoke to find his school bed wet with the evidence, devastatingly happy with himself. The experience was so perfect a counterfeit that his hands held the memory of touching her . . . this evanescent . . . Suddenly he knew who it was: Margery, one of the goddesses who had scorned him at Christmastime. How could he have imagined himself in her embrace? She was not the sort of girl to think such thoughts about, certainly not anything like entering her sexually. And Margery was quite obviously smitten with Peter. He remembered the particular way she angled her chin up to him as they danced, smiling a little poutingly, as though asking to be kissed; the way she held his finger for a long moment after dancing. Stewart had just ravished the girl who was longing for Peter—but of course not in that way; nice girls did not long in *that* way. That is why there were whispers of other women, the women they heard about in houses on Hollis Street, women who were paid.

Stewart looked at Peter in an English class, thinking, If you knew what I was doing with Margery in my dream last night . . . He experienced a little thrill in sending the secret thought. Even at sixteen Peter still seemed indifferent to such matters. How could he not feel it? Stewart wondered. Peter seemed above it all, precisely like the boys in the *Chums* annuals, full of adventure, good at sports, with no sexual existence, like a doll born without genitals, while Stewart sometimes seemed all sexual existence.

Stewart tried to be as he imagined Peter, on a plane above such things. On a particular night, in an agony of remorse at having again succumbed to the temptation to masturbate, Stewart made a resolution: never again! That was the last time. He would reform, become as pure as the others around him, obviously not including Wade and Jeffreys. He went to sleep happy, already feeling cleansed, a better person, his mind on higher things.

An aunt had given him a small pocket diary with pages of very thin paper. The next morning Stewart got it out of his trunk and

turned the empty pages to that day's date. He put a small cross by
the date to indicate that he had resisted temptation. But was that
cheating, since in fact a whole day of temptation stretched before
him? Should he not have waited until the next morning, when he
could fairly record twenty-four hours of abstinence? No, just putting the cross made him feel more virtuous. He was a reformed
sinner; he knew the joy of repentence.

In morning chapel, "Lead us not into temptation" came illus-
trated in Stewart's imagination with a clear depiction of the sin he
had so resolutely abandoned. To this day, that line—"lead us not
into temptation but deliver us from evil"—could conjure up images of his little blue diary. That evening before lights-out he took
it from under the pillow and looked at the cross. Why a cross?
Naturally, Christ died for our sins that we should be made pure.
There was a large crucifix behind the altar in the chapel. Christ
died to help Stewart be stronger. Did Christ abuse himself when he
was a boy? Of course not! Don't be disgusting!

Stewart was studying the catechism in preparation for confirma-
tion. At baptism his godparents on his behalf had renounced "all
the sinful lusts of the flesh." Those sinful lusts were obvious now,
and he had renounced them for himself. Stewart put the diary
under his pillow and settled for the sweet sleep of those who know
they are without sin.

The next morning, before breakfast, he made another cross and
held his head up proudly the rest of the day. The culture, religion,
education, all taught that self-denial ennobled human nature, base
human nature. Stewart's self-denial ennobled him. Curiously, it
made him feel more manly, more like the sinewy, healthy fellows
around him. People who said no to temptation *were* made better
people.

For thirteen days, with growing pride in his self-control, Stewart
made the daily mark in his diary. With each added cross, he believed himself more worthy of Peter's friendship. Now that Stewart had purified himself, purged himself of sin, he could really be
Peter's friend.

It passed through Stewart's mind that if he could so discipline
himself as to keep his hands off his privates for two weeks, he could
also train his body. He could make himself stronger, tougher. He
could work the little roll of fat off his midriff, make his thighs as
muscled as Peter's.

It was a late spring afternoon and very warm. A group of boys went to the pond to swim. Sitting on the dam, drying off in the sun, Stewart felt there was nothing he could not master by self-discipline. Peter was sitting a little apart, his legs in the water, his hands flat on the boards of the dam. Stewart noticed that Peter's stomach was so lean that when he bent forward, it made only tiny creases, like the forehead of someone frowning, but Stewart's stomach protruded flabbily. He could not separate the tautness of Peter's stomach from his other virtues—courage, honesty, cheerfulness in adversity, slowness to anger, and, above all, sexual purity. Peter's stomach was, in the words of the Book of Common Prayer, "the outward and visible sign of the inward and spiritual grace." Stewart's flabby stomach was the sign of his sloth, his self-indulgence, his postponement of grace for immediate gratification.

Now he was becoming worthy of such a body. He would rise above his humiliation, make an effort at games—run more.

Stewart had been born with an ability to see himself from outside his body. He never imagined, as many people do, that he was thinner or more graceful than he actually was; if anything, he exaggerated the other way. But now, sitting in the sun on that glorious May day, the air full of springtime perfumes and bird song, Stewart felt that his awkwardness was not inevitable.

Alas, no fourteenth cross entered the diary. Whether it was the stimulation of the swimming, or the balmy air, or being naked out of doors, the demands of Stewart's body betrayed the resolution of his spirit. Left behind as usual because everyone walked or ran faster, he dawdled in a languid mood until he felt a pool of warmth gathering in his loins and a sweet ache creeping through his genitals. In a second, he was off the path into a mossy glade. The merest touch produced an explosion of detumescence. For a few seconds he was the slave of an overwhelming imperative that blocked all reasoning and will power.

Then the remorse. Standing on his trembling legs, Stewart knew himself not only weak in body but weak in spirit. How could he be lithe and vigorous with taut muscles when he was morally corrupt?

Sadly depleted in spirit, his newfound manliness drained out of him, his pride abased by his weakness, he resumed his walk back to the school. And yet behind his disquiet there crept in an emotion that Stewart was beginning to recognize—a soothing equanimity that balanced his self-revilement with a soft little lecture in common sense: what you cannot control, you cannot control.

Even so, Stewart's failure made Peter seem all the stronger to him, as if their lives were a game of moral Snakes and Ladders. Peter always seemed to be climbing steadily higher toward sublime perfection. Stewart would painfully mount a few rungs only to be dealt a throw of the dice that sent him snaking down to perfidy, forced to start his moral climb all over again.

That cycle of disgust, resolution, reformation, fall from grace, and remorse repeated itself many times in his years at school and beyond, until psychology and Ernest Jones gave him comforting rationalizations and relieved the guilt. It became one of the patterns in his life, like a biological rhythm. Even the enlightenment of psychology and the insights from analysis did not break the power of that cycle.

Attempting to analyze it, Stewart related it to the seasons, a surge of new concupiscence in the fall. Associated with what? The quickening that comes from the resumption of the educational year? The time of year when he escaped from home? Obviously not unconnected with the choice of an academic career, to perpetuate that rhythm, and to gain long summers for travel.

The cycle governed small habits. The state of his clothes, his shoes, his need for a haircut, the length of his fingernails, all tended to reach the level of noticeable neglect, which he observed complacently, then ruefully, then ashamedly, until he felt goaded to correct it—to buy new clothes, new shoes, to get a haircut, to trim his fingernails. His pride restored, Stewart would vow that this time he would maintain it, as most other people seemed to do, not swinging from spruce to seedy, as he did. Jones traced it to conflicted feelings about his mother.

It surprised Stewart now to see that he had never thought of Peter as a prig, a goody-goody, smug, pious—all the rationalizations the morally ambivalent snatch at to explain the maddening superiority of others.

But he hadn't remembered the Margery dream for years.

Stewart got up and pulled aside the heavy velvet draperies to find it snowing heavily; snow had drifted in through the shutters.

Coleman groaned when he put his leg to the floor; pushing on the sofa arm, he forced himself to stand.

"You know, you could take it easy here today," Stewart said.

"Not a bit of it."

Stewart did not want to embarrass him by pressing it. The major said he had to be properly turned out, and borrowed a razor. Stewart made a fire in the wood stove in the kitchen and heated water. They drank their tea black and took a thermos of it in the car. They had no further discussion: it was taken for granted that they were going back to the work of the day before.

The wind was blasting out of the northeast, but in the lulls they could hear tapping and hammering, as people covered windows with boards or strips of tar paper. The other new sound was the jingling of harness bells on the merchants' boxy delivery vans, their wheels replaced by sleigh runners. The few motor cars on the streets were already having difficulty with the snow.

The two men stopped at City Hall to inquire about gasoline. In the corridors and offices a crush of people was clamoring for food, clothing, places to stay, repair materials, missing relatives. Many people were talking or shouting over the noise of typewriters, telephones ringing, and hammers pounding. Volunteers and city employees were harried by people besieging the desks arranged as improvised counters. There was no sign of the patience and resignation in the hospitals. These people were frantic, pressing against the desks, pleading, demanding. Receiving baskets of food, clothing, and blankets, or tickets for hot meals, they quarreled over the amounts, shouting, "But there are seven people in my family!"

Repair crews had not reached all the offices, and volunteers were working in their coats near broken windows open to the driving snow.

A group of well-dressed men and uniformed officers came out of the city council chamber. Stewart recognized leading citizens, friends of his parents, men who wore morning coats to take the collection at the cathedral. The tallest was Arthur Halliwell, a stockbroker with a vigorous mustache and a reputation as a yachtsman with an eye for the ladies.

"Hello, Stewart." He looked pleased with himself. "We have just set up a Relief Committee to take charge of the disaster. They've pushed me into being chairman—God knows why. Anything we can do for you?"

"Thanks. Major Coleman and I have been helping pick up wounded in the North End. We need gas for the car."

"We'll find you some. Go to the armory. Military supplies.

We'll get you a chit. That's wonderful work. Jolly useful. I think it's marvelous that everyone is pitching in."

Halliwell, talking to Stewart, frequently glanced around. Hearing this authoritative voice, volunteers stopped typing and men nailing up beaverboard let their hammers hang down. Halliwell's conversation became a speech:

"I was just saying to Stewart MacPherson, and it may interest all of you to know; our American friends have acted with extraordinary promptitude. The people of Massachussetts have already dispatched a trainload of emergency medical supplies, a complete field hospital with doctors and nurses. We've heard by telegraph that it has passed through Moncton, but the snowdrifts are so heavy they've had to disengage the locomotive and charge the drifts to break through. They should be here by late afternoon."

A few people started clapping.

"So we see that Halifax is not alone. No matter how bleak things look, help is on the way. The premier of Ontario telegraphs that they have sent two train carloads of glass, putty, beaverboard, nails, and so on. We've had telegrams from around the empire. If other members of the committee will permit me, I should consider it an honor to read one to you. It's headed Buckingham Palace, London."

There was a little murmur in the crowd.

"It was addressed to the governor general, the Duke of Devonshire, and His Grace has immediately telegraphed it to us from Ottawa. It reads . . ." Halliwell cleared his throat importantly.

MOST DEEPLY REGRET TO HEAR OF SERIOUS EXPLOSION AT HALIFAX RESULTING IN GREAT LOSS OF LIFE AND PROPERTY. PLEASE CONVEY TO PEOPLE OF HALIFAX WHERE I HAVE SPENT SO MANY HAPPY TIMES MY TRUE SYMPATHY IN THIS GRIEVOUS CALAMITY.

"It is signed," Halliwell said, "George, R.I."

A well-dressed woman was sniffling and dabbing her eyes. A man at the back shouted, "God save the king!"

"Hear, hear!" Halliwell said. "God save the king!" Many others repeated it, and a woman with a high voice began singing,

> God save our gracious king,
> Long live our noble king . . .

A few other voices straggled in to join her, when another woman, wearing a man's overcoat, shouted roughly, "Never mind the king. What about food?"

People said "ssh!" while more singers joined in:

Send him victorious . . .

The woman shouted louder than the singing, "We're starving and you're standing there and singing God save the bloody king!"

"This is terrible!" someone said.

"Who is she?"

The singing faltered, and the woman pushed rudely through the crowd. Her hair was uncombed and her eyes were red. "It's you kind of people always have the say. All you think we're good for is to scrub your goddamned floors."

"Shut her up," someone said. "Get her out of here."

"I won't shut up and I won't get out!"

"I think she's drunk."

"She's wearing a man's coat."

"My good woman—" Halliwell began.

"I'm not drunk. I'm hungry and I'm bloody sick and tired of the likes of you. It's not your precious South End and your grand houses that got blown up, is it?"

"That's right," a man called.

"It's not your children smashed up in their school and dead, like my sister's, is it? Eh?" She wiped tears from her eyes with her fingers.

A policeman was pushing through the crowd. "Now, come along, lady."

"I think she's drunk."

"I'm not drunk. I wish I was." The woman was crying. Stewart had never seen such misery in a face. A nurse in a St. John's Ambulance Brigade uniform hustled the woman away, still shouting, "We've got nothing. We need food. We need coal. We need clothes." People looked away, embarrassed.

Halliwell found his composure. "See that she's taken care of. Well . . . not surprising that nerves are a little frayed. If we all pitch in, we'll get through magnificently. Do you know the people at the *Herald* have managed to get an edition out today? Look at that!" He held up a copy.

One of the volunteers sat down and began typing, and the hammering resumed.

"Wish I could join you," Halliwell said, "but we've got another bally meeting."

Snow was accumulating on the black car as they got in and headed for the armory.

Coleman said, "I get the feeling that a lot of your bigwigs are tickled pink this happened. They've never felt so bloody important."

"Halliwell's always been important around town. Old family, old money. You find his name in the paper for something or other."

"It's odd," Coleman said. "In western Canada you really feel you've left all that nonsense behind—who your father was, who you went to school with. But it's strong in the army. Some officers treat the other ranks like dirt, like a lower class of people. Perhaps the damned war's turning me a little Bolshie."

Stewart could see why Coleman would never be at ease with officers. He carried himself too stiffly; his uniform was too meticulous.

To change the subject he asked, "Is it true most of the troops are British-born immigrants? That's what Laurier claimed in the conscription debate. Was he right?"

"In my division, about half and half. But in the ranks the British-born soldiers take the class attitudes very hard. And they'll bring it back with them."

"It's not something I've ever thought much about," Stewart said.

"Astonishing performance back there," Coleman said. "God Save the King and all that. Sometimes you Canadians are more British than the British."

The scene had embarrassed Stewart. There was a type of Canadian who always seemed eager to snap to attention, as though he imagined a superior just about to appear.

"When did the king spend time here?"

"In the navy," Stewart said. "He was stationed here."

"Strange little place for a king to be," said Coleman, looking at the snow and the desolation around him.

They drove up Barrington Street, avoiding pieces of wreckage and abandoned vehicles. Electricity had been restored, and a few trams were running, their headlamps a small cheerful gleam through the blowing snow that was beginning to cover the visible horrors. At the North Street Station was a landscape of whitening wreckage. A locomotive and several passenger cars lay on one side under the broken glass and twisted girders of the fallen roof, all the outlines rounded and softened by the coating of snow.

"My God!" Stewart said.

"Unbelievable!"

Both sides of the harbor, from the naval dockyard south, looked as though a war had been fought over it. Behind them, up the rise to Fort Needham and beyond, was a wasteland to the horizon. Of hundreds of buildings nothing was standing but an occasional brick chimney, a remnant of wall, some splintered tree trunks. The only color in the white landscape was the khaki of soldiers in greatcoats and balaclava helmets still digging for bodies or survivors.

A priest came out of the shell of St. Joseph's Church, and Major Coleman called to him, "Anyone in there, Father?"

Under his black homburg the face was haggard. "There is no one here. The dead have been taken away. Hundreds just from our congregation." He looked at Coleman's uniform. "They're saying it was the Germans. Do you think that is possible?"

"Pretty unlikely, Father," the major said. "How do you arrange a collision in that place with a ship loaded with munitions? Even as a suicide mission, it seems pretty far-fetched."

"I agree with you," said the priest, "but people say that. Well, I mustn't detain you. You have work to do."

Down the street a young officer signaled, indicating a row of bodies on the ground. "Can you take some of these? All dead, I'm afraid."

They lay awkwardly, not in repose, but with arms or legs frozen in the positions they had been flung into at death—crouched, curled up, spreadeagled, gesturing; a fist clenched in the air. A woman's hand was raised delicately as though about to touch her brow. When they lifted her, a blanket covering her head fell away, disconcertingly forcing Stewart to look at a face that destroyed the anonymity: a middle-aged face, like that of a teacher he remembered. Her body, frozen all night, went into the back of the car with difficulty.

"I can't believe we're not hurting her," Stewart said, as the desire to be gentle gave way to practical need. He had to bend her stiff arm to load her on top of the others. He shuddered when his bending her arm made her frozen hand touch her cheek, completing the gesture she had begun.

"Be glad they're not rotting," Coleman said when they were driving again. In the presence of the dead, they talked quietly.

"After some of the battles, we couldn't collect the dead for days. Shelling too intense. In summer they'd be putrid. I hated ordering the chaps to pick them up. Pieces broke off in their hands. At least these don't smell."

The major's laconic words made Stewart feel more horror than he had when lifting the bodies. The other feeling he acknowledged was a deep and primitive pleasure that he was alive and healthy, beginning to feel hungry. He dug out a packet of Craven "A" cigarettes, gave Coleman one, and accepted a match. Sucking the fragrant smoke into his lungs made him feel even more alive. In the rearview mirror, his face was a healthy pink, but immediately behind him was a dead face the color of plaster.

"Careful," Coleman said. The heavily loaded car swerved in the thickening snow.

It was worse unloading. The woman who had to come out first was now a person to him. He recognized her expression.

The storm became a full blizzard, bringing darkness early. The drifts deepened, and white mounds grew over abandoned cars and vans. More teams of horses appeared, their presence palely marked kerosene riding lights. When the trams stopped running, the city fell unusually dark; streetlamps were off and shop windows had been boarded up. In Stewart's headlamps, the snow blew almost horizontal as the screaming wind backed to the northwest.

Hardly able to see through the windshield, he swerved to avoid a plunging team of horses on South Street, and the Paige ploughed into a snowbank. He had no shovel, and no spinning the wheels or pushing would get them out, so they abandoned the car. Coleman confessed that his leg was giving him hell; it was all he could do to manage the few blocks to the house.

# PART TWO

## *The Diary*

THE HORSE WAS FALTERING in the heavy snow but quickened his pace when Peter turned his head south. Together they found the lane leading to the stable. In the sudden quiet when the sleigh bells stopped jingling, Peter could hear a foghorn from the harbor. He gave the horse water and hay before removing the harness and brushed the accumulated snow off the quilted leather seats. When he shook out the rugs, something hard fell to the ground. He climbed down and found a book. With his mittened hand he pushed it into his overcoat pocket.

Wearily, up to his knees in snow, he turned toward home. He had left Margery and the children for virtually two days. She would be frantic . . . or perhaps the immense suffering of others had made her see how fortunate she was. To be blessed with good health, an affectionate and conscientious husband, two charming children, a comfortable home, when thousands were suffering every kind of privation, all might play upon a personality like Margery's. Peter had long believed, along with her doctors, that one day she would just "snap out of it." He thought of her depression as willful, perverse; she was like a child in a black mood, needing to be humored, or talked to a little sternly to bring her around. For four years he had expected the change, while his own cycles of anger and resentment, charity and forgiveness, grew shorter.

So tired he could scarcely lift one foot out of the snow to move it ahead, Peter convinced himself that the affectionate, practical Margery he had left that morning might be there now. She might have the children in bed, dinner cooking, the table laid nicely, her hair done up prettily. For the last few yards the picture was so convincing that he was surprised to find the house dark and the front steps a foot deep in untrodden snow. On the kitchen table was a note in the messy scrawl typical of Margery on the edge of hysteria.

*Peter. Sorry. Couldn't find food or milk. Can't stand it here.*
*Taking children to Mother's.*

He could see she had been scarcely able to get the words down.
He could imagine her scribbling, the children bundled up, hot and
impatient to go; her coat undone, her hair untidy, her expensive
hat set slightly crooked; a frantic search until she finally ripped a
corner from a sheet of good writing paper, then scrambled for a
pencil without a broken point. Nothing was ever where it should
be in her kitchen. Unlike his mother's, nothing had a fixed place.

When she was well, Margery had exquisite manners; her notes
were extravagantly courteous. That Margery would have called
him "darling" and asked him come over or telephone her, or told
him what he could find for supper if he felt like not coming. But
tonight, nothing. The few words of the note said everything.

He was still in his old coat and boots, and snow was melting on
the kitchen floor. The house was chilly. He went into the cellar
and found the furnace almost out. He shoveled in coal and opened
the draft, but it would take half an hour to produce real heat. He
took a scuttle of coal and the kerosene lamp to his small study
behind the dining room. Crunching up newspaper to put under
the kindling, he saw on a front page a drawing of a wounded
soldier with a caption in bold type: "A Cry from the Trenches. In
the name of Freedom, Humanity, and Christianity, We Appeal for
Immediate Reinforcements."

In a surge of anger he ripped the page and twisted it into a small
ball. Going overseas would relieve many pressures. Margery's parents could look after her, and war service overseas was bound to
speed advancement in the church. He had already seen clergymen
with medal ribbons and regimental insignia on their black stoles.
Would anybody be made dean, in the future would anyone be
elected bishop of Nova Scotia, who had not put his life at risk in
this paroxysm of sacrifice and patriotism? But would any man be
made dean who had a sickly wife, weeping uncontrollably? Might
one cancel out the other?

Peter laid kindling and lumps of coal on the balls of paper in the
grate and lit the fire. The crackling flames cheered up the study.
He remembered there was still a piece of ham in the larder. Enjoying the feeling of no responsibility except to himself, he took
the lamp and padded in his socks, found the ham, and cut several

slices. He was ravenous. There was no bread, but he remembered the rest of his mother's oatcakes and a bottle of beer. He brought the food into the study and ate rapidly, looking at the flames.

The fire had warmed the study; as he removed his coat, he noticed the book he had shoved into the pocket. Putting the lamp by his reading chair, he flipped through it and saw handwritten pages with dates—recent dates. It was someone's diary. It looked like a woman's handwriting. He turned to the last page. The entry was dated December 6, 1917. Yesterday—the day of the explosion. He turned the pages back to the first entry.

Monday, May 22, 1916—

It is a mild spring afternoon, dark with quiet rain, and I am filled with such longing. Outside there is a bird chirruping. That is exactly the sound—chirrup, like "cheer up" said very quickly. The sound of the bird is very close but it seems to come from long ago. It makes me lonelier as it echoes through the moist air of the neighborhood. The elm leaves have just opened and the air is sweet with that fresh smell you can almost taste. A delivery wagon goes by, clop-clopping, the horse's back glossy with rain. I haven't heard a motorcar for ages. It is as though everyone has gone away from the city.

On an impulse this morning, I bought a bound notebook, and now I have brought it to my writing table in the window in our bedroom.

Apart from bread-and-butter letters, the only writing I do is to C. So this pen is how I touch him. It is spring in France too. Is it ever quiet enough in the trenches to hear the birds? He never mentions things like that.

C is so uncomfortable with some of the things I say that I must have a place to write what he doesn't want to know. His letters are cheery, uncomplaining, brisk. I think I am going a little mad with the emptiness of it. Yesterday was my birthday but it didn't feel like a birthday.

My need for him overwhelms me and there is no one I can tell that to. Ever since I got up this morning, I have had flashes of vividly imagining making love with him in the bed behind me. Not imagining: stronger, like a hallucination. I could feel *everything*—the touch of his hands, the little hurt when he tries to enter me, and then the delicious, delicious feeling of him sliding into me. He does it too quickly often, but sometimes, if I ask him, he slides it so slowly. I'm trembling. I'm out of breath. My hand is moist and the pen is slipping.

Later: I will burn this notebook before C comes home, but until then it can be my confidante, my secret confessor.

Tuesday, May 23, 1916—

Would anybody understand the things I do? I am convinced that ordinary people would consider me very odd—even abnormal. It frightens me to think so. Or would another woman in my place understand?

When C went overseas, I couldn't believe how empty it was. I walked from room to room looking for traces of him. In the study I picked up the pipes he had left, smelled them, put them in my mouth, tasting not him but the bitterness of the stem. I looked in his wardrobe and felt the clothes. I took the trees out of his shoes to put my hand inside where his foot had been. I took out a tweed jacket he wears a lot and pressed my nose against it. Outside it smelled of pipes and I smelled inside the lining of the armpit. Then, I could smell him—the odor of him. Miraculously for a moment it brought him back.

It became a secret little pleasure that I save for times when I miss him terribly, when I ache to hold him.

Recently, I can barely detect any odor of him in the clothes. I noticed his worn military brushes on his chest of drawers. He took the new ones I bought him as an early Christmas present. I could smell the Yardley's brilliantine he uses. In the bathroom cabinet was an oval tin of it. It was very difficult to open without breaking my fingernails. When the lid came off, I felt for a moment that he had come back, because the room smelled so like him. I brought the tin into the bedroom and kept it in the little drawer of the bedside table. At night, I take it out and open it in the dark to smell just before going to sleep. I touch myself as I smell it and think of him vividly. Sometimes I keep it under the pillow.

Last night was a bad time. Mollie was out and I wandered from room to room, with an ache of wanting him. Finally I pulled one of C's suits out to hold it against me. I looked at myself in the long looking glass with my arm around the suit as though I were dancing with a very thin, floppy man.

I felt my nipples so full of feeling that anything touching them hurt slightly. I want him to kiss the nipples and put them in his mouth. I once tried to put myself in a position where they would be near his lips, but he did not do it. Perhaps he finds the idea distasteful. He is very prudish in some ways. And I was too shy to come right out and ask him. Perhaps after longing for him so badly I won't be as shy when he comes back. Perhaps I am disgusting even to think of it. What does it mean if you think of such things?

Peter was breathing rapidly. He looked up, as if fearing someone might be watching, but saw only the kerosene lamp and the fire-light and heard only the wind outside. He shouldn't be reading this: a clergyman reading a lonely young woman's private yearn-ings. Not at all appropriate. Quite dishonorable. He closed the diary and put it on his desk.

But where had it come from? In his mind he retraced his route . . . up South Park Street . . . a load to City Hall . . . down South Park. That was another load. Would it have fallen from one of the early loads and remained hidden or come later? It could have been in any one of dozens of houses. And there were many coats.

He couldn't give it back if he didn't know to whom it belonged. And if he did, would the owner suspect he had read it? He would worry about it tomorrow. Dear God, he would have to start on some plan for the cathedral.

He got into bed, stretching a hand into the cold space Margery usually warmed. His thoughts returned to the woman longing for her husband to come home and make love to her. Peter was fully awake. This woman ached for her husband. Shocking that she would write it down. Her nipples. Wanting them kissed.

As a divinity student, determined to restrain his sexual urges until he and Margery were married, he had heard the others boast-ing of conquests, of how such a girl had let them do this or that, of visits to prostitutes—like those women yesterday, with their dead rouged cheeks and immodest underclothing. But he had always been able to remind himself of the enhanced humanity, the sense of exaltation, of coming nearer to God, from the act of will that kept one pure.

He had always believed that partakers of the divine spirit escaped the corruption that lust created in the world. Any animal automatically said yes to a sexual invitation, to a female in heat. The animal could not refuse. But man could refuse, and that was the God-given gift of will which distinguished man from the other creatures. God made man suffer because Adam, the primal man, fell into temptation. It was the mark of the stronger man, the greater man, to refuse, as Joseph refused Potiphar's wife, leaving his garment in her hand.

The more Peter had controlled himself, the more certain he was that he was earning God's approval. The discipline itself meant that God was present.

Now, married all these years, Peter knew the stronger hungers of sex and disappointment. Years of self-control had brought God no closer, and even in good spirits Margery had never been eager.

Peter lay there, his mind filled with swelling curiosity about the author of the diary. She wanted her husband to put her nipples in his mouth.

In his nightshirt and bare feet he went downstairs to retrieve the diary. Back in the bedroom, he found a match and lighted the bedside lamp.

Wednesday, May 24, 1916—

I feel the ache of C's not being here and anxiety over where he is. It is worse today because the war seems to be going so badly. I always feel safer, or feel that C is safer, when the news is good and we seem to be winning. For weeks now it is German advances day after day at Verdun.

Funny how different we are. C simply will not talk about these things. He'll smile, blush, turn away, or change the subject. It started with our wedding night. I had dreaded it a little, in spite of the experience with J long before—no, perhaps because of that—feeling a little guilty about that. If I had listened to Mother, I should have dreaded it enormously; not that she gave me any specific advice. But in all the admonitions over the years, all the little side remarks about "what a wife must put up with," little bits of feminine guile about ways to avoid IT, postpone IT; old wives' tales about a woman's duty and constant little references to pain.

Peter thought, Margery's mother must have told her precisely the same things, and she believed them.

Something in me pushed most of that out of my mind. But when C and I actually got into the same bed together, in the hotel at Quebec the night before we sailed for Bermuda—it was bliss. It did feel a little painful at first, but then it was *just delicious*. The touching, the kissing, the stroking, the holding, and the weight of him lying on me, the feel of him inside me— quite inexpressible pleasure. So shudderingly wonderful.

Fascinated, Peter read on.

The next day, the ship was sailing from Quebec City, down the St. Lawrence, so exciting! I was standing with C at the rail, wrapped in my fine new paisley shawl, watching the outline of the Citadel turn misty as we moved away. I was holding his arm very close and pressing against him—not only for warmth. The wind was blowing my hair about. I had to hold it away from my mouth when I moved close to his ear to tell him I had loved making love.

He turned to me, his sandy eyebrows looking bristly with surprise, and he glanced around to see if there was anyone near us. He looked back at me, smiling shyly, and when I asked whether he had liked it, too, he said of course but "you don't *talk* about it." So I said I thought when we were married we could talk about anything.

He looked at me as though he saw something that worried him. Then he smiled and said in one of his joking voices, "Nice girls don't talk about it."

I didn't say anything more, and just stood there pressing close to him and—to be frank—wanting to do it again and becoming aware that he did too, which of course was why I had raised it in the first place.

Later, settled in this house, in bed together, he did not like me to say anything while we were doing it. I wonder why. To me, it makes it even more exciting to put it into words. I don't mean all the time—chatter, chatter, chatter—just a few words now and then. I know he was too shy to tell me directly. But I could tell, so I stopped.

Thursday, May 25, 1916—
I have just read over what I wrote yesterday and am a bit taken aback by my brazenness. I know C meant nice girls don't

*think* about it and nice girls don't *like* it. It is generally felt, but almost never said—it doesn't have to be—that a nice, well-brought-up woman, meaning what I think myself to be—would naturally find sex distasteful. Mother emphasized that pain, duty, submission are the woman's lot. She never even hinted that I might enjoy it, let alone long for it, as I do now.

Mother and Daddy slept in separate rooms. The excuse was she always "needed her rest." I often wondered how much she pretended, lying there in a darkened room, too ill to come down to supper. She apparently had a ghastly time at my birth, probably why I am an only child. She always dressed me very nicely, but what a to-do she made about my periods and not showing myself too much, especially breasts; about keeping my knees together.

I am *supposed* not to like it. If I *do* like it—and I do—what does that make me? A depraved woman? It sickens me to think I could be abnormal, like a glutton or a drunkard, driven to excess but for sex. But I don't feel that. It is so confusing!

If it is enjoyable for a woman to make love with her husband, why must it be hush-hush? If nature made us this way, why is it wrong to talk about it, even think about it? This is the way we are. Girls at twelve to thirteen begin to bleed once a month. It is perfectly healthy. Why is it all, as Mother calls it, "infra dig?"

Why does the C of E say "conceived in sin?" What is sinful about doing what God made us to do?

The question was so simple and so impertinent that it startled Peter. His instinctive response was: Well, I could put her right about that. It was so deeply embedded in church doctrine that you never thought about it. It was the kind of question Stewart Mac-Pherson asked to provoke him. But this woman's question did not anger Peter. It made him want to know more about her.

Friday, May 26, 1916—

Watched Mollie polish the dining room floor on her knees, with a folded cloth, working wax into the newly scrubbed floor. She was humming, half-singing to herself. When the whole floor was waxed, she struggled back with the heavy cast-iron polisher that I can just manage to lift. She pushes it back and forth quite easily with a jerk at each end. I can still hear it clanking distantly from up here.

Watching her strengthened my resolve to do something besides looking after this house, and I'm not really doing that, merely supervising. I don't want to do the Altar Guild like L. Rolling bandages one day a week is not enough. Besides, rolling bandages makes me either very sad to think how they will be used or very—it is a shock what the mind can do! Yesterday, amid the chattering of the other women, suddenly I had a clear image of C's body and someone, me I suppose, wrapping him with a bandage. It wasn't a gory sight. There was no blood. But I was wrapping him around his most private parts, and the image, daydream really, filled me with intense longing for him. I could almost feel him swelling in my hands, and then I snapped to, noticing that I was perspiring inside my St. John's uniform. The noise of the other women at the big table, gossiping in their silly white headdresses, had so faded away into the distance for me that I might have been alone.

I wonder what it is like for the nurses in France who have to undress those poor men, and bathe them as well as tend to their wounds. I suppose the horror of it all and the desperate condition of the men puts all those thoughts out of their minds. And when the men feel a little bit better, but still need help to move or change or bathe? When C was so desperately ill with flu, the moment his temperature began to go down, he was suddenly very well that way. And his temperature was still 103. Surely those women must be aware when they are touching them. It's not like washing a dog or a horse—although brushing and currying a horse has quite often made me think of that, even a gelding. It is so enormous on a horse. Well, it seems pretty enormous on a man at first, at least on C, which is the only evidence I have from a grown man.

She kept startling Peter. One part of him was deeply shocked: this was almost salacious. But he also noticed an amused tolerance creeping into his feelings. Her candor was ingratiating.

Time to put on my coat and gloves and walk down to his mother's for tea. Misty and a little drizzly today. I'd love not to wear a hat. The mist feels so good on my face and hair. But if I got there hatless with my hair all dewy, Mrs. R would be a little shocked and, since I like her so much, I don't want to shock her.

Mrs. R? Who on earth could that be, who had a son, C, in France? He could not stop reading.

Saturday, May 27, 1916—

Oh, it is useless being a woman in these times! Sometimes I think I can actually feel a man's spirit creeping over me. On the days I feel womanly, I want to stay in, near a fire or radiator, to sew or read, to be still and quiet, to feel protected. In other moods, like now, I feel much bolder, wishing to be active, out of doors, doing something physical. I think of that as manly— brave, adventurous, able to go anywhere. In this mood I could join up and be a nurse in France.

If I'd been a man I might have had the gumption to stay in Paris, trying to paint. I don't mean I was good enough to be really good—I wasn't—even if James Morrice was encouraging, mostly because he was Daddy's friend from Montreal. Not good enough to get into the Julian, which took the good Canadians. Of course I suspected there was another reason for Morrice's interest, even though he was in his forties and often the worse for drink. I did my best to behave primly when he painted me in his wicker chair.

I love the freedom of that life. A lot of it was just being on my own in Paris after years of supervision. And a city big enough that people didn't know one another's business. And being a foreigner there—with no family to account to. I could sit in the cafés till all hours when the French girls of good family had to rush home to dinner. But it was more than the physical freedom—and the moral freedom. Who would have known if I had responded to Morrice's little hints—not so little hints. If he had drunk less, perhaps I might have. But all that is less what I mean by freedom than the spirit of the artist at work. Artists work enormously hard but they do as they wish. No one tells them how to work. Everywhere else in life people have to do what they are told, or what convention tells them. C is like that. Matisse does what he thinks is right. But, alas, you need talent for that freedom, which is why so many of us hung around the real talents, feeling their freedom and pretending, by sharing their way of life in the cafés and restaurants, that we had it too. I would love to be there now—in June.

It's good we are going to the country soon. I am very restless. No letters from C.

Monday, June 12, 1916—

We drove down to the Rs' cottage in Chester on Saturday, that is, Mr. R drove us in his new Oldsmobile, L and me and her two girls. He talked very depressingly about the war and the death of Lord Kitchener. He is really torn because it is so good for his business and so awful otherwise. He left us here for the month and drove back to town.

Mr. R, who had a new Oldsmobile—there weren't many of those in Halifax—and a daughter L, and a business that was doing well from the war.

We could smell the freshness and the presence of the sea as we got closer, even though we had the car windows up tight because of the dust from the road. I love it here. The house is large but still a cottage, with walls left rough inside, and the outside shingles weathered into a soft gray. The Rs call it Chester, but it is miles away from the town on its own land running out to a little point. From the front window you look out to sea past the islands, and from the side windows you look back at Mahone Bay and the smaller islands off Chester. I love the looser clothes we wear here, with nobody from town to put on corsets for.

There is a path along the shore that wanders in and out of sweet mossy woods and meadows. I love to walk through the bayberry bushes up to my thighs. My dress smells of the perfume afterward, and I crush a few leaves in my hand to smell it more strongly. The shore is rocky near the house, with a small beach in a little cove, perfect for swimming or picnics or landing a boat. If you walk far enough on the path you come to a much longer beach with the sand firm enough to walk on quickly. June is a perfect time here. Cold in the mornings and evenings but sunny and warm with cloudless skies when the morning fog burns off. The smells of the sea seem sharper, with the foghorn sounding from the lighthouse and the clanking and moaning of the buoys. I love the deep *oooooh-aaaah* sound the foghorn makes. I can hear it as I fall asleep. L wanted me to have her parents' big room at the front or the guest room with the large double bed, but I prefer C's room. It has cupboard shelves filled with summer boyhood things, the clothes very carefully put away by Mrs. R with tissue paper. It is the first time I have been in this room alone, able to look at things closely. I unwrapped a sailor's outfit he must have worn when four or five, about the size of L's girls, Elizabeth and Sarah. The little shorts, with the front buttoned upward in the sailor's style, and the tiny middy blouse gave me a sweet feeling; I think of him so little, so protected . . .

The woman who cooks for the Rs down here is Alice, Mollie's married sister, younger than Mollie and ruddier from being outdoors more, and just as cheerful. Her husband is a fisherman. She comes in the morning and lights the large range. You can smell the pleasant wood smoke coming up the stairs. When we throw on dressing gowns and go down—very informal—the kitchen is toasty and smells delicious, with a pot of porridge and coffee. Lizzy and Sarah, the two little girls, love having breakfast in their flannel nightgowns with the two big girls, L and me, all with our hair hanging down. We eat huge breakfasts of porridge and eggs and toast made from fresh country bread. The little girls get bored and run off while L and I sit lazily, feeling irresponsible, like children ourselves, gossiping with Alice, watching the girls run barefoot in the dewy grass, the early light shining through their flying hair. If Mrs. R were here, we would be dressed, with our hair done and all the sleep out of our eyes before we came down to breakfast.

Before she leaves, Alice builds a large fire in the sitting room, and we light it in the evenings. We sit around in the creaky wicker furniture, reading, playing card games or checkers or Snakes and Ladders with the girls. When it needs more wood, L and I together lift one of the large birch logs and, with a lot of clumsy heaving and laughing and squeals from the girls as the sparks shower out, we get it on.

Sitting there, our fronts warm from the fire and our backs a little chilly, the sound of the sea on the rocks just audible over the crackling logs, I feel a pull from upstairs. All those books and papers of C's waiting there. For two nights I have slipped away, saying that I am too sleepy to stay up, taking a kerosene lamp with me, just to have time here looking at his things.

Tuesday, June 13, 1916—

I am consumed with new curiosity about C, looking for anything that will give me new ways of understanding him. Last night I found a lot of papers from his school—essays, term reports—and pored over them by the oil lamp like a detective looking for clues.

Peter grew impatient and skipped ahead, skimming pages for more evidence of who she was, but also wanting to find more intimate thoughts.

Wednesday, June 14, 1916—

In her parents' bedroom looking over the sea, L pulled out a drawer full of photographs, and I took them off to C's room, sitting tucked up in the window seat. I noticed that C as a little boy always seemed to be looking off somewhere else.

In one picture taken when C was twelve or so, he looks wonderful, his hair messed up by the wind but falling in an adorable way. His arms are bare. I looked at it and wanted to touch the boy's body. I wanted to feel his thin muscular arms up to the shoulders above the shirt. I wanted to kiss his neck and chest where the shirt was open. I imagined looking at his whole body naked in one of these bedrooms with its windows on the sea. I could imagine his skin cool with a taste of dried salt from bathing in the ocean. I could imagine me, the grown woman, making love with the boy who would just be on the verge of becoming a man. Yet I couldn't get the face that is looking way off into the distance to turn to me.

I long to reach back into his childhood. I want to be the little girl where he is looking, the one he is anxious to break away from the annoying family picture to be with. To be with me, on that point, on the beach beyond it, in the soft woods above the beach, lying with him on the moss, listening to the waves on the beach and reading poetry together. Except that C isn't much for poetry.

I want to be the grown woman who knows and the girl his age who does not; the girl who does not threaten him but is his closest friend; the friend he doesn't tell any of the others about. But he takes me everywhere with him, and when we are alone he turns his blue gaze back to me. I am the one he is looking at when he is looking away in all the other pictures. I want to taste his hard little boy's body all over. I want to put him in my mouth. I want to carry him in my arms and put him to bed like a child but be with him in the bed like a woman. Then I could be his mother and his sister and his friend and his lover all in one.

Thinking of C as a little boy suddenly made me remember J at the lake. Those summers seem so far away and innocent now. I had not thought of him in a long time. I remember what we did in the barn and in the attic on rainy days. I can remember the feel of his body and the warm yet frightening feelings he gave me. Mother always said, "Now, you can't get too serious about J. You can't marry your first cousin." But we could investigate each other's bodies.

Her cousin?

Thursday, June 15, 1916—
Today we all went to visit C's boat, the *Seagull,* resting on props of wood, and it made me very uneasy.

I was sitting on a bunk beside the table where he worked on his charts. It had a thin layer of dust and with my finger I wrote his name slowly, with the sensation that I was touching him. I was going to write underneath, "I love you," thinking what fun it would be when he found it, but something stopped me, some feeling that it was bad luck—tempting fate.

After we had closed the boat up and retied the tarpaulin, walking back to the cottage, I kept looking at my dusty fingertip as if I carried something of him away with me. But when I thought "his dust," it gave me such a shudder that I was quite cold for a moment.

L just seems to be such a good sport about the war and H being away. I wouldn't dare talk to her about the intimate things. I'm afraid she would dislike me. Perhaps she has the right attitude, and like her I should try just to put all that out of my thoughts until he comes home.

Peter's lamp wick had burned down. It was nearly 1 A.M. He had to stop. Reluctantly he closed the diary and settled down in bed.

Who on earth was she? C.R. rang no bells. Her sister-in-law was L. He felt hypnotized by her. Everything about her stimulated him. Several explicit passages had aroused him. No wonder she wanted to burn it.

It would be a kindness to burn it myself. I'll put it in the furnace tomorrow morning.

It was full daylight when he awoke, but immediately he thought of her. Somewhere near him in the South End lived a woman whose intimate thoughts he knew better than he knew his own wife's.

The diary was on the bedside table. He took it downstairs and locked it in the desk drawer with his private papers.

He would have go over to the Tobins' to see how Margery was. The gas was still cut off, and he shaved in cold water.

His good suit of clerical black was too stained to wear. He put on his only other black suit, the trouser knees and jacket elbows beginning to be shiny. He had a fine gray suit Margery had ordered, but it remained in the cupboard. Gray, like wide collars, was for Low Churchmen.

As he tied the tapes of the black rabat behind his collar, Peter thought he could make a few discreet inquiries and return the diary to the woman, anonymously, with no embarrassment to her. He closed the front door and headed for the Tobins'.

When he turned into South Park, he was back on the clothes-collecting route. He began looking closely at the houses. She was in his thoughts as he mounted the steps of his in-laws' house.

"Oh, Peter, dear, do come in! We've been so worried about you," Cynthia Tobin said. "Margery's been telling us about the marvelous things you did on Thursday. How awful for you. It must have been simply ghastly. But have you had any breakfast?"

Cynthia Tobin had a faded prettiness, a dried look, and her throat sounded parched.

"Actually, no," Peter said.

"Well, come in, come in."

George Tobin was a big cheerful man with a balding head; he had started as a building laborer, created his own business, and now owned the largest construction company in the city. Marriage to Cynthia, who came from an old Halifax family, had made him quite respectable.

"Hello, Peter." George, wiping his face broadly with his napkin, rose from the dining room table, where Abigail and Michael were sitting before boiled eggs, and Margery, in a flouncy robe he hadn't seen before, was buttering a piece of toast.

She smiled weakly at him. "Good morning, darling. I'm sorry to desert you. But it was just awful. Did you find my note?"

"Not until it was too late to come over," Peter said.

"George is just off to see whether he can get his carts and vans back."

"They took everything we had to carry dead and wounded and supplies—horses, drays, trucks, vans. I hear they've wrecked a lot. If they couldn't find our driver, they put some soldier behind the wheel who'd never driven anything. God knows what I've got left."

"Do sit down," Cynthia said. The years were giving her heart-shaped face a pointed jaw; she was beginning to look like a pretty arrowhead.

"Tell me what you'd like and I'll tell Cook. Some porridge, eggs, a kipper?"

Food, like everything else, was plentiful at the Tobins'.

"If it's not too much trouble, I'd like a kipper, please."

"Of course it's not. You have such lovely manners, Peter. And some toast?" Cynthia went out, pleased to demonstrate the capacity of her domestic machinery.

Peter circled the table, kissing the children and Margery, who looked less wan today and very attractive in the lace-edged robe.

George Tobin came back with his overcoat on.

"The cathedral's hit bad, Margie says."

"Yes, a lot of stained glass was smashed. I don't know yet if there's any structural damage," Peter said. "That's my job this morning. To start planning what to do."

"It didn't need any more damage. The blasted place was jerry-built to begin with. I tried to tell them at the time. They wanted everything on the cheap. But I've told you before. Well, if I can be any help to you . . . I know they haven't got two cents to rub together over there."

"I suppose we'll have to start an emergency rebuilding fund," Peter said.

"Fat lot of good that'll do. Pennies. I think the government will have to pay for most of this. After all, it's war damage. A ship full of munitions wipes out part of the city, that's not an act of God. That's Ottawa."

He was wrapping a heavy scarf around his neck and shrugging on his overcoat.

"I don't care if it was the Germans, like some say, or an accident, or what. It's Ottawa's war and they have to pay something. It's going to take millions. I was up there yesterday. The whole

North End's gone. Well, Peter"—with a smile, George patted his shoulder—"that's your department, the people and their souls, in this life or the next one. My department is houses, and I don't know where in bloody hell we're going to get the materials just to keep the winter out of all these places, before we even talk about rebuilding. Half the city's got no glass in its windows. There's no window glass—or tarpaper or beaverboard, shingles, nails, putty— for a hundred miles. I've sent telegrams all over to send me stuff. It'll have to come in by the trainload. Even coffins. A friend tells me they've run out of coffins, but that's not my business, thank God. Closer to yours. Oh, Margie told me about your windows. I can scrounge a bit of glass and get a man over there to fix you up."

"Thank you. That's wonderful," Peter said.

"Least I can do. God bless."

Tobin put on his furry winter hat and left.

"Isn't that sweet of Daddy, Peter? I didn't think you'd mind my telling him about the windows we lost."

"It is very kind," said Peter. George Tobin was always being kind. In fact, he had given them their house.

MAJOR COLEMAN could not walk on his leg. He sat on the sofa in the study, drinking whiskey to numb it, unwilling to discuss it. But Mrs. Bethune, the housekeeper, found him and insisted on examining it. Mrs. Bethune had been a maid for the MacPhersons since before Stewart was born.

The major's leg was so swollen he could not pull up his uniform trouser leg. She made him remove the trousers and long under-wear.

"Don't be silly! Do you think an old thing like me is going to care about that?"

Meekly, he obeyed. Stewart was sickened by the appearance of the leg, ashamed that he had not stopped Coleman from using it so brutally. It was badly engorged, the inflamed skin a mass of recent scars, purple and bluish-red swellings, badly covered with stale bandages. When they were removed, he saw fresh openings run-ning with a mixture of blood and pus.

"Not very pretty, I'm afraid. No dancing with the Gaiety Girls for me."

Mrs. Bethune scolded, "What are they doing, letting you run around with your leg like that? Stay there a minute. I'll put some warm poultices on it to take the swelling down." She came back with dry towels and hot cloths in a basin. The major bit his mustache when she laid the hot compresses on the leg.

"Good thing my regimental sergeant major days are over, isn't it? No more square bashing for me. Always hated it anyway, but it's good for the troops."

The whiskey must have been working, because he rambled on. "I don't suppose it matters. In this war it's how many men you put in, and when they're killed, how many you replace 'em with, and when they go, how many more still. That's what it's about. Hardly matters whether the poor buggers can shoot straight."

Stewart got a passing team of horses to pull his car out of the drift and drove to City Hall. Halliwell, looking unshaven and rheumy from a sleepless night, grabbed him.

"Stewart MacPherson. Just the man I need. Do you still have your car?"

"Yes."

"Then for God's sake help us out. We're desperate for transportation at the station. The medical train from Boston has come in, and we need to move the equipment and people."

"But the station is wrecked," said Stewart.

"The south terminus by the ocean pier is working. The track is open through the cutting. Can you help us? The prime minister's train is there, too, and we're in a shambles here."

"Of course," Stewart said.

"I'd go with you," Halliwell said, "But I've got to make myself presentable before the PM gets here. Just time for a shave."

Stewart drove to the station and found the American train. He offered his services to the man in charge, Commissioner Frohlich of the Massachusetts Public Safety Committee, an energetic little man who held himself as erect as the major. As they got out of the Pullman car, Commissioner Frohlich said importantly, pointing to another track, "That, sir, is the private car of the prime minister of Canada, Sir Robert L. Borden. He received us very graciously a short while ago, and offered us the deep gratitude of the Canadian people for our quick action. A real gentleman, your prime minister."

When Commissioner Frohlich saw the battered Paige alone by

the curb, he said, "Is that all? Well, it'll do as a start." He acted as though he had expected a grander welcome.

"I'm afraid it's not as tidy as I'd like," Stewart said. "It's been used for two days as an ambulance."

A senior nurse and doctor got in with Frohlich. Disregarding Stewart, the commissioner said, "We come here with a trainload of doctors, nurses, and equipment, a fully equipped field hospital. We come through a blizzard, all day and all night, and they can't get a few buses or trucks down here."

"It's all pretty desperate," Stewart said. "The snow has stopped everything. And they're still digging people out."

At City Hall, Halliwell and others made speeches of gratitude. The Americans looked impatient. Finally, Frohlich said, "Well, let's get on with it. Who's in charge of the Medical Committee, the Transportation Committee, the Housing Committee? We're going to need cooperation from all of them."

"We don't have such committees," Halliwell said huffily. "It's all we've been able to do to set up the Relief Committee. There's been simply too much emergency work to do."

"Well, sir," the commissioner said, "I don't want to step on any toes here but I have had experience with disasters and you don't get anywhere without organization and we need some organization fast. I suggest you get together and make separate committees, for food, housing, sanitation, medical care, and transportation. And while you do that, show us a building where we can set up our hospital, and we'll get going. I hear you've still got wounded lying on hospital floors untreated. That's two days after the explosion. Those people will die if they don't get treated."

"We've got a building set aside for you." Halliwell turned to Stewart. "Look, old boy, you know the Bellevue Building—the Officers' Club. Take the Americans along there, and let them set up shop."

More quietly he said, "And get this officious little man out of my hair before I shoot him."

The Americans climbed back into the Paige.

"Looked like a scene of mass confusion in there," Frohlich said primly. "No organization. Everything happening in one big room. All those people shoving and pushing."

"It's a very small city," Stewart said. "They're doing their best. No one was prepared for anything like this."

"That's just it, young man, you've got to be prepared. That is how the Commonwealth of Massachusetts could ship a whole trainload of us with a fully equipped field hospital—"

Stewart wished the man would stop saying "fully equipped field hospital" like a gramophone record. It sounded like an advertisement.

"—and why we have a shipload of supplies leaving Boston tonight for Halifax. Because we were prepared for disaster."

Stewart thought even Mr. Frohlich might be staggered by what he was going to see. It was hard going on the unploughed streets, but he made it to the Bellevue Building and they went in.

"Why, this place is a wreck," Frohlich said as his colleagues stared at the gaping windows and doors, the wind blowing in, snow and ice on the floors of every room. "But if this is it, I guess this is it. We'll do our best. But we'll need some help. Say, driver, take me back to City Hall and I'll jump on them for some assistance. We're going to need soldiers and construction workers and a bunch of trucks to get our stuff in here. You can take this doctor and nurse around the hospitals to survey the medical problem. OK? Let's go!"

Stewart drove them to the North End for a quick look at the devastation, then to two hospitals, Camp Hill and the Victoria General. And that was enough for the doctor from Massachusetts.

"My God, I've never seen anything like this. Those men are dead on their feet operating and they've still got people waiting in the hallways."

They passed through a ward of children with beds and cots jammed so close there was almost no space between them. Stewart noticed the little girl he had brought in on Thursday with the blinded mother, the girl who had carried the dead baby. She was sitting on a folding cot, with one eye bandaged. Her other dark blue eye looked him gravely.

"Hello, Betty, do you remember me?"

"You brought me here."

"I didn't know you were hurt."

"My eye hurt after."

"Is it all right now?"

"They took it out. They couldn't keep it." The laconic statement made Stewart's stomach contract. She still talked in the flat voice of the day of the disaster.

"Where is your—mama? Her eyes were hurt too."

"She died." The child was quite without emotion.

"Oh, I'm very sorry."

"Anyway, she couldn't see," the little girl said.

"But you can see, with this eye."

"Yes, but it's hard if I look that way." She turned to the right, the side of her bandaged eye.

"You're a brave little girl."

"I'm nine."

"Well, you're a brave big girl."

"My baby brother died, too."

"I remember him. You were holding him."

"He was dead when you brung us here. Mama died later."

"Well, Betty, I hope you feel well soon."

Moving down the ward, he asked the American doctor, "What happens to a girl of that age who loses an eye?"

"She can wear a glass eye. The eye doesn't grow much larger. She'll be able to wear one now."

By lunchtime Frohlich had commandeered fifty sailors from the U.S.S. *Old Colony* and a company of Canadian soldiers. They had cleaned the slush off the floors, removed the furniture, washed all the walls, covered the windows with beaverboard, and got a heating system going. By six o'clock they had installed an operating room and a hundred beds. By midevening they had moved in ninety patients. Frohlich's amazing efficiency had even caused the Stars and Stripes to be hoisted over the building.

"Damned cheek!" said Arthur Halliwell when he came to visit. "But beggars can't be choosers."

"I think the only thing he forgot was the state flag of Massachusetts," Stewart said.

"Do you know, Stewart," Halliwell said, "the prime minister has fixed the Americans up at the Halifax Club. No one ever slept there before. There are no bedrooms. But he wanted them to have a decent place to sleep, so we moved some beds in. Hotels aren't good enough, apparently. Can you believe it?"

THE UNKNOWN DIARIST would not leave Peter's thoughts. Leaving the Tobins' house for the cathedral, he made a detour to his own house. He unlocked the desk and read a few pages to remind himself that she was real.

Friday, September 1, 1916—

Our second wedding anniversary! I have not felt like writing for a while. I have been trying to exercise a little self-discipline, to keep my thoughts on other things. I hated myself that all I could think of was *that* side of things. So for two months or so, ever since we came back from Chester, I have reformed and made myself as cheerful and positive as L.

The shops are advertising autumn millinery. I have no desire to go and look at pretty things. It seems selfish, even unpatriotic. The truth is I find the things in the Halifax shops a little dreary. If I wait, as I did last year, until I go to Montreal, Mother will press me to go shopping, and it's true—everything is much smarter there. The summer dress I bought there last winter, the white embroidered voile, is the smartest thing I've seen here. So I've worn it again and again.

Monday, September 4, 1916—

I am always happier when the war news is better. The *Herald* says we are "smashing" the Germans at the Somme. Mind you, the *Herald* manages to sound cheerful about the war every day even when things are very gloomy for our side.

The paper says that "only $3800" remains to be raised so that the consecration of All Saints Cathedral can take place in November. The figure seems so little, and the cathedral so huge and imposing. This summer Mr. R bought his big new car, and I see from the advertisements that Oldsmobiles cost $1299. What people spend on three motorcars would do it. I know that C wants to buy a car when he comes home and we have the money. There is still my money, or "your" money, as he calls it, which Daddy gave me when we were married. I could pay all the cathedral needs myself. But I won't. I go only because C went, and I don't go every Sunday.

The cathedral gives me mixed feelings: from the outside it is grand and dumpy at the same time, inspiring and homely, uplifting to the spirit and depressing. Perhaps that suits Halifax. From some angles it soars, from others it squats. It is better inside, more graceful, more perpendicular, when you can't see the depressing gray-black stone of the exterior. It is no Salisbury or Chartres! Of course it is still unfinished.

Peter had never seen Salisbury or Chartres. Her remarks made him feel he'd been criticized, discovered in his provincialism. It had never occurred to him that the cathedral was anything but grand, inspiring, and uplifting to the spirit from all angles, in all eyes.

Wednesday, September 6, 1916—

A letter from C. Why does it give me such a feeling of remoteness from him? He is my life, my soul. I long to hear from him. I live from letter to letter. I weep over them. Well, sometimes I weep over them. But I do read them eagerly, thirstily.

I take the letter to the window and look for the tiniest sign of the war, some trace of where he is, of the trenches—a speck of mud, of blood. I smell each letter carefully, holding the paper to my nose, sniffing like a blind dog all over the surface, sniffing the inside of the envelope. I would look ridiculous if anyone could see me. Nothing. No smell—or only a smell I imagine.

I hold his letter to me, embrace it, hug it, press it to my bosom, like a silly heroine in a novel, as if something of him will pass into me from "somewhere in France."

I am sick of that "somewhere in France." They use it in the papers all the time, when someone is killed or wounded. Somewhere in France! They could quite easily tell us where they are. How is it going to help the beastly Germans if C tells me where he is? Have they got squadrons of nosy old busybodies with teakettles to steam all the letters open? Well, I am sick of it. Was C part of this marvelous victory at the Somme? There is no hint in his letter. Of course, he wrote a month ago, from "somewhere in France." I mean, he could be sitting at a café in Paris or lolling at Biarritz. But I am being silly. I seem to feel the bad time of the month a little more severely each month. It makes me irritable.

I'll go shopping for some chocolate and tobacco and really nice things to make up another package for him. Something practical I can do. Then I must force myself to do some sewing —which I hate—but the waist that goes with the black skirt needs a button, there is a tear in the lace on a petticoat where I caught my heel in it—and so on. Dreary!!!

Sunday, October 15, 1916—

Awoke from a frightening, awful dream, so real the feeling
stayed with me all day. In the dream C came back from France,
not wounded or anything, but so ugly that I did not recognize
him, and, when I did, he repelled me. His face was coarse and
awful, and when he wanted to kiss me, it made me ill. I woke
up perspiring and wanting to be sick. The feeling was so strong
that I went down to the kitchen and drank some baking soda
mixed with water. The sick feeling went away, but the feeling
of dread hung over me. L and I took a long walk to see the
glorious trees across the Arm. The man rowing the ferryboat
said his brother had been killed in France. It made me terribly
sad. We walked the path through Boulderwood and had tea at
the Saraguay, where it was warm enough to sit on the lawn.

The Saraguay, Peter thought. Margery's parents were members.
He could ask—indirectly.

I told L about my dream, and she said in her brisk way,
"Don't pay any attention to it. You probably just had
indigestion, and that can make you dream anything."

Peter could hear his mother saying just that. He closed the diary
sharply. He could not sit there like this. He must get to the cathedral to get on with his duties.

Reading her words made him lightheaded. Remembering her
explicitness, and anticipating more, had actually awakened a small
sexual ache. He had to find out who she was.

At the cathedral, he made a careful inventory of the wreckage. It
soothed him to draw a plan, systematically recording the damage to
the stained glass. He picked up a fragment, holding it to the light.
It was like looking through an amethyst at the cold sunlight of the
northern winter. The Greeks, he remembered, thought amethysts
prevented intoxication.

Each window had been paid for by people with grief or love in
their hearts; the brass plaques attested to years of human joy and
pain, an enormous accumulation of emotion, back into the distant
reaches of the small British colony. Finally, after several false starts,
a decade into the twentieth century, it had its own stone cathedral.
It was a focus for the devotional energy in hundreds of white frame

churches in little harbors by sparkling blue seas, under ancient elms in deserted Loyalist villages, nestled in deep valleys in Cape Breton, bosomed in growths of balsam fir, white spruce, feathery hackmatack: all those communities lifted up their eyes unto this place. Fog-bound, forest-bound, sea-bound people had quite literally saved their pennies, sockfuls of big, blackened Victorian and Edwardian pennies. To see it now, only a year after its consecration, so savagely ripped open, was tragic.

While studying for the ministry at King's College, Peter could think of nothing sweeter, once ordained, than to be given one of those small churches. But after one summer as assistant rector in Annapolis, he was snatched up for preferment. He served as secretary to the prolocutor of the committee revising the Book of Common Prayer. That put him in the very small group of young Canadian-trained clergymen with high potential. The church powers still preferred English priests trained at Oxford or Cambridge.

Two years later Peter was asked to assist another senior Nova Scotia clergyman. When the dean he was helping became seriously ill, Peter functioned for a time as an acting member of the committee, among men whose knowledge and experience vastly exceeded his but who commended his scholarship and good judgment. Thus, very early Peter had found himself traveling on a special track, active in church politics, constantly bidden from one special task to another.

He completed his plan of the damage. The larger stained glass windows were intact. Heavy leading must have helped them. But all the small memorial windows, the St. Stephen's Chapel window, and some of the tinted glass in the transept and sanctuary were missing. They would need an expert to estimate the cost of replacement. Next, he met the sexton, the cathedral's handyman, caretaker, furnace attendant, and snow shoveler.

"Well, it could be worse," he said. "You'll pay for a lot less coal for a while. Them people using the crypt for two nights have been moved out, but I'm just keeping the heat on down there so's the pipes don't freeze. Just won't run so much heat up here. No sense keeping that big furnace going full blast, with all the heat going out the windows. And it means I don't have to set no mousetraps up here for a while. No smart mouse hangs around in a cold building in the middle of winter. They're likely all downstairs right now keeping warm with me."

Peter laughed and asked how they could cover the broken windows.

"Can't just nail tarpaper onto it, like people are doing to their houses. Nothing to nail into but the stone, and that concrete flakes out if you look at it. It's going to take some firring in them pointy windows."

"What's firring?"

"Strips of wood you set in there. But it takes a real good carpenter to do it right and a lot of wood. How long you reckon it'll have to last?"

Peter said, "I don't know. But it could be a long time. Even if we had the money—thousands of dollars to order new stained glass —and could order it today, it would take a long time, perhaps a year or eighteen months. So I suppose the covering will have to be able to stand up to a lot of weather."

"Then you need real construction people. That's too much for me. Can't do them windows up the end of a ladder. Got to put scaffolding up. Most they could do right away would be hang some big tarps down to keep the rain out while they're putting up the scaffolding. That's some big job. Only big companies have got them tarps."

"Well, thanks for your help. I'll have to speak to the dean about it."

Peter presumed the dean was still out. He went into the office and quickly scanned the names on the Altar Guild list. The members were all listed by their husbands' names. Mrs. Walter Belcher, Mrs. John Colvin. He didn't know L's married name nor her father's first name. R——? Peter thought for a moment. The office was empty. He went over to the desk where the dean's occasional secretary worked and pulled out the file of parishioners who made regular offerings in weekly envelopes. The list of Rs was long: Rafford, Rainey, Raleigh, Ramsey, Rand, Rankin, Ransome, Rawden, Rawson, Raymond, Read, Redfield, Reed, Reid, Renfrew, Reynolds, Rhodes, Rice, Richards, Ritchie, Robbins, Roberts, Robertson, Robinson, Rogers, Roper, Rose, Ross, Roy, Russell. It was tantalizing. Somewhere in that list was the answer.

She had been married for three years. The date was in the diary:

September. September weddings in the cathedral for 1914. He could look that up. No. They would have been married in Montreal, where her parents lived.

Stewart MacPherson might know who she was.

The dean opened the door, his black gaiters showing beneath his winter coat, and hung up his shovel hat.

"Saint Paul's have offered to share their church for two services on Sunday. And the Scouts have volunteered to take all the prayer and hymn books to Saint Luke's Hall. They're bringing their own toboggans and sleds."

Peter told the dean about his conversation with the sexton.

"We'll have to convene the building committee as soon as we can, although most of the members will be desperately busy. Our sister churches believe that some kind of compensation will be coming. But what can we do immediately?"

Peter had an answer. "If you'll let me, sir, I'll speak to George Tobin. It needs a big firm to cover the windows. Tobin's is big enough, and if we could promise payment whenever relief money comes in, he might do it."

"Capital thinking," said the dean. "Mr. Tobin wouldn't be willing to do it as a gift to the church, a contribution?"

"He's not a member of the congregation, sir."

"What church does he go to?"

"None."

"I see."

"The fact is, as he has often told me, he was one of the firms that tendered to build the cathedral. His bid was rejected as too expensive. He thinks the firm that was chosen used inferior materials and did a very poor job. He tweaks me about it now and then."

"Well, it never hurts to ask. It would be a godsend now."

Talking to Tobin meant having dinner, which meant a stop at Tower Road to change. Cynthia Tobin liked to dress on Saturday nights, war or no war. He hurried into his dinner jacket. That left him half an hour for the diary.

Wednesday, October 18, 1916—

The Diaghilev ballet has opened in New York for the first time. Seeing that brought back to me so clearly the day Mother and I went to see it in Paris, the summer she came to meet me. *L'Après-midi d'un Faune* and *Le Sacre du Printemps,* both with

Nijinsky. She hadn't the slightest idea what she was taking me to, except that I had said it was the exciting thing to see that season. She was terribly upset, but there was no getting out. We were in the middle of a row and I was hardly noticing her. I was in something like a dream, a swoon. *L'Après-midi* was so very sensual that it excited me physically, not directly, but half-directly, and a little frighteningly. *Le Sacre* also excited me, but differently. Some of the Stravinsky music was so shocking, unpleasant, and brutal, and yet thrilling, as though the composer imagined the sounds of war coming long before this real war. Yet other parts were haunting and lovely. I have never forgotten that evening—the leering, primitive, suggestive, Eastern look in Nijinsky's eyes, his silky movement, like a cat's, the huge leaps and the velvet landings. I wish I could see it again. The moment I caught the name Diaghilev out of the corner of my eye in the *Herald,* I began to feel a tingling of excitement through my body.

It has made me itchy to be going somewhere, to make a trip anywhere, to do something exciting. My life is so— boring!

I am restless. Mad schemes pop into my head, like simply getting on the train and going to New York for a week. I could afford it, but it would shock the Rs and my mother.

The casual references to money made Peter cold at the pit of his stomach. She said the cathedral fund wanted "only $3800" and that she had that amount. Her nonchalance suddenly made the universe of relative wealth—the spaces between the big planets and the little—much vaster to Peter and more frightening. That was more money than he made in three years. Even the cheapest motorcar was hopelessly out of reach.

She was tempted to hop on a train to New York. What would that cost? Not just the ticket but tips for porters and dining-car people. In New York, taxis, hotels, restaurants, theaters, concerts . . . He could not estimate the cost; perhaps hundreds of dollars. It angered him that she was so casual about it.

His anger made him read faster, impatiently skimming pages about Halifax architecture, about people and manners, about music by Stravinsky, her pleasure in reading Tolstoy. He felt excluded, as by her indifference to money. She seemed to be talking to some-

one else, who knew things Peter did not. Peter skimmed until she
resumed her most private voice and seemed again to be confiding
in him.

Sunday, December 24, 1916—

Mollie can be so vulgar, but she has a way of getting to just
what I am thinking. Her husband was drowned, and when her
son-in-law moved to Halifax to work in the dockyard, Mrs. R
brought Mollie to town to be near them. We both went to the
Rs' this afternoon to help in the kitchen, because a lot of
officers from out of town are coming to Christmas dinner
tomorrow. Mollie and I were in the scullery, cleaning the huge
turkey. Mollie cut off the long neck and pulled the skin off. She
looked at me with a wink and said in a loud whisper, "It always
makes me think of something I shouldn't think of," and then
she laughed until she had to wipe her eyes on her apron. I
blushed from realizing that I knew precisely what she meant and
even more from knowing that she knew I knew.

Peter read the passage again. It had never occurred to him that
women joked about such matters.

Mollie's a tough old thing, indestructible and always cheerful
—actually, not so old, only fifty-five. She came in last week,
shaking with a cold, after spending Sunday with her family and
insisting on coming through the slush from the North End. She
was sniffling and coughing. I offered her some hot tea and she
looked at me slyly and said, "There wouldn't be a sip of
something stronger, dear?" Of course she knew exactly what we
have in the sideboard. She knows everything about this house.
The new laws make everyone so negative about liquor that I'm
sure I should have been shocked, but I simply asked whether
she'd like rum or whiskey.

"Rum, thank you," she said firmly. When I came back from
the dining room with the bottle, she suggested I have one too.
So I did! I poured two small glasses and we sat down at the
scrubbed kitchen table, sipping—like the old women in the
Montparnasse cafés.

I had never tasted neat rum before, except a drop on my
finger when making hard sauce. It smells a lot better than it

tastes. Mollie pushed the wisps of graying hair back from her face, blew her nose, and told stories.

Thursday, February 22, 1917—

Thank God C did not join the navy. The German submarines are sinking ships so rapidly that it must be more dangerous at sea than in France.

Like the war, winter drags on, not as cold here as in Montreal, but damper and foggier. I feel it in my bones more. Along Barrington Street this morning, the cold pounced on me from the harbor, making me scurry across the intersection, trying to keep my boots out of the deeper pools of slush. And the fish smell! It rides the wet wind up from the docks and somehow makes it seem colder. I hold my fur muff up to my nose and mouth to block it off. Sometimes it's as strong as a whiff of smelling salts. It makes my eyes water.

An advertisement for Bermuda caught my eye on the shipping page. "Forty hours from frost to flowers." S.S. *Bermudian,* two days from New York. That is what C and I should do when he comes back. Get on a boat to Bermuda and start our marriage all over again, surrounded by bougainvillaea and hibiscus. How enchanting it seems now, our walks on the beach with my skirt hitched up and C's flannels rolled up to the knee, the waves coming and going over our feet, the water so silkily warm that we scarcely noticed it touching our skin. No matter how we washed our feet, there was always a little sand in the foot of our bed, and his skin tasted of sea salt.

And here I am daydreaming about that—a winter woman with my paisley shawl wrapped around me, my skirts tucked around my ankles, my fingers and the tip of my nose cold in spite of the radiator hissing and spitting by the window.

Thursday, March 15, 1917—

In the legislature they have introduced an act to extend the vote to women in Nova Scotia. I suppose that's important, but I haven't thought about it very much. I really must pay more attention to the world outside my own selfish feelings. The paper says today that 115 people died in Halifax in February, fifty-one of them children and thirty-nine children under two years of age. That is just frightful! Why don't more people make a fuss about it?

The Anglican Church *is* making a fuss, Peter interjected. Some ministers have raised it repeatedly in public meetings, in letters to the mayor and city council.

Friday, March 16, 1917—

Anna Case of the Metropolitan Opera is coming to Halifax! It gave me quite a flutter until I read the advertisement more closely. "Anna Case is not coming to Halifax but her real voice is." Phinney's is selling tickets to a concert where they will play Anna Case recordings in their shop, on a gramophone. Proceeds to the Red Cross. That is when you know you live in a very small place!

I have thought of the war and C's absence as something to endure as an injured animal endures, curling herself up with her nose in her paws and sleeping until it goes away—hibernating. But that feeds my tendency to think about myself too much. Mrs. R introduces me to the daughters of her friends, the girls C knew from childhood, and they are very pleasant, although bound up in their homes and children. They all look as though they have nothing but wholesome thoughts, Ovaltine at bedtime, and Friar's Balsam for their children's colds. Can other women switch off that part of themselves like an electric light in an unused room when their men are not around? Don't they think of it and feel their knees go weak? If hard-bitten old Mollie with her work-roughened hands and heavy body thinks of it, doesn't the young doctor's wife, with her delicate wrists and rosewater scent? When she goes to bed alone, doesn't she press her breasts against a pillow and hug it to her with longing?

These women make me forget that for nearly three years I listened to the most uninhibited talk in the world. There were all sorts of students in the ateliers on the fringe of the Julian and the Beaux-Arts: intense women with unwashed hair and rumpled clothes who lived with artists, or pretended to, and *jeunes filles bien rangées*, like me, daughters of the bourgeoisie, raised even more starchily than I. Our small talents quickly pushed us into the ranks of the dilettantes, but we were never excluded. We talked all together for hours in the little cafés, and talk about sex was taken for granted, like politics and food and drink and tobacco, a background to what was really important, arguing about ART. Stifling now to be among women with whom I can't even mention it.

No wonder she is so outspoken, Peter thought; she lived like a bohemian in Paris.

The czar of Russia has abdicated. Since all I know of Russia is *War and Peace,* I thought of Natasha and what that will mean to people of her class. The czar looks so much like King George, they could be twins instead of first cousins. Imagine our king abdicating. No, it is unimaginable. The British people and the people of the Dominions love him too much—or we're always saying we do.

Monday, March 19, 1917—
The end of the war is in sight, the *Herald* says! I ran into the kitchen and read it to Mollie: a great Allied victory, the Germans on the run. Mollie was ironing and asked if that meant our men will be coming home. I said I hoped so, and she said, "Don't get your hopes up too big, dear." But she couldn't dampen my spirits. I looked at the heavy iron she was lifting from the stove—she calls it a sad iron. In a rush of happy feelings, I told her that if the war was over I'd buy her one of the new electric irons.
"What's wrong with this one? It works right good."
I told her she wouldn't have to heat it on the stove; it stays hot all the time. You just plug it into the current like a lamp.
"Sounds like a waste of good money to me" was her comment.

Wednesday, March 21, 1917—
The first day of spring and a driving blizzard! I tried to get *Anna Karenina* from the library, but it had been taken out again.

Peter skimmed what she wrote of her reading, of visiting wounded men at Camp Hill. Then mention of her cousin J caught his attention.

Tuesday, April 3, 1917—
A telegram from Mother. It terrified me when it came.

Instant fears of the worst, but it was good news. J is coming
through Halifax tomorrow on his way overseas. Haven't heard
anything about him for months and didn't know he had joined
up. I must get the guest room ready and think of something
nice for dinner.

And the Americans are coming into the war! Wonderful, if
that helps us to win or get it over with.

Tuesday, April 10, 1917—

J's regiment sailed today and I watched them go, with such a
full, sad heart that he might have been my husband and not my
cousin. The men used to board the transports with an air of
wild gaiety and adventure. No more. The grimy trains squeal
into the new ocean terminal siding, and the men tumble out,
tired, rumpled, and cross, carrying their huge kitbags and rifles.
They form into ranks and march off with the band playing, but
the lilt is gone. Towering behind them is the huge converted
passenger liner, menacing in its ugly Cubist camouflage, like the
presence of war itself. The day was grim and desperate; the
chilly air and gray sky threatened rain. Standing at the rail, some
of the men sang, "Keep the Homes Fires Burning," which made
us all weep.

J has grown more serious, much more self-important, and I
don't like him as well. He looks marvelous in his uniform,
almost a dandy, with his very dark hair and dark eyes from
Daddy's family. And he hasn't married yet. I wish I could think
of someone.

I loved showing off the house, but I felt odd, knowing he
was under my roof with C away. I lay in bed the first night
when the house was quiet with the thought that he might
actually creep down the hall and steal into bed with me—as he
did when we were at the lake at Grandmother Montgomery's.
At supper, chatting across the table (pretty with the candlelight
and silver I have so little chance to use), I kept thinking how
strange it is that physical acts between two people can seem to
be fully erased. They meet years later and it is as though nothing
had ever happened.

I was sure, looking at him carefully while he talked about
Montreal, that those things had gone out of his head completely.
I had a wicked little desire to tease him about it—he looked so

upright and proper with all his brass buttons buttoned and his Sam Browne buckled.

I really didn't want any revival of that—it was childish; we had silly names for everything—and would never have made the slightest move to provoke it. But I couldn't help thinking about it in bed and, as I thought, becoming both frightened and aroused. I heard the floor creak in the hall outside my bedroom, and it sent a flash of fear through me, but a tingle of excitement too. I strained to listen but could hear nothing, so I must have imagined it. I was both relieved and a tiny bit disappointed.

My mind is a very dangerous creature. It remembers everything and imagines everything. It is ten years since those summers, almost half my life, yet some things are as vivid to me as if they had happened yesterday. Lying in bed, knowing that J was just down the hall, I could remember what his young body felt like when I touched it. After the second summer Mother and Daddy sent me to Switzerland. It never occurred to me until now that perhaps they knew more than I thought. Perhaps Grandmother saw more and quietly warned them. If so, in one sense, her warnings were too late. I did things then I haven't done with C, even though we are married. We didn't have any sense of what was right and what was wrong because we knew it was all quite wrong. I have never told anyone, even the girls at school when we traded deep secrets. My secrets were darker than theirs.

When I told Mrs. R that J was coming, she insisted on having a small dinner party, which turned into a debate about the war. I sat there, only half-listening through the cigar smoke, while we drank port and cracked walnuts.

Mr. R said he agrees with Winston Churchill, who says the most terrible months of the war are still to come, even with the Americans now involved.

J said he thought it would be wrapped up very quickly, because the Americans could send so many soldiers and their factories could turn out so many tanks and weapons.

Mr. R said, "Bloody Americans!" and went on about how long it had taken the Americans to see their own vital interests while they watched the British Empire bleed itself to death. He said, "President Wilson crows about saving the world for democracy. Well, dammit, it's Englishmen and Canadians and

Australians who have been giving their lives for democracy
while the Yanks have talked. Now, like everything else they do,
they have to make a big noise about it."

We have heard that argument before. I sat there patiently
listening while I tried to see in J the half boy–half man who had
once been the most exciting thing in my life. Oddly, though
now a man and on his way to war, he looked callow to me, and
his arguments sounded like wishful thinking. When he kissed my
cheek and saluted at the gangway, he didn't look like a soldier—
too thin and nervous.

Friday, April 13, 1917—

At last spring has come. I had a brief creative tingle, thinking
about painting the daffodils gleaming through the black railings
of the Public Gardens but remembering how muddy my
attempts at Impressionism always came out, I quickly banished
that idea.

My spirits are down again since J left. I am more uneasy
about what will happen to him than I am about C, because I
have grown almost used to that worry. Every day I go down the
list of casualties, the Roll of Honor, as they call it. I have a
morbid superstition that if something happens to C, they may
forget to send me a telegram and I will just find his name in the
paper. They now print rows of little tanks, guns, or soldiers
between the lines of Killed in Action, Wounded in Action, and
Missing, as though we need reminding. Today there is worse. A
Major MacKenzie of the 85th Battalion—thank God I don't
know him—has been seriously wounded by shell fire. The
wretched newspaper practically gloats over it, calling him "one
of the finest men physically who ever enlisted in the King's
service . . . His personal character nobly matches his splendid
physique. Tall, splendidly made he was when he set out for the
firing line, a superb specimen of manhood." Why in heaven's
name are they saying that? I can't believe it. Why do they go on
talking about the perfection of a body that is now torn apart by
shells? What must his family feel? And his wife?

Monday, April 16, 1917—

I cannot read the paper. Canadian regiments have been in
four days of solid fighting at Arras. The *Herald* says large

numbers of officers have been killed. I cannot read it. I cannot bear it.

Peter had to stop. He was late. He ran to the Tobins', arriving just as they were sitting down.

At the dinner table, Margery looked withdrawn but in control. The Tobins had two guests, the Gastonguys, father and daughter. Jeffrey Gastonguy was a reserve colonel, too old for active service, but he was helping at City Hall. His wife was dead. His daughter, Susan, a childhood friend of Margery's, had been working as a volunteer typist in the City Hall Relief Committee office.

"I forgot to tell you, I saw Stewart MacPherson the day of the explosion . . ." Peter said to Margery and noticed Susan's immediate interest. Margery, who liked Stewart, had tried unsuccessfully to interest him in Susan.

". . . in the North End. He was using his car to carry injured people."

"He's such an odd man. You just never see him anywhere. We still invite him to things, but he never accepts," Susan said.

Her father, a lean man with bony cheeks and a little mustache, was arguing angrily, tapping with his spoon for emphasis.

"The damned Americans are charging in here as if they owned the place. Put their own damned flag up right away, for God's sake! I heard as soon as they got their hospital open, an American woman was transferred there from Camp Hill. They're putting it out that she wept when she saw the Stars and Stripes. Did you ever hear such claptrap? Just the sort of propaganda nonsense Americans are putting out all the time. They seem to think no one else feels anything about his country or flag. The Union Jack is a damned sight older than the Stars and Stripes, and people don't go around caterwauling about it all the time."

"Well, it isn't really our flag, is it, Father?" Susan said, with a wink at Margery, who gave a weak smile.

"What do you mean? Our chaps are dying for that flag. The Americans come in here and simply take over. Shoved us aside at City Hall and began organizing us."

"But, Daddy, look what they did! Someone needed to take over!"

"Well, what are we for, for heaven's sake? Lots of us are trained to take over in a moment of crisis."

"But I saw what was going on down there. Everyone trying to grab control. It was like children. All those self-important, would-be majors."

"Well, I'm no would-be major—"

"Oh, you know the people I mean! Anyway, I think the American man, whoever he was, really straightened them out. He gave them the push they needed. Now they have some organization. And the Americans got their hospital going in one day!"

"Well, no one ever said they weren't efficient," Cynthia Tobin said.

"Yes, but what's all the fuss about?" the colonel persisted. "One hospital, a hundred beds, well and good. Jolly good work, to be fair about it. But you'd think the Yanks had come in and saved us, to see the prime minister and Halliwell fawning on them. The official estimate now is nearly ten thousand people wounded. We've got hospitals all over town, hospitals in schools, the Ladies' College, hospitals in private homes. We're looking after thousands and thousands of patients, performing operations, dressing wounds. And they make all this commotion over one hospital of a hundred beds."

"Well, shall we have coffee in the drawing room?" Cynthia said.

Gastonguy was still fuming as he gallantly held her chair. "It's the way the damned Yankees have come into the war. All the hullaballoo about their finally getting off their duffs, and you'd think they'd done the whole thing themselves . . ." His irate voice faded across the hallway.

Margery beckoned to Peter. Avoiding his eyes, she whispered, "I'd like to stay here another night. Do you mind? The children are very happy and they're just getting over their colds. Do you want to stay?" She looked at him tremulously.

"No, that's all right. I should get back to the house. I have to keep the furnace going. But I need to talk to your dad first."

"About what?" She looked alarmed.

"About the damage to the cathedral."

"Oh, that!" She seemed relieved and went off to join her mother.

When the Gastonguys left, George Tobin fell into the leather chair in his library with a big sigh and loosened the waistcoat of his dinner jacket. He listened carefully to Peter's summary of the damage, and asked a few questions. How many windows and what size? How high? Would they replace the windows with stained glass or plain?

The heavy man sat, compressing the leather chair cushion almost flat, doing the calculations in his head. Finally he said, "Well, I know the size of it. You're right about the firring. We can't nail anything into stone."

Peter noted the "we."

"We'd have to have the windows measured and frames made to set in. They could be prefabricated at the mill. That's the cheapest way. Save labor on the spot. It's about two thousand dollars' worth of work. Just to cover up and keep the weather out until some permanent work is done."

"Would Tobin's do the work and accept payment when the relief money comes through?" Peter asked.

"What relief money?"

"As you said this morning, the money Ottawa will have to send."

"And if no money comes—what do I do?"

"Do you think there won't be money?"

"No. There'll be money. The prime minister's a Nova Scotian. He rushed right down here to be on the spot. Just over a week till the election. Halifax is vital for the war, shipping troops out, food, munitions—all that. The explosion's the greatest disaster that ever hit Canada, maybe the States too. The Americans are sending trainloads and shiploads of supplies. Forget old Jeffrey Gastonguy. He's been half-balmy for years. There'll be a lot of money and, let's be honest, Tobin's will do fantastic business. So will all the construction firms. We've got to rebuild a third of the city. Needed it too. There were miles of rotten housing up there. I never showed you the house I grew up in. It's gone with all the rest, thank God. I couldn't even see the street, Roome Street. Miles of matchsticks covered with snow. And still digging bodies out. That house was so flimsy I'm surprised it took a big explosion to blow it over. The whole stinking North End needed rebuilding anyway. So there'll be money. But should I do it?"

He looked at Peter speculatively and shrewdly for a few moments.

Then he spoke once more: "Margery is bad again, Peter. You know it and I know. When she came running in here yesterday, her mother was shocked. I didn't see it; I was out. She couldn't stop crying. Cynthia cleaned the children up and fed them, got Margie to lie down and calmed her. She's very bad, Peter. And we've got to do something about it."

"Yes," Peter said, warily.

"We've talked about this a lot. When you stood up and told me you two wanted to be independent, I tried; Cynthia and I tried to stay out of it. I know what a man's pride is, Peter. I'm full of it myself. I hate people pushing me around. It's why I started my own business. But you can't let your pride drive that girl into the madhouse. Because that's what it looks like to me. I know you don't beat her or use her bad. If I thought you did, I'd kill you. When this first started I actually asked her, Is he beating you? What is it he's doing? And all she'd say was, No, Daddy, he's very sweet to me. It's just that I can't manage. You've been doing half the housework, Peter. What does that do to your pride, for God's sake, washing diapers? You hear what I'm saying?"

"Yes, I do," Peter said. "It's a really bad period right now. Nothing seems to cheer her up."

"Right. So we've got to try something different. Look, my friend, I'm a businessman with rough edges. All the refinement in this family comes from Cynthia, not me, as she'll tell you quick enough. You're a far better educated man than me. But it just makes sense, in a business or anything else in life, it just makes common sense, if a situation is getting worse, you've got to try something different. Waiting won't do it. Waiting makes it worse. You agree with me?"

"Yes, but—" Peter began.

Tobin reached out a large hand to stop him. "No buts. I'm going to make a deal, Peter. I'll fix the goddamned church—I'll do it for free—no cost, a donation to the Church of England, which has never done anything for me, but . . . This is the deal: you get a maid in that house to help Margery. If it takes it, you get two maids. You get some of the drudgery off that girl, and we'll see if that doesn't brighten her up."

"But you know I can't afford a maid."

"But I can and I'm going to see that she has one. You stopped me the last time. If you stop me now—and I admit you're the master in your own house—no help for the cathedral. The rain and snow can rot the place, for all I care. So do we have a deal?"

"I just need to think a moment," Peter said. He hated this, yet a kind of relief swept over him. He was being forced. He had no choice, but he would also go back to the dean triumphant, with a contribution of major proportions. Of course a maid would make things easier. All he had to do was make it comfortable in his conscience.

"Peter, I'll throw in a free survey of what it will cost to do the permanent job on the cathedral, search for any structural damage, look at the masonry, foundation, the whole thing."

"That's very generous," Peter said, thinking Tobin probably also calculated that he'd be rewarded with a much bigger contract for the final repairs—a coup for him. Yet it would be a coup for Peter with the dean and chapter to garner such a windfall.

"I would be a fool to refuse so generous an offer," Peter said. "I accept. You are extremely kind."

"Kind? Peter, I don't know whether that's your minister's politeness talking or what, but surely to God you understand things better than that! I'm not being kind! I love that girl, and I want to protect her. You're her husband. You're a fine fellow, but you've got yourself into a profession where you'll never have a red cent. Smart clergymen marry rich wives. You were smart. You picked Margery, and she fell in love with you. We're not rich, but we can certainly make life easier for you if you get over being pigheaded, thinking that it's demeaning to take help from us."

"Right," Peter said. "I think I've always been a bit ashamed because my mother had almost no help. I thought that's what clergymen's wives did."

"Your mother is a wonderful woman. One in a thousand; tough as nails and ladylike at the same time. She was bred that way in Scotland. No pampering. Like my mother. Do you think she had maids and stuff in Roome Street? Don't be balmy. And my mother had nine kids running around under her feet. But that doesn't mean I can do that to Cynthia. Goddammit, Peter, sometimes I wonder whether you're as smart as you think you are."

Peter reddened. He got up. "I am really grateful, Mr. Tobin. It is extremely generous of you."

"When are you going to stop calling me Mr. Tobin, for God's sake? Come on, Peter, loosen up! Life's for enjoying. Have a whiskey!"

Peter wanted to leave quickly, to get out into the cold night, to cool his embarrassment and think. But he accepted, clinked an expensive crystal tumbler with a smiling George Tobin, and drank the whiskey and soda.

As he opened his front door, he could not wait to get to the diary.

Thursday, May 3, 1917—

I have the sweetest letter from C. I have cried and cried over it because it makes me so happy and so sad at the same time. It begins "My dearest," which he never says! It's funny that two words can make my heart swell so. He says it is spring in France and things are going better. The victory at Vimy Ridge seems to have turned the tide. The spring flowers and birds singing there make him think of spring in Halifax and me. "If I were there on your birthday, I would get you some mayflowers. To see your lovely face as you smell their rich perfume would make me the happiest man alive. Pretend I am there with you. Take this (a $1.00 bill enclosed) down to the market and ask the Indian women for their nicest bunch of mayflowers." For C that is poetic. The idea fills me with tenderness and longing for him. I read the words "your lovely face" about ten times, then went to my dressing table and looked in the mirror. Not so lovely, in my opinion: always a little too angular in the cheeks and jawline. No Bellini Madonna!

Monday, May 21, 1917—

My twenty-sixth birthday! A lovely day, the air warm and delicious, the huge lilac in our garden bursting with blooms, almost falling over the fence into the street, and the shadowy strip beside the stables thick with lily of the valley.

I kept my "date" with C, put on the blue lawn dress he likes and a wide straw hat, and walked to the market. I could have bought ten bunches of mayflowers with his dollar, but the little blossoms are so delicate they should be in small bunches. I settled for two.

Wanting a place to be alone, I went into St. Paul's and sat in one of the old pews. Only then did I lift the little bouquets to my nose. The smell was so innocently sweet and my feeling for him so strong that I cried with happiness. I knelt on the prayer bench and asked God to be kind to him, and to bring him back to me. Walking up Spring Garden Road, I wondered about my

wanting to say a prayer and decided I had done it to please C.
He believes and I don't, but sometimes I feel the need to
pretend, to speak to C's God. I couldn't really explain that to
anyone.

Then more mayflowers! L brought me some. So I had to
show her C's letter, which I'd meant to keep strictly for myself,
and we had a sisterly weep over it. Mr. R let L use his car to
drive her mother and me out to Herring Cove. We had an
elegant birthday picnic on the rocks, with the surf breaking and
the sun shining very hot. Mrs. R had a parasol and looked quite
Edwardian, sitting erect under it in the shade of one of the huge
granite boulders. She has such poise that she always looks as
though she belongs just where she happens to be. I was too
warm and took off my stockings to paddle in sun-warmed tidal
pools. L said this is where C always dared her to go swimming
in the ocean on the twenty-fourth, the queen's birthday.

Bunching my skirts up, I sat on the granite with my feet in
the sea. After a few seconds, the water was numbingly cold, but
I left them in to see how long I could stand it. There was
something exciting about testing myself, as though it gave me
physical contact with C. The numbness crept up to my thighs
before I finally got up.

When I got home and undressed, I sat on the bed and lifted a
knee up to lick the salt left by the ocean. It made me think of
C and Bermuda and made me want him very badly.

The description stirred Peter's feelings. The image of her bare
legs in the sea, of her licking the salt from her knee, sent a small
sexual current running through him. He assumed that her legs
were shapely and thin.

Wednesday, June 20, 1917—
We have come back to the cottage, and it feels like coming
home, yet my mood is quite different this year. I no longer feel
the frantic need to know more about C. I suppose I have grown
more fatalistic about him. I am not going to solve his
mysteriousness by snooping around his childhood books.

Thursday, June 21, 1917—
The longest day of the year. Last night L and I sat on the
verandah after the girls went to bed, watching the afterglow

over the sea and behind the islands. I had my feet up in the big
rocking chair, cradling my knees with my arms for warmth. The
night was growing chilly. Our talks are always a little guarded, as
if we are afraid to get too intimate about C. She surprised me
by suddenly asking whether we wanted a large family. I said I
wasn't sure I wanted children, that it would just be nice to have
some time to ourselves when the war is over to get to know
each other. She said I probably wouldn't have much choice,
because "men make demands," and a really bad feeling came
over me at her assumption that sex is an imposition on women.
I felt a pang of exclusion, the moment of terror I have often
that what I feel is not right. I couldn't speak for a moment but
couldn't stand the silence, and said women make demands too.

L said "sshh." I couldn't see her face in the dark, but I
knew she was glancing at the girls' window upstairs. L moved
her chair closer and whispered that women do it mainly to
please their husbands and constantly worry about having
babies.

I thought about it afterward in bed. The fog had crept in and
the foghorn moaned from the point. Will that happen to me?
That I'll have children and then dread having more so much
that I'll fear making love with C? If that's the real meaning of all
the pretense that women don't like it, I won't let it happen to
me! When they talked about birth control in Paris—and the
students talked about everything—I just nodded, as though I
knew. But I'm determined to find out.

The mention of birth control produced a swirl of thoughts in
Peter. Stewart MacPherson had suggested it when the arrival of
two children had made Margery unhappy. Peter had said, "Absolutely not!" It was against God's will. He shuddered to remember
Margery's terrible voice when he thought she was asleep: *If you've
started another child, I'll kill myself.* Peter did not want to hear it. To
block it out, he went back to the diary.

This afternoon I sat on the beach watching the girls play. I
had brought a big parasol and was trying to start *Anna Karenina*
(which I finally secured!), but the sun was too bright and the
wind kept whipping the pages back. I watched Elizabeth and
Sarah as they ran shrieking in and out of the waves. There was

another family from a nearby cottage and their boy, about Lizzy's age. I watched them as though composing a painting, noticing how differently they behave already. The little girls were being giggly and throwing their arms and legs into all sorts of flighty gestures, their yelps and squeals at the bigger waves going right to their fingertips. When Lizzy talked to the boy, she was in constant motion, one hand on her hip, her back arched, the other hand gesturing from the elbow or wrist, her eyes constantly shifting to see who was watching her. Everything she said, every laugh, was matched by a gesture—bending her knees, arching her neck to let wet hair fall back. The boy stood still, pointing a few times down the beach. Interesting to see the girls showing all that extra feminine movement so early. Do they copy it from us, or do they do it instinctively? That's what I would paint: the boy quite still, the girl gesturing self-consciously.

There is a sense of incompleteness in being a woman that makes us need something added to make us whole. Is a woman made by nature to feel that? I envy men their air of seeming more complete in themselves.

Friday, June 22, 1917—
Raining. We all put on stiff fishermen's oilskins and rubber boots and sloshed down the road to the fishing village to visit Mollie, who is staying with Alice. The house sits up the hill a few yards from their dock and the fish house that stands on long seaweedy legs at low tide. The little house is white with a big peak in the front and two bay windows looking down the cove, with nasturtiums planted outside. We had a lovely cheery time in the steamy kitchen for tea with hot scones Alice had just baked and jam made from wild strawberries.

I like the two sisters, Mollie and Alice, red and freckled, and Alice's daughter, Mary, a young version of the same. She has a little boy but no husband. When I asked Mollie, she said, "some man came in a fog and left in the morning."

They are very poor, with little money for "store-boughten" things. The women don't wear stockings unless they are really dressing up—just put their bare feet in their shoes or boots. But they have vegetables and fruit trees. They shoot duck and deer; they have their own ham and preserves in the winter and plenty of lobster and fish. It must be healthy. Mary's little boy looks so much sturdier than Mollie's white-faced granddaughter and the new baby in town, where there is so much tuberculosis and diphtheria and other diseases.

Saturday, June 23, 1917—

Sunny. Afternoon of washing my hair, drying it in the sun, doing my nails, after picking wild strawberries with Mollie this morning. Crouched down in the field among the granite boulders, feeling pleasantly perspiry in the sun, strawberries so ripe that they squished if picked too firmly; the warm air filled with their scent, and my lips and fingers stained with them. While I squatted until my knees ached, Mollie plumped her bottom down in the grass with her legs stuck straight out and picked all the berries within reach. I got her to talk about C when he was a boy down here and she made me feel better about him. She said there's nothing wrong with him "just because he's no chatterbox." And she added, "You've got sparkle enough for the both of yous, the way I see it."

I didn't want to tell her my dream. I miss him and turn to see him behind me on the path near the beach. He steps around a bend out of sight. I run frantically after him, but when I get there, he has vanished. I keep running down the path till I come to the sea and he is nowhere in sight. I shiver just remembering it.

Monday, June 25, 1917—

I had a moment of panic while trying to go to sleep last night because I simply could not remember what C's face looked like. I had to strike a match to light the kerosene lamp and get the picture I have of him from the dresser. I brought the silver frame back into bed and pulled the covers up against the chilly night and stared at his face to burn it into my brain. When I was sure, I blew out the lamp and the face stayed with me, so I felt better.

Sunday, August 26, 1917—

A glorious summer Sunday afternoon. We had tea at the Saraguay after swimming. One of those late August days when the sky and sea are sparkling and the afternoon shadows are already longer. There were small sailboats and rowing boats and canoes, the men looking a little stiff in their straw hats and bow ties, paddling by, their girls reclining on cushions, but needing such a different palette from the French boating scenes.

The Rs had invited some officers from a British warship for the day. They were very sweet: funny and terribly polite. Very willing to be helpful with rugs or baskets, putting a cushion behind Mrs. R, all that "fussy stuff" C hates and she expects. It is hard to tell with Englishmen. Their manners are so polished, their voices so soft, they seem feline, almost feminine. It was apparent that one of them, Lieutenant B, was not in any way feminine. His bathing costume fitted him very snugly when it was wet. I noticed it on the dock when we swam and we were sitting with our legs in the water. The bulge in his wet suit seemed obvious to me. I tried not to look at it and concentrated on his face. Quite different type from C; very black hair, which he slicked back smooth on his skull when he came out of the water.

I found my eyes again glancing down at his lap and imagined that it was becoming larger. His eyes were smiling at me in a knowing way. I suddenly had a very strong desire to kiss him and to touch the lump in his swimming costume. I can't imagine what he read in my face, but I panicked, pushing myself off the dock and plunging down into the very cold water. I could see the bright sun shining down through the bubbles. I swam out a few strokes and turned to look back. He was still sitting there, smiling at me, showing nice even teeth. He probably doesn't swim well. He got a ducking but never left the dock. When I swam back, I had an urge to grab his feet under water and pull him in, as we used to do as children at the lake. Decorum prevailed. I climbed out and ran up to change. When we were having tea on the lawn, he kept giving me meaningful long looks. Fortunately, he was facing into the sun and had to squint and couldn't really see me properly. He looked very trim in his blazer and flannels. He used a striped tie for a belt.

It's the first time I have ever felt the slightest urge toward another man since I fell in love with C, and that is years and years. And it disturbed me. I must find ways of keeping busier and putting my mind to better things.

Monday, August 27, 1917—

I am worried about yesterday and an idea that frightens me because it slipped so innocently into my mind. It just suddenly came to me: if C were killed, I would find another man. He has gone so far away, and for so long, that another man could replace him—not replace him but arouse *those* feelings. I loathe myself that I could think such a thing. I am truly ashamed. Longing and loneliness must make the mind sick to let such thoughts in.

In a few seconds of daydreaming, an entire life goes by. A phone rings, a telegraph boy comes to the door. C is dead. We regret to inform you. Or his name is in the *Herald*. In seconds— faster than seconds—I have been stricken with grief, wept with his mother, worn black at the funeral, watched his coffin, wept alone, dried my tears, and *married another man!* Before I wake up and realize what I have been doing, I have discarded C, all because some smirky Englishman in a tight swimming costume began to give me that particular feeling.

It's good that his ship is sailing sometime this week.

Saturday, September 1, 1917—

Our third wedding anniversary. I did not hear from C specially, although I had a letter last week. Mother is again urging me to come to Montreal. She must detect a mopy tone in my letters. I want to go and I don't. I have a shadowy worry that I will miss something if I leave. I think I really dread having to talk with Mother for several weeks. She'll start picking in the way that gets under my skin. She always finds the loose thread and pulls it and pulls it until she has me furious and out of control. No matter how I tell myself in advance not to let her bother me, she does. She'll pick up some hint that I am uneasy about C—not just worried about the war—but worried about who he will be after the war. She'll pick at it until it will seem far worse than it is, which will exasperate me so that I'll blurt out more than I mean to. Oh!!!

I'd better wait until I'm calmer. Besides, it'll be very hot still in Montreal, and dusty. Perhaps I should go in October, when the leaves will be glorious in the Laurentians. I don't know. I don't know what I want to do. I feel so irritable!

Sunday, September 9, 1917—

I really am in a stupid state. The British admiral asked the Rs to lunch on board ship yesterday to thank them for entertaining so many officers ashore. He also asked L and me. The moment I heard about it, the idea jumped into my head that Lieutenant B would be there. So I told myself firmly, You'd be a stupid girl to go. And then I asked myself, Whatever are you afraid of? And then I told myself, You go out so little and you couldn't be better chaperoned than by C's mother and father and sister. But there was a strange feeling in the bottom of my stomach, because secretly I was curious to see whether he had the same effect on me as before. I wavered over whether to go or whether not to go, and did not sleep well Friday night because my conscience bothered me. But yesterday morning, I said to myself, You have nothing to be ashamed of. You didn't flirt with him. Just because he flirted with you doesn't mean you have to run away and hide, for heaven's sake! Then, having firmly decided it was too unimportant to fuss over, I found myself dithering over what dress to wear and taking a lot of time with my hair.

I might just as well not have bothered, because we went out to the ship in a motor launch. It rose and fell a huge distance in the waves, so the companionway we had to climb was one instant far above our heads and the next several feet below. Two laughing sailors lifted me bodily and almost threw me to two others, who caught me and set me firmly on the steps. Mrs. R and L came off the same way, and we arrived on deck with our hair blown all whichway and our hats clutched fearfully in our hands. It was three very blown-about ladies who were piped aboard H.M.S. *Knight Templar*.

I glanced down the row of officers waiting to receive us but did not see Lieutenant B and felt easier. An elegant lunch in the wardroom served by stewards in white jackets. I drank some wine, which made my cheeks flush. The other officers were very jolly and the lunch was lively and noisy. The nice old admiral with red cheeks made toasts and said sweet things about the hospitality of Haligonians being a legend in His Majesty's service across the seven seas. And Lt. B never appeared! (Serve you right for making such a big fuss about it!) I relaxed and enjoyed myself. I had forgotten about him when I heard Mrs. R

mention his name with those of several other men who had
been in the Saraguay party, and the admiral told her they were
in another ship. So he has sailed away and I don't have to worry
about him.

Tuesday, September 11, 1917—
Today an invitation came to a ball at Government House on
October 6 and I accepted. I haven't been to anything as elegant
since C went away. Immediately I thought if I'd gone to
Montreal I could have had a new gown. But I really need usable
day dresses more, now that the skirts are getting shorter. Ball
gowns are still floor length, thank goodness, and my silk taffeta
is very fresh.

Monday, September 24, 1917—
Everyone is talking about the Compulsory Military Act. For
the first time the government is forcing men to go to war. Some
people are hysterical, calling men who don't enlist cowards and
weaklings. It just makes me wish I were a man, because I'd go
right away. There was a picture of British girls going to France
and a funny story. The first time the women soldiers saluted
officers in one of the Scottish regiments, the Highlanders lifted
their kilts and curtsied. I'm glad people can still laugh about it.

Sunday, October 7, 1917—
It is six o'clock on Sunday morning and I can't sleep. I
tiptoed downstairs to make a cup of tea without waking Mollie
and brought it back to bed. I must hang up my ball gown. It is
lying on the chair where I flung it last night with everything
else because I wanted to crawl into bed and hide with shame.

I went to the ball full of keyed-up feelings. I knew I looked
nice. The emerald taffeta looked good with my pearls. L looked
gorgeous in her black velvet.

Government House was dazzling with electric lights in the
chandeliers and hundreds of candles. We had just left our wraps
and powdered our noses when I ran smack into Lieutenant B. I
was quite startled and instantly felt a sort of tiny inner leap of
fear or excitement. He was tall and elegant in his mess kit, with
a high color running up his cheeks into his dark hairline. He
recognized me at once and looked at me just as directly and
insinuatingly as on that Sunday at the Saraguay.

He asked me to dance and I hesitated a moment, but L and Mrs. R had gone on into the ballroom and I could hear music. Since we were there to dance, I accepted, with a mixture of excitement and dread.

He was a good dancer, making me feel lighter on my feet and a better dancer than usual. His first name is Neville. His father is an honorable something, the younger brother of an earl. I introduced him to L and her mother, and he danced with them both. The ball was swarming with good-looking officers, old and young, and I was asked constantly to dance. But N kept coming back. I had supper and danced most often with him.

Mr. R had one dance with me and said the red and blue medal ribbon Lieutenant B was wearing was the DSO, which is given for doing something very special and courageous.

I asked Neville about it, and he said the destroyer he was in got shot up, the captain was killed, and he had to run the ship. That's all he would say. I liked the self-depreciating manner, and the wry humor around the edges of everything he said. He's now in *Changuinola,* an old passenger liner made into an armed merchant cruiser. He said they had acres of empty ballrooms and dining saloons dripping with rococo decoration and asked if I would come if he gave a party. I didn't answer.

Toward the end, from the candles and all the bodies, it grew very warm in the ballroom. I was perspiring inside my dress. He held me against him so closely as we waltzed that I could feel his body. When the orchestra stopped, I had an almost uncontrollable urge to put my arms around his neck and kiss him. My legs felt weak, as though my knees would not support me. I asked to sit down and to have something to drink. He took me to a sofa and brought me a glass of punch. When he sat beside me, I had to move my skirt. He looked at me intensely and said I was a very beautiful woman. I was afraid to open my mouth for fear that something stupid or dangerous would leap out. Finally I asked him if he was married, and when he said no, I said I had to remember that I was. Very stupid, because he instantly said, "Are you likely to forget it?" He had the same impertinent look as the day I saw him in his bathing costume, and his presence gave me the same feelings.

I said nothing, but of course I was in danger of forgetting it and he knew that perfectly well, from the way I had danced with him and held him and pressed myself against him when I could have backed away. He knew and it showed in his eyes. And without looking in the mirror in the cloakroom, I knew that my face was glowing and that my eyes glittered. I knew as I said good night and shook his hand how close I had come to disgracing myself.

Mr. R drove us home and L said, with a mocking edge in her voice, "Well, *you* had a good time!"

And Mrs. R said reprovingly, "Now, darling, don't begrudge her because she captured the most attractive young man of the evening." But I sensed a slight edge in her voice too. And when Mr. R walked me to the door, gave me a peck on the cheek, and said, "I'm *glad* you enjoyed yourself, my dear," I felt as though they had all been discussing me.

My cheeks were still flushed when I sat down at my dressing table and looked at myself. The silk of my dress was stained with perspiration under the arms. We read about women like Anna K and their lives seem a million miles from ours. Yet how easy it is to find ourselves standing at the edge of the same precipice.

There were moments last night when I felt as I do in a nightmare: something frightful is chasing me and my legs turn to liquid and I am powerless to run away. Only last night I could not wake up and find it had evaporated. What was pursuing me was flesh and blood, and much of me did not want to escape.

I do not trust myself. I will write to Mother and suggest my coming to Montreal right now.

Monday, October 8, 1917—

I can't stay here. A delivery boy brought a large bunch of roses with a note from N.

> Thank you for a blissful evening. Will you dine aboard next Saturday?
>
> RSVP, H.M.S. *Changuinola,* Dockyard

Wrote him immediately saying I'd be out of town, took a cab to the station to buy a ticket, and telegraphed Mother that I'm arriving on Wednesday. I must get myself under control, and the best way is to go away. Now, to explain to the Rs why I'm leaving so suddenly without making it seem like an emergency.

Wednesday night, October 10, 1917—

I feel relieved, as though I have cleverly escaped. I am on the Ocean Limited, a drawing room because I booked so late and the compartments were taken. The Rs accepted my explanation that Mother had been urging and urging me to go and a sudden impulse made me accept. But I think they suspected. Mr. R is so sweet. He took the trouble to drive me to the station and help with the luggage.

He kissed me and then held me firmly for a moment by the shoulders and said, "A change of a air is a very good thing, now and then. Just remember you are dear to *all* of us."

On the platform outside the window of my drawing room, he tipped his hat to me in the old-fashioned way and walked off. The words *"all* of us" stayed in my ears, and I knew what he meant.

Deep into New Brunswick now, after dinner. I felt a little strange eating in the dining car by myself because there were a lot of men in uniform. But there was no awkwardness. The nice colored sleeping-car porter has made up my bed. I want to get into it and think all this through before I go to sleep. I love sleeping on the train.

Thursday, October 11, 1917—

It is morning and we are rushing through the Quebec countryside, patches of crimson maples and burning gold amid the groves of dark spruce. Just because I am on the train, I ate more breakfast than usual. I like the crisp starched tablecloth and all the little silver pitchers and jugs and sugar bowls tinkling and the waiter in his floor-length apron swaying down the car with his tray over his head. I always feel happy when I am traveling. I love the simple pleasure of going away and being somewhere else.

But I took a long time going to sleep last night, and my eyes feel scratchy this morning.

I lay with the blind open and my lamp out to see the rushing dark trees against the starry sky. I thought of the flowers N had sent me. All flowers are a little erotic to me. Roses are more subtle, but some flowers look naked and obvious, like the inside of an iris.

I could not stop my thoughts going back over the time I

spent with N. Memory played little tricks as I lay in the dark,
with the pleasant movement of the train rocking me a little. If I
said to myself, I'll just go over that from the beginning, my
mind wouldn't let me. It would skip the uninteresting parts and
dash straight to the erotic bits. Even if I tried very hard to come
to them slowly, trying to relive the moments as they happened
—being introduced to him on the Saraguay verandah, chatting
with the others, going to change, coming out and walking down
the lawn—my mind wanted to skip all that and go right to
when we were sitting on the dock and I first got that strong
feeling sitting beside him in his wet swimming costume. Then it
would flit past all the preliminaries in Government House right
to where I was in his arms dancing and pressed up against him
so close that I could feel him. I became terribly aroused, lying
there, and let it build up, sending my thoughts back and trying
again to delay the time when the most exciting moments would
arrive. When they did come, I tried to prolong them, make it
seem a half an hour that I was beside him on the dock, not a
few minutes. Then I imagined him in this bed with me on the
train until the excitement was unbearable and I tried to replace
him with C, but the effort of trying to imagine C at such a
distance made the pleasure recede and I went back to imagining
N. Then it was C and N and J, sometimes one, sometimes
another; then it did not matter, because thinking about it had
raised me to such a pitch that I shook all over and found myself
perspiring and shivering.

Thinking about it this morning, in the trance I fall into when
watching the trees and telegraph poles go by, I reasoned that no
one can punish me for what I think. If I have done nothing
wrong, then I have no reason to feel guilty. Since I quickly took
myself out of a position where I might have done something
wrong, there is nothing to worry about. What a person thinks is
her own business. What she does is a different matter.

A young woman in the dining car a few tables away smoked
a cigarette after breakfast. It looked shocking and common. It
made me imagine all kinds of things about her life that may not
be true. When she looked at me in my conservative outfit, what
did she think? That I am a well-off goody-goody who would
never say boo to a goose? Well, she can have her thoughts and I
can have mine.

Thursday, November 1, 1917—

In the train on my way back to Halifax. Just read what I wrote on the trip up and I can't believe how overwrought I sounded. Didn't write anything at home because I suspected Mother would snoop through my things, as she always did, pretending to look for stockings that needed mending. I found the hiding place at the back of my bedroom cupboard, under the old dresses and shoes, a loose piece of floorboard you can pry up with a nail file. Several notes J wrote to me years ago and some silly things from the girls in Switzerland—not for Mother's eyes—were still there.

I read J's notes with such a strange feeling. The enchanting messages I thought he had written were unromantically blunt: Can you sneak out Thursday afternoon because I have a half holiday? But if what we were saying was childish, what we were doing was not. Seeing his pinched handwriting suddenly gave me an entirely different feeling about it. The idea of undressing and being touched by a boy who still had ink on his fingers now seems a little revolting to me.

The first time was in Grandmother's barn. J found a way to climb up to the highest beam and jump down into the hay. At first it was very scary. Terrifyingly high, almost under the roof, with the trapped summer heat thick around my face, and the spiders' webs on the beams. When I finally forced myself to jump, the falling sensation and the soft bouncy landing in the sweet hay made it the most exciting thing I had ever done. I didn't care that it made my dress fly up and that he was looking. We did it again and again until we were too exhausted to climb and lay panting where we had fallen deep in the hay. He said that if I let him really look at me, I could look at him. I had never seen a boy. We started going to the barn and pretending to jump, but really to undress and touch each other. Perhaps because his parents were dead and he had been in boarding school all those years, J knew a lot more than I did and wanted to do more things.

When he had to go somewhere else for the day, I would sneak back into the barn by myself and imagine him there. I can remember all the tingly feelings and the excitement of being so daring and secret, which may have been the biggest part of the thrill, but it all seems so—I don't know—so grubby to me now.

I wonder whether doing that somehow spoiled me, made me more keyed-up about sex than I should be; that it strained my nerves in some way. That was the feeling I got from finding his schoolboy notes. I tore them in small pieces and flushed them down the toilet.

The notes made me dislike J even more than I did when he passed through on his way overseas. That helped put me back in control of myself. It made me feel a very grown-up woman now, happy to be who I am and married to C. Whatever he may lack in "sparkle" (Mollie's term), he is a fine man. I am going home to act my age and learn to run the house beautifully so that I can be a better wife than he ever imagined. And when I have a safe moment by myself, and a good fire going, I will burn this for safety!

As I guessed, the moment I got off the train Mother was at me. When she kissed me, the smell of her face powder reminded me that I was in Montreal as much as the horses waiting outside and the sounds of French all around us. She clutched my arm with both hands and trotted along, asking, "What is it, dear? What is it?" I had to tell her something to shut her up or I'd have gone mad. So I told her I was just very, very lonely waiting for C, suddenly woke up one morning and couldn't stand it, and had to come to Montreal to get my mind off it all.

She looked at me suspiciously and scratched around for more, like a cat reaching her paw under a chair in case there's a mouse. But I stuck to the same story and she had to accept it.

The best times in my childhood happened when Mother went away on a trip and Daddy and I were alone in the house. He made me feel very grown-up, not noticing if I stayed up late, taking me out to a restaurant sometimes for Sunday lunch. Once he let me help him when he was having a little bridge party. I helped cut the best pieces of celery and arrange the little hors d'oeuvres. His partner was Mother's friend Mrs. W, very thin and elegant, who I always suspected had a crush on Daddy. When I went to sleep I could hear the occasional laughter and the delicious perfume of cigars coming up the stairs. It was very comforting to fall asleep and know there were happy grown-ups downstairs. The atmosphere was different when Mother was home.

Daddy still makes me feel more grown-up than Mother does. He said some comforting, practical things about C and the war. He thinks that the sacrifice our men are making in France will pay huge dividends for Canada after the war. Terrible as the loss of life is, it is not in vain. Canada will be able to hold its head up as a nation, more independent of Britain, a country the world must respect and listen to. The war means that Canada is growing up.

Friday, November 2, 1917—

I am back in my own bed and Mollie has brought me a cup of tea and toast "because it's special coming home." I gave her a pretty sweater from Morgan's, a cardigan in the delphinium blue that matches her eyes. She was very touched and gave me a big hug. I have brought Mrs. R and L really fine little Habitant carvings, and Red River coats with hoods and sashes for the little girls.

Bringing them presents, like coming back to my own house, makes me feel I really belong here and that they are my family. I can't wait for C to come back so that I can fold him back into my life and curl up around him in this bed on the cold nights.

Two letters from him when I got in last night. He sounds cheerful and confident and says he misses me and loves me. Those are big things for me, because he doesn't say them in every letter. The Americans have finally moved into front-line positions, and that has made everyone optimistic.

The next letter was mailed from London, where he was on leave for a week. He met friends and had a splendid time, going to restaurants and the theater. Why does that make me slightly jealous? I should be thrilled that he is out of danger if only for a week. I am thrilled. I just can't help feeling that if he is having a good time, I would like to be having it with him. Pout! Pout!

Wednesday, November 7, 1917—

"Canada's Soldiers Again in Great Victory," says the *Herald*. They have taken Passchendaele—"the most signal triumph in the history of the corps." I get frightened when the *Herald* boasts like that. I never know whether they are exaggerating to keep our spirits up, because they are also straining every nerve these days to force men to enlist. Single men and widowers without children, age twenty to thirty-four, have just three days to report. They have taken us up and down emotionally so many times, and the big victory stories are always followed by longer lists of casualties. Oh, dear!

Thursday, November 15, 1917—
Something has changed in C. A letter today has a very different tone. I thought it must be due to the big battle they have been through—Passchendaele—but his letters always take about a month to get here, and this was written on October 8, weeks before Passchendaele.

Now, after nearly two years, he is doing exactly what I have longed for him to do, to confide in me, and, just as suddenly, he is a real person again! And I love him. I love him. And I want so badly to hold him.

Friday, November 16, 1917—
Woke up early with the awful thought that he feels some premonition and that's what has changed his tone. It was still dark, so I turned on the light and reread his letter from yesterday. I was wrong. He sounds elated. He sounds free. It was chilly and only 5:45. I turned out the lamp and snuggled down in the warmth again to think of him. I am so proud of him. Imagine being man enough to admit that you have been afraid. How stupid to pretend you aren't. Women are like double agents, aren't we? We want our men to be strong and brave and do heroic things, but we also truly want them to be careful, not to be too brave, to protect themselves.

Friday, November 23, 1917—
A whole week. I've been hoping every day for another letter but none came. I hope he doesn't stop writing like that. I have read it so many times, it is almost worn out with unfolding and refolding. When he wrote, they must have been getting ready for Passchendaele, and that didn't end until a week ago. So it may be weeks until I hear again. I can't bear to look at the casualty lists.

Tuesday, November 27, 1917—
A wonderful sharp early freeze-up before any snow has fallen. L and I took Lizzy and Sarah skating across the Arm. We took the tram to the end of the line at Oakland Road and walked down to the ferry. The poor ferryman was huddled by a fire on

the shore. He had to row farther out because the skin of ice
reaches past the normal landing place. That saved us some
walking distance, and he looked so cold, we gave him ten cents
each instead of five—and to make sure he waited for us on the
way back.

Williams Lake was like glass. Perfect black ice without a wind
ripple in it. I glided off right to the other end, which must be a
mile. I had to sit down and rest because my ankles were
burning, but I loved the skate back.

I was so exhilarated that when we got back to the tram stop,
I ran down the car like a child, flipping the cane seat backs the
other way before the driver could do it. I think L and the girls
were a little shocked. As he carried his driving handle to the
other end, the driver said, "Well, young lady, do you want to
drive it too?" I would love to drive one of the trams and bang
my foot on the little pedal that makes the bell ring.

Wednesday, November 28, 1917—

Stiff from the skating, I lay in bed, stretching my leg muscles
and being lazy about getting up. Then I noticed that the
bedroom windows were covered with beautiful frost patterns,
because Mr. O'Brien hasn't finished putting up the storm
windows. Thinking of childhood and Jack Frost's painting, I put
on my wrapper for a closer look at the fantastic shapes, like a
Gaugin jungle frozen white. I put one finger against the pane as
we used to do to melt a little peephole. With my fingernail I
wrote a name. And then I erased it with a kiss that melted the
ice.

Thursday, December 6, 1917—

Woke up early with another of those waves of physical
longing for C. So strong I shuddered. Soon it will be two years
—on the fifteenth it will be two years—since he left for France.
Two years without touching him or having him touch me.

I needed fresh air, so I bundled up and walked briskly up
North Park and Sackville to the Citadel and up the road to the
fort. I was out of breath and had to undo my scarf because I was
too warm. It is such a beautiful mild day.

Peter realized he had come to the day of the explosion. She had
been out just before the ships collided. He read on, tantalized.

The view from the top was glorious, the sun just coming up over Eastern Passage and a thin film of mist covering the harbor. Found myself wondering whether one of the ships anchored in the mist was Lieutenant B's. Bad sign. I was sure I had put him out of my thoughts.

Came home and suprised Mollie by banging the front door knocker because I had locked myself out. I have got out all the paintings from Paris and stood them around the room. I'm going to have a cup of coffee and

The broken-off sentence startled Peter out of the trance the diary induced. It was like waking up. Her spell was so powerful, it made him forget everything else. And she had left a tumble of disturbing thoughts. The explicit passages had electrified him. He felt swept away by her words. It was past midnight, already Sunday morning, and he had to be up early for communion service at St. Paul's.

STEWART MacPHERSON was not interested in children. His own childhood had been so largely unpleasant—experiences his sessions with Ernest Jones had only partly undemonized—that he had long ago concluded he was created to be an adult, with a long and messy gestation completed, like a marsupial's, outside the womb.

So it was strange to him on Sunday morning to find himself telling Mrs. Bethune about the little girl at the VG. The housekeeper had come back out of concern for the major's leg.

"She's is a very appealing little girl," Stewart told her. "Very beautiful, with black hair, white skin, and incredibly blue eyes."

"Sounds as if she's made quite a conquest of you," Mrs. Bethune said. "But the poor little thing, to have an eye taken out. And her mother dying. Does she have a father still?"

"I don't know. I think I'll go back tomorrow and find out."

"Well, be careful you don't get too involved now."

Mrs. Bethune went on with her work, then came back to Stewart to say, in a softer tone, "You know, there's some dolls your mother had in a trunk upstairs. She thought she was going to have a little girl, poor soul, and she kept them. Nobody's ever going to use them. Why don't you take the little thing a doll?"

"That's a splendid idea, Mrs. B. Can you find them?"

"Oh, yes. I know more about what's in this house than what you do."

She insisted that Major Coleman see the doctors at Camp Hill, and he gave in. Stewart drove him there and went on to the VG with a doll wrapped in Christmas paper and some cookies Mrs. Bethune had produced. But Betty was not in the ward. Another, sicker child had replaced her. He looked at all the bandaged little faces, some sad, some blankly staring. The hospital was frantically busy. Even three days after the explosion the doctors were operating on people who had been forced to wait. The ward nurse in charge was hard to locate and very tired when he did find her. She stood erect before him in her large winged cap and starched apron bib.

"She was transferred last night to the Sacred Heart Convent. Are you a relative?"

"No, I was the one who brought her here on Thursday, with her mother. Betty told me her mother died. Is that true?"

The nurse looked exhausted and impatient but produced the medical record.

Betty O'Shaughnessy, 9, of Roome Street, admitted December 6, 1917, with mother, Winifred O'Shaughnessy, 31, who died of injuries, and infant brother, Thomas, dead on arrival. Fine glass splinter removed from intercranial cavity. Optic nerve damaged and right eye removed. No complications. Patient ambulatory. Discharged December 9, 1917, to temporary orphanage for unclaimed children, Sacred Heart Convent, Spring Garden Road.

At the convent a nun went to inquire while he waited on the heavily waxed front hall floor, looking at a picture of Madeleine Sophie Barat, Mother Barat, who had founded the order in France. The name Madeleine evoked a train of associations, cut off by the return of the nun, who introduced herself as Mother Nesbitt.

They found Betty gravely watching other children with her unbandaged eye. They were of all ages, from infants to children of ten or eleven. When he looked in, they stared with expressionless faces. If these children had seen a fraction of what he had seen after the explosion, they would be deeply traumatized.

Mother Nesbitt said, "If you give her a doll in front of all the others, they'll be very hard to manage. I'll bring her out."

Betty O'Shaughnessy came out, holding the nun's hand; her good eye did not show she recognized him.

"Hello, Betty."

"Hello."

"Is it nice to be out of the hospital?"

"Yes."

"I've brought you a present."

She eyed the Christmas paper. "It's not Christmas yet."

"But this is a special present. You may open it."

"Oh, what a beautiful dollie, Betty!" Mother Nesbitt exclaimed on seeing the porcelain head and fancy clothes. "It's a very good doll, dear. I hope it won't be damaged in the rough and tumble here."

The little girl sat and laid the doll across her knees, smoothing its clothes. She didn't say anything.

"Are you going to say thank you to the gentleman?"

Betty looked up at Stewart then. "Mama said I can have a doll for Christmas if I'm good."

"Well, she was right. You did get a doll."

"Did Mama get it for me?"

"No, this gentleman brought it for you."

"Can I keep her?"

"Yes, she's yours to keep. What are you going to call her?"

"I'm going to call her Dollie."

Still the flat, composed little voice. Mother Nesbitt opened the cookies and offered Betty one; then the nun took the tin into the room with the other children and passed it around.

"Betty, what's your daddy's name?" Stewart asked.

"Tom O'Shaughnessy."

"Do you know where he is?"

"He's at work. He went to work."

"Where does he work?"

"In the dockyard. He works on ships."

"Do you know what kind of work he does?"

"He's a welder."

"Do you know the name of the company he works for?"

"He just works at the dockyard."

Mother Nesbitt returned. Stewart did not know how to say goodbye to the child. Should he kiss her, or would that disturb her? He decided to risk it and found it was a very long way for a man of his size to bend down. He had never kissed a child. Her cheek was softer than anything his lips had ever touched. She appeared not to notice. The nun briskly shooed her off. "Go back and play with the others. Mind you take good care of the dollie."

Stewart drove to the dockyard, thinking of the Madeleine he had known.

At King's College there had been more opportunities for theater. Stewart had gobbled them up, romping through several parts to become the principal male performer.

He was invited to join a group of amateur players in the town of Windsor. They were a very literary group, who mounted plays and held private readings of works unsuitable for public performance. Ibsens's *Ghosts* was in that category, and Stewart had read Oswald.

Then they mounted Stephen Phillips' *Paolo and Francesca,* an earnest verse drama, rapturously received in London seven or eight years before.

Another man, thirtyish, clearly expected the part of Paolo by right of past glories in the company. Yet when he read, a slight lisp made him silly as the tragic lover, and the director chose Stewart. In the way of these things, with a small pool to choose from, the actress cast as Francesca had read his mother in *Ghosts.* Her name was Madeleine Fraser. She was perhaps thirty-five, very dark and striking, but to Stewart, at twenty, decidedly an "older woman." She had lovely hands and wore a ring, but he never saw anyone who resembled a husband.

The names Paolo and Francesca carried heavy connotation, and from the first read-through everyone's attention was fixed on the kiss that seals their love and their doom. There were little jokes about it.

"Stewart, you won't be afraid of the big love scene with Madeleine?"

Madeleine laughed coolly. Clearly the others were titillated by the accident of casting that would force them to play at being lovers.

With the books still in their hands, they came to the scene where Paolo and Francesca, reading together the story of Launcelot and Guinevere, succumb to their own passion and kiss. Stewart and Madeleine simply looked at each other and said "Kiss," and the director quickly said "Curtain," for it was the end of the act.

But with lines learned and the playing more realistic, the moment of actually kissing Madeleine became unavoidable. Stewart determined not to shrink from it at the next rehearsal, and he must have signaled the determination because he left his glasses off.

To this day he remembered Paolo's lines:

> Now they two were alone, yet could not speak;
> But heard the beating of each other's hearts.
> He knew himself a traitor but to stay,
> Yet could not stir: she pale and yet more pale
> Grew till she could no more, but smiled on him.
> Then when he saw that wished smile, he came
> Near to her and still near, and trembled; then
> Her lips all trembling kissed.

And Francesca, in the stage directions "drooping toward him," says, "Ah, Launcelot!" and he kisses her on the lips.

Madeleine drooped, Stewart kissed—a frightened, tight-lipped kiss. But her mouth opened and there was a hot little tongue flicking over his. His genitals tingled. The director said sharply, "And curtain! Very nice. That will ease up a little. A trifle stiff, but you'll feel it more as we get into it." Everybody laughed in a worldly way.

Madeleine looked as though nothing had happened, and Stewart, glancing around, couldn't see a hint that anyone had noticed. Lightning had flickered, but only he had felt it.

Back in his college room, he could think of nothing but the next rehearsal and how to respond to Madeleine's clear invitation. Or was it an invitation? Was that how real actresses behaved to make it convincing? He devised schemes for private rehearsals to deepen their understanding of the characters, but all seemed too transparent. Then Madeleine arranged it. On Sunday she invited the cast to her house for a light supper after a late afternoon rehearsal. She found a moment to say, "Why don't you stay when the others go and we'll talk about the play?"

Stewart stayed, nervous about what the others might think; but, whatever they thought, they left, and he and she were alone on her sofa, with a bottle of Cointreau. He learned that that was all she ever drank. It was spring, and she wore an afternoon dress to her ankles, closely fitted around her bosom and small waist. There was a large vase of freshly cut lilacs; the room was filled with their scent. Madeleine rose to straighten one stem of heavy blossoms, and as she came back toward him, Stewart noticed the outline of her thighs pushing forward against her dress. She sat and crossed her legs. They chatted, making little jokes about this or that player. She poured more Cointreau into the tiny etched glasses and they sipped. She told Stewart how very good he was in the part, "a natural, far better an actor than anyone in town." She had seen a lot of theater, had dabbled a little herself, until her marriage.

Her marriage?

"I was married but I'm not really now." She had a soft way of talking, as though from great distance in time and place.

"What happened?" he asked tragically, imagining a young husband killed in the Boer War or succumbing picturesquely to tuberculosis.

"It's a long story." She sighed and laughed.

His first seduction rolled like a velvet ball down a hill of satin. He did almost nothing. They talked and she got up to draw the curtains. They sipped and talked as though they had been friends for years. It seemed too bright, and she lowered the lamps. They laughed about the kissing scene in the play and discussed from how many removes the story came to them, from the ancient legends, through Dante. She suddenly remembered that she had found the place in Dante and came back to the sofa, sitting a little closer. She read the Italian, inviting him to look over her shoulder as she translated, an exercise apparently quite familiar to her.

"*Quando leggemmo il disiato riso* . . . when we read the desiring smile . . . *esser baciato da contanto amante* . . . being kissed by so much love . . . *questi, che mai da me non fia diviso* . . . this that from me will never be divided (she means Paolo)"

To read with her he had to lean very close to her shoulder.

"*La bocca mi baciò tutto tremante* . . . the mouth that kissed me was all trembling . . . *quel giorno più non vi leggemmo avante* . . . that day we did not read any further."

Madeleine turned, smiling wistfully. Her mouth was. a few inches from his. They kissed. It lasted a long time, and they gradually subsided back onto the sofa.

Trying to reconstruct it afterward, as he did a hundred times, it seemed that almost imperceptibly, with no awkward scrambling or tugging, by stages so gradual he did not notice them passing, garments were moved, undergarments parted, and he was living what so far he had only dreamed. They never removed the rest of their clothing. When they separated, she smoothed her petticoats and skirt down to her ankles, and he noticed with some surprise that she still had on her delicate buttoned boots and he his shoes.

Madeleine smiled at him and smoothed his hair into place. They had another Cointreau and continued to talk.

He felt elated that night as he walked back through the sleeping town, the wide streets dark under their arching elms. Not feeling sleepy, he left the rickety board sidewalk leading to the college and made a detour to the town waterfront. The enormous tide had flowed out of the Avon River into Minas Basin and the Bay of Fundy. The moon shone upon the exposed mud and a schooner, sitting on it beside the dock. All was still. He was, after all, a man. She had wanted him, he had wanted her, and it was as deliciously unburdening as in the dream.

Later, if any guilt attached to what they did, he attached it to Madeleine. It was a sin to make love outside marriage. But since both activities were expected of a young man, the sinfulness must lie with the woman who urged him. When he did, later, let such thoughts sidle in, when he was beginning to find reasons to stop seeing her, another crept in to reinforce it.

What if the man with the lisp had been cast as Paolo? Perhaps the Cointreau and the marked page in Dante had awaited him too. But his heart overflowed with gratitude to this beautiful woman, who, giving herself, had banished doubt and insecurity.

He writhed in the nights when he could not be with her, re-living their encounters in his imagination. Yet, afterward, he was impatient to leave, to be away.

He never saw Madeleine undressed, but as he observed her more closely, he concluded that she was older than he had guessed, perhaps forty or forty-five. They never got into bed together. She never invited him above the ground floor of her house. He came at night, usually fifteen minutes or so after a rehearsal, and entered through the kitchen. If there was a maid, he never saw her. Nor did he learn any more about Madeleine's marriage, or why such an apparently worldly woman was living in Windsor.

"You know Italian so well."

"Yes, is it so strange? I lived in Italy for several years."

"Before you were married?"

"Yes—and no!"

He learned nothing more about her than the smell of her scent, the sound of her voice, the slither and rustle of her garments as she moved, the furniture in her handsome drawing room, and the impenetrable look in her dark eyes. Their relationship remained frozen in one act, repeated each time precisely as before, speed the only variation. Thimbles of Cointreau and smiling conversation made them languorous with anticipation; more conversation and smiles; more Cointreau as they slid down. She appeared to want it just like that, and he made no objection. She did it with an air of pleasant complaisance, bordering on indifference, like a cat permitting herself to be stroked but not arching to reach for the attention. She did not get excited as he did. It did not disturb the rhythm of her breathing as it did his. She did not talk about it afterward.

*Paolo and Francesca* was well received in the little Opera House, and they played once more in Hantsport, a few miles away on Minas Basin. Stewart was relieved when it was over, because he was afraid that their intimacy would show. Perhaps it did to wiser members of the company, but no one mentioned it.

The rest of the world carried on as though such things never happened, as though the original Paolo and Francesca had lived in a different universe bound by different biological rules. In this tidy, churchgoing market town, life still seemed Victorian, although the queen had been dead for eight years. The more self-indulgent morality associated with King Edward had not altered the moral climate in Nova Scotia.

Stewart was told at the dockyard that there would be no one to answer any questions until Monday. The day had cleared a little, and he drove up Citadel Hill to look again over the landscape of destruction.

Whether the relief efforts were well organized or not, although miles of the city had been wiped out, an estimated two thousand people killed, nine thousand wounded, fifteen thousand homeless, and a blizzard on top of it, the city had begun to work again.

Electricity was restored. Bakeries and dairies were functioning. Newspapers were published. The streets were cleared better than before. Trains were moving again through North Street Station. From Citadel Hill he could see the little yellow trams bustling along their routes. Altogether, the small city showed remarkable resilience after a disaster greater than the Chicago fire or the San

Francisco earthquake. Despite the catastrophe, the city's vital war effort never faltered. The convoys that fed the Allied war machine continued to assemble and sail for Europe. Only two vessels had failed to join them: the Belgian relief ship *Imo* lay, a battered hulk, on the Dartmouth shore; the French munitions ship *Mont Blanc* had vanished in a million fragments of hot metal.

AND THERE SHALL BE SIGNS in the sun, and in the moon, and in the stars; and upon the earth distress of nations, with perplexity; the sea and the waves roaring; men's hearts failing them for fear.

Peter listened to the naval chaplain read the gospel as the clergy of All Saints held their first service in St. Paul's. The words of St. Luke were eerily fitting.

The choir and the congregation sang, "Thanks be to thee, O Lord." The chaplain left the lectern, and the communion service continued with the recitation of the creed,

I believe in one God the Father Almighty, Maker of Heaven and Earth, and of all things visible and invisible . . .

Peter faced the altar and mumbled the words with hundreds of others. He wondered how many worshipers, how many of the clergy, gave them any literal meaning. One did not have to believe the words to find comfort in saying them.

The elderly bishop of Nova Scotia now slowly mounted the pulpit, the skin of his face and hands as paper white as the starched ruffs at his wrists and neck.

He said that the hearts of all of those fortunate to be alive went out today to thousands of fellow citizens who had suffered from events unprecedented in their violence and cruelty; cruelties that had struck with particular and unfair severity on many of the poorer members of the community. All felt drawn together into closer communion with the church in times like this as fellow beneficiaries of God's love and grace . . .

Peter's seat permitted him to see almost half of the congregation. His eyes roved over the rows of worshipers. Each time he found a young woman, he paused for a moment and asked himself, Could she be the one? And then moved on.

Would she have come today? Perhaps the whole R family had

come. If he joined the senior clergy by the door, to shake hands after the service, a name might slip.

He had no idea of what she looked like. He looked from woman to woman, thinking each had the potential to be the one. The bishop was expressing the deepest and most heartfelt thanks for all that friends here, across our great Dominion, our generous cousins in the United States were doing.

"And now the United States government has offered the munificent sum of five million dollars. Such generosity leaves us gasping for adjectives . . ."

Even though it was raining, Peter had walked down to St. Paul's, to give himself a chance to study all the houses on South Park and Spring Garden Road. She had given one clue.

"Down South Park and the streets leading off are wooden houses that look quite unassuming, even pokey from the street, like ours, nothing grand." He had walked slowly, peering as he passed many houses that could answer her description.

Having narrowed it down, he could concoct an excuse to go door to door, as clergymen do, inquiring after parishioners, looking for the sick or the lonely or the reluctant, for new worshipers. It was work that fell legitimately to a young curate.

The sermon over, the congregation rustled and coughed and the communion service proceeded. It was lovely, poetic, and musical to Peter, heard even when he wasn't listening, words said and sung so many times that they were like his skin and his hair.

Let your light so shine before men, that they may see your good works, and glorify your Father which is in heaven.

He had told the dean about George Tobin's generosity in a hurried moment during the robing.

"That's marvelous, Peter. We'll talk about it later."

Peter joined in the general confession.

We acknowledge and bewail our manifold sins and wickedness . . .

It was the first time he had taken the sacrament since he confessed the woman in the burning building, and the words, in a great hum by hundreds of people in the old church—

We do earnestly repent and are heartily sorry for these our
misdoings—

did not seem sufficient. This general confession was too easy; the
words beautiful and rhythmic on the tongue but essentially empty.
The individual conscience might intend specifics as the gracious
words slid by, but the confession was not demanding enough. It
did not force a person to leap the barrier of his pride, as the Roman
confession did.

He rose, waited respectfully for the bishop and other senior
clergy to kneel, then himself knelt to receive the bread and wine.
From his earliest understanding, he had wanted to feel the mystical
communion with Christ. As he grew older he had deliberately
suspended his own disbelief in the doctrine of transubstantiation.
He had studied it thoroughly, its historic origins and its later modi-
fications. The idea attracted him, but the observance had always
left him with a sense of something missing, something eluding him.

The congregation began to line up the rail, and Peter took a
salver of wafers.

The Body of our Lord Jesus Christ, which was given for
thee . . .

Young women knelt at the rail and he pressed wafers into their
crossed palms, thinking each time that he might be touching the
hand of the woman. He tried to banish so inappropriate a thought
from his head by concentrating on the words he was saying:

Take and eat this in remembrance that Christ died for
thee . . .

But he was aware that he looked carefully at which hands bore
wedding rings, and stole a glance at each lowered profile. As one
group left the altar rail and another arrived, he waited with the
salver held in dignity before his chest.

THE NOVA SCOTIA HOSPITAL stood on the Dartmouth
shore, a gaunt building overlooking Halifax.

To reach it, Stewart had to take his car across the harbor on the
small ferry. The asylum smelled like all such institutions to Stewart,
sour, suggesting vomit or incontinence mingling with the disinfec-
tant used to clean it up. He also knew that in part the smell was in

his imagination. The institution housed not only the mentally ill of normal or high intelligence, but all the human deformities and monstrosities that survived infancy: idiots and feeble-minded; hydrocephalics whose necks barely supported their watermelon heads, and microcephalics with tiny monkey heads; normally shaped men and women who snarled or barked or cried like gulls; people who continually tore off their clothing, or masturbated openly, or dirtied themselves, or smashed furniture and the walls; who tore at their skin and hair; who huddled, rocking naked in the fetal position; whose eyes saw everything and nothing; all the dreaded genetic errors and syphilitic brains; all the marginally human material society abhorred but the law protected. Conditions in such institutions were improving, the Nova Scotia Hospital was humanely run, but that did not lessen the dread that always accompanied Stewart on such visits.

He found Dr. Hart visiting the seven shell-shocked patients from Camp Hill in a room overlooking wintry trees and snow-covered grounds. There were bars on the newly glazed windows.

"I meant to come sooner, but I got caught up. How did the men take the new trauma?"

Hart was glad to see him. "Immediately after the blast, general terror, trying to hide under the beds, trying to get out, then calmer. I sedated them all a little. Mathers, the red-haired fellow over there, needed more. For two nights he screamed, keeping the others awake."

The patients were eating lunch from trays at their beds. A smell of turnips pervaded the room. A nurse was feeding the man whose hands never stopped shaking.

"Are they bothered by coming here? They look quite settled in."

"No, I was probably wrong about that. They're well away from the unpleasant sights in the other wing. But some of them know what it is. And if we can't cure them, many of them will have to live in places like this."

Stewart said, "No one should have to live here unless he is absolutely incurable—and violent."

Hart said, "Everything has been tried that the Medical Corps and the psychiatric profession are willing to try."

"But the treatment is all designed to get them back into the trenches," Stewart said strongly. "The men obviously know that, and knowing it must deepen the neurosis."

"Making them fit to go back to the front is the only reason the military authorities tolerate any treatment. Most of the senior people agree with that numbskull Bell at Camp Hill. But they don't know what to do with the rejects."

The turnips gave way to the sour hospital smell in the corridor. In the staff dining room they were joined by Dr. Hattie, the superintendent, for a lunch of overcooked liver and mashed turnips.

"How did your permanent patients react to the explosion?" Stewart asked.

Dr. Hattie replied, "People who think of this as Bedlam should have been here Thursday night. No light, except a few hurricane lamps and candles. In the dark, there was every imaginable kind of noise from the wards. Darkness is very frightening when you don't expect it. It terrified them. We had to put restraints on some. And we haven't been to find out which of our patients have lost relatives. That will be the next crisis."

"I suppose it's possible for civilians to be shell-shocked just like soldiers, in equal circumstances," Stewart said. "It occurred to me, looking at all the mangled bodies the last few days, appalling sights, as you know. You physicians are used to cadavers and pieces of bodies, but civilians aren't. The sight suddenly transforms our precious humanity into mere chunks of meat. Soldiers aren't used to it at first. It made me think how reasonable it is for a soldier to be traumatized by it."

"You're right," Hart said. "And he can't help relating it to his own survival. He sees people next to him blown into fragments, men with their heads blown off, limbs torn off, viscera spilling out."

Dr. Hattie smiled. "May I remind you young fellows that men have been seeing that in wars for thousands of years? Think of a battle like Culloden or Waterloo. If there was shell shock or psychogenetic illness in those days, no one ever mentioned it."

"But it was different," Stewart said. "One theory about warfare now—it's been written up; someone noticed it first in the Russo-Japanese War—is that it's much more frightening for the infantryman. He's trapped in the trenches, under artillery bombardment for days on end. It comes from the skies. He can't move, he can't defend himself, and he's lost the one ability that always gave soldiers their collective courage—the ability to take the offensive. It makes him impotent and terrified.''

Hart said, "I've just read a paper by Dr. Russel, the army psychiatrist running the special hospital for nervous cases in Kent. He has a plausible theory, I think. He agrees with Freud that sex is a powerful unconscious drive, but Russel says there must be another equally powerful one, the instinct for self-preservation. Obeying that instinct collides with a soldier's duty to the state: the tension overwhelms him, and he becomes dysfunctional.''

"But why do some break down and others continue to function?" Stewart asked. "Are there different personality types, as some believe? Is there a predictable hysterical type, and a warrior type? I've just been sent a test produced by Woodworth at Columbia. He made a list of questions using symptoms of neurotic behavior.''

Dr. Hattie said, "I've heard about that. They've started giving it to U.S. army recruits."

Stewart asked, "Could you work backward from our shell-shock patients and find which had neurotic symptoms before their army experience? Are we treating a trauma inflicted on the battle-field—"

"A lot of them get shell-shocked without going near the battle-field," Hart broke in, "which was why so many get accused of malingering.''

"Then are we treating a neurotic condition caused by war or a prior condition aggravated by war?"

Dr. Hart said, "Well, at least we now agree we're treating a condition that arises in the mind. We've been battling for years against the idea that all mental illness had a physiological cause. The medical establishment thought shell shock must be physiological damage caused by the concussion from exploding shells, microscopic changes in neural tissue—all those excruciating lumbar punctures they inflicted to demonstrate abnormal albumin and blood in the spinal fluid.''

Dr. Hattie said, "The war may be a very good thing for psychiatry. If shell shock forces us to accept that illness can arise in the mind, it will vindicate Freud and all the others.''

"Have you tried the Freudian techniques yourself, Dr. Hattie?"

"Yes, I've experimented with dream analysis and free association. I got encouraging results in a few cases of hysteria, but I'm too busy to give individual patients the hours that would take."

"I've been trying to persuade Dr. Hart to try psychoanalysis on his shell-shock cases." Stewart smiled at the younger doctor. "But unsuccessfully."

Hart said, "I'm not opposed theoretically. But I have no training in psychoanalysis. Ernest Jones left such a bad odor at the U of T, they wouldn't teach it. So almost no one can use the technique. And the army would never permit us to spend hours and hours a week with each patient. We have thousands of these cases and only a handful of psychiatrists."

"That's my reason," Dr. Hattie said. "Hundreds of patients, too little staff, even if they were trained."

Hart grinned at Stewart. "So why don't you get out of your dry academic psychology? You're far more interested in our business. Come back to psychiatry, and you can try all the psychoanalysis you want."

"But I'd have to stop my Ph. D. and start all over again on a medical degree."

Dr. Hattie said, "I'm not so sure about that. It may be heresy, but I think one might be quite good at psychoanalysis without medical training. It may be more an art than a science."

THE BISHOP, a widower, had Sunday lunch with Dean and Mrs. Creighton. The old man looked smaller and more frail in his gaiters and short cassock. Everyone assumed that he was close to retirement and that the dean, as the next senior churchman, would succeed him.

When the sherry was drunk, the leg of lamb carved, the mint sauce, Brussels sprouts, and roast potatoes passed by the maid in her best apron and cap, the bishop said grace.

Then the dean said, "Young Peter Wentworth has talked his father-in-law into patching up the cathedral windows without charge."

"That's very generous of him. Who is the father-in-law?"

"George Tobin, Tobin's Construction."

"I didn't know he was Wentworth's father-in-law."

"He gave his daughter, Margery, away when you married them about five years ago."

Margaret Creighton said, "A girl with wide dark eyes. She was very pretty then."

"Oh, yes. Oh, yes. Perhaps I did know," said the bishop.

"Tobin says it's about two thousand dollars' worth of work and materials just to cover the windows properly until the replacements can be made. He also agreed to do a free survey of what it will cost to put things right."

"Well, that's very generous, I must say."

"Probably quite good business, too. It'll give him a leg up on the contract when it comes. Do you remember that Tobin was one of the unsuccessful bidders when the cathedral was built? He was passed over at the time. He reminds Peter quite often."

"He's just the sort of man who would bring it up," Margaret said. "Quite a rough fellow, really. He married Cynthia Smiley, who was always a bit pushy herself. I think she set her cap at a rather grand Englishman who was here with the army years ago. Someone with a title. But he upped and left her and she found George Tobin. With his money she now plays the grand lady anyway."

"Now, now, darling," said the dean.

The bishop laughed. "And Peter Wentworth? Still the high flyer?"

"Oh, absolutely. The best young curate I ever had. Works like the devil—well, like a fiend. Very spiritual. A deep, spiritual commitment. You know that varies."

"Well, his father has always been a very deep chap."

"No, Peter is deep in a different way. More passionate about his faith."

"Not too passionate, I trust." The bishop sipped from his water glass. "No evangelical tendencies creeping in? A lot of people today go for all that shouting and breast beating."

"The other way, in fact," the dean said. "If anything, young Peter feels more at home with the Anglo-Catholics. He's very discreet about it. But I see the signs." He leaned over conspiratorially. "Narrow collars!"

"Narrow collars?"

"You look the next time you see him."

The bishop sighed and put down his napkin.

"Everyone always wants something different. That's the trouble with Protestants, always splitting up into smaller bits, quarreling with each other. Like a farmer dividing his land, generation after generation, as they did with the French seigneuries in Quebec. Now everyone has a narrow strip. I envy the Roman Church, I must say. They just plough the same huge fields, generation after generation, and keep their schisms pretty well hidden. I wish we could."

"Is that a new parable?" Margaret laughed. "The wise land-owner hoardeth his land and the foolish landowner divideth his?"

"If you like," the bishop said. "But shouldn't Peter Wentworth get a parish soon to season him a bit?"

"Yes, but I'd hesitate to put that kind of responsibility on him just yet. Things aren't quite right at home."

"There could be a multitude of sins in that phrase," the bishop said.

Margaret Creighton said, "Margery Wentworth's a mess. She's a charming little thing in her way, very pretty, but ever since they've been married, as far as I can see, she just mopes around, looking listless and limp. I think Peter does half the housework. His hands look as red as a washerwoman's. You couldn't put a young woman like that into a parish where she'd have to carry half the rector's job. Believe me, I know how hard it is."

"What is the trouble, do you think?"

"I think he's too soft with her. She was probably spoiled by her family—she grew up just as they were making pots of money—you should see the clothes Cynthia Tobin still puts on that girl's back. I think if Peter were firmer with her, she'd snap out of it."

"Sometimes, you know, people just don't snap out of it if they're of a melancholy disposition."

"She was a gay enough young thing, at parties and balls before they were married. I don't think she has anything as romantic as melancholia. I think she needs her mother—or someone—to be firm with her."

"Have you suggested that to him?"

"Oh, heavens, no! I tried at the beginning to give her a few tips about the duties of a clergyman's wife, but she's got her own mother around the corner and Dorothy Wentworth down the road. I wouldn't dream of interfering."

"So this girl is really going to hold him back?" the bishop asked. "Not the first brilliant church career I've seen blighted that way. I wouldn't be bishop if Louise hadn't been as good at the job as I was—better, in fact. God bless her."

Mrs. Creighton put her hand on his translucent white fingers. "We miss her, too. But you're right. Margery is a serious drawback for Peter."

"Well, apart from her personality, her money might be a spur," the bishop said. "I've seen young men driven even harder to get ahead because they married wives who came from more money."

"There's no question that Peter is ambitious," Mrs. Creighton said, in her emphatic way.

"Well, selfishly it suits me very well to keep him here," said the dean, rising from the table. "For the smooth running of the cathedral, I'd rather have him here than off as a rector somewhere else— or overseas, which he's wanted so badly."

"Just a pity to clip the eagle's wings," the bishop said. "We noticed Wentworth right away at King's and on the prayer book revision committee. A bright young man. What a pity about the wife."

"Come and have a glass of port in the drawing room. We've got the fire in there."

TOM O'SHAUGHNESSY was missing. On Monday morning, the foreman told Stewart that Tom had been on the dock, waiting for a tender to take him out to work on a ship at anchor. The explosion had almost emptied this part of the harbor. Divers at the bottom twenty feet under water were suddenly standing in dry air. All the water that had submerged them had vanished into the tidal wave that engulfed the shore. Hundreds of people on the docks and in the waterside streets were drowned or washed away.

The men weren't working. They were all talking about the disaster, missing friends, miraculous escapes. No one had heard from Tom O'Shaughnessy.

"He's most likely dead," the foreman said.

"Has anyone gone to the mortuary?" Stewart asked.

"No, we're just getting ourselves to rights here."

"Would you be willing to come with me and look? It's that or taking his nine-year-old daughter to look at all those bodies. I think it's too much for her. She's seen both her mother and baby brother die."

"Tom's wife's dead?"

"Yes, and the baby. Only the little girl survived, and she's lost an eye."

They looked at each other. No one wanted the awful task.

"I'll come," said the foreman. "Tom was a good fellow."

Stewart drove to Chebucto Road School, where the army sentry let them in.

"Why do they have to guard a place like this?" the foreman whispered in the basement, where rows of bodies were neatly arrayed on wooden trestles and covered with sheets.

"Looters," the soldier replied. "People sneaking in and taking rings and stuff off the bodies. Some tried to cut fingers off that had rings on them."

"Jesus!" the foreman said.

Stewart walked with the foreman as an attendant lifted the sheets from the still forms of students and workers caught in a moment of agony or, it more often seemed, indifference to death.

The foreman held his tweed cap to his mouth as if afraid to be sick. It is natural, Stewart thought, to feel awed by the dead, who have passed a dreaded test we still face. Yet it is natural also to feel, however stealthily, relieved; the same silent complacency of the well to the sick, the young to the very old. It is you, not I, but that same relief could be tinged with guilt. He looked around at other people searching for dead loved ones, trying to read from their faces what they were suffering. If soldiers who survived combat had psychic disorders, it was reasonable that civilians surviving a disaster might also. Civilian shell shock.

"That's him. That's Tom," the foreman whispered over one body. The white skin and black curly hair made him recognizable as Betty's father.

"He looks like nothing's happened to him. He's not hurt."

"What color eyes did he have?" Stewart asked.

"I don't know. I never noticed."

"You want to see the eyes?" The mortuary attendant lifted an eyelid on the corpse. The eye was the same dark blue. It was a pity it couldn't be taken out and given to Betty.

The mortuary attendant said, "Will you collect the body for burial?" and Stewart said yes.

"Then we'll embalm him right away. We've set up in there." He indicated a partition at the end of the basement. "We're embalming the children first, but we'll do him today."

Betty was indeed an orphan now. But should she see her father before he was buried? At the convent, Mother Nesbitt wanted to ask her superior, the reverend mother.

That lady had none of the doubts of the professional psychologist. Of course. The child should not grow up with a fantasy that her father was still alive.

"But not at the mortuary. When they have laid him out for the funeral, she should see him to say goodbye and say a prayer for him. One of us will go with her. She'll have the comfort of knowing that he's gone to be with her mother and the baby in heaven."

At this simple statement of faith, Stewart the atheist, who agreed with Freud that religion was an illusion, found his eyes moistening. It was sentimental and comforting. What else could one say to a little girl of nine?

The reverend mother asked, "But what about the mother and the baby? Have they been buried?"

"I don't know. I never thought to ask. I suppose they just— disposed of them."

"Nobody is just disposed of. A funeral home can arrange to have the bodies brought here from the hospital morgue."

"Here?"

"We have a chapel here. We have funerals. Her church, Saint Joseph's, is completely destroyed. But I know the priest, Father Mahon. I'm sure he would come here to conduct the funeral."

"Won't it be a terrible shock for Betty to see her whole family buried all at once?"

"It would be worse in the long run not to know what happened to them. And you can come too, as her friend. It will be very beautiful. And it will make her feel better."

Stewart had another errand. The *Herald's* front page proclaimed that "practically all the Germans in Halifax are to be arrested." The *Herald* was demanding that blame for the explosion be fixed on the Germans. Stewart was appalled at this pandering to hysteria.

It was snowing again and blowing hard. As if the explosion were not terrible enough, followed by a sixteen-inch snowfall, then freezing rain, now it looked as if another blizzard was coming. Incredible.

Arthur Halliwell was at the City Club, where the Relief Committee now had its own offices. Stewart found him in a madness of ringing telephones and people dashing in with papers and questions. He noticed that, despite the chaos, they already had their own letterhead.

"Thanks for helping with those Americans, when was it?—Saturday. Suddenly we couldn't find even one damned motor anywhere. We had to move some of their gear in milk delivery sleighs. But we've got ten motor trucks coming in by sea from Boston, and they should help. You've got to hand to it to the old Yanks. They may drive you up the wall with their self-importance, but they do deliver the goods. Do you know their government has promised us five million dollars? Ottawa has just come up with one million. That says something, doesn't it?"

Stewart said, "I hate to bother you, but can you do anything about this business of rounding up the Germans? It is really absurd. A man I know at Dalhousie, a young philosophy professor, called me. He expects to be hauled off to jail. Is it really necessary to do that?"

"Well, I suppose they can't be sure. But it's all out of my hands. It's the politicians and the military command and the police. Tumbling over themselves to look responsible. Mind you, someone was damned irresponsible, or it wouldn't have happened. What I want to know—and I want them to get an inquiry started—is how they allowed that ship in here, with no warning to anyone. I'd tell your friend just to keep his head low for a bit. They'll be starting the official inquiry. That'll give the newspapers something to write about. Now, I've got to get jumping. Got a relief train coming in from Toronto and one from Rhode Island. And, believe it or not, something called Christian Science Relief. God knows what they do to the victims. Pray over them, I suppose! And we've got to find places to put all these people and their gear. We put the Maine relief unit in the Ladies' College, but we're running out of places with roofs on them."

Stewart helped Halliwell put on his coat.

"Anyhow, I think we're beginning to get a grip. They're still finding bodies up there. But the hospital situation's improving. Saint Mary's College has opened a hospital, the Red Cross has started a dispensary at the Technical College, and we've shipped some more injured out to a hospital in New Glasgow. So it's looking up a bit. They even tell me most of the prostitutes have packed up and gone off to Montreal and Toronto. Business is too hard here. Marvelous, isn't it?"

Halliwell was clearly thriving on the job and had lost the self-congratulatory air he'd worn the first day, although the other Halliwell was not far underneath.

"Oh, I forgot. We got a cable of sympathy from Queen Alexandra. Isn't that nice?"

"Bit late, isn't it?" said Stewart. "Oh, but of course. She's deaf. Probably didn't hear about it for four days."

Halliwell looked genuinely injured. "That's a little rough, old man. I think it's jolly decent of the old lady."

Stewart was beginning to see that Halliwell, like the whole city, was behaving sensibly—after an initial bout of panic.

He drove home reflecting that if Anne-Lise were still in Halifax, the police might be arresting her now.

Anne-Lise had replaced Madeleine. Madeleine and he were apart for the summer, and that fall she was less exciting to him. On his first visit she looked older and less appealing. It was a hot evening, and she wore a dress that left her shoulders naked. While the unaccustomed display of flesh attracted him, he observed when they kissed that there were many small wrinkles in her neck. The artificiality of their lovemaking left him impatient for something freer, more complete. The affectation of the little Cointreau glasses was irritating, and he stopped drinking it. He had exhausted his curiosity about her, and she had none about him.

So he went less often. Once or twice she sent small, exquisitely written notes that carried her scent into his fusty college rooms. A fortnight went by and then desire outgrew his indifference and he went back. She scolded him mildly, the conversation was desultory, the need to pretend a social purpose abandoned. Everything became abbreviated.

There never was an absolute rupture. The winter closed them in, the snows deepened around Windsor so that the distance to her house felt greater, and he stopped going. In early spring, he was invited to read for another town play but refused, pleading studies. He assumed Madeleine would be in it, and he didn't want to go through it again.

The King's College drama group was asked to do a reading—some scenes from Shakespeare—at the local hospital. It was a success, and they were asked to repeat the performance at the Victoria

General in Halifax. The staff was serving tea when a smiling young woman approached him. She had a white smock over a day dress.

"I liked so much what you did." Stewart was wondering about her accent when she added, "In Germany, where I come from, we are, too, great admirers of your Shakespeare. In school I studied his plays, first in German, then in English."

She had a cool, sculpted face, with hollows beneath the cheekbones that made her look hungry, and very candid eyes. She had the look some Germans have of being almost English but different. Her accent falling on Stewart's impressionable ears made her most mundane remarks exotic.

"Are you visiting Halifax?" he asked.

"No, I work here, at this hospital. I am a doctor. My appointment here is for two years!"

If Stewart had been aware that there were such things as women doctors, it had not registered consciously; it took him a little aback, particularly in a woman so young and pretty. Her name was Anna-Lise Graumann. She came from Berlin—the most advanced city in the world in scientific and medical matters, a place of social and artistic ferment and daring. What an aura that instantly gave her for Stewart, who was just beginning to perceive the provincialism of Halifax! And there was an openness about Anne-Lise, a lack of coquetry, as though the chasm between the sexes (and their ages) should simply be dismissed in these modern times. Perhaps he divined that so rational and unaffected a twentieth-century woman would also have progressive ideas about love and sex. Stewart fell in love with Anna-Lise Graumann on the spot.

"Do you have a special friend, a woman friend?" she asked him very directly the next afternoon. They were walking in the Public Gardens.

"Not really," he said, trying to imply both experience and availability.

It was late in April, with a sweet warmth in the air. In the bright sun some of the women carried parasols to protect their complexions. Anna-Lise not only had no parasol but wore no hat, and the filaments of her loosely pinned chestnut hair glowed with the sunlight behind it; she looked as though she had dressed in haste.

"How old are you?" she suddenly asked when they sat on a bench. A band from one of the regiments was playing on the bandstand in the distance.

"Only twenty-one, I'm afraid. Still very young."

"Why be afraid to be young?" she said. "We will all be old soon enough. My mother already thinks I am too old, an old—how do you say it?—my English is so terrible—an old . . ."

"Maid?" he suggested.

"Of course! So! My mother thinks I am already the old maid, too old to get married."

"Well, that's absurd," he said. "You're very young, very pretty."

"I am already thirty-one," she said, with a little smile, mock-forlorn.

"But you're beautiful!"

"Do you think so? Honestly?" She looked at him gravely, and he noticed her eyes were greenish, with thick lashes. The invitation in them made his stomach turn over.

She asked him back to tea. She had a flat in a house on Robie Street over looking Gorsebrook Golf Course and near the hospital.

"This is not my taste," Anne-Lise said, taking off her coat. "Do not think I would have such furniture at home. But it is not so unpleasant. Just old-fashioned. In Berlin everyone is modern." To Stewart's eye the room looked quite agreeable, with soft armchairs, a fireplace, flowers, and pictures.

She made tea and they talked and talked. She was the first person he could talk to about all the novels he had read. She had his enthusiasm for the Russians.

"I have read *Anna Karenina* three times," Anne-Lise said. "You have a lot of time to wait in the hospital life. And I weep every time. It is so sad. It makes such a longing in me. It is like the music of Chopin."

He knew nothing of Chopin or Schubert or any of the composers she mentioned that long afternoon. He knew almost nothing about music.

The spring twilight softly gathered, and it was dark. They had not lighted any lamps. They talked in the dark until he said, "I must be going. I have to get back to college. The train is at nine o'clock."

"You could stay here—with me," said the calm voice out of the dusk. "Are you hungry? I could make us something to eat."

Anne-Lise was hungry, and they ate. Stewart was so nervous that he had no appetite. She moved competently around the little kitchen and talked at the table as though they had been eating together for years. She did not make coy allusions to what might come next. She did not rush the meal. She methodically cleared the table and washed the few dishes. Finally she turned, held out her hand, and when he took it, said, "Come." He had a momentary image of a doctor taking a reluctant patient into her office.

She led him into her bedroom. Immediately but delicately she took off her clothes and helped him undress, again as though it were a wifely duty she had been performing for years. She was thin but beautifully proportioned. He had never before seen a woman naked, or been naked with one. When she leaned against him, her hard breasts burned into his chest.

She was as hungry, as avid, yet as matter-of-fact in bed as over supper. She was all over him and he all over her. She was angular yet soft, demanding but giving, resistant and yielding. When he entered her, she panted and made little cries, and crooned, *"Lieber, Lieber, Lieber."*

He awoke to a brilliant sunny day and the sound of Anna-Lise clattering in the kitchen. The coziness of that sound, the intimations of domesticity, enchanted him. He did not move but waited under the covers, watching the new leaves outside stirring against a perfectly blue sky, wondering with both fear and amusement what his parents would say if they knew where he was.

Anna-Lise came in, wearing a long Victorian nightdress with frills and lace. She put a cup of coffee on the bedside table and leaned over him.

"You promise to come back to me as soon as you can?"

Why remember all this? Because it gave him such pleasure to remember and such sadness now.

At King's, his overnight absence had not been noted in the bustle of preparation for graduation exercises, further complicated when King Edward died suddenly of pneumonia. They lowered the college flags, raised them when George the Fifth was proclaimed, and lowered them again for Edward's funeral. The college canceled all festivities.

Stewart sat in the chapel for an interminable memorial service, at which every bishop, dean, canon, and rector for miles around came to put his fealty on record, extolling "His Most Gracious Majesty, Edward the Peacemaker"; uttering prayers for the repose of the soul "of our great, good, and well-beloved king, whom God took to himself on Friday last," blazing with hypocrisy for the man who had led the moralists of the day a merry dance. Compelled to attend, Stewart absented himself mentally by reliving his night with Anne-Lise, every part of him humming with the memory and already aching to be with her again. The windows of the chapel were open onto the glorious countryside. Bees blundered in and buzzed against the mullioned windows until the perfumes of spring, the scent of nectar, drew them out again, as they drew Stewart.

Peter was on the other side of the chapel, looking rapt, as he always did there, probably swimming in reverence, lost in the mystic bond between subject and monarch.

Some students delighted to repeat the salacious rumors about the portly king, his reputed affairs, his appetites for all the pleasures of the flesh. They teased the devout Anglicans like Peter that such a decadent man was the head of their church. It didn't faze Peter; just gave him another cue for a sermon: "Even if what they say were true, one man's frailty does not corrupt the church. Its authority is too well founded. It has flowed for nineteen hundred years from the founders of the church, through the great saints and martyrs, through the British Reformation and Anglicization, from king to king down to the present day." If you let him, he could go on and on.

With the term over, Stewart was back in Halifax, which had become *her* city. He was terrified to be seen by his parents or others, like Peter's parents, knowing that they would be shocked by this liaison. Carefully choosing his time and reasons, he borrowed his father's car, and he and Anne-Lise had picnics down the coast. The roads were unpaved and almost deserted in those years. They could turn off the Herring Cove Road and follow small farm tracks into fields above the shore. They sat out of the wind behind huge granite boulders in the meadows overlooking the sea.

Anne-Lise was seriously athletic. She plunged enthusiastically into the cold Atlantic in a bathing costume briefer than any he had seen. He worried that someone might see him with a woman so immodestly dressed. But in that summer of 1910 there was never anyone around. They had nature to themselves, and Anne-Lise gloried in it. She said, "It is so difficult in Germany to find a place so alone—to be as alone as this. There is a place I like to go in

Germany, Rügen on the Baltic. I go with a woman friend. You are very alone there. You can do this!"

She took off her bathing costume and stood naked beside him, facing the Atlantic swells, letting the gentle sea breeze dry her. He lay back in the grass watching her, his heart and body filled with both satiety and longing. The slight wind blew her hair back and even stirred her pubic hair. She came astride him and they made love in the sunshine, in the field of wildflowers, Queen Anne's lace level with her head, and the surf booming on the rocks below. She was uninhibited. If it pleased her, she did it, knowingly but innocently. She had brought scones and strawberry jam. She dipped a finger in the jam and smeared some on his lips and then licked it off. She giggled excitedly, put some on her nipples, and he licked it off.

With her trim, athletic figure, she looked different from the stiff, unreal figures Stewart was used to seeing, bent into a shallow S-shape with their bottoms and bosoms squeezed flat in the bent forward-sway back fashionable then. Anne-Lise's freedom privately thrilled him but embarrassed him in public. She was criticized for it at the hospital. She told him, mockingly, how the old matron had said, "Doctor Graumann, would you be kind enough to come to my room for a moment?"

Wickedly, Anne-Lise imitated her haughty manner. "Oh, it is just teatime. Do have a cup of tea. I do hope you will forgive my forwardness, Doctor, but I feel I must speak to you on a delicate personal matter."

Anne-Lise rolled her eyes and exaggerated "delicate personal matter."

"You are the only woman doctor here and perhaps no one else would say it. Perhaps also things are different in Germany. But here it is not considered nice—how can I put it?—for a woman to appear too loose. No, I did not mean loose; I mean to say that to appear in public without your corsets is to appear undressed. It shows too much. Your body moves too much when you walk. It is considered a little indecent for a lady to show herself that way, when there are men around and they cannot help noticing. It might even encourage them, God forbid, and we know they need no more encouragement. I have observed how the younger doctors and the medical students look at you."

Anne-Lise laughingly told Stewart this one day in Point Pleasant

Park, looking out to sea. There were other people walking in their Sunday clothes. All of the women, he now observed, were corseted; only the girls were not. In one part of his Haligonian mind he thought the matron was right. To see a woman's breasts and buttocks in motion as she walked in public, even as youthful and firm as Anne-Lise's, was faintly—what did they think then?—vulgar, in bad taste, suggesting morally a looser woman. Yet like everything else about Anne-Lise, the free spirit thrilled him; that was probably what she intended, because her laughter grew more suggestive and she touched him more.

They got up and hurried into the woods of the park but could find nowhere private. At times like these, they fed each other's wild anticipation so that he reached such a pitch that everything about her—the fit of her sleeve at the wrist, the look of her shoe—inflamed him more until finally they panted up the stairs to her flat and tore at each other's clothing.

On this day, as they came in, Mrs. Gagnon, Anne-Lise's landlady, was standing by the door of her apartment on the ground floor. She was a French Canadian from New Brunswick. Her husband, now dead, had made money renting houses. She was a handsome woman with a stocky figure, her hair only beginning to go gray.

She said, "I got some beer from a friend today. Would you like some?"

She was a lonely-looking figure, and to keep on her good side, because she tolerated his comings and goings, they accepted. They went up to Anne-Lise's flat, so desperate to throw themselves at each other that they could scarcely stay apart. A few minutes later Mrs. Gagnon came up the stairs with an armful of beer bottles. In good humor they sat with her in the living room and drank beer. It was very hot. They perspired and wiped their foreheads with handkerchiefs. Anne-Lise and Stewart exchanged frequent glances as Mrs. Gagnon settled in happily. She told funny stories about her husband in her accented English, putting the stress on the last syllables. They thought she would have two glasses of beer and go. But no, she clearly wanted to make it an evening. They wanted to her to go quickly. Their bodies felt held apart like stretched elastics, straining to snap together.

Anne-Lise said, "Well, I think it is getting so late!" But Mrs.

Gagnon said, "Oh, no. I don't mind. It is very nice to get to know the both of you. I will go down and get some more beer, eh?"

They embraced hungrily, only to hear her panting back up the stairs. Her hair was beginning to come loose with the exertion and the heat. There was nothing to do but join her, and her capacity was greater than theirs. Anne-Lise pulled him into the bedroom and whispered, "She won't go! I can make her to feel sleepy. I have some powders from the hospital." She opened her case and found some sleeping powders. In the kitchen they put the white powder in Mrs. Gagnon's glass and stirred the beer until it dissolved. It made the beer froth up and a few white specks were still faintly visible when he took it to the guest, who was fanning herself in the heat.

They settled down. She said, "This beer is beginning to taste funny." She said, "FunNEE, like bi-TTER, you know?" But she forgot the taste and went on drinking. The sleeping powder showed no effect. Half an hour later Mrs. Gagnon was still drinking and talking freely. In the kitchen, Stewart said to Anne-Lise, "I'll pretend to fall asleep. That'll make her go home."

There was a sofa opposite their easy chairs. A few minutes later he said, "I'm a little sleepy," yawned, and lay down, pretending to go to sleep. That made Mrs. Gagnon talk even more freely.

"He's a nice boy, that one," she said to Anne-Lise. "You going to get married to him, eh?"

Anne-Lise laughed. "But he is so young!"

"Younger is better, you know what I mean?" said Mrs. Gagnon, now slurring a little.

"What do you mean?"

"I mean for this!" Anne-Lise let out a yelp of laughter and Stewart peeked through his eyelashes to see Mrs. Gagnon poking herself between the legs. "For this, a young man is better. But at my age, any man is better than no man."

Then he heard her saying, "What you think? I could pour some beer on him? You know, down there? Wake him up? Then we could have fun with him. You know?"

Anne-Lise said, "No, let him sleep. Poor boy. Let him sleep. He is so tired. And so am I."

Mrs. Gagnon said, "Sometimes I get such a big longing for it. I'll pour some beer on it myself. There you are, pussy! Have a little drink." She was talking in a singsong like a child to a kitten: "Nice pussy! Pussy, have a drink of beer!"

Stewart opened his eyes and was astonished to see her with her legs apart, her skirts up, holding her underwear open and trickling beer between her legs. Anne-Lise was doubled up with giggles.

"Pussy, pussy have some beer," crooned Mrs. Gagnon. It was the first time he had heard that pet name for the female part. Anne-Lise called hers Gretel and his penis Hansel.

Then Mrs. Gagnon began to cry. "You are so nice to me," she cried on Anne-Lise's shoulder. "I have no one to have a party with. But now it is time to go. The boy is fast sleep." She bent over, breathing heavily, and gave him a beery kiss on the lips. He pretended to wake up, and she left.

They went to bed and made love and held each other, saying, over and over, "There you are, pussy. Have a drink of beer."

The matron was not alone in noticing the way the other doctors looked at Anne-Lise. Stewart noticed and, being younger than all of them, tried to stifle his anxiety.

One weekday evening he came unexpectedly to town, full of excitement at surprising her. He had rehearsed, all the way from Windsor in the train, the scene of delight heightened because unexpected. The door of her flat was not locked. He opened it and tiptoed in—and heard her voice saying, *"Lieber, Lieber!"* in that throaty, panting way he knew. The reality hid itself from him for one more moment. He imagined she was saying it to herself, thinking of her times with him. Then Stewart heard a man's voice say "There!" in an exultant tone of finality, relief.

Stewart crept out and away, sick with images of Anne-Lise with another man, doing so exuberantly what she did with him. He took the train back to Windsor, visualizing over and over again the scene he had only heard.

He resolved never to go back but weakened when the weekend came. He went, determined to confront her, be hard, demand explanations, issue an ultimatum. Instead, he said nothing. She said nothing. The moment he saw her, he hungered for her. If anything, he wanted her more fiercely and felt a strange license to be rough with her, which she enjoyed, because normally she was the more aggressive. Afterward, however, the feeling was different; she sensed it and asked him why.

He told her, noticing that, despite his pain, he enjoyed holding the unknown card.

"Oh, but that was just a friend!" she said, with no trace of apology or guilt. "He is a doctor I have seen now and then since I came here. He is very nice. Sometimes he comes to see me. You should meet him. You would like him."

For days afterward her words played like a record under a stuck gramophone needle. He would hear her say, "He is very nice. Sometimes he comes to see me."

Stewart would smell her scent as he heard the words and see, half-formed, the image of a man. It was easy to convince himself that Anne-Lise had other lovers because he wasn't handsome enough, mature enough, proficient enough in bed, witty enough —anything enough.

Again he swore he would not go back but found himself on the way to see her before he was aware that he had made the decision. The moment he was with her, the familiar scent of her eau de cologne, which suffused her clothes and her flat, made his skin crawl with desire. He could not control it.

He tried to be casual. "Have you seen the doctor again?"

"No, he is out of town, I think."

Anne-Lise did not mention him again, and Stewart gradually stopped asking, convincing himself that he had faded away until she said one evening, "I can't see you next Saturday. A friend is taking me to a ball at the hospital."

"A friend? You mean the doctor."

"Which doctor?"

"The doctor who was here."

"Oh, no. This is another man. A very nice man. No, *that* doctor is married. He could not very well take me to the ball."

"Well, who is this other man?"

"He too is a doctor. There are many doctors in the hospital."

"And do you know them all?" Stewart snapped, all the agony returning.

She kissed him. "No, of course I do not know them all."

Stewart could not make love to her that night. The idea that another man had lain there and touched her put the stranger there with them. Something in the feel of her skin and the taste of her mouth suggested his presence. Tiny details that had no importance before began to come forward. The sculpted hollow between her cheekbone and jaw, which he had so admired, now gave her a ravenous, insatiable look. Her sweat, he noticed, was very strong. When she touched him, he was not erect.

"What is the matter? *Was ist loss, Lieber?* Tell Anne-Lise what is wrong."

He had no pride. "If I think of you with other men, it comes between us. I think of them with you and I can't think of us. It is on my mind too much."

"Go to sleep now. You are tired. Go to sleep, *Liebchen.* In the morning, we will make love. Go to sleep. *Schlaff gut, du.*"

She stroked his forehead like a fretful child's, and the hateful images evaporated. She was right. In the morning he wanted her as badly as ever.

He grew to dislike some things about her and even then could not stay away. He noticed that she was not as beautiful as he had thought, merely quite pretty. Her front teeth were a little uneven —a trifle. The skin around her nose, he now noticed, had larger pores than the rest and when she was too hot, perspiration appeared there instantly. It gave him a faint disgust. She sat naked on the bed to clip her toenails. He had found that charmingly uninhibited; he had never seen a woman at her toilet. Now he found it crude. She grew more casual with him, not minding what he saw her do, asking him to wait while she washed her hair in front of him. She was, to his inexperienced and fastidious mind, more matter-of-fact than he found comfortable about her menstrual cycle. Nothing was hidden. Stewart put it down to the clinical atmosphere of the medical life, where he supposed nothing was sacred. In a positive mood, he thought, How worldly and sensible! Yet he was privately shocked and repelled.

She practiced birth control with a diaphragm—all new to him. Afterward he was grateful for all the information, not widely available then, and for the experience, however painfully acquired.

Gradually, the trace of disgust in his feelings for her receded or became a pleasurable ingredient in their lovemaking. He accepted the situation with her and re-established pleasant relations. His desire to be with her was a force greater than his pride or his slight revulsion at some of her indelicate ways. She grew discreet again about other men, and Stewart persuaded himself they did not matter; in fact, he convinced himself that she saw them less often. He and she became friends again. They did not love each other but became even better lovers.

The pragmatism raised his confidence, sexually and emotionally. She demystified the other sex: she showed him what gave her pleasure. If he was slow to take the cues, she was explicitly demonstrative, with all veils of prudery drawn aside, as in an anatomy lesson. The clitoris, such a mystery to a young male, was revealed, explained, demonstrated. She had no guilt about masturbation; indeed, she thought it a perfectly reasonable substitution for a partner, often preferable, and she showed him how she did it.

To use the vocabulary he subsequently learned, she had a strong oral orientation as well as genital. Her residual penis envy took the form of her wanting that member, vaginally and orally. She would gaze at it, caress it, murmur endearments to it. She also wanted oral stimulation herself and talked matter-of-factly about a homosexual episode with the woman friend at the resort on the Baltic. She made it sound not only innocent but intriguing.

At times this education moved a little rapidly for Stewart and her aggressiveness made him uneasy. He wondered whether she was quite sane: he did not know the word *neurotic* until later. Apart from Madeleine, he had no experiential context for Anne-Lise. Where Madeleine had been so casual about their couplings as to seem almost indifferent, Anne-Lise was avid, at times voracious, driven, fierce. Then the act became sinewy and fibrous and muscular, her consciousness descending to a lower level. When Stewart's own desire was on the ebb, he disliked hers as too desperate, too primitive; when his own urges flooded back, his finickiness vanished, and her slavish quest for pleasure excited him and drove him further.

She showed total concentration on whatever physical act they were performing, as though she were driven to it, an ecstasy of duty, the willing slave to desire, pursuing it down the darkest labyrinth of her nature. Stewart worried that he was locked physically with a woman slightly demented by lust, well outside the ordinary. He had no vocabulary to verbalize what he meant. Her appetites and her efficiency in satisfying them gave him tinges of uneasiness. He thought Anne-Lise lost her personality in sex.

But these were fleeting doubts, and when sex was exhausted, Anne-Lise was wonderful company in other ways. She was funny. Her impersonations of the matron, later of Mrs. Gagnon, were hilarious. Her intolerance of Halifax's provincialism found a greedy listener in Stewart.

"How can you have a city this size, this old, the head city of Nova Scotia, with no opera house, no concert hall, no music, no museum, no gallery. What about bookstores? Almost nothing. Restaurants, cafés, terraces? Nothing. In Germany even very small cities have such things. Your architecture is primitive and ugly. Here is nothing beautiful to look at except the nature. That is beautiful."

Stewart lapped it up, his soul aching to be away. She embodied all the European sophistication he began to crave. And she introduced him to Freud.

Until his third year at King's, he had been loitering through his education without any serious intent. In his third year, King's established a chair in philosophy and he took that course, which included an introduction to psychology. It was no more than a gesture, with only one general text, but he found it fascinating. He read the text straight through and then had a fortuitous conversation with Anne-Lise.

They were discussing a dream, he couldn't remember now whether hers or his, and she said, "Have you read Freud on the meaning of dreams?"

"Who is Freud?"

"Who is Freud?" It was Anne-Lise at her most explosive. The first time Stewart heard the great name, it was spoken by a pretty woman who was sitting naked in bed, drinking coffee.

"*Gott in Himmel!* Stewart! How can you be educated and not know who is Sigmund Freud?"

Thus he heard about *The Interpretation of Dreams.* Anne-Lise remembered that Freud had recently been lecturing in the United States, and searched the medical library for *The American Journal of Psychology.* There in English were five lectures Freud had delivered at Clark University on "The Origin and Development of Psychoanalysis."

Stewart began reading in the train back to Windsor. He read like a man crawling into an oasis after days in the desert. He read walking from the station up the hill to King's College and he read in his room that night and all the next day. He did not want to go to meals because the noise and conversation would distract him. He ate biscuits and apples. He did not stop until he had finished both the introduction and *The Interpretation of Dreams*. Then he went for a long walk along the Avon River. He felt like a man given his freedom after years of imprisonment. He had been handed the key to the intellectual prison represented by his upbringing and his education, by this small Church of England college in a tiny town in a forgotten outpost of the British Empire. Yet liberation was just one gift: Freud also gave him a sense of coming home spiritually, of immense cultural knowledge synthesized and domesticated; of medicine and science, philosophy and literature, anthropology and religion distilled and put to the service of the human mind and heart.

And Stewart decided that this was his calling: to understand himself and his fellow man through the seductive medium of psychoanalysis; to share in this humanistic discipline which considered nothing sacred except truth.

From *The Journal of Psychology,* he learned that a colleague of Freud's, Ernest Jones, had established a department of psychiatry at the University of Toronto.

Stewart wrote, and Jones replied that psychoanalysis was a discipline for students of medicine. However, if Stewart wished to pursue psychology at Toronto, Jones would be willing to guide him in Freudian theory and methods on the side.

His father was torn. Against his passionate dislike of anything associated with Toronto, the Nova Scotian's bitterness about slights from Upper Canada, he had to set his son's first sign of ambition.

"You won't make any money. Do you know what professors get paid?"

When told of his plans, Peter had said, "Well, I suppose I'll miss you. We've been chums for a long time."

The word *chums* made Stewart writhe. Then, quite unself-consciously, Peter said, "Good luck. I'll pray for you." That sincere but, to Stewart, embarrassing remark brought into focus his instinct that it was good to be leaving.

With a young man's sexual optimism, Stewart parted from Anne-Lise too easily. The torments of withdrawal almost blotted out the exhilaration of being in a bigger city and the joy of studying what fascinated him.

He could find no way to satisfy the sophisticated appetite Anne-Lise had created. The confidence her free-spirited sexuality had given him made it easy enough to approach female students at the university, but the pursuit of intimacies took weeks, and, in the event, the girls were prim or frightened or very conservative. Then Stewart knew what he had lost in Anne-Lise.

Inevitably he imagined how she repaired his absence. They wrote often, and he poured out his frustrations. She was as explicit and uninhibited in her letters as in person, and they only excited him more. And then she was gone.

Her two years at the Victoria General were over. She wrote in November that the children's hospital in Berlin wanted her back before Christmas. There was a convenient sailing from Halifax to Hamburg, and she went.

From Berlin she wrote that she was thrilled to be back in her exciting city, and urged him to come to see it with her. But their correspondence waned. More than a year later—he was already working on his M.A. in Toronto—she wrote a charming letter to say that she had been married to a doctor.

Stewart's life moved on, and various women moved in and out of it. Some relationships were brief, some longer. But with whoever it was, whether he felt strongly about her or casually, Anne-Lise never completely left his thoughts.

Only a week ago, watching Christine Soames put on a stocking, he had remembered Anne-Lise performing the same act and realized that it was six years since she left.

Stewart sat at his desk. The thought of Christine had reminded him: he had to write to the chancellor.


MARGERY WENTWORTH was sitting in the rocking chair in her old room in her parents' house. Her bedroom occupied one of the bay windows on South Park Street at the front of the house, her parents' bedroom the other. She was watching the rain on the windows and hiding from her mother and the children. Abigail and Michael were downstairs, baking cookies.

On her lap she held a stuffed rabbit, hers since she had been Abigail's age. She had caught the children's cold. In her fingers was a handkerchief so sodden that she could not blow into it again, but she had been unable to get up and get another. In the chest of drawers across the room were at least half a dozen handkerchiefs, embroidered and lace-edged. Her mother kept clothes in the room as though Margery still lived there. She could come and stay, needing to bring nothing.

The room had not been changed since she left it to marry Peter. Across the pillows of the double bed were ranged all the stuffed animals she had grown up with. After making the bed meticulously this morning, she had replaced them—her bear, her knitted squirrel, her rag doll, her mouse, her calico cat, her bristly hedgehog—each in its usual place, calling each by its name. Sometimes these friends of her childhood felt more real than her children. She knew the stuffed animals better. They had lived with her longer. She could easily hug the animals and pour her feelings into them as she held them close. They made no demands on her. She did not feel the same desire to hug the children, who always wanted to pour their feelings into her.

When she tried to recapture the idyllic picture she had dreamed for her life with Peter, it was the children who got in the way. They were never in the original picture. When Abigail came ten months after their marriage, then Michael, she felt they had come between her and Peter. The less attention she was able to give them, or the less efficiently she looked after them, the more of his time it took to do so, so in every way they took time from her and Peter, driving them apart, causing her to cry, to feel inadequate, to disappoint him, to look like a mess instead of the poised, elegantly groomed girl she knew had won him.

A pulse of anxiety moved in her when she thought of the children. How long would they be content downstairs? They would come scratching at the door, or her mother would march upstairs, her heels and her mood audible all the way up the central staircase and across the upstairs hall, her dry plaintive voice at the door. "Darling, you must come and see to the children. Cook's got to do dinner and I'm at my wit's end trying to amuse them. Margery!"

Margery hated her mother.

Making the bed and dressing herself was all she had been able to do that day. She had slept for ten hours and still had no energy when she got up. She was exhausted now, just sitting and staring at the rainy winter street.

She had been worrying at one thought, trying to recapture a feeling. Intellectually she could, not emotionally. She knew she had been a happy in this room. A happy little girl, a happy bigger girl, a happy young woman. All the nice things in her life had originated in this room. She had gone from here full of expectation and come back here to cherish the event in her thoughts. She had sat in this chair, waiting for something exciting to happen; in an evening dress, waiting for Peter to pick her up for a dance. It was her thinking and feeling chair. She had been happy, looked forward to things—Christmas, birthday, a party or an outing, being with Peter, being married. She had longed for days to go by, for whole months to disappear until something wonderful, dazzling happened to her—like marrying Peter, so long waited for. Yet trying to remember the feeling was like trying to think of a girl in a book, a story she knew but could not remember exactly. It was like trying to be someone else.

It was incomprehensible to her that she could ever have thought that just to be alive was glorious. Life to her now was like a gloomy, rainy, miserable day to a child of Michael's age, stuck indoors. There was no joy in anything.

A maid wasn't going to help. Her father had announced Peter's agreement with such enthusiasm. "Now things will be better, my girl!"

They wouldn't be better. There were still two little alert, demanding faces looking at her, expecting things, needing their clothes washed and mended and sorted and put away and hung up and taken out and laid out and picked up again . . . and endless meals.

"But Michael doesn't like liver!" Abigail meant that she didn't like liver. Margery had hated liver when she was a child and had never been forced to eat it. Peter had been and thought it was good for children. There was a lot of iron in liver, and iron was good for the blood.

"Margery, if you'd eat a little liver, perhaps you'd have stronger blood. A little iron would give you more energy."

"I detest liver."

Peter knew everything. His mother had brought him up so infuriatingly well that he seemed from the beginning to know more about household management that Margery herself—and was more interested. If Peter made scrambled eggs, they were better than Margery's. She always left something out, or burned them, or forgot to put water in the frying pan immediately, so that it took hours to scrape off the dried-up mess of half-burned eggs. The thought of congealed egg residue made her sick.

The maid wouldn't make a difference. Her father saw the maid as a new dawn, a whole new day, when everything would be cheery and happy. That was the way he woke up each morning. Her mother didn't, but that was another story. And once upon a time Margery herself used to wake up like that. She knew. But she couldn't recover the feeling.

She held the wet ball of a hanky to her dripping nose and began to cry again. Making an enormous effort to overcome her lassitude, she got up and opened the drawer. Her fingers fidgited with the handkerchiefs. Unable to pick up one, she impatiently snatched at the pile and took several. That seemed like another failure. She fell listlessly across the bed, mopping her eyes and pushing her hair away from her nose.

If only Peter had weaknesses too, something to balance all she reproached herself for. But he did not have any. She knew the look on his face when he told her about the maid—not excitedly, like her father. His look meant, Now we've given in to your helplessness. Sometimes she saw the edges of his mouth harden with impatience. And he was right. She was useless to him. She couldn't do anything he needed. She hated ironing the damned surplices! He didn't notice, but sometimes she slipped over to her mother's house and had Ruth iron them. Now, at everything she did, the look in Peter's eyes, even his words of encouragement, meant a reproach.

In the morning when I first know I am awake, even before I open my eyes, I dread it. My heart is heavy with fear of—I don't know what—fear of another long, empty day. I want to go back to sleep and not wake up. I wish now I could go to sleep and never wake up. Then I would not hear the children clattering upstairs, as they will any minute. I would not have to find the energy to be nice to them; to wash my face and powder it, to comb my hair, to smile. If I could stay asleep I would not have to talk to Peter, who will come soon and make me think about going home. I do not want to go there. I don't want to go anywhere. I want to be left alone. I no longer want him to touch me. When he puts his arms around me, I can feel in his way of holding me that he is being patient, that he is being kind; I can feel that he is telling himself he must do it. But I can feel it. Or I feel the other reason for his touching me. Oh, God, if that has happened! I can't go through that again. Not another baby, not through all that again. Michael is still on the potty. All that disgusting mess. Disgusting mess! And feeding them and smelling of milk! Constantly worrying that I won't have enough milk, and their crying, crying, crying until I am frantic! I could not do it again!

It might have been better if Peter had gone overseas. He talked of it casually, but I know how much he wanted to. All the men want to feel manly, to feel like heroes. Everyone we know has someone there. It is very hard for Peter, being a minister. But in a way it would have been easier. I could have stayed here with the children and not felt the constant guilt at not doing things right. Not have to watch him doing the laundry, washing nappies. It is so humiliating. I used to think, No, please God, don't let him go to the war. Please God, do not let him go; I couldn't stand it if anything happened to him. I don't know. I feel so tired.

Margery heard the front door close downstairs. Peter? Her father? She sat up and saw her face in her dressing table mirror. At the same instant an idea entered her head, as though a door in her mind had opened, letting in a bright light. And with it came a great feeling of relief, an immense weight lifted from her. Now she knew what she meant. The certainty calmed her. If she were pregnant again, she knew what she would do. And she knew exactly how to do it.

She sat down at the dressing table and combed her hair. She sprinkled eau de cologne on a handkerchief and freshened her face, then put on some powder. She heard Peter's tread on the stairs. In his step she could hear his reluctance to find her collapsed and weeping, his hope that it would be different.

"Hello, darling. Feeling better?" He kissed her cheek.

"A bit."

"That's good." How little it took to cheer him up. One atom of improvement, and he took it as the world changing.

"My cold's still awful," she said and sniffed.

He sat on the bed. "Well, you chose a good day to stay in and rest. It's miserable out. I got soaked every time I went out."

Margery felt pleased with herself that she had been able to please him. She had found the secret way out. It was so simple. Now she could be nice to him because he was kind to her. Now, if she chose, she could give the man she loved such a great gift, taking all the trouble of herself away from him. How simple it was!

Peter had closed the door to give them some privacy. With a

little shock, she realized she had never been in her childhood room with him like this. Occasionally, he had come into the room, chatting or to collect a child, but he had never closed the door and sat down on her bed. She was very conscious that he was sitting on her bed. Her bed. It was somehow invasive. Her animals were all behind him. He looked tired and strained. Margery was conscious of infinitely tiny changes in his expression. This look meant that his mind was on something quite different from what he was talking about. He was wearing his worn clerical suit. She wondered how many clean collars he had left.

"Your dad's men started work on the cathedral today. It's amazing how quickly something goes when professionals do it. They've got a lot of the windows covered already. The dean is thrilled that it can all happen so quickly without all of us having to go around begging for the funds. The dean says the bishop is very pleased that any further damage will be prevented and we can all get on with the parish business. So many people are still homeless—someone told me fifteen thousand. And thousands more with no way to cook food. More than anyone can cope with all at once. They're setting up a relief committee of all the clergy, different denominations, so I suppose I'll be the one the dean asks to represent us."

She knew Peter would not talk on like this if she had not given him the small sign that she was feeling better. It showed how relieved he was.

"Did you get any names of possible maids?"

"I didn't feel up to it."

"Margery, you should get moving on it. The sooner you have something, the sooner things will get easier for you around the house."

"Yes." Margery sighed. All the dread, the grimness stretching endlessly ahead, came back to her.

"Do you feel like coming home now?"

"What, now? It's already nighttime!"

"What difference does that make?"

He got up and stood behind her at the dressing table, lifting his hands to stroke her shoulders and arms.

"Don't you want to come back to our own place?"

She recognized the change in his voice, and his touch became more sensual as his hands came near her breasts. She panicked and shook herself out of his hands to stand up.

"I think Mother will be expecting us to come down."

A surge of anger went through Peter, but he subdued it and followed her downstairs.

The maid had bathed the children, and they came down to say good night. Peter went back upstairs with them to hear their prayers. When she jumped into bed, Abigail put her arms tight around his neck and said, "Are you going to stay here with Mummy and us?"

"No, I have to go and keep an eye on our house."

"When are *we* going back to our house?" Michael asked.

"I don't want to go back to our smelly old house," said Abigail. "I like this beautiful, beautiful house because we make cookies . . . and the bathroom is nice and warm—"

"—and Grampa gives us horsey rides," said Michael.

Abigail switched to a serious voice. "Daddy, is the explosion going to be over soon?"

"Well, it is over," said Peter. "It was just a big bang last Thursday. It broke a lot of windows and hurt a lot of people. But it happened and then it was over."

"Are people going to die from it?"

"Yes. It is sad to say that a lot of people died."

"Were they good and will they go to heaven?"

"I'm sure many of them will go to heaven. The children will."

"Did even children die from the explosion?"

"I'm afraid some did."

Abigail frowned, but suddenly a mischievous look took over. "Do you know where Michael was when the explosion came to our house?"

"Where?"

"Don't tell!" Michael said sternly. "Don't tell! Don't tell!"

With a wicked smile, she whispered through her curled hand, "He was on the potty. He was on the potty!" She began to sing, "He was on the potty. He was on the potty."

"Stop it! Stop it! Stop it!" Michael shouted with rising volume.

"Abby, don't excite him just before bedtime. Now settle down, both of you. Pull the covers up. After your prayers it's supposed to be a quiet time."

Peter tucked each of them in, kissed them, and turned off the lamp.

"Night, night."

"Good night,"

"Good night, Daddy."

Abigail pulled him down and whispered, her mouth hot against his ear, "I like it here because Mummy doesn't cry—so much."

It filled him with sadness, and he swallowed. "I know."

As he was closing the door, Abigail sang out gaily, "He really was on the potty, doing his job, and the explosion made him fall off. Ha, ha!"

Peter closed the door and went downstairs.

The woman in the diary would adore Abigail for her little spurts of daring. Only around Margery was Abigail subdued, as anxious-looking as Margery herself. Peter stopped himself on the first landing. He had to get himself under control.


COLEMAN WAS JUDGED well enough to be discharged officially from Camp Hill. The authorities were eager to clear Halifax of unneeded people. He could start immediately on his three-day train journey to Alberta. There was a train with officers' accommodations late that evening.

"How does your leg feel?"

With a groan not quite stifled, the major had gratefully put it up on one of the leather sofas.

"Not too bad. Still a bit swollen up and hot but better than yesterday."

"You know, you don't have to clear out. You're quite welcome to stay, now that we've got some heat again. And I think Mrs. Bethune wants to mother you. She was shocked by the sight of your leg."

"Shouldn't have let her see it. No, I'd rather get back. You know, I haven't seen my intended for two years."

"Well, let's have a drink and a good supper. Mrs. B has brought us something that smells wonderful, and I've got some wine my father was kind enough not to take with him."

"Very considerate of him, I'm sure," said the major.

Over the wine and Mrs. Bethune's lamb stew, Stewart asked, "Are you going to get married right away, as soon as you get back?"

"That's what I've been counting on all this time. I'll have to see, get the lay of the land, as you might say."

Stewart felt the pause indicated something else. The creases in the major's worried forehead ran up into his thinning hair.

"You feel a bit shy going back to her with your leg in that shape?"

"Well, in a manner of speaking. She knew me as an active fellow, fit and able. She knows I got banged up a bit, but hearing about it isn't the same as seeing it."

Coleman sounded like a man asking himself questions.

"It worries you, does it?"

"Oh, I'm not worried about her running off with another chap, if that's what you mean. It's just—well, people at home have no idea what it's like. She hasn't seen anything. Could turn her stomach, looking at that." For comfort he had extended his leg to the side.

"How old is your fiancée?"

"A bit younger than I, thirty-three."

"Well, she's not a child."

"No, and she's a hardheaded girl. She was determined to join up when I did and go to France as a nursing sister. I'm bloody glad she didn't. The school begged her to stay, and so did I."

"She doesn't sound like the kind of woman who'll be squeamish about a healing leg."

"No. I just have to remind myself that it is healing."

"If you wanted to give it a little longer, you'd be welcome to stay."

"No. That's good of you, but I'd better get there and face the music."

After dinner, Stewart drove Coleman to Camp Hill to pick up his kit and then to the station. As they were leaving the house, he noticed the canes in the umbrella stand. He pulled out one with a handsome, silver-tipped handle and offered it to his guest.

"No one has used this since my grandfather died. I should have thought of it before. See how it feels."

"Oh, I couldn't accept anything as good as this."

"Don't be silly. Try it out."

The major walked with the cane a few steps.

"I have to admit, it's quite a help."

"It's looks just the thing with your uniform."

He watched the major walk down the train platform. The cane restored his dignity, minimizing the painful, dragging limp. But it did something else. Holding it, Coleman no longer looked as though the regimental sergeant major in him were waiting to slam to attention. With the cane, he had relaxed.

Peter left the Tobins' after dinner. At Inglis Street a tram car was making the sharp corner, its wheel flanges shrieking on the steel track. The sound frightened two large dray horses hauling a flat sloven laden with crates for the docks. They broke into a gallop, thundering past Peter, the steel-rimmed wheels showering sparks as they ground against the granite curb. They could easily have mounted the curb, their great hooves or the wheels crushing him instantly. It might have been Margery and the children walking there, killed just a few steps from her parents' house. All dead. If they were dead he would be free of all these concerns, free to do with his life what he wanted.

He caught himself, ashamed of the thought. He walked on. The shame brought back the terrible dream he had dreamed when Abigail was not yet two and Margery, just delivered of Michael, was so emotionally spent that she could not feed him. The baby cried constantly, and she remained a collapsed, sobbing heap. Peter had to be away for weeks at a time at the prayer book revision conferences; the work was intellectually demanding. It was an extraordinarily privileged position, and he had to do well to justify the committee's trust for future preferment.

Home was a nightmare of unwashed dishes, squalling babies, the house smelling of their diapers; Margery distraught, drained, harried, a child held awkwardly on one hip, stirring something, her hair undone, her eyes swollen from weeping.

On one of those nights Peter dreamed that he was holding Abigail in his arms at a beach. He walked slowly into the sea, which gradually deepened, like John the Baptist with an early Christian child. Eventually the water covered Abigail, and Peter held her under until she stopped moving. She did not struggle. In the dream, it seemed the decent, humane solution, as simple as a parable in the Bible. But the instant he realized the little girl was dead, Peter awoke in terror, trembling and sweating. Perhaps he screamed, because Margery awoke suddenly, as terrified as he. "What is it? What's the matter?"

Peter couldn't tell her. He couldn't inflict it on her, and was too ashamed to admit what monster his sleeping mind had conceived.

Margery settled back to sleep. With his heart still thumping, Peter got up and went to the children's room with a candle to look at Abigail, her hair damp from the warmth of her sleep, pressing golden curls against the pillow. Her cheek was rosy in the cool room, her eyelashes thick and dark against it. He took her up and crushed her hot little body to his and asked God for forgiveness. She murmured and tried to nestle against him to go back to sleep. He put her back in her cot and tucked her in. Looking at her sleeping form with an intense ache of relief and remorse, he prayed to be forgiven.

But he carried the dread of it for weeks; there was no one he could tell. It was then he began to wish for the ritual of confession. He had read some of the penitential books of the medieval church. Then, every kind of human depravity had been recognized and afforded its appropriate penance.

The Church of England never demanded anything so fervent, never tested your faith once you had memorized enough of the catechism to be confirmed. For the rest of your life, you could be a model Anglican by attending church now and then, taking communion, and putting something in the collection plate. You didn't even have to have faith to observe the social conformity the church required. Even a priest's faith was not tested.

He passed Stewart's house on the corner of Victoria Road. The lights were out. Again the thought: Stewart might know who she is.

Peter walked slowly up Lucknow Street, with its black trees growing out of high snowbanks. He considered each house, remembering her description: *quite unassuming, even pokey from the street, like ours, nothing grand.*

What Peter could not see he felt. In this house, or that one a little farther on, this woman might be walking through the rooms —vibrant, warm, sensual.

SEVERAL TIMES during the funeral service, and again at the graveyard, Betty twisted and looked around, as if searching for someone. To see on the side of her missing eye, she had to turn her whole body. Mother Nesbitt gently turned her back again.

Stewart's eyes filled with tears at the pity of her situation, but Betty's one hyacinth-blue eye was dry and unblinking. Its color was striking against the drab clothing of the those present, like a crocus glimpsed through tired snow. They had found her a coat for a small woman, nipped in at the waist, too old for the girl, and a black felt cloche. It made her look like a tiny woman. She held the nun's hand and the Victorian doll. They had tried to take the doll away, but she held it too tightly, and the sisters, overcome with grief at the sight of two large coffins and one very small, had let her bring it.

When the coffins had been lowered, earth sprinkled on them, and the final prayers said, they returned to the convent. As they entered, Betty turned again and looked toward Spring Garden Road.

"Grandma didn't come." She said it as matter-of-factly as she said everything.

"Who is Grandma?" Mother Nesbitt asked.

"Do you have a grandmother, Betty?"

"Yes."

"What is her name?"

"Grandma Webber."

"Where does she live?"

"She works for a lady in the South End."

"This is the South End. Do you know the street?"

"It's called South Park Street."

"Do you know her name, the lady your grandma works for?"

"Mrs. Robertson."

"Do you know the address, the number on South Park Street?"

"It's a pretty house."

"Do you know where it is?"

"Yes."

"Did you go there?"

"Grandma took me there and we had cookies."

"If I took you there, could you show me which house it is?"

"Yes," the child said.

"Well," Stewart said to the nun, who was shaking her head, "if she has a grandmother who's living, we'd better find her, hadn't we?"

"Yes, of course. The poor little thing has no one else. Why didn't she tell us before?"

"Apparently no one thought to ask her," Stewart said. "Would it be all right if I took her to look? I have my car here. I'll bring her back."

"Yes, I'm sure it would be all right. Betty, Mr. MacPherson is going to take you to see if you can find where your grandma lives."

Betty looked up at her. "Can I still use this coat and hat you lent me?"

The nun smiled. "Of course you may, dear."

Stewart was intrigued by the mechanisms of Betty's emotional defenses. She had retreated into herself. Yet if you asked the right questions, she showed no reluctance to give information,

In the front seat of the car, she turned to look back. "That's where Mama and me sat when she was hurt, and the lady died."

"Do you remember everything that day?"

"Yes."

Stewart waited, but she said nothing more.

"Betty, this is South Park Street. It's a long street. I'll just drive slowly down this side and then up the other side, and you tell me which house it is. Take your time. A lot of the houses look very much the same."

Betty said, "It's that one."

"Which one?"

"That one, down there." She pointed down the block on the far side.

"Which one; which color?"

"It's black and has white around the windows."

He stopped opposite the house she pointed to.

"Are you sure?"

"Yes."

Stewart turned the car around and parked in front. As they walked up the steps, he took the child's hand for the first time and was surprised again by how far he had to reach down. He said, "Now don't be disappointed if it's the wrong one."

"It's the right one," Betty said.

They knocked, and a strong-looking, middle-aged woman opened the door.

"Grandma, you didn't come to the funeral."

The woman screamed, "Betty!" She picked up the child and hugged her desperately. "Oh, my little darlin'! Oh, my little darlin'! I thought you was dead."

She sobbed into the child's neck.

"Let me look at you. Your eye's hurt?"

"They took it out, Grandma."

"Oh, you poor baby!" She cried and then said fearfully, "Is your mama—?" and she looked at Stewart, who shook his head.

"Mama died in the hospital. She couldn't see, Grandma, and her eyes was all blood. And my dad died and the baby. I was holding him when he died."

"Oh, my God. I can't take it in. We was sure you was all dead." She hugged the child to her fiercely, crying. "Nobody knew for sure. The house was gone, the whole street was gone, but we didn't know a thing."

She picked the child up and carried her into the hall, calling out, "Mrs. Robertson! Come down! For God's sake, Mrs. Robertson." She was sobbing and calling, "It's Betty! Betty's come. Betty's alive!" She couldn't talk anymore. She sat down on a chair in the hall, hugging the child and sobbing, then standing her up at arm's length to look at her again, then pulling her back.

A slim young woman came running downstairs, calling, "Mollie? Mollie?" She had blond hair pulled back in a chignon. She glanced at Stewart in the doorway, and he glimpsed a pretty face before she turned back to the woman and child.

"Oh, Betty!" She knelt and put her arms around them both. She laid her clear cheek against the old woman's; she was crying.

"Oh, Betty," the young woman cried, "we're so glad to see you. Mollie, I can't believe it! I'm so happy, I can't believe it!"

Stewart, watching in the open door, had to wipe his eyes.

"Grandma, they buried Mama and my dad and the baby, all together in the earth. And his coffin was little and white and Mama's coffin was black and Dad's coffin was black. And all the sisters came."

The young woman got to her feet, drawing a handkerchief from her sleeve to mop her tears, and said softly to Stewart, "So, they're all dead—her mother and father, and the baby?"

"Yes, I'm afraid so."

"Oh, how terrible for her, and for Mollie!" She buried her face in her hands and sobbed. In a moment she straightened up and wiped her eyes again, and he noticed what a truly beautiful woman faced him, more beautiful for the tears in her gray eyes, the flush on her cheek, and the strands of honey-colored hair escaping from her pins.

She held out her hand. "I'm sorry. I'm Julia Robertson. Do come in and close the door, or we'll freeze."

"How do you do? I'm Stewart MacPherson."

"Come in, please. Are you a doctor?"

"No, I'm a psychologist at Dalhousie."

"Oh, yes, MacPherson. I know about you. It's the big house on Victoria Road—with the tennis lawn in the garden?"

"Yes, that's right."

"I went there to play tennis once, with Charles and Lucy, my husband and his sister. Goodness, it seems a long time ago—before the war. There was a party."

"I was away a lot of the time in those years."

Julia turned to look at Betty and Mollie and back at Stewart, and lowered her voice. "So you know how it happened?"

But Betty was telling Mollie the story all in a rush:

"I was eating my porridge. Dad had gone to work. The baby was sleeping. Mama said I couldn't go to school because I had a fever, and they were picking the Mary and Joseph. I was by the window. I said, There's a big fire in the harbor. There's a ship on fire. It was shooting out different colors. I saw the big fire going up to the sky; then the baby cried and Mama asked me to pick him up and everything went white and the windows broke and everything was falling on top of me. For a long, long time I couldn't move, but I smelled smoke and Mama screamed, and I tried and tried to get out 'cause there was fire all around. I used all my strength and squeezed out, and Mama said, My eyes are hurt. I can't see! Betty, help me, help me! Get the baby, and help me, Betty! And then everything was on fire and the smoke hurt my eyes. I picked up the baby and there was no wall anymore and I pulled on Mama's dress and we walked out, and Mr. MacPherson"—she pointed at Stewart—"was there with a big black car and an army man and the army man shouted, Get in here; we'll take you to the hospital."

As she talked, the monotonous, flat little voice began to take on more intonation. When she quoted her mother, Stewart could hear the woman's voice, first relaxed but excited as she watched the fire, then screaming in terror as the glass shot into her eyes and blinded her. Mollie was weeping and stroking Betty's black curls. Julia Robertson stood against the doorframe, her fingertips to her lips.

"There was a woman in his car with blood all over. She

bounced when the car bounced 'cause he drove real fast. I was never in a car before. The baby was very heavy. At the hospital, I said, The baby is sleeping but he's cold, and Mama screamed and felt him, and he was dead. And they ran in to get help for the other woman, but she was dead and leaning against me. Mr. MacPherson and the army man pulled her out and laid her on the cold ground. When Mama went in the hospital she said, Someone stay with the baby, and I said, I'll stay with him. And they laid him down on the ground with the woman that was dead. He gave me a blanket to wrap up in 'cause I didn't have no coat on. And I never saw him after, because I was with Mama and a nurse came and I said, My eye is starting to hurt and it's getting dark and fuzzy to see. And they looked at it and put me on the table and the doctor put a cloth over my mouth and nose and put stuff on to make me go to sleep and he said, Count to ten. And I counted and when I woke up I could only see out of this eye and there was this bandage and they said they had to take my eye out because there was a piece of glass in it. And Mr. MacPherson came to see me and brought me this dollie in Christmas paper and I thought it was a present from Mama, because she said I could have a doll for Christmas and the sister said it was a present from Mr. MacPherson."

She had said it all in a rush, not seeming to pause to take a breath.

Mollie kissed Betty's face all over and then turned to Stewart and Julia Robertson, who was wiping her eyes again.

"And what happened to your mama? Can you tell Grandma?"

"Mama died."

Mollie looked at Stewart.

"Her mama was my daughter Winnie. She was married to Tom O'Shaughnessy. They came here because of the work in the dockyard and the good pay. To think this is how it ended. How did she die?"

Stewart said, "They thought it was only her eyes that were injured. So did we. That's what we saw. They operated on her eyes, then put her to one side. When they went back, she was dead. She had bled to death from internal injuries. I'm very sorry."

"Oh, my! Oh, my!" Mollie put her hand over her eyes. "She was such a good girl, Winnie. And Tom? How did he die?"

"He was missing for several days. Betty told me where he worked and I went to the dockyard. His foreman came to the morgue at Chebucto Road with me and found him. He must have died in a second from the pressure of the blast. There was no mark on him."

"Oh, my God." Julia put her two hands together in a praying position in front of her lips and wept. "Excuse me." She moved into the drawing room and sat on the edge of a chair.

Stewart followed her quietly.

"I cannot bear to think of it. There's been so much horror, and to think this little girl has seen so much."

Stewart said, "I don't think she has felt anything yet. I've been with her often since last Thursday and I have yet to see her cry. Eventually her feelings will catch up with her, so it's good that she's found her grandmother before they do. Where does Mollie live?"

"Oh, she lives here. She works for us. And Betty can stay here. It's the only thing." She got up eagerly. "Mollie, of course Betty must stay here with us. There's the other room beside yours."

"Oh, that's good of you, dear."

He noticed that Mollie talked to Julia more as an aunt than a servant.

"Until we can find something else."

"I'll have to go back and explain to the nuns at the convent. They've been keeping her since she got out of the VG."

"She was in the VG? Just over there, and we didn't know?"

Julia Robertson had an eager, open look and a mouth that seemed just about to smile. She kept pacing the few steps between Mollie and Stewart.

"Mollie," she said, "I can't believe it! She was at the VG and the convent all these days, just around the corner. Your dollie is so beautiful, Betty."

"Mr. MacPherson gave it to me, for Christmas."

"I know. How very kind of you. And you went to the funeral? You have been kind. Let me think. Can I offer you something? What time is it? Oh, I'm so confused!" She laughed, again putting her fingertips to her lips. "Let me think. Would you like a glass of sherry?"

"Very much," said Stewart and admired Julia's trim shape as she swept out of the room.

Betty said, "When I came here before, the lady said I could have a cookie."

Mollie said, "Of course, my darlin'. I'm just going to bring you into the kitchen and you can have alls you want. Where did you get that funny old coat?"

"The sisters gave it to me. It was the only one they had that fit me. My coat got buried when the house fell down."

There were photographs in silver frames on a table, one of a young army officer. Stewart was looking at it when Julia returned with a sherry decanter and glasses.

"That's my husband, Charles. He's in France."

She poured two glasses and smiled. "Did you know him? Charles Robertson?"

"I was just wondering. I think so—when we were boys."

"His family called him Sandy."

"Sandy Robertson. He may be a little younger—"

She came closer to give him a glass of sherry. He saw that there was a permanent little smile line etched in each corner of her mouth.

She smiled now. "They called him Sandy, but he's much more a Charles." As she said Charles, she pursed her mouth in a mock serious way.

"Perhaps his sister was more your age group. Lucy Robertson; she's now Lucy Traverse. Do you know Harold Traverse?"

"Oh, of course I know Lucy. We played together as kids. She was at dances and parties years ago. But I was away at school."

"Oh, where?" There was a pleasant urgency, an eagerness about her that reminded Stewart of something.

"RCS—and then King's, and then the University of Toronto."

"Ah, yes, well, Charles was at Lower Canada College and then McGill, so you probably missed all along the way. And, you see, I'm from Montreal."

She was so attractive that he had to struggle a few seconds to remember something he wanted to say.

"You know—about the child. I'm concerned about her eye. The dressing needs to be changed every day. And she hasn't seen it yet, as far as I know. It may frighten her when she does. It won't be nice to look at. I've had a preliminary chat with the eye people at the medical school. They think it's important that a prosthesis, an artificial eye, be fitted soon, so that the socket doesn't shrink and the muscles atrophy."

She listened to him with a sympathetic attention he found deeply appealing.

"For her own confidence, too, I think it's a good thing. She's a beautiful child. I didn't know until now that she had any family. What I mean is I was thinking of making arrangements for the eye myself."

"That's sweet of you. How very thoughtful."

"Well, I've become rather attached to her."

Julia looked at him gravely; there were still tears in her eyes.

"Obviously, Betty found a real friend."

"Well . . ."

"I'm just beginning to put together all that you've done."

He could not take his eyes from her. "It may involve taking her to Boston. That's where the best people are."

"Oh, that's sounds an awful lot to do."

"Would you want to see that beautiful child grow up disfigured?"

"No, no, I wouldn't! Not for a moment," Julia said earnestly. "It's just a little—well, it makes me squeamish to think of her with a glass eye." She shivered. "No. But I agree completely. I just meant it was a lot for you, as a stranger, to take on. We could help. I could help. I'd love to help. Mollie is almost family to me and to the Robertsons."

Stewart felt a strong desire not to break the connection, but he said, "I'd better go and tell the convent. The sisters may want to meet Mollie themselves. But we can worry about that later."

"We can't thank you enough," Julia said. "Oh, goodness! I never asked you to take off your coat. I must be in a daze. We've had a lot of people camping here. They've just moved out. Do come back to see us."

"I will."

Stewart walked the few steps to his car, taking deep breaths of the cold air. He could not remember when he had felt so happy. To see the little girl in the arms of her granny, her terrible story bubbling out of her, like any child breathless to tell. And the charming Julia Robertson. She was quite unlike all the young women of the South End group she had married into—the Robertsons, Gastonguys, Tobins.

Now he had to give the good news to the convent.

•   •   •   •

That evening Julia wrote to Charles.

My darling,

At last I have something nice to tell you after all the horror and ugliness I told you on Saturday. Today—wonderful! Unbelievable! Mollie's granddaughter Betty turned up alive! We were sure, as I told you, that they had all perished. The house was completely destroyed. I had gone to see it with Mollie. Your father got us permission to go through the soldiers patroling the edge of the devastation. Apparently ghouls are still sneaking in trying to steal from the dead. Can you imagine such a thing in Halifax?

It was very frightening to see what the explosion had actually done. Until you see it, you can't imagine. That whole part of the city is just flat, as flat as can be, with only part of a tree or a snapped-off telephone pole standing here and there.

But seeing their house was even more frightening. Not a very nice place, a four-family wooden tenement. But it was gone! Just pieces of boards in heaps covered with snow, but where some of the boards poked through you could see the burning from the fires that had raged afterward. It was terrible for Mollie. We stood there in the freezing wind sweeping up from the harbor, in all that desolation, and the total wreckage of their house seemed to confirm that Tom, Winnie, Betty, and the baby had all died. We had heard nothing and it was impossible to get information. The hospitals and first-aid posts were swamped with casualties for days and days. I went around studying the lists of people treated—they were pinned up outside—but we found nothing. Even the awful lists of the unknown dead the papers publish didn't match Mollie's family.

Here I was in the bedroom this morning when I heard Mollie yell. As you know, nothing excites her very much. The only other time I've heard her shout like that was at the explosion itself last Thursday. I ran downstairs, and there was Betty, the poor mite, looking like a miniature woman in some old coat, with a bandage on her eye and Mollie hugging and kissing her like a mad fool.

With Betty was Stewart MacPherson—do you remember him? He says he vaguely remembers you but he knew Lucy better. Tweedy, and teaches psychology at Dalhousie. We've

been at the MacPhersons' house to play tennis—on Victoria
Road, remember? Apparently he was driving wounded to
hospital, and he found Winnie and Betty and the baby and took
them to the VG. Winnie died from internal injuries. The baby,
little Tom, born since you left, was already dead. Betty was
holding him in the car, and they found him dead. Can you
imagine a little girl remembering that all her life? MacPherson
seems nice, big, and a little rumpled-looking (after all, he is a
professor!), and he must have a lot of feeling. He kept going
back to see Betty. She had to lose one eye. A piece of glass
went into it. It's so awful, Charles! Do you remember how
gorgeous she is? Those fabulous Irish looks—raven black curls
and the most extraordinary blue eyes.

MacPherson even found Tom's body in the morgue. Betty
has been staying with the sisters at the convent (they were
Catholic), but tonight she's with us. I've given her the other
maid's room beside Mollie's, but I'm pretty sure Mollie has the
child cuddled up in her own bed with her tonight. Mollie is so
thrilled. She can take a lot, but this morning she just cried her
eyes out, I suppose for all the years she hasn't cried and for all
the family she has lost. But the little girl hasn't cried yet. Not a
drop.

MacPherson wants to pay for her to get an artificial eye, if
needs be taking her to Boston. He must be quite well off. Did
his parents have a lot of money? Their house was splendid. You
know, when I told Lucy about all this, she said, "Oh, Stewart
MacPherson!" with a funny laugh. Apparently he's considered a
bit odd. Lucy says he leads a "naughty life"—ladies of a not
very nice kind, a lot of trips to Europe—and you know what
*that* implies! I think she really means—in fact she said—he's a
black sheep and won't settle down with any of the nice little
South End ewes bleating their heads off for him. She mentioned
Susan Gastonguy, for example. I'm being mean. Anyway, I
found him pretty nice—not at all weird—and very feeling.

Julia paused and sat back in her chair. She wanted to say something more about Stewart, but what exactly? And did she want to
say it to Charles? It was that a feeling of warm sympathy came from
the heavy man, a feeling that made her want to curl up at one end
of the sofa and talk to him for a long time about all sorts of things.

And something else—well, that wasn't quite what to write to Charles.

So, it makes me so happy, darling, to have something good to tell you. It has really lifted my spirits after all we have been through.

She stopped again. All she had been through? Charles knew about the windows breaking and the front door crashing in. He knew they had filled all the rooms with homeless people, that she and Mollie (with a cut head and all the uncertainty about her family) had moved furniture, found bedding, cooked and served food to people whose lives had been spared but who had lost everything. That had been easy to do. It felt good to be doing something useful, and now they had gone. The last had left yesterday and the house was almost back to rights. But she could not write to Charles about the diary. A cold, sick shiver possessed her again. She had been over it many times. She took a deep breath. She couldn't even make a big fuss about it with Mollie. In the moments after the explosion everything was confusion. It all happened in seconds. If only she had had a moment to think sensibly. She was writing in the diary. The windows of one side of the bedroom blew in. There was a frightful crashing noise. Mollie screamed. Julia snatched up the diary and ran downstairs. Blood was streaming down Mollie's face. Julia dropped the diary on the sideboard and pulled out several linen napkins. She folded one as a thick pad to put on the cut at the top of Mollie's forehead. Mollie sat on a dining room chair while Julia held the napkin in place and looked around in bewilderment. The floors of the dining and living rooms were covered with glass. The light curtains inside the heavy draperies were blowing slightly in the open air. The front door was lying flat in the hallway. People were running by in the street. They were shouting.

Mollie said, "Must've been one of them German submarines, come right into the harbor blowing us up."

"Does your head hurt?"

"No, it don't hurt much."

"It's still bleeding, though. Can you hold this?"

Julia ran to the front door to look out. An army truck was driving slowing down South Park Street. A soldier was shouting, pointing a megaphone this way and that: "Everybody outside!

There's going to be another explosion. Get into the open air. Get to safety. Another explosion."

Julia ran back in. "Mollie, do you hear? We have to get out. But it's cold outside. Can you get your coat?" Mollie hurried toward the kitchen. As she pulled her coat from the hall cupboard, Julia remembered the diary. She got it from the sideboard and plunged it into the pocket of another coat at the back of the cupboard.

Julia and Mollie crossed the street to Victoria Park in front of the cathedral. Some of its windows were gaping spaces. Other people were gathering in the park. Some had wounds. A woman took off her petticoat and tore it into strips to make bandages. Suddenly remembering her St. John's training, Julia removed her petticoat and did the same. This was something she really knew how to do. She bandaged Mollie's head neatly; it had almost stopped bleeding. Then she professionally bandaged other people with cuts in the face or hands. There were no serious injuries. It was sunny but cold. People were shivering and rubbing their hands. Some had come without coats. A family of two parents and two children came out, each with a thick wedge of bread spread with jam. The northern sky beyond the Public Gardens and the Citadel was fearsomely black with smoke.

Half an hour later, the soldiers drove by again, saying there was no longer any danger; it was safe to go home. In the house the two women swept up the broken glass. They closed the inside shutters of the old windows. Mollie produced a hammer and carpet tacks, and they tacked the heavy draperies over the shutters to keep out the cold. Julia walked over to Lucy's and Mrs. Robertson's to make sure they were all right. No one had been hurt. Mr. Robertson had gone to see the damage to his shipyard. Coming back up South Park Street, Julia saw a horse-drawn dray piled with bodies. She stood numb, unable to believe the sight. Later, Mr. O'Brien miraculously appeared and temporarily rehung the front door.

There were still eight or nine people, mostly older women, shivering in the park. Julia walked over and asked them to come in where it was warm. She and Mollie gave them cups of tea and made sandwiches. They had nowhere to go, so they stayed, using all the beds, some sleeping on the floor. The house was cold. Mollie and she covered the visitors with everything they could find —blankets, quilts, picnic rugs, old coats.

On Friday morning Mollie got the wood stove going and made

porridge for a dozen. The visitors wandered off to look for relatives and places to stay. Julia bundled up and walked down into town to see what she could find out about Mollie's family. A policeman guarding a smashed shop window directed her to City Hall. It took nearly an hour to work through the shouting, pushing mêlée of people trying to get information or help. They had only begun to keep a file of missing people. A woman told her, "If they're alive, they may have been to the dressing stations on the Common or at Camp Hill or at any one of a dozen makeshift hospitals."

Through the thickening snow, Julia walked up the steep hill and around the Citadel. The driving snow and wind made the walking very hard. Parts of the city north of there were burning again as the rising wind fanned embers of Thursday's fires. She visited all three first-aid stations in the barracks on the Common. Even to read the handwritten lists pinned outside, she had to wait and push people as frantic as she. There were no O'Shaughnessys.

Julia walked on to Camp Hill Hospital. It was Bedlam. People had lain all night on stretchers or on the floor in the corridors. Wounded were still being brought in. A rush of nurses and doctors ran back and forth. At the information desk a harried NCO said, "No lists. It's too soon for lists. We've got so many hundreds in here, more than a thousand, we don't know who's here and who isn't. There's three to a bed in some of them rooms. Nobody's had time to count."

Julia began walking home, emotionally numb. Her feet were aching with cold, her hands cold even in her muff. The blizzard was strong enough to blow her off balance as she crossed Spring Garden Road.

Her house was still full of strangers. She stepped over and around them and collapsed, shivering, on a chair in the kitchen.

"I'm sorry, Mollie. I couldn't find them. Tomorrow we can look in other places."

Mollie gave her hot soup and they sat in silence.

"I'm used to people going," Mollie said eventually. "Down the shore, everyone's used to it. There's not a year goes by, someone doesn't get himself drowned out fishing. Sometimes two and three together. Man and his two sons. But it seems the natural way. You live almost half-expecting it. But you don't live to expect something like this."

Only after she went up to bed did Julia remember the diary. She rushed downstairs again but couldn't find the old coats in the hall cupboard. She went back into the kitchen.

Mollie said, "There was that pile of old stuff we used for all the people was here last night. It was in the hall there. A man come by today asking for warm clothes for the victims. He said they had nothing. I gave him some. I knew you meant to give that stuff away."

Julia felt as she had when her finger accidentally touched the electric light socket; a throb of fear.

"Was there anything in the pockets of the coats?"

"I didn't see nothing, dear. Have you lost something?"

"You didn't see a small book?"

"No. No. Nothing like that. To tell you the truth, I didn't look in the pockets."

"Who collected the things?"

"Some young minister. It was already blowing up into a living gale, so I didn't look at him too hard. Is it important, what you lost?"

How could she scold Mollie? The poor thing was drawn and white with anxiety about her family. It wasn't Mollie's fault anyway.

"No, it's not important," Julia said and went upstairs. But lying in bed, wearing a flannel nightdress and woollen stockings, she shivered with embarrassment. How stupid of her! How careless! But could anyone read it and know who she was? She was sure she had not used any last names. But the things she had said! She tried to remember. What had she said? She had not been prudent. That was the point of the diary. But to imagine some stranger reading it! Or worse, someone who might know her. Julia rolled over to hide her face in the pillow, then realized that was silly. Calm down, now, and think. No one could really know. It was all right. It had actually been like playing a game as she wrote, to hide behind the initials. Like daring someone to guess, part of the fun of writing. She mustn't keep worrying about it. Have to assume it's lost, somewhere in the confusion of the disaster. If some poor soul, desperate for clothing, finds it in a pocket, what sense could he make of it? *He* because it was in a man's coat pocket she had slipped it.

Again and again the next day she thought the same thoughts.

She would have a sick remembrance, then think it through and try to calm down. It was better not to worry.

Now Julia looked at her unfinished letter. It was one of those moments when Charles seemed very far away—almost nonexistent. That was what had driven her to the diary, her longing to bring him closer, to make him real, like taking out one of his suits and smelling the jacket lining. She had written that in the diary. How mortifying! On an impulse, she got up and went to the cupboard and looked at the same tweed suit. She felt only sad. The longing had gone away. She closed the cupboard.

The letter? She could finish it tomorrow. No, that wasn't fair! She forced herself to sit down, pick up her pen, and reread the last line she had written.

It has really lifted our spirits after all we have been through.

She added,

My darling, I do so hope that you are well, and warm, and safe tonight. Our troubles are nothing to yours. I wish I could hold you tight and tell you I love you.

Good night, dearest.

> My warmest love,
> Julia

DESCRIPTIONS of the unidentified dead began appearing in the newspapers, and many people came to the morgue. Stewart went to watch their reactions, making notes, obtaining names and addresses. He wanted to know whether the experience of the explosion, the horrible sights many had witnessed, the shock of finding a dead relative, would affect civilians the way similar experiences in battle affected some soldiers.

These people were governed by the mood that he noticed still gripped the city. It was as though everyone knew he was under observation and would be judged later on his behavior. If this was shock, it seemed to tighten people's grip on propriety. Few wept or broke down.

Then a young woman came in, modestly but decently dressed. She said she was looking for her brother and asked to see three bodies by ages and descriptions printed in the paper. She moved confidently, like a discriminating shopper. She looked at two and sadly shook her head. When a guard lifted the sheet from the third, she laughed, actually laughed with pleasure; the laughter sounded odd in that cold echoing basement. She said, "Oh, Jack, it's you!" and bent down to kiss the face.

"I'm sorry, miss"—the attendant was reading a tag—"but that body has just been identified by someone else."

She looked bewildered and then said, "But he's my brother. Jack Dalrymple."

"He was identified by his parents. The tag says, 'John Winsor, twenty-three, a factory employee at Moirs.'"

"Twenty-three. That's Jack's age," she said, as though they were discussing a pleasant coincidence.

"Was your brother married?"

She laughed. "No, of course not."

"Well, this gentleman is wearing a wedding band. You see?"

She looked carefully at the band, then at the dead man's face, and said, casually, "Then it's not my brother at all. I'm sorry," and quickly walked away.

Stewart stopped her and introduced himself. "I'm making a study of people's reactions to the explosion. May I talk to you about what happened?"

The young woman wrapped her coat more tightly around her and shivered. She had a thin freckled face, with short sandy hair under her winter hat.

"Couldn't you get another person to come with you who knows your brother? Then you'd convince them."

"There is no one else to come. They're all dead." She did not break down, and she gave Stewart her name, Mary Dalrymple.

Then she gave him the oddest smile. Did he read it correctly? It looked decidedly seductive.

"I have no address now. Only the Salvation Army. That's where they put me, because my home's gone. I was at work when it happened, and when I got home, there was nothing. They found my mother half-burned and the rest all burned."

Other people crept apprehensively along the forlorn rows, speaking in whispers, as if in an empty church. They looked half-ashamed to have survived unhurt.

Robert Ferris was a salesman at Colwell's, the men's clothing store on Barrington Street. He had a puffy white face, and his black hair was combed very precisely. Ferris was there to look for his missing sister. He did not find her, but when Stewart talked to him, Ferris said suddenly and rather crossly, "You know, I saw the zeppelins."

It was conventional that people were numbed by shock, but some reactions seemed bizarre.

"Oh? Tell me about them."

Ferris looked relieved. But he would not face Stewart. He stood beside him, talking as though they were both watching something in the distance.

"No one else believes me, but I saw them. I was just reaching under the counter to pull out some socks, the shop had just opened, and the explosion happened. Our front windows were smashed, and a wind blew everything around. I ran outside, still holding the socks, and looked up, and there were two zeppelins with bombs spilling out of them."

"What did they look like?"

"They looked like zeppelins. Haven't you seen pictures of them? They were long and silver and had the big German cross on the rudder fins."

"Where did you see them?"

"They were flying over the harbor. I saw the bombs fall out, and then they disappeared behind the smoke over the North End."

"Are you sure you saw that?"

"Absolutely. I would swear to it, but no one believes me."

Stewart took his name and address to do a further interview. This was different from shell shock. These people showed no physiological symptoms, no obvious signs of anxiety. They were not twiching or perspiring heavily. Both the young Dalrymple woman and Ferris seemed rational and in command of themselves. Yet they were apparently talking nonsense—very plausibly. A dissociated psychic state. Was it a form of amnesia in the woman's case? A form of dissociation arising from the emotional shock of the explosion? Or had these two people shown neurotic symptoms before the explosion?

Intrigued, Stewart began a tour of the hospitals, asking physicians and nurses. By the end of the day he had thirteen cases, which the medical people lumped as "bad nerves . . . hysterical . . . uncommunicative." He took the names and had quick interviews with the patients. There was a man with a concussion who walked in his sleep. There were three people with amnesia, one apparently total, the others partial. There were patients with screaming nightmares, whose cries affected the other patients. There was a man who had seen shells from German guns whizzing over the city. There were conversion cases just like the shell-shock symptoms, emotional distress converted into physical conditions: a woman who was blind but showed no damage to the eyes, two cases of paralysis, with no physiological cause.

A man believed all his family, wife and children, had been killed, although they came every day and stood around his bed. He would not be consoled.

There were people with escape stories so farfetched that they sounded like fantasies: a man said he had been in a rowboat on the harbor but was lifted by the blast and flown through the air for half a mile, to land softly on the grass at Fort Needham.

As far as Stewart knew, no professional had ever analyzed the psychological reactions in a disaster. That was what he might do: a thorough study, "Psychic Trauma in Disaster." Perhaps that should be his Ph.D. project.


MARGERY WENTWORTH walked from her parents' to her own house. It was the first time she had been out in days, and she felt like a child emerging weakly after the measles.

She did not want to move back, but she had an important purpose. In her dressing table drawer was a small calendar. The house felt warm but unwelcoming. She left her coat on and went upstairs. She noticed that Peter had not made the bed after getting up. His side of it had been slept in. Hers was untouched.

She sat down at the dressing table and found the little calendar in which she marked when she expected her periods and when they began. They were always almost identical. From November she counted forward into December. She was due on the seventeenth —four days away. If her period did not come, she was pregnant.

It was less than two weeks to the twenty-fifth. She had done nothing about Christmas. It was always left to her, because Peter was busy with extra services, carol singing, children's crèche services, visiting the sick and bedridden. Her mother always did well by the children. It would have to wait. She put the calendar in her bag and looked at herself in the mirror. Against her black coat and hair her face looked very white, and there were blue shadows under her eyes. She picked up the silver-backed comb and tugged it listlessly through her hair. She said, I am not pretty. I am no longer pretty. It doesn't matter now.

On her way out, the sight of the unmade bed made her uncomfortable. She made it carefully and neatly, as she always did, fluffing up his pillow and pulling up the spread. She felt better, but halfway downstairs she stopped. Peter would know she had been back in the house. She climbed the stairs and unmade the bed on Peter's side, leaving it as she had found it. She dented the pillow, took out his pyjamas, which she had folded, and dropped them on the floor.

Margery left hurriedly in case he came back and surprised her there. The unaccustomed time, midafternoon, the children out, and the house empty might make him think she wanted him to make love to her. It had happened before when they had been alone together on an afternoon. The unusual time excited him more. She hurried down Tower Road, going away from the cathedral, in case he came, thinking of that.

Her mind was much clearer now, clearer than it had been for months. She had stopped the constant crying. Her cold was getting better. Her mother thought she had really "come out of it." It was easier to think. She felt more like her old self, able to think things out, the way she had decided when she was only fifteen or so that Peter was the boy she wanted, and had thought through all the ways to make it happen.

Margery turned into Victoria Road so that she would not have to pass his parents' house. She had not called on them for weeks and felt guilty about it. Dorothy Wentworth was the kindest soul on earth, but she made Margery uneasy. Her sensible clothes were an implied reproach to the elegance of Margery's in a household otherwise so pinched. Margery deliberately dressed down to visit the older Wentworths. Dorothy Wentworth did everything too efficiently and with invariable good humor. And Canon Wentworth was just as predictably good-natured, if a little removed, looking at her for several minutes before finding an appropriate question to ask. She should have brought the children to see them. That would have to wait.

She would not be in this terror if Dr. Menzies had been different, or younger. When she was really down after Michael's birth, Stewart MacPherson had suggested they consider birth control. He knew people at the medical school. His unorthodox ways made Peter uneasy, but Margery trusted him. Peter had been dead against

210 BURDEN OF DESIRE

it, but she went to Dr. Menzies anyway, while still nursing Michael. Menzies was an old man, an elder in St. David's Presbyterian Church. He had been her mother's family doctor. His hands examining her were rough, and so were his words when she asked whether he knew about methods to limit the number of children.

"Yes," he said contemptuously. "I have heard of them and other things people are doing nowadays. I'm surprised to hear you speak of them. Do you know it is against the law for me to interfere with conception? As illegal as if I performed an abortion on you. Did you know that?"

He had a Scottish accent and bristling, overgrown eyebrows.

Margery was shocked. The idea of birth control embarrassed her, but she had never connected it with anything as heinous as abortion.

"Against the law. I could be sent to jail for receiving literature and birth control materials through the mails. In forty-five years of practice, I have never aborted God's handiwork. I do my humble best to abet it when I can. And I am not going to turn my faith upside down now, no matter what nonsense people are talking about birth control. If you want fewer babies, you'll have to work that out like everyone else. Your husband is a man of God. Well, God invented one sure, foolproof way to prevent babies."

Margery blushed and went away, cowed by his stern manner and his masculine authority. In one sense she was relieved; she would not be deceiving Peter.

Her feelings had always been mixed. There was a strange pleasure in giving in, despite the risk. The other night when she had felt awful, the night she had collapsed over the surplices, came back to her. She had been exhausted, with hardly enough strength to lift herself onto the bed and collapse. Then he had come to lie beside her, stroking her.

She had felt him there at a great remove. There, not there. She was too tired. She kept almost slipping off. She was famished for sleep. Yet he was faintly there, stroking her. She roused herself to say no. Then something made her say, I don't care; do what you want. She felt outside her own body and inside it. From a distance, as though she were floating near the ceiling, she watched more than felt him remove her clothes. It was as though he were doing it to someone else. Yet the idea of surrendering, of just giving in, of letting him do anything, was as appealing as slipping into sleep. She scarcely felt him enter her and leave. He felt strong, and she felt so weak, so listless. His muscles were hard, and hers were limp, like fronds of seaweed in the waves.

Later her other mood had snapped back. When he got into bed, she was suddenly wide awake and filled with black terror. She wanted to be sweet to him—and she wanted him damned.

"Hello, Margery."

She looked up, startled, to see Stewart MacPherson smiling down at her. Walking with her eyes on the sidewalk, she had seen no one approaching.

His strength and cheerfulness, his ruddy color and shining brown eyes, made her feel weak and helpless. Odd that such an ungainly boy had become so attractive a man. He never wore a hat in winter, but he took off his glove to shake hands.

"How are you, Margery? I haven't seen you in months." In his eyes she could read anxiety at her appearance.

"I'm just out for a walk. I've had a cold, a bad cold."

She knew he was noting her lank hair, her pale complexion, her unsmiling mouth. She knew what he was seeing, and it didn't matter.

"I saw Peter the day of the explosion, in the thick of it up there." He gestured up South Park Street.

"That's right. He said he'd seen you."

Margery looked deeply preoccupied, scarcely able to keep her mind on their conversation.

"He told me you were all right. Just a few broken windows."

"Yes, I'm all right."

She liked Stewart.

"Perhaps, when things settle down, you and Peter could come to dinner. I'll ask Mrs. Bethune to make something special."

"Yes" was all Margery said, and looked past him. He would have expected her to say, "Oh, how delightful. You are kind. We'd love to . . ." and to bubble on graciously. Instead, she took a step away, barely managing to smile.

"I'm staying at Mother's. She'll be expecting me."

He watched her walk away, thinking that she was smaller than he remembered, then noticed that she was slumped over, with her head down.

She was a woman whose waist came very high under her breasts. Unless she held herself up straight, she looked bent, like a rag doll folded on the stitching lines. Her high waist made her arms seem too long, and she had a way of letting them dangle from the elbows in front of her, with the wrists limp, as a kind of signal of helplessness. That and the folded look gave Margery the appearance of something collapsed within.

He had noticed it soon after Abigail was born. The girl who had looked so vibrant appeared washed out, anemic, lusterless.

Margery had very wide-set eyes framed by dark curly hair, giving her the unreachable, ethereal look that had attracted Stewart as an adolescent. But the same look could quickly turn haunted; the wide mouth, which smiled so easily at dances, could turn down and look haggard.

It was obvious that she had no talent for household management. Stewart had learned that simply by going to her house one day for tea, soon after her marriage.

When the doctors were of no help, in desperation Peter had asked Stewart for advice. Flushed with confidence from his first studies with Ernest Jones, Stewart guessed that Margery's depression had its origins in some sexual dislocation.

He remembered talking to Margery one afternoon, during a tea on someone's lawn. They took a stroll together. She looked so wan, so gray and dispirited, that he felt moved by her defenselessness and, in a shadowy corner of his consciousness, moved sexually. The realization was fleeting, but he noted a second when he thought that the woman he had lusted after as a boy, and who had no interest in him, was now hungry for comfort from any quarter. And coloring his thoughts was the Freudian orthodoxy that her problem might be sexual.

Back in Toronto, he described his conflict to Jones, who said disarmingly, "Oh, I always find myself sexually attracted to my women patients. And it's not hard to see what has attracted you to Margery."

Stewart was not reassured. Privately he felt Jones made too light of the danger. He wrote to Peter delicately, suggesting that psychotherapy might help. Peter rejected it, saying she had to pull herself together and ask God for the strength to cope with life. Besides, there were no psychoanalysts or therapists in Halifax.

Then Stewart had tried another tack: if having two children caused Margery such unhappiness, practicing birth control would give her time to adjust and to plan whether she wanted more. He offered to make discreet inquiries. Peter rejected it right away. The Church of England opposed birth control: he said the Lambeth Conference had specifically condemned it.

The rebuff had made Stewart back off. There was an unnerving difference between plausible theories in a book and their application to the complexities of real people.

Stewart now entered his own house, marveling that he could ever have been so stirred by Margery. Compared with Julia Robertson, the poor thing was pathetic. But perhaps he should speak to Peter again.

JULIA KNEW SOMETHING had happened to Charles. Mollie had taken Betty to the convent, and Julia answered the knock at the front door. Her parents-in-law had never visited her together on a weekday. Elizabeth Robertson kissed Julia and walked into the living room with her arm around her; her husband closed the front door.

The older woman faced her, her sweet face set, holding both of Julia's hands.

"I think you've guessed, my dear. We have some very sad news about Charles. He's alive. But he's been badly wounded."

The words sounded familiar to Julia, as though she had heard them many times and had been expecting them now.

"How badly?"

Archie Robertson put his arm around her shoulders.

"We don't know exactly. Here it is." He pulled an envelope from his pocket. "For some stupid reason the telegram came to us, and Beth opened it."

MD OTTAWA ONT DECEMBER 14
MRS CHARLES ROBERTSON
HALIFAX N S
5041 SINCERELY REGRET INFORM YOU EIGHT NINE SEVEN SIX EIGHT FOUR ACTING MAJOR CHARLES ARCHIBALD ROBERTSON 42 BATTALION OFFICIALLY REPORTED SEVERELY WOUNDED DECEMBER ELEVEN TREATED FIELD HOSPITAL EVACUATED HOSPITAL ENGLAND. DIRECTOR OF RECORDS

"Julia," Elizabeth said, "I am awfully sorry I opened it. I thought it was for me. The moment I read it, I called Archie, and he came right away."

Julia smiled. "Well, we don't know what *severely* means, do we?"

"But I'll do my damnedest to find out," her father-in-law said. "I'm going to army headquarters and make them find out up the line. The main thing is, he's alive."

"Yes," Julia said.

Archie's normally ruddy face was pale; his eyes were red. He looked uncomfortable, wanting to leave.

"Let's hope for the best. As soon as I get any details, I'll ring or come round. I'm terribly, terribly sorry, my dear."

"I'm sorry for you—both of you," Julia said, and then her eyes filled with tears, for them.

Archie kissed her cheek, gave her an encouraging hug, and went out. His wife pulled Julia down beside her on the sofa.

"Sit with me a moment."

"Honestly, I think I have been expecting this every day since he went," Julia said.

"So have I, dear—and worse."

"Even when I hated to do it, I've read the casualty lists in the paper. Every day I've wondered how the families felt. Now that it's happened, I don't know what I feel."

"I feel quite numb myself." Elizabeth looked at her from under the heavy eyelids that gave her face a sweet, sad look.

"You know us quite well by now, dear, and I hope you know how fond we are of you. Really fond. We're not a demonstrative family. It might be hard for you to know that. I should say *I'm* not demonstrative. I think Charles takes after me. Archie is more so. I know he's fond of you. I just want to tell you—between us—that I have come to feel—very attached to you. In some ways you feel closer to me than Lucy."

Mrs. Robertson's pretty blue eyes were filled with tears, but she gave a little laugh.

"I don't know why that should be. But I think Charles was a very lucky fellow to find you for his wife. I just pray to God he comes through this to realize it himself."

The older woman's lips trembled. Julia leaned over and put her arms around her, and Elizabeth, almost against her will, it seemed, raised her arms to clasp her daughter-in-law. They both wept.

When they separated, Elizabeth Robertson sniffled and reached for a handkerchief. Julia said, "I just posted a letter to him this morning."

"He'll want mail more than ever now."

"You know, I didn't know he was an acting major. He's had a promotion."

Both women laughed through their tears.

MRS. BETHUNE'S HUSBAND, who used to do odd jobs for Stewart's father, had covered the broken windows with tarpaper. It made things very dark by day, but the house was warm. It would be weeks before they could get window glass.

Even before the explosion, to save fuel during the war, Stewart had been living in only part of the old house, keeping many rooms shut, using the study as his living room. In the years since his parents died, he had changed little. It was one of the unconscious patterns he was always meaning to analyze.

He had never completely removed his father's papers and odds and ends from the desk. With a little effort, Stewart could smell his pipe tobacco, Dobie's Four Square Blue from Edinburgh, richer than his own Craven "A" cigarettes. His mother's green velvet draperies hung there. In front of the gray marble fireplace, the brass scuttle, the brass-handled poker, tongs, and shovel had all survived from his grandparents' time. Apart from a few books and journals of psychology, in that room it could as well have been a cold winter night in 1887 as in 1917.

It was midevening on Friday. The room was snug and a little airless, because the fire had been burning for several hours. Stewart was reading when the doorbell rang.

He was astonished to see Peter, who had not been to the house for a long time and never just dropped in. The clergyman stamped the snow off his overshoes and shook his coat. In his lean, handsome face, the high color in his cheeks, and the glittering gray eyes, there was a vitality Stewart remembered from Peter's days as a star rugby player.

He looked exhausted but excited, as though the disaster had called forth all his competitive energies and purpose. By contrast, Stewart felt sedentary and indolent in his warm study.

Peter at first refused a drink—he could stay only a minute—but when pressed he accepted a sherry.

"You know the other businesses can close until they get them-

selves together," he said. "Board up their windows and go home.
A church can't. It's needed more than ever. The cathedral's a mess,
and one of my jobs is to get it back in operation. We hope to be
ready by next Sunday. We had to use Saint Paul's yesterday. You
should have seen us. The Scout troop brought their sleds and toboggans on Saturday. They piled them up with prayer books and
hymnals and pulled them downtown. Quite a procession down
Spring Garden Road." Stewart felt he had gone back to school and
one of the masters was telling a story about school life that made
him feel an outsider and much older.

Margery must have told him they had met, but Peter talked just
about the explosion. His description of giving absolution to the
woman in the burning house was very emotional.

"Can you imagine what it's like to lie there pinned down and to
feel the flames coming closer?"

"Like the poor wretches the church in its mercy used to burn at
the stake," Stewart said, then regretted the facetiousness. Peter's
religious pronouncements always provoked it. Usually the jibes
started an argument, but Peter looked at him as though he might
be considering the truth of what Stewart had meant as a joke.
Something was different about Peter.

"Can you find a satisfying theological explanation for the explosion?"

Peter looked at him questioningly, then turned away.

"I haven't had time to think about it."

"Surely it's no derogation of faith to believe in accidents? Why
not simply recognize this as an accident? Tell yourself that God was
looking the other way?"

That brought the old sententious Peter snapping back: "God is
never looking the other way."

In other days Stewart would have enjoyed picking up the cue,
but it was obvious that Peter was disturbed, exhausted, so he resisted the temptation. The trauma of Peter's encounters in the
explosion was evident—and that was on top of the daily strain with
Margery.

"I ran into Margery on South Park Street yesterday," Stewart
said, tentatively.

"She's staying at her mother's with the children. We had a lot of
windows blown out."

"Has the explosion been a great strain on her nerves? She looked depleted to me."

"She's had a bad cold," Peter said. "They've all had bad colds. Did you hear her father is paying to cover all the damage in the cathedral windows?"

"Peter," Stewart said sternly, "I don't want to interfere, but Margery looked ill to me. Seriously ill. You must know what I mean."

"Well . . ." Peter seemed to have to drag his unwilling mind to the subject. "Well, yes. She's been having very bad spells again. Nothing snaps her out of them. But her father's going to provide us with a maid. He thinks that will take the strain off her, and I agree. So perhaps we'll see some improvement."

"I hope so. You know there's a very talented young psychiatrist in Halifax now, with the army. His name is Hart. I've been working with him on some shell-shock cases. I find him very sympathetic. I'm sure, if I asked him, he'd be willing to have a chat with Margery. Just a chat to see if she wanted to talk out some of the things that are bothering her."

Peter got up.

"I've tried for years to get her to talk about what's bothering her. And if she won't talk to her own husband, why would she talk to some stranger?"

"That's the point. You may the last person she could talk to."

"Well, I think that's nonsense. We've been through this before." All of Peter's arrogance came back in the remark.

As well as he knew Peter, Stewart could not read his mood this evening. There was less of the moralistic Peter who always irritated Stewart; instead, the clergyman seemed distracted and vulnerable. It made his handsome features less stern than usual, and more appealing. He kept changing the subject away from Margery. "Did you hear about Bill Jamieson being killed?"

"Poor fellow. I'm losing count of how many from King's it is now."

Peter said, "The day of the explosion someone stuck a note in my letter box, accusing me of cowardice. It wasn't signed. It upset me very much."

"But you've got a wife and children. You're under no obligation to join up."

"Well, you know the papers have been calling on young clergy-men to go,"

"Forget them. The war's bringing out something very nasty in people. All this strident patriotism."

Peter looked at the fire. "I've asked several times to go overseas as a chaplain."

Stewart was astonished. "I never knew that."

"The bishop has refused; the clergy are too shorthanded as it is."

"Do you really want to go,?"

"Well, I feel—I don't know—I feel left out, on the sidelines."

"You make it sound like a rugby match."

"No, but it's thrilling. I can feel just what made them all join up right away."

"It's the same irrational appeal that has always sucked young men into war—"

"But it's patriotism, too!" Peter said fervently. "As cynical as you are, you must feel the pull of king and empire, like everyone else."

"Yes," Stewart said, "I'd rather live under King George than the kaiser, if that's what you mean, but I'm not sure we have to sacri-fice millions of men to prove it. It seems utterly barbaric to me."

"The right cause always justifies the sacrifice."

It was a typical conversation stopper, but Stewart let it go un-challenged. It was the most human conversation Peter had permit-ted in years, and Stewart want to come back to Margery.

"In any case, you can't leave Margery in this condition."

Peter looked at him vaguely. "Right." He got up. "Well, I'll just be getting back."

It was only then that Peter revealed the reason for his visit, although he made it look casual. As he was putting on his overcoat, he pulled out a book.

"I forgot about this. I spent the day after the explosion—was it Friday? That's a week already. I can't remember—the day of the first snowstorm—I was using a sleigh—I went around collecting clothing. That evening I found this in the bottom of sleigh. It must have fallen out of something, but I had handled such mountains of stuff, I had no way of knowing what."

He held it in his hands, self-consciously.

"It's obviously a woman's diary, a well-to-do woman—she must live somewhere in this part of town—young, husband away in

France. Judging by the contents, she must be deeply distressed that it's missing. It's clear she never intended anyone to see it—even her husband—perhaps especially her husband."

It was also clear from the new light in Peter's eyes that he was more interested in the diary than in talking about Margery.

"Is it indiscreet?" Stewart asked.

"It's more than indiscreet."

Now he was beginning to intrigue Stewart.

"It distresses me a little," Peter went on, "to compound the violation of her privacy, so to speak, but I have no way of knowing who the woman is, so I can't simply return it."

Stewart's training suggested that "violation of her privacy" meant more than Peter consciously knew.

"It's mostly initials and dashes. She was worried that someone might read it. But you're the student of psychology—" Through his weariness he managed a smile that made the stiff lines of his cheeks break up. "—especially female psychology. And perhaps you'll know who it is." He finished wrapping his neck in a scarf. "Now I'd better be off."

Before closing the door, Stewart watched him walk away in the driving snow. Peter had always been too purposeful to have come over without a mission—on such an awful night—in so casual and offhand a way, as though he were in and out several times a week. And in his manner there was something different, a current setting across his usual air of certainty about everything.

Back in the study, Stewart put the poker through the bars of the grate to shake down the red coals and added new lumps. He picked up the diary and began reading.

The woman's appeal rapidly gained possession of his attention as she took shape in his mind, sensually and spiritually.

Then the name Mollie made him pause. Mollie was the name of Betty's grandmother. The initials—C, L, Mrs. R—tantalized him for a few moments, until it all came together in a flash. Describing breakfast in the cottage kitchen at Chester, she mentioned L's daughters, Elizabeth and Sarah. But those were the names of Lucy Robertson's little girls, who lived just up Lucknow Street. Lucy Robertson, Lucy Traverse . . . he had just been talking about her yesterday with—Julia Robertson! C was Charles Robertson. The delight of discovering that made him say it aloud: "For God's sake, it's Julia Robertson!" He was reading the diary of the woman who had so beguiled him just the day before. He could see her, smiling eyes and mouth, her crown of blond hair; could hear her pleasant voice in the words of the diary.

How extraordinary that he would meet her one day, be attracted to her, and the next evening be plunged into her very private thoughts. Imagine such a sensual, passionate woman lurking beneath that decorous surface. Well, not so astonishing; quite natural. Sensual, passionate women exist under many sedate surfaces, conforming to the conventional image; that is what makes the individual discovery so exciting in each woman's case. But to have it thrust before him like a book, as a book, in fact . . . It was unfair. It was taking advantage of her. What should he tell Peter?

He did not want to tell Peter. Instantly, he wanted to protect Julia. Why should anyone else make the connection? If he told no one, he could protect her. It would amuse him to keep the secret from Peter.

By pledging himself to secrecy, Stewart rationalized a license to go on reading. He could not stop himself, anyway. He was so accustomed to case histories of female neurotics and psychotics that this was like a case history in normality, something the professional literature almost never covered, except by inference from the abnormal. He thought he could hear her voice, see her smile, watch her toss her hair, and laugh. She was captivating.

He felt a twinge of regret when Julia's affection for Charles welled up, as with the mayflowers on her birthday; a quiet sense of satisfaction when she felt estranged from him.

He read every word: he didn't skip, as Peter had. A passage about the people she knew in Halifax intrigued Stewart. He learned more about Betty's background.

Perhaps it is because Halifax is so much smaller that I notice the differences money makes here more than I did in Montreal. The contrast between the wealthy Haligonians like the Rs and the working people is very distressing. When I went with Mollie to visit her daughter and husband and children in the North End, it was quite awful. Their place was tidy enough, but the little houses were so mean—just boxes with shingles, or larger wooden tenements that sagged and leaned together. The hallways were smelly, as if sour cabbages were cooking, and the streets were smelly, as though the sewage were leaking. The children looked peaked and unhealthy. And these were the homes of honest, working people, dockyard workers like Mollie's son-in-law, men and women who work in the factories up there, the families of sailors and soldiers overseas fighting for all of us. The streets were unpaved and muddy. The cinder sidewalks gave off an unpleasant decaying smell on the hot day we went there. The children had nowhere to play but the streets. I suppose it's just as bad for the poor in Montreal. I just never saw it there.

The rich people in Halifax (they would think it terribly gauche to say *rich),* the well off, do not show it ostentatiously. There are a few big houses you might call mansions down on Young Avenue or by the Arm. But the real secret is the houses that try almost deliberately to look dowdy and unprosperous. Down South Park and the streets leading off are wooden houses that look quite unassuming, even pokey, from the street, like ours, nothing grand. Some of them are double-fronted with two bay windows and a little Victorian decoration, but they have very plain shingled sides. They are painted somberly, gray with lighter gray trim, brown with cream, white with black. But inside, my goodness!—the gleaming floors and marble fireplaces, the paintings and silk draperies, the chintzes. Some of the furnishings look as though they had been here for a hundred years or more: the rugs, the old mahogany, and fine silver. I think that the fronts of these houses are a façade to mask the comforts inside.

Stewart looked around his study and laughed aloud.

Everybody pretends not to be well off. "Oh, my dear, the prices today! I don't know how we're going to manage!" Mrs. R said the other day, pouring from her gorgeous old silver teapot into her equally gorgeous Spode cups.

It is a quiet comfort, nothing show-offish, but comfortable and lived-in. The chintz is faded, and they don't worry about it. Of course, a lot of the money is old, like the Rs'—two or three generations. So when they sit at Sunday lunch, the lovely old table, whose mahogany has faded to tawny, and the well-rubbed Georgian candlesticks are taken for granted.

The houses are adorable, magnified Victorian doll houses. I'm tempted to get out my things and paint them. One in particular:

the upstairs bay windows have little roofs with elaborate scrolled buttresses extending down between the arched windows. It looks like a church pulpit. There is all sorts of Victorian whimsy, gingerbread, and finials on the roof peaks.

How self-assured the inhabitants seem! You do not impress them easily. They have been everywhere, and nothing suprises them. They do not swoon when someone comes from far away, because people have constantly come in and out from the most exotic places.

Mrs. R, without giving the slightest show of "putting on airs," as Mother would say, seems more worldly than all of us. I love her sense of humor (I wish C had inherited it), always ladylike but quite sharp. She told me at tea the other day about Mrs. W, who takes her entertaining, and herself, too seriously. She had a dinner party for a visiting British admiral, Sir Somebody-or-other. It was actually a cold Sunday night supper, and the maid was off. At the end of the main course, several of the officers, including the admiral, got up to help clear the dishes. Mrs. R said the woman rapped out, "We don't stack the plates!" The admiral said he was sorry and carried the plates out, one in each hand.

She has us down perfectly, Stewart thought. That's the advantage of being an outsider. Preposterous little town of fifty thousand people giving itself these grand airs. Yet in a curious way these are not airs. To many, the town looks mean and scant. Its grandeur lives in its psychology, the disproportionate self-assurance, out of scale with its assets. For two centuries these people have rubbed shoulders with princes and dukes and sons waiting for their father's titles who came and went as junior officers in army or navy, streams of titled Englishmen who served some time in Halifax, as they did in Gibraltar or Bermuda or the West Indies or India. Her Lt. B, DSO, was just the latest in a long line.

Stewart acknowledged another twinge of jealousy. The flirtation was innocent enough. It just showed the cruelty of wartime separation: natural longings giving her tides of guilt.

What on earth did Peter think when he read this? He must envy the woman's life, because his is so constricted. But also, he is censorious. The episodes with her cousin J and with Lt. B must have shocked him to death. Could Peter want to return the diary?

Could he do that with a straight face, having read it? Well, Peter could do a lot with a straight face. Straight-faced . . . straight-laced. Peter was so straight-laced about sex that he was surely shocked by the woman's frankness. Straight-laced suggested Anne-Lise, who spurned lacing. Peter had been self-righteous about Anne-Lise. But at least she had been single. This woman is married. He must think her almost a fallen woman.

Far better to keep her identity to himself.

"PETER, have you heard about the Robertson boy?" Margaret Creighton passed a cup of tea to Peter, who had come in to see the dean.

"No."

"The paper's just come. It's on the front page. He's been badly wounded at the front. You must know him. Charles Robertson? They call him Sandy. You certainly know the family, Archie and Elizabeth Robertson. Robertson's Shipyards."

"Oh, yes."

"Have a sandwich or a bit of cake with your tea. You look famished. Donald will be here in a minute. The paper's on the piano. And their daughter, Lucy, has been very active in the guild. They're such a nice family. Beth was in my wedding. I'll have to go and see her."

Peter looked at the paper. He knew Sandy Robertson. He had played tennis with him in the holidays. He had danced with Lucy. Lucy and Margery were friends.

"Yes, I know him," Peter said.

"Oh, Donald, there you are. I'm afraid there is some very sad news. The Robertsons' boy has been wounded."

"Archie's boy? Oh, dear, no."

"Sandy Robertson. He married that beautiful girl from Montreal."

Peter's heart quickened. He knew. Of course R was the Robertsons and C was Charles Robertson and L was Lucy. He knew them all. He knew them to talk to. He had been to their house. He had met her.

"Dear God," said Dean Creighton, sitting down with his tea. "Oh, that is dreadful news. Poor old Archie. He's such a good fellow. He and I match up at golf quite often," he said to Peter. "How bad is it?"

"It says severely." Peter passed the newspaper.

"That could mean anything. But obviously it's grave. Severely must mean very grave."

Mrs. Creighton said, "I think I should go over to Elizabeth's this afternoon, don't you?"

"Perhaps I should go with you."

"I don't remember his wife's name," Peter said. "Charles's wife."

"It's Julia," Mrs. Creighton said. "She lives right over there across the park. You can see the house from here. The black one with the unusual white trim. I often think it looks like pillars."

Now he knew that too. His heart was beating more rapidly.

"Julia. It's such a pretty name, and she's a very pleasant young woman. Considering that she's from Montreal, that's saying a lot."

"Now, my dear."

Peter wanted to dash out of the room and run across the park.

"I'm just saying what Elizabeth says about her. A lot of people from Montreal and Toronto, if they have a bit of position, come down here and are quite sniffy with us. Oh, Donald, don't look like that! You've seen it enough in the church! But Beth says this girl is an absolute delight. And how many of our friends say that about their daughters-in-law?"

"I don't ever see her in church," the dean said.

"That's true," said his wife.

"Don't you think we should telephone first?"

"Not with such close friends. It's too impersonal. I think we should just walk down there. It's the least we can can do. Poor Beth. She must feel so awful."

"Peter, did you need me for something urgent?" the dean asked.

He had to wrench his mind back. "No, sir. It can wait. We need to discuss our part in the mass funeral. The committee has settled on Monday to bury all those still not identified."

"How many is that?"

She lived just across the park.

"More than two hundred. And they think it's appropriate to have a senior representative of each denomination."

"So it's a question of who. I see. Well, let me think about it. And I'd better talk to the bishop. We have evensong this evening.

Perhaps you could take that, Peter. This business with the Robertsons' boy is very upsetting."

"Yes, of course."

Peter left the deanery and entered the cathedral. Although the heat was on, it was still very cool. But he was in a fever. He walked rapidly down the side aisle to the east door and gazed across Victoria Park to South Park Street. The house stood out sharply. Of course he had stopped there when collecting clothes. He knew it instantly. The room in the bay on the second floor must be where she wrote, at her desk facing the window. Sitting there, she had experienced all the emotions in the diary, the feelings that had made her shiver, perspire, weep. If she were sitting there now and looked up, she would see him.

The Creightons were coming out. Peter closed the door and moved rapidly up the other aisle and into the vestry. He put on his overcoat and took his black homburg.

Back in the transept, habit urged him to turn and genuflect to the cross on the high altar. He suppressed the urge but went down the side aisle so as not to feel the cross at his back.

The snow in Victoria Park was deep, so he walked around, going up to Spring Garden Road, past the statue of Robert Burns, and down South Park Street. It gave him a few minutes to prepare.

He felt exhilarated, without trepidation, at one with himself, as sure-footed as on the best days on the sports field, when a hand, not his, guided him on a wave of mysterious force to the goal. The people he passed were misty and out of focus, the noises of the traffic muted.

Lucy Traverse opened the door. Her eyes were red.

"Hello, Lucy. Peter Wentworth."

"Oh, Peter! Yes."

"I am deeply sorry to hear about Charles. The dean and Mrs. Creighton have gone to see your parents. I just heard and came over to see if I might comfort his wife a little—and you."

The words come out smoothly.

"It's kind of you to come. Please come in. I haven't seen you in ages—except, you know, up there in your robes, handing round the communion cup."

Lucy was a jolly, freckled girl whose femininity never dismayed him.

He could feel Julia's presence in the house; he forced himself to keep asking questions.

"What's the news from Harold?"

"He's fine, I suppose. Always makes the war sound maddeningly like it's the jolliest thing he ever did. Let me take your coat."

"And do you know any details about Charles?"

"Almost nothing. I'm terribly worried, Peter. If they say *severely,* you know, it's probably very, very bad."

"Well, perhaps not."

"Come in and see her. Julia, it's Peter Wentworth from the cathedral."

Julia was sitting in a straight chair turned away from a tea table. He saw a woman who was blond, lovely, composed, and smiling politely, offering him a cool hand.

"It's good of you to come. I recognize you from the cathedral, although I'm not a very faithful churchgoer." She said it unself-consciously.

"I've tried to get her involved in the Altar Guild," Lucy said cheerfully. "But no luck."

Peter knew that. He knew what Julia and Lucy had discussed on a chilly summer night at the cottage, when this golden young woman had sat, clasping her legs, her feet in the seat of the rocking chair for warmth. He tried to keep his eyes on her face.

"Would you like some tea? It's a little cold, but I can get some hot water." Her look was clear, level—startling.

"No, I had some with the dean and his wife just now. It was she who told me about your husband. I was deeply sorry to hear it."

"I didn't think so many people knew already."

"It's in the evening paper. On the front page."

"Oh, dear!" Julia looked at Lucy "The papers write such wretched things when the men are wounded. I couldn't bear to read it about Charles."

He knew what she felt about that.

"I wonder if they know any more than we do?"

"I read it," Peter said. "It gave no details."

"Did it say severely wounded?"

"Yes, that was the word."

Lucy said, "It could mean anything. My father is trying to find out more."

All the comforting phrases he was trained to say sprang to his lips

—he is in God's hands; we must pray for him—but he held them back. They would have sounded empty to this lovely, self-possessed woman.

"Did you know Charles?" Julia asked.

*Did?* Does she consider him dead?

"Of course Peter did," Lucy said. "We all knew each other. But Peter is my age." She laughed. "Peter was the handsome one all the girls wanted to dance with."

He met Julia's eyes. She seemed to be watching for his reaction to the compliment.

The young clergyman was good-looking. Julia noticed the lean, disciplined features as he came in. His black clothes framed them and drew her eyes to his face. But his mouth was wrong. It should have been thin-lipped, yet the lips were full, although drawn back at the corners as if in discipline. Each time she glanced up, she found him staring so intently that it made her uncomfortable, but she was drawn to glance back to see if he was still staring. He was. He did not have the soft, indulged look of churchmen. He looked hard and urgent, even desperate.

Peter slipped effortlessly into the part of the clergyman meeting her for the first time, paying a call of condolence. But his mind went back and forth between the clergyman and the man who had almost memorized parts of her diary. He wanted to let his gaze stray all over her, to drink in the physical reality, to match it piece by piece with the thoughts she had confided to the diary. It took little effort to remain on the stage, playing the other part, saying the lines fluently.

"I should go," Lucy said. "I was hoping to see Mollie and Betty. I still can't get over that."

Julia got up and walked to the window. She was wearing a white waist with a dark skirt. The clothes strained along her figure as she bent to look through a crack in the curtains tacked over the shutters.

"Goodness, it's almost dark."

He noted the smallness of her waist and swell of her breasts. She came back and sat down.

"An amazing thing happened on Wednesday. We have a woman who works for us, Mollie Webber, a dear soul. Actually, Lucy has known her much longer, because she worked for her parents."

I know about Mollie and her earthy humor.

"Mollie had a married daughter in the North End. Their house was totally destroyed, and for days we heard nothing. She assumed they had all been killed. Then, two days ago, she opened the front door, and there was her granddaughter—quite alive. It was like a miracle to her."

Lucy broke in, "But, Peter, do you know who found her? Stewart MacPherson! Peter knows Stewart very well. Weren't you away at school together? Yes! But can you imagine anyone more unlikely—"

"Stewart came here?" Peter said. Now he struggled to stay in the part.

Julia said, "The poor little lamb lost her mother, father, and baby brother."

"But not Mollie!" Lucy said. "Apparently right after the funeral, Betty suddenly piped up and said Mollie hadn't come."

"And how is she now?" asked the concerned priest.

"She was a little strange at first," Julia said, looking at Lucy questioningly. "Didn't you think so? Withdrawn emotionally but quite talkative. She just looked at you with that one gorgeous blue eye. But Mr. MacPherson thinks that she hasn't felt any grief yet. She's still in shock."

A little fire of anger kindled in Peter. Stewart was reading the diary now and he would know immediately who had written it because he had met her.

"Well, I'm going to leave you." Lucy got up. "I'll see them tomorrow. Mollie can bring her over to be with my girls. The schools are going to be shut for ages. Peter, it was so nice to see you; really kind of you to come over. We should get together. How's Margery?"

"Fine, just fine."

"We never see you. I haven't seen Margery since she brought Abigail to Sarah's birthday last summer. She puts her in such adorable clothes. Anyway, I must be off." She gave Julia a long hug and patted her back. "Telephone me the minute you hear anything."

"I will." Both women began to cry.

"And I'll do the same. Cheer up. It may not be as bad as we think. Bye-bye for now, Peter. Come and see us!"

When the door had closed, Peter and Julia looked at each other awkwardly for a moment.

"I should be going," Peter said.

"No, no. Please stay. Why don't you sit over here where you'll be more comfortable?"

He sat in an easy chair, noting the taste and probable cost of the quietly elegant furnishings. In the straight chair Julia folded her hands in her lap.

Those hands which held the pen, which rested on Lieutenant B's arm while she danced pressed against him.

"I suppose you must think it's awful. The Robertsons are all such loyal churchgoers, and clearly I'm not." She laughed.

She had called her own face too angular. He could see what she meant. The line of her jaw was sharp and her cheekbones distinct. But the effect was not hard or strained. And the honey-colored hair, pinned loosely on top of her head, softened it. He pictured that hair loosened, falling about her face.

"I can't pretend about it," she went on. "I do go now and then. Mostly to please Mrs. Robertson and Lucy."

"Were your parents, your family, active in their church? You come from Montreal, I believe."

She smiled. "Well, not much. Dutifully, I suppose. Weddings, christenings, funerals."

She was thinking of something else, and when she spoke again she had dropped her social voice.

"It's very hard, not knowing how bad it is with Charles. We got the news hours ago, but it's left us in terrible suspense. My mind keeps leaping from one possibility to another, and each possibility brings such different feelings with it. Do you know what I mean?"

Her accent was different from the Haligonian he was used to, but her voice fell sweetly on his ears.

"And you don't know which emotion to fasten on."

She smiled at his understanding so well.

"Yes, exactly. If Charles is badly hurt but will get well, be able to walk and live a normal life, I will feel one way; I suppose actually relieved, almost happy. If he's really—oh, it seems awful even to think it!" She pressed her fingers together against her lips as if to prevent herself from crying.

"If he is—well, I have spent some time with the wounded men at the military hospitals. I know how terribly broken up some of them are. They'll never lead normal lives again. If it's that, I would feel an entirely different thing. If he were to die—I know I should not be considering the more terrible possibilities, but you can't help your mind doing it, can you?"

Again that eager, intelligent look.

"I mean, you can't stop your mind from thinking?"

It was the voice of the diary. Her presence caused too many impressions to swirl in his thoughts for him to make order of them. She was talking about the man whose spirit was so elusive to her, so hard to grasp, yet whose body she ached for. *Ache* was the word to describe the feeling that now suffused him. A sweet ache for her.

Peter said, "I think uncertainty is a greater cause of suffering sometimes than the worst certainties."

Too portentous, too vacuous? Should he tell her? He wanted to very much.

"I had an experience on the day of the explosion. I was helping get people out of the destruction up there. We found a woman pinned down by a large beam. The house was burning around us, and there was no way to lift the beam and get her out."

"How awful!"

It felt good to tell her the story, to see her listen intently. He told her about giving the last rites but not about his embarrassment and shame.

One part of his mind could watch how her slim neck rose from the small pleats at the throat, observe her breasts, the shape of her knees beneath her skirt; another part told her the story, more fully that he had told it to Stewart, and enjoyed telling her.

"When the one uncertainty, whether she would be absolved, was removed, the certainty of death seemed almost comfortable to her."

"Do you believe that?" Her question was so direct, it seemed nearly impertinent.

"It would be intolerable for me to believe anything else." And yet he didn't.

"You think she was comfortable in death because she had such pure faith?" Julia asked.

"Only someone who believed could have faced such a death smiling." She had forced him into a reflexive hypocrisy.

"How ghastly that must have been for her—and for you. You know, I still can't grasp what's happened. I read the numbers of people killed and injured in the explosion. I can't comprehend that many tragedies . . ."

He could hear her mind switching to something else. He followed her eyes to the silver picture frames on a table. There was Charles, pale eyebrows, still looking like a boy.

"Charles has faith—I think. To be honest, I really don't know. He went to church as his family does. But we never talked about it." She turned back to Peter with a sad smile.

"We had been married only a short time before he went overseas. Religion is one of the things people like us don't talk about very much."

"Many people don't think about it until they need it," Peter said.

She smiled. "And you think I need it now . . . ?"

She had this way of letting a thought trail off, impatient to be making small talk when she wanted to say something real.

"You know, what really troubles me—excuse my being so frank with you—I didn't say this to Lucy—what really troubles me is that Charles was wounded three days ago! The telegram said December eleventh. That was Tuesday. Three whole days have gone by. Now nearly a fourth. What's happened to him has happened. The people with him, the doctors and nurses, wherever he is— they know precisely. And we don't know! We don't even know where he is!"

"In England, the paper said."

"Well, there you are! England, for heaven's sake!"

"I'm sure you'll know very soon now."

"But I woke up this morning not knowing anything."

It was probably the room above this one—awakening with that hair strewn on the pillow. Going to the window in her nightdress and scratching a name in the frost, melting it with a kiss.

"If only I could have gone on knowing nothing until—I knew everything. Does that sound ridiculous?"

"No, that's understandable." His mind was only fractionally on the conversation. "It really is the human condition, isn't it, to know too little?"

He knew it sounded fatuous, and he felt her impatience.

"But, Mr. Wentworth, there is no mystery about this! What has happened to poor Charles has happened to him, and he has lived more than three days with it. The only mystery is that we haven't been told. Other people know. We don't."

"Sufficient unto the day is the evil thereof."

A more impatient look, strongly felt by Peter.

The front door opened, and there were noises in the hall.

Mollie Webber came in with Betty. At the sight of Julia, Mollie began weeping. Betty stood in the hall doorway, staring with her one eye.

"Mrs. Robertson told me." Mollie came over to Julia and gave her a motherly embrace. "I'm so sad to hear it, dear. Oh, I'm sorry, sir. I don't know there was a visitor."

"Mollie, this is Mr. Wentworth from the cathedral."

It was the maid who had given him the clothes. She did not recognize him.

"Pleased to meet you. This is my granddaughter, Betty. I took her to Eaton's to get a coat. The other one looked so sad on her. And we took it back to the sisters. Then I thought I'd take her over to see Mrs. Robertson. And that's where we heard about Sandy. I hope it's all right with him. I knew him from when he was a baby."

"It's a lovely coat, Betty," Julia said. "The blue—I love the color."

"She's some shy, today." Mollie said. "Not a peep out of her. Come, sweetheart, so's Grandma can make your dinner."

Peter said, "I'll be getting along. I have to take evensong."

"You were very thoughtful to come. I suppose many people would draw a lot of comfort from the church at a time like this. In any case, you were kind to come."

"If there is anything I can do," Peter said. "I'm just across the way in the cathedral. If you need any help. Perhaps I could call again, in a day or so?"

"You think I'll weaken and become a good Christian again?"

That intoxicating smile. She opened the front door. As he shook hands, he was close enough to smell her faint perfume, unfamiliar. It reminded Peter that this woman was a stranger, not an intimate friend.

As he went down the steps, Julia said, "Yes, if you like. Good night, Mr. Wentworth."

"Good night, Mrs. Robertson."

Julia closed the door. Why had she said that? Something about the Reverend Mr. Wentworth made her very uneasy. Yet she was able to talk to him more directly about her feelings than to Lucy or her mother. His eyes disturbed her. His stare was too intense.

Thank goodness everyone had gone. She wanted to think by herself, not have to make conversation. As Mollie said, "Everybody needs a pool of still water."

Julia climbed the stairs and closed the bedroom door behind her. She unbuttoned and removed her high boots, then lay back on the bed with a sigh. She was very tired. She pulled half of the bedspread over her for warmth.

She wanted to bring the fact of Charles's being wounded into a place in her feelings where it was real. She wanted to domesticate it, bring it into the house, into this room—now.

How often had she imagined it. The images had gone though her mind hundreds of times, wounds in his legs, his arms. Those wounds they survived, though sometimes they lost the limb. She shuddered. Was that severely wounded? Probably not. A wound in his head? That was severe. They survive those too, although the results can be ghastly, faces that are not faces, or faces crudely remade like blundered sculpture. But even those imaginings had been hypothetical; like imagining a lover or a sexual encounter, the feeling could be explored—even lived almost—without danger, without the commitment of reality, with the ability to awaken tomorrow morning and know that it isn't so. She could always shake her head and snap out of the daydream, or, feeling the stitch of terror, tell herself it was not real, it would go away. Now she would awaken tomorrow morning knowing it was not a dream.

With the changed awareness came guilt. Was this punishment for the way she had behaved? Julia shook herself. Ridiculous. To believe that she was being punished, she would have to believe in a punisher. She did not. The intense young clergyman had had the good sense not to push it on her, although she could see that he was fidgeting to use his professional wares. No punisher, yet still guilt. She could not erase the idea—no, be sensible!

If her mind strayed from Charles because she was lonely and longing for him, must divine retribution strike *him* down? Was that her punishment? Then why not punish her? Why hurt him? Charles had done nothing. He was a good man, more moral than she was. But that wasn't the point. He was lying somewhere tonight, in pain, with a wound, or several wounds.

She tried to imagine wounds to his body. His smooth white body with its faint fuzz of fair hair, like one in the hundreds of paintings she had studied in Venice and Florence. Crucifixion scenes, Christ removed from the cross. But in the paintings, Christ's body was never tanned at the neck and the arms like Charles's, although Christ's probably was in real life.

To imagine metal tearing into that flesh, creating bloody gashes, made the muscles in her vagina compress involuntarily. To think of his body being cut into, the body she had held in her arms in this bed. She wanted to caress him, hold him gently beside her so that no movement could hurt his wound. Some of the men at Camp Hill groaned when they moved even slightly. She wanted to put no weight on him, but to kiss his cheekbones and eyelids, his forehead; to soothe him to sleep; to say, Charles, I'm here, my darling. It's all right. The hurt will go away. I'll make it go away. Lie still, my sweet. Go to sleep. It will be better when you wake . . .

And she slept.

Peter could not sleep. He was in torment. The face and form and voice of Julia Robertson had haunted his thoughts from the moment her front door closed. He lay tossing in bed, remembering.

He had had to run to the cathedral. There had barely been time to change into a cassock and surplice, his King's College hood and preaching bands, and make his appearance. The two dozen worshipers for evensong were huddled in their overcoats, because the cathedral was still cold. The verger had lighted the minimum number of candles.

Peter's clear diction vanished into confused echoes in the long space between the altar and the lonely cluster of worshipers. The familiar prayers, the words so often said by rote, began to deliver themselves of a fresh and personal meaning.

> If we say that we have no sin, we deceive ourselves, and the truth is not in us: but if we confess our sins, he is faithful and just to forgive us our sins, and to cleanse us from all unrighteousness.

It came to Peter, as it often did, that the Book of Common Prayer, which he had helped to revise, shone through the centuries with the genius of its original authors. No matter what a person might have on his heart or conscience, the ancient formulas sought it out. It served both the simple mind and the subtle. It served even the mind without faith: a priest did not have to believe to say them movingly.

Almighty and most merciful Father, We have erred and strayed from they ways like lost sheep, We have followed too much the devices and desires of our own hearts. . . .

A priest could go on for many years without thinking of the meaning of the words.

Spare thou them, O God, which confess their faults, Restore thou them that are penitent . . .

I have coveted my neighbor's wife. I covet her now, and there is an innocence in my covetousness.

But there was a new thought, not innocent, that could not be put into words. It lived in a dark pool, with an occasional flash of silver, as something darted beneath the surface . . . If a team of dray horses frightened by a tram mounted the sidewalk pavement and killed . . . Something hateful and desirable; hidden, half-forgotten, until another silver dart of fear flashed in the darkness of his feelings: if Charles did not come back . . .

As the priest, Peter was empowered to forgive the sins of the congregation:

He pardoneth and absolveth all them that truly repent and unfeignedly believe his holy Gospel.

Worse, at dinner, the Tobins talked ceaselessly of Charles and the Robertsons. What a tragedy for them! What a nice, quiet boy!

Cynthia Tobin said, "He must have been one of the first to enlist; he's been gone such a long time."

Margery had looked at him with frightened eyes when he appeared, searching his face for something, but had said little. He felt a spasm of panic when he heard her mention Julia.

"I met his wife. She was at Lucy Traverse's for Sarah's birthday when I took Abigail. She's a lovely girl. Very worldly and well traveled. She spent years in Europe. She has really elegant clothes."

"Not any more elegant than yours, Margery," Cynthia said reproachfully.

It annoyed Peter to hear his wife talk about Julia. He interrupted by saying to her father, "The cathedral's beginning to warm up. It was still chilly this evening, but by Sunday services we should be fairly comfortable."

"It didn't take the explosion to make that place a drafty old barn." Tobin laughed. "You'd need boilers the size of the *Mauretania*'s to heat it properly. By the way, you can tell the dean or the bishop I'll have the estimate for the full job in week or so. We're up to our ears at the moment. All these American ships and trains are moving supplies in here so fast, they can't unload."

"Now, George, how often have I said no business at the dinner table?"

"It isn't business. I'm talking to my son-in-law."

"Well, think of something else to talk to him about, and not just construction."

"All right. When are you two going to do something about the maid we agreed about, eh?"

Margery looked beseechingly at Peter, who looked away.

"I've done my side of the deal, and I'm going to pay for it."

"Ssh, George! Not in front of—" Cynthia whispered, indicating the maid bringing in dessert.

"Cook's had to use corn syrup. It's getting so difficult to buy enough sugar. If you ask for five pounds, the shops think you're hoarding. And all those wretched posters to make you feel guilty for buying at all."

"We're a damned sight better off than the chaps who are doing the fighting, and the people in Britain," George said. "Just be thankful we haven't got a boy over there ourselves, getting his guts shot out like the Robertson boy."

"George!"

Peter excused himself, saying he had to work on something for the dean.

"At this time of night?"

"It's about the mass burial for all the dead they haven't identified." Peter said.

"How ghastly!" Cynthia said. "Do you have to go and see it? You know, the descriptions of the bodies they publish in the newspaper are really quite revolting. The details are just too—well, the sort of the thing you don't talk about. I think the explosion is causing a lot of people to forget what decent behavior is."

Tobin laughed. "It's a bit much to expect some poor old biddy blown up in an explosion and found in nothing but her drawers to be on her decent behavior!"

"George, don't be disgusting! You're just trying to provoke me. No, it isn't their fault, of course. But the newspapers don't have to say every gruesome detail."

George snorted and got up from the table. "Want to have a cigar with me before you're off?"

"No, thanks. I'd better be going."

"No rest for the wicked."

Peter walked rapidly down South Park to Victoria Road and knocked on Stewart MacPherson's door. He had to have the diary back.

The look in Stewart's eyes as he handed it back suggested something like sardonic amusement.

"What did you think of it?" Peter asked.

"Well, I can see why she'd be unhappy to lose it. It's certainly very frank."

"Yes, it is."

Peter felt relieved. Obviously the diary had not told Stewart who she was, even though he had actually met her.

"Won't you come in for moment?"

"No, I've got to be getting back."

"What are you going to do with the diary now?"

"I haven't decided."

"Why don't you just burn it? Then it can't cause anyone any distress."

"Perhaps I will."

Alone in his dark house he would read her diary one more time. He welcomed the night and the quiet house. He wanted to reread passages that had become familiar, matching them with the woman he could now clearly visualize.

Now he could go with the real woman into her bedroom, to the cottage near Chester, to the beach with the little girls, watch her remove her stockings to put her legs in the sea. He would watch her sitting, withdrawing the pins from her golden hair, letting it tumble down around her face. He could see her in her own fantasy carrying the little boy to bed, turning in loneliness to crush her breasts against a pillow, moving a breast so that the nipple might be kissed. He could see her in the barn as a little girl, leaping into the hay with her dress flying.

Now he could also hear her voice, feel her intelligence and independence of mind. He could relive the look from her level and appraising eye. He could see the tiny wrinkle of an imminent smile at the corner of her lips. He could see the fold of skin under the eyes that made her look a little tired, or newly awakened, or having recently cried. Now he knew the smell of the perfume she wore.

He read quickly, skipping rapidly. There was almost no need for the diary. He carried it all in his head. But what to do with it? Burn it, as he had intended that first night? How different things would be if he had obeyed that urge. But he did not want the sweet ache for her to leave his system, like honey flowing through his veins, deliciously but painfully. The ache of sexual self-denial was familiar from his disciplined youth; the feeling that had been part of his faith that would bring God to him; the pain in his testicles and inside his groin that came from desire not indulged, passion not released. He felt that now, remembering her: the shape of her thighs under her skirt as she sat, the shadow beneath her breasts in the finely pleated white material of her waist. But there was another ache, a yearning in his soul, a yearning such as he used to feel on May nights, when he and Margery saw each other too briefly, when he walked in the moist air, heavy with the scents of spring, the air so thick that he seemed to breathe love. He felt that now, but a hundred times more intensely.

The Anglican community in Canada must be filled with people whose private lives and consciences would bear public scrutiny no better than hers. That was the weakness offered by Protestantism, especially the Church of England. It was all in one's own conscience.

I will go back to her to ask if there is more news. People who resist the church often welcome us in times of trial. If you ask, they say no, they can manage, thank you. Yet if you come and sit with them, they become dependent. This afternoon she began to unburden herself. If she began, she may continue.

MARGERY WENTWORTH woke up frightened. Perhaps her period had started, although it was two days early. To be sure, she tiptoed down the hall to the bathroom, but there was no sign.

She settled back in bed, trying to recapture the sense of dread that had awakened her. She had been dreaming about Charles

Robertson. They were at a party near Chester. A large house with weathered shingles. The Robertsons . . . probably Lucy who gave the party. They had gone in cars: Peter, Susan Gastonguy, Stewart MacPherson, Lucy's beau, Harold Traverse. A fire on the beach. And Charles was standing shyly apart from his older sister's friends, very helpful with the fire. They had dug a pit and lined it with beach stones for a clambake and built the fire on top of the stones. Lobsters and corn and clams were cooking under a tarpaulin.

Charles had rowed her and Susan out to his boat at its mooring in the cove. They sat in the cockpit, the setting sun reflected on his face . . . freckles so numerous they blended together . . . a shock of tow hair falling over his forehead . . . the line of spruce trees down to the water's edge, granite boulders with seawood exposed by the fallen tide, the water in the quiet cove as still as a pond.

She remembered more as she lay awake in the quiet night in the bed of her childhood, her stuffed animals moved to the chair for the night, except the stuffed rabbit, cuddled beside her. She had slept with the rabbit more nights in her life than she had slept with Peter.

Everyone had gathered driftwood for another fire to provide light and keep the mosquitoes off . . . the mingled smells of lobster, chicken, corn, and clams when the tarpaulin was lifted . . . the fire spitting sparks into the black sky . . . It must have been late July or August, to have corn; the sky was full of stars.

That night Charles, the boy almost a man, sat at the helm of his boat full of shy pride that the older girls had come aboard. The sharp edge of his profile was turned away into the setting sun. Margery had been looking at his hand on the tiller. It rested there, hardened by working the boat, the nails broken in places. Low-angled sun shone on the reddish-blond hair, no more than a down, running up the tanned arm under his rolled-up sleeve. Huddling on the cockpit seat, pulling her skirt down to keep her ankles warm, she had the strongest desire to lean forward the few inches that separated them and put her lips on the back of his hand. The feeling made her swallow and shudder.

When they climbed down into the dinghy to go ashore, Charles held the boat's side and gave her his other hand. She leaned her weight on it to find the thwart with her toe. The feel of his hand stayed in her hand as she clasped it in her lap, sitting in the stern. It was clear some message had passed between them, because he looked at her intently while rowing, the blue eyes half-hidden by the sun-bleached eyelashes.

She saw him in the firelight, watching her across the fire. Peter was near her in the dark but self-conscious about getting too close. Bolder girls and boys snuggled up, half-lying on the sand under the blankets as it got chillier and the fire died, and they sang all the old songs. But Peter kept his distance, sitting with his arms around his knees.

Peter was the best-looking boy, the fastest when they ran, the one who could jump the farthest. And he had come from school with the big prizes. He was the one they all knew would do great things. But when she slipped her hand into his in the dark, he gripped it for a moment, conspiratorially, then slipped it out again lest anyone see. Margery didn't care whether anyone saw. They had kissed in the dark on the way home from parties, and she knew it excited him, because he began to breathe as heavily as she, but it was always Peter who said, "We'd better not go too far."

And across the fire was the gaze of Charles, the lights in his hair shining in the firelight. Obviously he felt something about her, too.

As she listened in the quiet house, her parents asleep across the hall, the children in the next room, that sweet moment from years ago crept away. She tried to draw it back, but the feelings winked out like the fire embers on the beach, until it was too cold to stay and time to leave. They had spent the night with the Robertsons, doubled up, sharing beds, she with Susan. In the morning, they had driven back. As they got into the cars, she had glanced around, but Charles was not in sight. When the car rounded the point, there was his boat with sails set, heading out of the bay, the straw-colored head just visible, until the road turned inland and the trees hid the view.

She had never had doubts about Peter. He was the one all the girls talked about, although no one really understood him. Her mother thought she was sacrificing a lot to marry a man determined to be a clergyman. Her father was sure Peter would "wise up" and change his mind during his college years. Margery wondered whether the life of a clergyman's wife would be too confining socially. Could they give parties? Dances? She loved to dance.

She loved the image of herself dancing, her thin figure in a flowing ball gown. She knew her shoulders looked perfect in the low-necked dresses. Her mother warned her, "You'll have to cut your coat to suit your cloth . . . you'll have to trim your sails." But the money didn't matter; she was dying to be Peter's wife and live with him. Because he was confident and absolutely sure of himself, it gave her confidence. She never had an inkling of the grayness that would cast a shadow over her spirits, turning everything positive into a negative.

Or had she had a premonition? Was that the elusive feeling behind the dream of Charles, that tiny electricity that had passed between them?

Something in the shadows of her dream wouldn't come out, a feeling about Peter sitting carefully apart from her on the beach, the feeling that he didn't really need her. He wanted to marry her. They had discussed that, sealed it with a kiss, and confirmed it often. He wanted to marry her, but she came to believe that he did not find her emotionally necessary. That was how he made her feel: unimportant to him. His work was important. His work came before everything. No one outside the church could imagine how hard the work was.

"I have to go and work on something for the dean."

"At this time of night?"

He was always willing to expend himself, eager to volunteer for extra parish visits, to carry a message for the bishop or the dean to a rector in the country. The wartime shortage of clergymen made them use Peter almost as an archdeacon to the rural rectors. No errand was too little for him. Her father noticed it. "If Peter put a tenth of that energy into any business, he'd be a rich man by thirty." Her mother thought it was part of a wife's duty to understand that his work came before everything.

Margery was not necessary in his life. He didn't wish her out of the way. He loved her and he was very kind to her and the children. He was endlessly long-suffering and helpful around the house. He put up with all her miseries, but if she were to disappear tomorrow, he would still be there. If she had vanished from the dark by the firelight on the beach, he would still be there, sitting with his arms around his knees, self-contained. He would mourn, of course, he would be pitied, but would it tear his heart out if she were gone?

All this was clearer to her for having dreamed of Charles Robertson and awakened with a sense of dread around her heart.

She was unimportant to Peter.

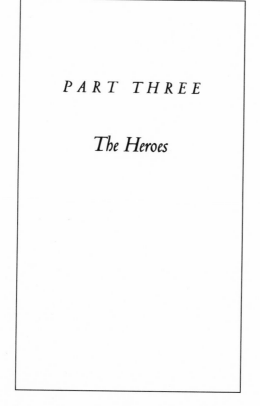

PART THREE

The Heroes

ARCHIE ROBERTSON'S TELEPHONE CALL produced instant action in Ottawa.

The parliamentary private secretary came out of the prime minister's office to give dictation to the personal secretary. "He wants a cable sent urgently to Sir George Perley: Prime Minister to Minister Overseas Military Forces Canada, Argyll House London. Highest priority you cable me personally full details medical condition hospital whereabouts Acting Major C. A. Robertson, 42nd Battalion, 7th Infantry Brigade, Third Canadian Division, Number 897684, reported severely wounded in action on December 11, 1917, evacuated to hospital in England. Repeat highest priority. Borden."

"He's never done that before," said the secretary. "Who's Robertson?"

"Son of a supporter in Halifax. Runs a big shipyard. Important for the war effort. Important for the election."

"I thought they canceled the election in Halifax because of the explosion."

In London, it was late evening when the corporal in communications brought the cable to the duty captain at Argyll House. The duty captain read it twice and went upstairs to waken the colonel, who said, "Where's Sir George?"

"Dining somewhere in Whitehall, I think."

"Well, it's a waste of time trying to find him, and he'd only want us to get cracking on this anyway. Go through the casualty lists for this week. When you find it, get on the blower to the whatever hospital it is for the information. Let's have it by the time the minister gets home from dinner."

"We don't have the lists, sir. New procedures. Casualty lists are now handled at headquarters."

"Since when?"

"New system, while you were on leave."

"Bloody hell. Well, get on to Shorncliffe and get them to read their list."

The captain spent a fruitless half-hour on the phone and woke the colonel up again.

"Duty officer says there's no one in the records department down there till 0800, but tomorrow's Saturday. Won't be till Monday."

"Monday! The prime minister's not going to wait till Monday. Get yourself a staff car and go down to Shorncliffe. I'll call the GIC to get a records officer in there to meet you. When you've found the file, locate the hospital and get the information. Call me back as soon you can."

"Who'll be duty officer here, sir?"

"I'll be the bloody duty officer!"

One staff car was being used by the minister, Sir George Perley, the Ottawa businessman whom the prime minister had sent to London to straighten out the chaotic organization of Canadian forces and give Ottawa a line of command separate from the Imperial General Staff. It took nearly an hour to locate a driver, and the captain left at midnight. It was slow driving through Southeast London to find the Old Kent Road, then on narrow country roads with no headlamps for blackout reasons. At nearly 3 A.M. they arrived at the headquarters of the Canadian Expeditionary Force. A major, resentful at being awakened by a captain, opened the records office and went through the lists of men recently evacuated from field hospitals near the front. They found Acting Major Robertson's name on the list of a military hospital near Winchester, in Hampshire.

"That's a British army hospital. Had an overflow in the Canadian hospitals after Passchendaele. There's a drill to follow. You have to contact the British army medical liaison officer for information about our fellows in British hospitals."

"Where's the liaison officer?"

"London. But you won't get him in the middle of the night. They keep regular office hours."

"On Saturdays?"

"Not on Saturdays."

With difficulty, the captain put through a trunk call to London. The colonel said, "Bloody red tape. It's worse than France. At least people know what they're there for. You'd better go directly to the hospital and find out there."

"That's in Hampshire, sir. We're in Kent."

"Well, drive there! Do I have to come down and show you the way? Use your goddamned initiative. Drive there!"

"Yes, sir."

At half past four the captain and driver began the long drive across Kent, Sussex, and most of Hampshire. The December dawn did not show itself until after 7 A.M., but away from the smoke of London the sun burned through the mist and shone weakly over the pretty countryside.

They pulled up at the British hospital after nine. The captain told the driver to find some breakfast and asked for the senior medical officer. There was a delay because he was operating. The chief nursing sister said she would like to help, but they could not give out information without the authority of the senior medical officer. Would he like a cup of tea?

At 10 A.M. the surgeon came out of the operating theater and lit a cigarette.

"We've got five hundred cases in here, and I don't recognize the name immediately. Robertson, Canadian major?"

"Captain, acting major."

The doctor took a file of forms on a two-hole binder and began to flip through.

"There's been so much traffic through here, it's difficult to keep the files up. Here we are. Robertson, Major, Charles A., Forty-second Battalion, Third Division, Canadian Expeditionary Force. He's in the officers' pavilion at the other end of the building. Bad case. Grenade wound. Multiple injuries."

"What's his condition now?"

"A bit dodgy yesterday but holding on. We'll go along and find out. If I don't come with you, the sister will put you through a rigamarole. Come on. The fresh air will do me good."

They walked on crunching gravel the length of the hospital, a Georgian mansion with ugly temporary structures tacked on for new wards.

"Is this Major Robertson someone special that you've come all the way down from London to ask about him?"

"It's a personal interest of our prime minister's."

"In my experience the politicians usually want to put as big a distance as they can between themselves and the casualties. Not good for civilian morale."

"Actually, Borden hasn't been like that. When he toured the front, he visited thirty-seven hospitals."

They went into the temporary building. Through glass panes in the doors they could see two long rows of beds, with Christmas decorations festooning the ceiling.

"Morning, Sister. Special request. This officer has come down from London. He needs to visit one of our customers. A Canadian, Major Robertson."

The nurse's handsome, countrywoman's face was expressionless. She said, "Come in, sir." Both men entered.

In her office, she closed the door. "Then it's bad news you've come for, sir. Major Robertson died last night. I was just completing the forms." She looked apologetic. "I never thought he had much of a chance, Doctor."

The doctor looked at the forms. "Acute peritonitis from severe abdominal wounds. They did their best at the field hospital to clean him up, and we operated again here. No way to stop the infection. They kept him on morphine to damp down the pain. Did he say anything, Sister; any messages?"

"He never really regained consciousness, sir."

"Where's the body?"

"It was moved to the mortuary during the night."

"Do you want to see it?" he asked the captain, casually.

The captain swallowed. "I suppose I'd better, in case I'm asked."

"Any personal effects?"

"Yes, sir. I was going to send them on through the usual channels."

"I think we can safely entrust them to the captain."

He was handed an OHMS envelope, asked to sign for a watch, a wallet, some letters, and French coins.

The nurse softened for a moment. "I'm very sorry you had to come all that way for this, dear."

"Thank you, Sister."

"God bless."

They walked on the dewy gravel to the main building. The doctor smoked another cigarette.

"You had breakfast?"

"No."

"Nor have I. Come and join me after we've viewed the body. We have quite a good mess. Eggs, bacon, and toast. That suit you?"

The captain dreaded what he had to do. He had not yet been to the front.

"Nice morning, sir," the mortuary attendant said cheerfully to the medical officer, and put down his mug of tea.

"Do you recognize him?" the doctor asked when the covering was drawn back.

"I don't know him," the captain said, looking at the silent face covered with faded freckles.

"Good-looking chap. Our men seem so weedy beside you Canadians. Especially other ranks. Must be a healthier life, better food, better exercise. I've been meaning to do a systematic comparison, skeletal structure, general musculature. It's most obvious in shoulder and chest development. Look at this. Length of the clavicle."

The doctor spread his hand to span the collarbone on the corpse. The pressure of thumb and little finger left slight depressions when he lifted his hand away.

"Full span. Nine inches or so. But I've never had the time to make the records. Too much work dealing with the daily traffic through here. Well, you can tell them his face wasn't banged up, but the rest of him"—he indicated the body still covered by a sheet —"I don't think you'd want to see that. Come and let's eat."

"I think I'd better telephone my HQ first."

"Suit yourself. You can use my office."


The telegram caught up with Sir Robert Borden in Cornwall, Ontario. His private railway car had left Ottawa overnight for a day of election speeches along Lake Ontario—Prescott, Brockville, Kingston—and a major rally in Toronto that evening.

REGRET INFORM YOU MAJOR C. A. ROBERTSON DIED LAST NIGHT BRITISH MILITARY HOSPITAL HAMPSHIRE FROM EXTENSIVE ABDOMINAL WOUNDS CAUSED BY EXPLODING GRENADE. HAVE SENT URGENT SIGNAL GENERAL CURRIE GHOCEF FRANCE FOR FULLEST PARTICULARS OF ACTION IN WHICH ROBERTSON WOUNDED TOGETHER WITH ANY RECOMMENDATION FOR DECORATIONS. GEORGE PERLEY

The prime minister watched the wintry lakeshore slide by; giant slabs of tortured ice moved by incredible forces littered the shore.

How terrible to have to tell Archie Robertson. He could not leave it to the Records Office in the Department of Militia and Defense. The normal channels took days, the form letter from Buckingham Palace weeks, even months. From old friendship, not just political necessity, he owed Archie that courtesy.

"See if you can arrange a private place for me to telephone when we get to Prescott. A trunk call. To Archibald Robertson in Halifax. Probably at his home; it's Saturday."

"Yes, Prime Minister."

Recommendations for decorations. Perley's political instincts were sharpening. Decorations could ease the pain for the family. Not bloody much, but something. A grenade wound in the abdomen. Only very brave or very foolish fellows received such wounds. The ghastly sights from his own trip to the field hospitals remained with him: handsome young faces trying to grin through terrible boils around the neck and armpits from the mustard gas. The words of his campaign speeches were in the front of his thoughts. For whose future was he spending these young lives? Not just for the king and empire. How hollow Laurier's "Ready, aye, ready" sounded now with the conscription tearing the heart out of Quebec's loyalty to Canada. Even one of his own election meetings had been broken up by anticonscription rioters. Shouted him off the platform, in Ontario, the bedrock of imperial sentiment.

But that was the point. Only in name now was this terrible sacrifice for the empire. It was really to buy Canadian dignity and independence, almost as though Canada were fighting Britain for her independence. Ironically, Canadians were fighting Germans for their independence from Britain; even more ironically, fighting in France. In 1776 the Americans had fought the British directly. The price was far cheaper then. Primitive ordnance and fewer men under arms. How many men did Washington lose? A few thousand in battle? Eight thousand; something like that. Nothing like the slaughter in this war. Canada had already lost nearly forty thousand.

At least they had pulled the Canadian troops away from the hopeless stupidity of some British commanders. Max Aitken was right: the British generals were donkeys, willing to expend their men so casually, so ruthlessly. Would the Americans be more sparing with their doughboys? They hadn't actually gone into battle yet. If the Yanks had Canadian losses proportionate to their population, that would be nearly half a million dead. Inconceivable. They would go mad. Stage a revolution, storm the White House.

But you couldn't sell this war by calling it a war of independence from Britain. The very people most willing to fight didn't want real independence. Now there were very few eager to fight at all. Conscription was not working. For all the political cost, few were being dragged out by the law. Shame was a better recruiter than the law. Even the women handing out white feathers.

Shame and heroism make the brave juices flow in other men. They can't resist. Like the Highland regiments. Robertson's battalion, the 42nd, called themselves the Royal Highlanders of Canada. Brilliant recruiting device. If you put them in kilts and give them a pipe band, the recruits swarm in—Scottish background or not. You need heroes. Young Robertson might be a hero—and from a Highland regiment to boot.

Borden could warm to that. It was exploiting the dead, but compensation for the family. It would assist recruitment, and that would speed the end of the war; and it was effective politics, when the Unionist coalition needed strong support. It would make Archie and Elizabeth Robertson feel better. Pity it wasn't the Nova Scotia Highlanders, but no matter. A Highland officer hero. That was the tonic for Nova Scotians wearied by the war, prostrated by the explosion. An officer with a grenade wound in the abdomen must be a hero.

The prime minister was impatient for the facts. He wanted them before the train stopped and he had to put in the terrible call to Halifax.

AS A CHILD, Julia knew it had snowed the moment she was awake. Without moving her head from the pillow she knew the outside sounds were padded, as though the horses were wearing thick slippers. The snow drank up sounds.

With her eyes closed she could imagine the ceiling lighter because of the light reflected upward from the snow, faces freshly seen because the light came from below their chins and eye sockets, making them seem weightless. Snow made the house feel warmer, cozier.

Blond hair scattered on the pillow, nose burrowed under the

quilt, for a second Julia experienced the pleasure of a child waking to that muted world. Then she remembered. Today was different from yesterday; knowing made all the time before yesterday different from all the time after. The heartache was fresh each time she remembered.

The house was very quiet. She got up and opened the curtains to find it was snowing heavily. She got back into bed and watched the soft flakes falling past the black limbs of the trees. She felt a different person. Yesterday she was the wife of a man who had gone through two years at the front unscathed. Now she was a woman who knew that her husband had been badly hurt.

But how badly? It was intolerable not to know. Surely they could have sent more details. If they could send one telegram, they could send another. Perhaps it was a gas attack and they didn't want to say until they saw how he was recovering. The newspapers said that some men recovered completely with no ill effects, others didn't. Some were blinded. Again her thoughts went through the other possibilities.

She threw back the bedclothes and dressed hurriedly. She had to be busy.

Why doesn't my face show the anxiety I feel? She looked at herself as she combed out her hair, then pinned it in a knot on top of her head. She saw the shadows under her eyes from too little sleep.

Many times in recent days she had thought of the diary as a place to turn to, as a friend, then remembered it was gone. She clasped her hands on her dressing table and rested her chin on them.

I am losing my sense of certainty about things. But I cannot bear to sit still. I will go down and talk to Mollie and Betty.

Downstairs she found the house empty and a note from Mollie: "Mr. Stewart" had taken them to the doctor for Betty's eye. It added, "There is coffee into the pot."

She drank a cup of coffee at the kitchen table, remembering the comfortable feeling she had had when talking to Stewart MacPherson. How different it was with Peter Wentworth, whose eyes seemed to devour her, to be looking all over her at once.

What could she do? Write to her mother and father. But she dreaded it; besides it was pointless to write until she knew exactly what had happened. She could call on Lucy and the girls, who treated her more as a big sister than an aunt. No, she did not want to play Old Maid or Fish. She could go to the senior Robertsons. She could telephone them. They would telephone her as soon as they knew. She could buy a Christmas present for Betty. It was only ten days until Christmas. But the shops were so gloomy with their windows boarded up.

The diary had made her feel better, letting her pour into words whatever she felt. The familiar tremor of fear went through her with the thought that someone had read it and again the rationalization: they could not know who wrote it. It must be up there, somewhere in the wreckage and the snow in the North End.

You could start another diary. I could, but I don't have a book to write in. You could start in on writing paper. It isn't the same. She felt dithery, unable to make up her mind. She put down her cup with a clatter and walked to the front door, then stood, her arms clasped in front for warmth, watching the snow fall. Outside it felt soft and inviting. With a small flush of good spirits, she closed the door and started putting on her outdoor boots and coat. She would go for a walk in the snow. She put on the hat of a fox fur dyed black that her mother had given her and picked up the matching muff.

It was exhilarating to be out. The large white flakes landed delicately on the muff. All the sounds of the street were muted. Trees and houses receded into gray shadows behind the swirling curtains of snow. The nearest flakes formed one curtain and the others receding seemed to form other curtains, like successive layers of open lace billowing softly. There was no wind and the snow fell almost vertically; only the larger flakes side-slipped like white feathers. Immediately Julia felt better for the exercise of walking, difficult in the accumulating snow on the unshoveled sidewalks. She strode out, her skirt brushing the snow, her breath making a little cloud on the air. She was soothed by the quiet, softly falling universe, and calmer, as though by coming out she had left half of her anxieties behind her. She came to the end of South Park Street and entered Young Avenue.

Perhaps I will go as far as Point Pleasant and look at the sea with the snow falling on it.

She passed the Robertsons' house, looking in case anyone waved so that she could wave and say she would drop in later, but she saw no one.

Her feelings about Charles had been so varied: intense physical longing for him, efforts to make him feel closer. She had devoured all the evidence of his boyhood, worried that he had never been really close to her. And then, it was as though he had come back, starting with the letter for her birthday and the mayflowers.

Then his attention seemed to recede again and she had noticed Neville Boiscoyne. In the fall Charles again began sounding more present. He was like a man standing in a fog who suddenly steps forward and is sharply in focus.

It made her feel Charles knew that Neville was tempting her and had flashed back to claim his rights. Ridiculous—but it happened so fortuitously. The big battles of Hill 70 and Passchendaele had given Charles the new sense of mission and of himself. There he was, even more exciting a man than she had thought him before. A man brave and clear-headed.

In one of the last letters, he wrote, "After this nonsense is over, I would like to go with you to all those places you know and I don't: Venice, Florence, and the rest, and have you tell me all the things I am so ignorant about."

What joy it would be to go back to Europe with him after the war, to the magnificent places like San Marco or the tiny, humble places that give the Old World its delicious flavor. A lazy afternoon in early summer in Paris: slow lunch in a small restaurant. Asperges à la vinaigrette. A glass of wine. The smells of Paris. Its horses. Its tobacco. A small hotel room with tiny roses on the wallpaper, the long French window open, a thin white curtain idling in the warm afternoon light, the atmosphere in the Matisse interiors, the sounds of children distant in a courtyard.

She had reached the park. The snow was too deep to walk all the way to the Point. The ploughs had not been out. She walked in a little way under the spruce trees laden with new snow, and had to lift her skirt because the snow was deeper. She felt it cold against her stockings over the tops of her boots. She shook the snow off her hat and muff and stood in the silence, contented. From when she was a little girl, she had thought of snow as a protector. It was like thick woolly white blankets lying on everything. It kept the pine needles and the seeds of the wildflowers warm through the winter. Under the trees, where the new snow had not drifted, there were small tracks where mice had scurried about, out of their warm nests. Larger tracks where a squirrel had leaped, a little pile of reddish husks where he had shelled a pine cone. Outside the roof formed by the spruce boughs, the snow fell silently. She was deeply happy.

No matter what has happened to him, we will be all right and I will love him with all my heart.

She walked gaily back up Young Avenue. Two small boys, bundled up in woollen hats and scarves, watched her. When she passed, a snowball smacked into the snow just ahead of her. She glanced around. The boys ducked behind a bush. Julia bent down and quickly made a snowball herself but hid it behind her muff as she straightened up. The boys looked out from the bush, and she threw the snowball hard and true. It hit the bush, loosening a shower of snow on their heads.

One of them said, "That's not fair!" She laughed and walked on, feeling very young herself, conscious of the extra sense of healthiness that came from being outside and active in the winter.

When she came to the Robertsons' front door, her cheeks were glowing from the cold, and she knew Archie Robertson would say, "That's put a bit of color in your cheeks, lassie."

But he did not. He opened the door to her knock and looked at her with a face drained of good spirits.

"Julia! I've been trying to ring you."

"Tell me! Do you have news?"

"It's almost more than I can bear to tell, my dear."

"What is it? Tell me!"

"He died last night. The prime minister called me himself. I must say, it was very kind of him."

"But he was only wounded!"

Archie put an arm around her. "He was very badly wounded. It was amazing he lived at all. They got him to hospital in England. He held his own for a day or two. Then last night he died."

"Where is Mrs. Robertson?"

"Upstairs in her room."

"May I go up and see her?"

"Of course."

Elizabeth was not lying down. She was sitting in a chaise longue with her feet up, looking at the snow fall past the windows.

"Oh, Julia! My dear girl!" She held out her arms to Julia, who sat on the chaise, and they embraced and cried. Archie Robertson stood there and put a hand on each of the women's shoulders. He tried to say something comforting, but no words came and his throat was sore. He had to take his hands away because his own eyes were full. He wanted to tell Julia what else the prime minister had said.

"Archie, you can be very proud. Your son died a hero's death. He was a very brave young man. As soon as I learn the exact particulars, I will let you know. God bless you." It was the prime minister, after all.

That did not matter now. He wiped his eyes and looked at his wife and his daughter-in-law. Julia had forgotten to take off her coat and hat. Her bright cheeks and her blond hair showed beneath the black fur. She looked radiant, despite her tears. Pools of water from melting snow on her boots were forming on the carpet. It didn't matter. Charles the hero did not matter.

"All the same, I think it was very good of Borden to call himself."

Elizabeth Robertson reached up and took his hand. She said, gently, "Archie, please stop saying that."

BETTY CRIED OUT, "Oh, please! Oh, please! Oh, please! That hurts!"

"It's all right. I've finished now." Dr. McKenna lowered the instrument through which he had been examining Betty's empty eye socket. Stewart felt as relieved as the child. The doctor's manner was brusque, perhaps from exhaustion. The man was working eighteen hours a day. Even with help from eye doctors from the United States and the rest of Canada, he and his colleagues were overwhelmed by the number of cases. Too many people had gone innocently to their windows to watch the fire on the *Mont Blanc*.

He pushed the bright electric lamp away and rubbed his eyes under his own spectacles. He said to Mollie, "Take her outside. I need a word with Mr. MacPherson."

"Her bandage?" Mollie whispered, looking horrified that Betty's socket would be left uncovered.

"Quite so. My nurse will replace the dressing."

Betty slid down from the examination chair and went out with her grandmother. Dr. McKenna turned to Stewart. "There's something I can't quite see without going farther in. I'll hurt her too much unless she's asleep."

"What do you think it is?"

"The reason it hurts is that there's another sliver of glass in there, or the end of the original sliver. I'm worried about how far it's penetrated. It has perforated the lining in the nasal corner, across the optic nerve. Some strands of the nerve have probably been severed, which is why she lost the sight of the right eye. But—"

"Can you remove it?"

"I shall have to," he said crossly. "I have a hundred other patients to see, but I can't leave her with a piece of glass in there. I'll have to have her anesthetized and do it in an operating theater."

"When would you be able to do that?"

"Well, now! I mean right now."

"I'd better warn her what's going to happen."

"The less she knows, the better. Just worry her more." Impatiently, McKenna pulled a slim gold watch from his waistcoat pocket, looked, and snapped it shut.

"I have just time if I do it at once."

Betty did not want to be put to sleep again. She clung to Mollie when she saw the operating theater. She pressed her bandaged eye against Mollie's breast and whimpered in fear.

"There, there, sweetheart. It's going to be all right. The doctor just wants to put you to sleep for a few minutes so he can stop your eye from hurting."

"He'll make me die, like Mama," she wailed.

"No, no, he won't."

A theater nurse and the anesthetist came in, and Betty clung more tightly to Mollie.

"Betty." Stewart bent down and said quietly, "Come along and lie down, like a brave girl. Your granny can hold your hand while you fall asleep."

Stiff with fear, she let him lift her onto the table. When the anesthetist put white gauze over her mouth and nose, she raised her hands to take it away, but the nurse and Mollie held her arms. As drops of chloroform fell on the gauze, he said, "Now, Betty, can you count to ten?" She counted to three and her voice faded.

Stewart and Mollie sat in a waiting room.

"How is Mrs. Robertson taking the news of her husband being wounded?"

"She's quiet about it. They're all worried because they've heard nothing."

"I wanted to call her when I read it in the paper. But I didn't want to disturb her."

"Well, you come on in and see her when we get back with Betty. She could do with some cheering up."

McKenna came out, wearing rubber gloves and an apron over his waistcoat. His manner was gentler.

"She's going to be groggy for a while. If you'd like to be with her, the nurse will bring her out in a moment." To Stewart: "Come down the hall for a moment." He stopped in an alcove and said condescendingly, the medical professor to the student, "Do they teach you people in psychology any anatomy?"

"A certain amount."

"You know what the pituitary is?"

"Roughly speaking, yes."

"Small gland, under the hypothalamus, directly behind the optic chiasmus."

"Yes, I know."

"This child no longer has one."

"I don't understand."

"I've never heard of its happening before. I got the sliver of glass, like this"—he held up his gloved fingers. "It has cut part of the optic nerve, missed the chiasmus, penetrated the nasal cavity, under the brain, and severed the stalk that attached the pituitary to the hypothalamus. It is quite incredible."

"What does it mean?"

"Well, my area is ophthalmology. But I would guess that it means no growth."

"No growth?"

"Growth. People think of it as the growth gland. How old is she?"

"Nine."

"She may grow old as a little girl of nine—if other factors don't intervene and cause other conditions."

"Will she be healthy?"

"I can't say. The pituitary does things we can only guess at. I strongly urge that you consult a neurologist, like Lewis Watson here at Dal. But she'll be comfortable now, with the glass removed."

"What about the talk we had of replacing her eye?"

"Do you still want to bother with that?" McKenna glanced down the hall. Stewart took it to mean, It's only your maid's grandchild.

Stewart felt himself flushing. "Of course I want to bother."

"In a week or so, we'll look at that. It will be a little sore for now. I've put in a few small stitches to close the wound."

When he drove them home, Betty still drowsy, lolling on Mollie's shoulder like a little girl, he noticed that she switched back and forth, from quite grown-up to a much younger child.

"I think she'd like to have a lie-down, wouldn't you, dearie?"

"Is Mama ever coming back from being dead?" Betty asked. She looked ready to suck her thumb.

"No, sweetheart." Mollie kissed her. "I'll just take her upstairs and see if Mrs. Robertson is there. Ooh, you're a heavy load!"

He was sure Julia was not in the house and felt an intruder. He would say goodbye to Mollie when she came downstairs. He studied the cool room, with its gray marble fireplace, chairs in pale velvet and silk, yellow silk curtains with a fringe, a gilt mirror, a light-toned oriental rug on a polished floor. Colored engravings of the *Cries of London*. Formal and conventional but not stiff.

He looked more closely at the cluster of framed photographs. Beside the picture of Charles in uniform was their wedding picture.

He looked at her open face, her small waist, her bust and hips hidden by flounces and ruffles, at the way her long fingers held Charles's arm with light possession. Would Stewart have thought her so desirable, so intriguing, if he had never known about her diary? Obviously she was a beautiful woman. The groom looked shyly happy, and Julia looked poised and relaxed, as though she wore this fussy wedding dress frequently, part of her wardrobe.

How many people can look at a stranger's wedding photograph and have in his head information about the bride's private thoughts? This woman liked sex and admitted it to herself. Usually you knew that about a woman only when she became a lover. And when you knew it about a lover, it was overlaid with hopes, fears, jealousies, boredom, staleness, ungainly postures, a voice too shrill, an unpleasant odor, some coarseness of manner. Becoming lovers diluted curiosity as it satisfied it.

The wedding picture fed his curiosity about Julia.

Life does not permit you to read the other person's part before you enter the scene, to read the character in a novel and then become a character yourself.

Mollie came downstairs.

"She's not in, Mr. MacPherson, I'm sorry to say. She must have gone to the Robertsons' for more news."

"We can talk later. I think another doctor should see Betty. I'll inquire about that."

"I don't know how to thank you, sir. You've done so much for us. Poor little thing. She went right to sleep. She's no trouble to look after. In one way I would love it if she never did grow up."

JULIA GOT UP from Elizabeth's chaise longue.

"I'd like to go out for a few minutes. By myself. A few minutes alone. Please. I'll be all right. I just need a few minutes."

She wanted to run back to the protection of the woods. She walked quickly toward the park, where the dark shadows and the falling snow had wrapped her in a soothing bandage.

He is dead. I can't believe it. He is dead. Charles is dead. Charles is dead. My husband is dead. My darling is dead.

She came to the place where she had stood before. Her tracks were almost covered with new snow, but in the shadow of the trees they were as she had left them. She stood where she had stood with such happy fantasies an hour earlier. How could the heart stand such lurches from joy to despair?

He is dead. I am standing here in the snow. My body is warm. My head is warm inside the fur. My hands are warm inside the muff. My whole body is alive. My face is cold. The cold is beginning to pinch my toes. But I am standing in the snow with my warm blood moving through me, and he is lying somewhere cold —dead—no blood moving. His heart is not beating. If I touched him, he would be cold and still. They will bury him in England.

All his clothes are in the cupboard at home. He will not wear them now. They will bury him in a uniform. Bury him. There will be a cross in some graveyard in England. I will never see him again. I will never see him again. The pipes he left. All of those things from his boyhood that his mother kept in the cottage. His boat! He will not come back to sail the boat.

Still the snow fell, noiselessly, outside the shelter of the sympathetic trees. Julia felt the cold steal up her legs. Her feet were freezing, but she did not move.

On my birthday, I put my legs in the sea. Bearing the cold made me feel closer to Charles. I tried to feel closer by holding his letters to me. Touching his clothes. The smell has gone from his clothes. I thought he would come back and make them smell of him again. He will not come back. Now there is nothing to feel closer to. He is dead. If he were lying here now, with the snow falling on him, he would not feel it. He does not know anything. If I lay down, I would slowly freeze. Then the snow would cover me and I would not feel it. I would be a mound under the snow.

Yesterday, he could still feel, perhaps feel terrible pain. Now he can feel nothing.

Charles is dead. Dead. Now I have no husband. She cried like a little girl, her breast heaving, gulping sobs shaking her chest. The tears ran warm down her face. "It isn't fair! It isn't fair!"

After a few minutes, Julia found a handkerchief and dried her cheeks. She shuddered, noticing that she was very cold. She had to move. She started to wade through the snow to Young Avenue, her legs stiff from standing still so long.

As she crossed the bridge over the new cutting, a train was panting underneath, the engine just getting up speed. Giant clouds of smoke puffed up one side of the bridge and then the other. Julia leaned on the parapet for a moment. She could see it was a hospital train. Wounded men, freshly arrived in a ship from England, leaving for their homes across Canada. For some of them, days of jolting, rattling travel, with wounds aching, stumps still burning, minds tormented with anxiety about how their wives, girls, mothers, bosses, would welcome them. But they were alive—and going home.

Julia watched the rear car of the retreating train and saw its red signal light dissolve into the falling snow.

They would be home by Christmas, even those who lived in British Columbia. She and Charles had never had their own Christmas. The Christmas after their wedding they had spent with his parents.

We never had our own Christmas tree. Now we will never have a Christmas together.


MARGERY AGREED TO GO HOME with the children. Peter would come and get her after church on Sunday.

"You can have Sunday lunch with us and then go." Cynthia Tobin always wanted to keep them for meals.

The decision revived the pressure about a maid.

"If you're not going to do it yourself, we can find you a good strong girl from Newfoundland. You'll have to train her, of course. They don't know anything, these girls. They come straight out of the fishing villages, but they learn and they're hard workers. I will say that for them."

"Mother, I don't think I'd be very good at training a maid. I don't think I could face it."

Her father said, "Cynthia, it's far better to find someone already trained. If it costs a dollar or two more a week, what's the odds? The important thing is to get Margie some help right away."

"Well, it's *your* money, George! But you needn't snap at me! I was just trying to be helpful."

"I am not snapping, Cynthia. I was just stating the facts." He turned back to his paper and muttered, "Women!"

"What did you say, George?"

"I said women."

"And what did you mean by that?"

In these familiar exchanges Cynthia's tone grew haughtier and haughtier.

"Mother, I can't stand to hear you going at Daddy like this!" Margery got up and ran up stairs.

"Cynthia, you make her nervous."

"Who has made her nervous? Not I. Peter, do excuse our bad manners. I just find it all a little trying. I have trouble enough keeping an adequate staff in this house. The girls are getting so independent. Housework isn't good enough for them. They want to work in the factories so that they can go out to the pictures in the evening. It's going to be very hard to find someone suitable for Margery. She really needs some nice, comfortable, motherly woman."

Someone like Mollie. Peter thought of the comfortable woman with her South Shore accent and sturdy appearance, as capable of rowing a dory in rough weather as polishing the floor. His mind wandered. Mollie and the rum. Mollie and the turkey neck. The idea of Mollie had the pleasurable glow of Julia around it.

Cynthia was talking to him. "What Margery doesn't need, Peter, is some grand little parlor miss, putting on elegant airs and wanting two nights a week and an afternoon off. That's why I say someone not too fastidious but reliable and comfortable. Someone who can cook, simply and wholesomely, keep the house clean, do the laundry and the marketing, and take the children off Margery's hands when she needs a rest."

"That's sounds like two maids to me." George Tobin laughed.

"That shows how little you know how I manage, George. When I give a girl a home and a good position, I expect my money's worth."

"Factory jobs may not be so attractive now," George said. "In the Dominion Textile works, most of the girls died. The floors with the machines fell down on the others." He smacked his hands together. "Each one fell on the one below. Good cast-concrete and brick building too. I'm glad it wasn't one of ours."

IT TOOK STEWART SEVERAL HOURS to administer the Woodworth Psychoneurotic Inventory to Dr. Hart's seven shell-shock patients. At first they were sullen and suspicious, or apathetic. The test questionnaire was headed "Personal Data Sheet," and he had to explain repeatedly that its purpose was to help the men adjust to civilian life and discover what kinds of work they would be suited for. Mather, the deaf man, had to have everything explained in written notes.

"All you have to do is circle the answer you mean, yes or no."

He did not know how intelligent or even literate they were, or whether they could cooperate, but army discipline prevailed. They treated Stewart like an officer, docilely taking up the pencils he provided and bending over the sheets. Corporal Ransome, whose legs were paralyzed, carefully leaned his crutches against the edge of the table. Private O'Malley's hands continued to shake when he was thinking but stopped momentarily as he marked an answer. The concentration appeared to make Private Jenkins stop weeping and whispering to himself.

Stewart watched them silently. They were like obedient children in school, but exhausted, defeated children, resigned to yet another pointless exercise in military life. Now he could see clearly the psychology of patient/soldier relating to doctor/officer. As officers, doctors still held authority over the patients, and the military doctor's primary role was to convince soldiers they were not sick. Some army psychiatrists thought shell-shock was an assertion of the rebellious claims of the individual against the moral demands of the state. At worst, they agreed with the army command: shell shock was a cover for cowardice and effeminacy. If the patient as a soldier could not trust the doctor as an officer to make only a medical decision, the neurotic condition could worsen.

So could the new procedures these men had all come through. By the summer of 1917 the desperate need for manpower had convinced the British and Canadian armies to stop soldiers claiming shell shock as an easy way out.

Officers and doctors at the front were forbidden to use the term. A soldier showing such symptoms at field hospitals was labeled NYDN (Not Yet Diagnosed, Nervous) and immediately evacuated to one of the new neurological units set up at the five base hospitals serving the British armies. The specialist who examined him had to fill out a form, W3436, describing his symptoms and what the soldier said had happened to him. Form W3436 could become a passport to safety or death. The form went back to the officer commanding the soldier's unit. He had to declare in writing whether the soldier had been subjected to exceptional battle conditions, worse than other men had undergone without showing nervous symptoms. If the CO said no, the W3436 was sent to the adjutant's branch of the division for investigation and possible court-martial proceedings. If the CO said yes, the conditions had been exceptional, the soldier was classified a shell-shock case and sent back to hospital in England to undergo the "quick cure." These men had come through that process.

Stewart was impatient for them to finish. Each question had a favorable or unfavorable answer, unfavorable indicating the neurotic response, although many were answers a well-adjusted person might choose. Woodworth had already corrected for that by eliminating questions that too many normal people answered unfavorably.

*Were you unhappy when you were 14 to 18 years old?* The favorable response was *No,* but Stewart could truthfully have answered *Yes.*

An unfavorable response would be meaningful only if the subject gave unfavorable responses to enough related questions to indicate a pattern.

*Did you have a happy childhood?* (Unfavorable response: *No*)

*Were you considered a bad boy?* (Unfavorable: *Yes*)

*As a child, did you like to play alone better than playing with other children?* (Unfavorable: *Yes*)

*Did the other children let you play with them?* (Unfavorable: *No*)

*Were you shy with other boys?* (Unfavorable: *Yes*)

Unfavorable answers to all those questions would be an indication of unhappiness, or antisocial moods or behavior. But those were innocuous compared with later questions about phobias, nightmares, sex, suicide, family insanity, drunkenness, a drug habit, and the whole range of psychoneurotic symptoms:

*Are you ever bothered by the feeling that people are reading your thoughts?*

*Are you troubled with the idea that people are watching you in the street?*

*Does it make you uneasy to cross a wide street or open square?*

*Does it make you uneasy to sit in a small room with the door shut?*

*Can you do good work while people are looking at you?*

*Does some particularly useless thought keep coming into your head to bother you?*

It would be interesting, Stewart thought, to try to answer the questions himself, being as honest as he could be. Useless thoughts certainly came into his head to bother him; for one, Julia Robertson kept entering his mind, not a symptom of neurosis, just plain longing for what he couldn't have.

*At night are you troubled with the idea that someone is following you?*

*Do you find it difficult to pass urine in the presence of others?*

*Do your feelings keep changing from happy to sad and from sad to happy without any reason?*

A subject's score was obtained by adding his unfavorable answers and comparing the total with averages Woodworth had obtained by testing both normal individuals and groups of people diagnosed as neurotic.

The idea of the test fascinated Stewart. It was the first systematic attempt to measure differences in human personality, to identify possibly neurotic people. If administered widely, it could indicate what proportion of the general population suffered from some neurotic symptoms. It would be interesting to give it to all his classes. No, Dalhousie would never permit students to be asked these questions. If it had been available in 1914, some of the unfortunate men now in front of him might have been excused from military service. Thousands might have been spared the mental tortures they were now experiencing and the prospect of a lifetime of insanity, or something close to it.

He felt like a child eager to get home to try a new toy. He

wanted the men to finish so that he could take their questionnaires away and analyze their answers.

MR. POLANSKI, the tailor in the small shop on Barrington Street, looked up from his pressing iron.

"Yes? Oh, I didn't recognize you in the clothes, Reverend."

Peter was wearing a tweed overcoat with the collar turned up. The small shop was hung everywhere with uniforms being pressed, altered, or having new stripes, medal ribbons, or insignia sewn on. The military atmosphere made Peter feel out of place.

Polanski had a deferential yet sardonic manner. In previous visits, Peter was not sure that he was not being quietly mocked, either in himself or his profession. Polanski gave the impression of being much better educated than his profession suggested.

"You have been praying hard, Reverend."

The tailor brought forward the black suit Peter had left for mending.

"It was just after the explosion. I was helping with some of the victims. I couldn't think about my clothes."

"Yeah, explosion. I can't get anyone to fix the window. Look at it. Without daylight, I can't see. No glass. No men to put the glass. Look, I can't make good as new. I have to put patches here, see? Invisible weaving here, maybe. Here patches. Even very fine stitches and, believe me, I can do it fine, it will show. In a dark church you get away with it. Outside, it shows. It needs a new suit."

"I was afraid of that."

"Why be afraid? I can make you a suit. Better than this you got from Colwell's. What did you pay at that fancy place? A fancy price?"

The conversation was embarrassing Peter. "Ten or twelve dollars, I suppose."

"Ten or twelve dollars! They robbed you. You're paying for their fancy address. For you I can do as good a suit as this for five dollars. Come here. Look at this cloth. A special order. Navy cloth. Very fine for a minister's suit."

He looked through thick spectacles, his unlit cigarette in his lips. He could see the struggle in Peter's face. No gentleman had a suit made by the corner tailor. He should go back to Colwell's. As careful as his mother was with money, she would have said, "A man's clothes have to look right. Tailoring is not like dressmaking." Margery would insist.

"Look—four dollars for the suit, with vest. How can you go wrong? You've got to be well dressed or they don't respect you. Now, for Catholics is easier. They wear robes. Under robes, some old pair of pants. Just slip off the jacket. I'll take the measurements. Who's to know you got patches in your pants if you're a Catholic priest? It's an advantage."

"Are you Catholic?" Peter asked.

"Sure, what you think? Most Poles are Catholics."

Peter didn't say. He had assumed the tailor was Jewish. He was short, with a few strands of hair across his naked pate.

"So what's wrong with this suit?"

Peter was wearing the gray suit Margery had bought him.

"The color is wrong—for winter." How could he explain to a Catholic tailor from Poland that for Anglican ministers it was Low Church to wear gray. It bothered Peter, because he liked gray suits. He felt a lighter, freer person in gray, and this one gave him the pleasure of wearing a new suit. But he had put it on only to come to the tailor.

Polanski stood on a small stool to measure Peter's shoulder. The shop smelled of stale sweat from the clothes, and cigarettes, and singed wool from the ironing.

"Lucky you're a minister, even if it don't pay much. You're not over there fighting." He nodded toward Barrington Street and the Ocean terminal, where the troopships came and went.

"They're trying to get all young fellows like you."

The tape measure was across his chest. Peter saw himself in a mirror, his arms held up—crucified. He looked healthy and strong. Without his clerical collar, he might have caused anyone to wonder why he was not in uniform.

"I wanted to go, but I was told my duty was here."

"Count your blessings. You could be dead."

It was still snowing when Peter left. Across the way, ambulances were lining up at the Ocean terminal, and a train was waiting. Another hospital ship must have docked.

Walking north on Barrington Street, Peter considered the shift in emotions he had just experienced. Thinking Mr. Polanski was Jewish had created an attitude, very subtle, but an attitude. The tailor shop put the little man in a class to which Peter instinctively condescended. Yet the suspicion that Polanski was an educated man, perhaps an émigré intellectual forced to do tailoring, created a crosscurrent, less condescending. The religious identity gave the man an extrasensual aura, like an odor, but odorless; like a color, but invisible to the eye. The switch in his apparent religion required of Peter a change of attitude. It was like stepping into a stranger's kitchen when he was a small boy: strangers' houses had different smells, sometimes unpleasant. Now the Polish tailor had a different invisible color, the color Catholic. So it was for Lutherans and Baptists. They seemed to have different odors, different smells.

Why is this prejudice, this distaste, this shrinking from the unfamiliar, so deeply fixed that it causes us a visceral reaction, however faintly, an adjustment of the stomach? Peter thought, I recognize that aversion in me and I find it absurd. I recognized it putting on the gray suit. It was the feeling that caused me to shrink back from the woman in the burning house, until the sergeant shouted at me, "Absolve her or I'll kill you."

He was about to turn onto South Street when a middle-aged woman stopped boldly in front of him. She had a broad, hard face. She said, "Coward!" and handed him a white feather.

Peter froze in surprise and shame. He could not speak. He felt stupid, standing on the street corner with the white feather in his hand. People were passing and stared at him. The woman walked away.

Julia Robertson—what humiliation if she saw this scene. He wanted to throw the feather away but could not with people watching. He put it in his overcoat pocket and started up South Street.

Years ago at King's he had felt the thrill of self-abnegation on learning what Ignatius Loyola preached to the Jesuits: by obedience you surrendered to God the most valuable part of your humanity, your will power and your intellect. The saint called it a holocaust in which worldly goods were consumed by poverty, your body was consumed by chastity, and your mind was consumed by obedience. Now Peter had no sympathy with such self-immolation.

Protestantism destroyed obedience. It restored even to God's servants their will and their intellect. Poverty was a relative thing. He was poor, sometimes embarrassingly poor in this society, but he had many material possessions, and that was accepted. The more senior or well-born or well-married men in the church, like the dean and the old bishop, had more possessions. As for chastity, to face the facts, the Anglican Church was founded on the unchastity of Henry VIII. Some Anglicans chose chastity for personal reasons. The Reformation freed western man to decide these things for himself, to discipline his own appetites, to serve God in his own way.

Peter knew he had turned toward Julia's house. Now he was aware of going away from her and toward her. In the cathedral, walking toward the altar was away from her, away from the altar was toward her. He had known the feeling from childhood. In the small peninsular city, he always knew north or south from the line of the harbor and could orient himself by a glance at the Citadel. Then his lodestar was his parents' home. The cathedral was another, then his own home with Margery and the children. Now the house on South Park Street had risen over the horizon of his emotions, and he was constantly aware of its position—her position.

IT TOOK SEVERAL EXCHANGES of telegrams to satisfy the prime minister.

MINISTER CANADIAN FORCES OVERSEAS LONDON TO PRIME MINISTER OTTAWA
GOC CEF GIVES FOLLOWING ACCOUNT CIRCUMSTANCES WOUNDING OF ACTING MAJOR CA ROBERTSON. ROBERTSON SHOWED UTMOST INITIATIVE BRAVERY DEVOTION TO DUTY IN BATTLES HILL 70 AND PASSCHENDAELE. CO RECOMMENDED MENTION IN DISPATCHES THEN DSO BUT NO ACTION SO FAR TAKEN LONDON. THIRD DIVISION REGROUPING SINCE ATTACK ON CAMBRAI AND GERMAN COUNTERATTACK. BAD WEATHER PREVENTED AERIAL RECONNAISANCE. NIGHT OF DECEMBER 10 MAJOR ROBERTSON VOLUNTEERED WITH TWO NCOS TO RECONNOITER FORWARD GERMAN POSITIONS ESPECIALLY GERMAN INFILTRATION UNITS. UNDERSTOOD MISSION EXTREMELY HAZARDOUS. ENCOUNTERED UNEXPECTEDLY LARGE ENEMY FORCE MOVING INTO NEW POSITION FOR SURPRISE ATTACK. MAJOR AND ONE NCO WOUNDED. OTHER NCO KILLED. ROBERTSON ORDERED SURVIVING NCO BACK TO REPORT WHILE HE DREW GERMAN FIRE. NCO SAW GRENADE LAND AND ROBERTSON PICK IT UP AND THROW IT BACK KILLING SEVERAL GERMANS. SECOND GRENADE LANDED. ROBERTSON THREW IT BACK KILLING MORE. HIDDEN MACHINE GUN OPENED UP HIT ROBERTSON AND GRENADE EXPLODED

CLOSE QUARTERS. TRIED TO CRAWL BACK BUT COLLAPSED. VOLUNTEERS
BROUGHT HIM IN UNDER FIRE IN DARK. WOUNDS VERY SEVERE.
TREATED AT FIELD HOSPITAL BUT QUICKLY EVACUATED TO ENGLAND.
HIS ACTION PREVENTED POTENTIALLY FAR GREATER LOSS OR CAPTURE
CANADIAN TROOPS. BATTALION CO SAYS ROBERTSON EXEMPLARY
OFFICER AND WORD HIS DEATH DEEPLY AFFECTED MEN. RECOMMENDED
POSTHUMOUS DSO. GCO HEARTILY CONCURS BUT SUGGESTS OBE.
RESPECTFULLY PERLEY

PRIME MINISTER OTTAWA TO MINISTER OMFC LONDON
PRIORITY CONFIDENTIAL. STRONGLY RECOMMEND MAJOR ROBERTSON
BE AWARDED VICTORIA CROSS. CLEARLY SHOWED EXTRAORDINARY
VALOR WELL ABOVE AND BEYOND CALL OF DUTY. REGARDS BORDEN

MINISTER OMFC TO PRIME MINISTER
PRIORITY CONFIDENTIAL. USUAL WHITEHALL CONTACT OBJECTS VC.
CONTENDS DOMINION TROOPS PARTICULARLY CANADIAN RECEIVED
DISPROPORTIONATE NUMBER VCS RECENT MONTHS RELATIVE TO
IMPERIAL TROOPS. PLEASE ADVISE DEGREE IMPORTANCE. PERLEY

PRIME MINISTER TO MINISTER OMFC
ADVISE YOU MAKE STRONGEST REPRESENTATION MY PERSONAL BEHALF
VICTORIA CROSS HIGHEST NECESSITY THIS CASE. SAY CANADIAN TROOPS
WON MORE VCS BECAUSE DISPLAYED UNCOMMON VALOR TENACITY AND
INGENUITY IN BATTLE. SAY IMPERIAL GENERAL STAFF KNOW THEY OWE
RECENT VICTORIES IN IMPORTANT MEASURE TO CEF MEASURE
DISPROPORTIONATE TO SIZE. SAY WE HAVE MORALE AND RECRUITMENT
PROBLEMS AS ACUTE AS BRITISH. SAY I WILL NOT TAKE NO FOR
ANSWER. BORDEN

MINISTER OMFC TO PRIME MINISTER
WHITEHALL OFFICIAL SAYS ROBERTSON VC MATTER ONLY FOR DOWNING
STREET. PERLEY

PRIME MINISTER TO MINISTER OMFC
THEN GO DOWNING STREET MAKE PLAIN FUTURE COOPERATION HINGES
SATISFACTORY RESOLUTION THIS MATTER. BORDEN

MINISTER OMFC TO PRIME MINISTER
HAVE HONOR INFORM YOU DOWNING STREET ADVISES HIS MAJESTY
GRACIOUSLY CONSENTED CONFER VICTORIA CROSS ON MAJOR CA
ROBERTSON. PERLEY

. . . .

JULIA REFUSED Archie Robertson's offer to drive her home. She wanted to be alone and she wanted to exhaust herself with walking. It was almost dark as she left Young Avenue and started up South Park Street. Her house loomed in her thoughts.

I have a house and furniture. I have parents-in-law and a sister-in-law and nieces by marriage, but I do not have the man at the center. Physically, to me, he died nearly two years ago. He has not been in our house, at our dining table, in our bathtub, in our bed, for two years. Yet knowing he was alive made him present. Now that I begin to understand that he is permanently absent, cannot ever come back, cannot smile shyly when I whisper indiscreetly to him, cannot smoke a pipe in the little sitting room, cannot tell me he hates the Matisse or the Morrice portrait of me that I have now hung there.

I will have to go in and go through the house, room by room, telling myself he will not be coming back to this room. Even wounded, he will not come in here again. Even on crutches, even without a leg or an arm—those things I used to dread.

A block from her house, she looked across Victoria Park and saw a light through one of the cathedral stained glass windows. Without thinking why, she crossed the park and entered the church.

It was empty and dimly lit by a faint illumination from the chancel at the far end. Julia sat near the back, grateful for the quiet.

I thought I was alone before, but I was just feeling lonely. Now I am alone. It is not a feeling. It is one realization after another. One discovery after another, that all the assumptions on which my life is built are now false assumptions.

Even when I missed him most terribly, longed for him most feverishly, I knew that he was coming back; if I could be patient, he would be back. We would learn to sleep together again. We would be thirty together. We would have children. But we will not have children now. We will never be thirty together—or forty. I will be thirty alone. Charles will never be older than twenty-six. His gravestone will say 1891–1917. He did not live as long as Shelley. Shelley was thirty when he died. Drowned sailing. I have been to the place in Italy. So romantic. The places Charles wanted me to take him. I will never take him.

She saw a distant figure in a black cassock moving in the shadows by the altar. She recognized Peter Wentworth and watched him, coming and going, arranging things, eventually disappearing.

She sat absolutely still, staring the length of the cathedral in the thick silence. Far away a motor horn sounded, softened by the snow. Then she saw Peter in a side aisle, coming toward her.

"Excuse me for intruding on you."

She looked at him, but did not smile.

"I have been thinking about you, wondering if you had heard any further news, and praying that it was good news."

She looked at Peter, as if deciding whether to tell him. She took a breath, and looked away toward the altar.

"Yes. We've heard."

She paused again. She wanted to tell him and she did not want to. She did not want to share the information. It was too private. She looked down at her lap, then raised her head without turning to him. "We have heard that Charles is dead."

Then he could see that she had been crying, that the fold beneath her eyes was thicker than he had seen it before.

"I am most terribly sorry to hear that. Grievously sorry."

He was silent, absorbing the fact that the man she had longed for was dead.

"I wanted to be quiet for a while, so I came here—to think."

Peter sat in the pew near her but not close. Very quietly, he said, "I have no wish to intrude on your feelings, but if you would like me to say a few prayers with you, if that would help—"

She smiled politely. "No, thank you. I just wanted a quiet place to think."

He sensed, however, that she did not resent his presence. They were silent, sitting a little apart, the shadows gradually thickening, the lamp in the distant sanctuary glowing red.

"You will think it strange that I am here. As I told you, I am not a churchgoer." She turned to him assertively. "I am not even a believer. Does that shock you?"

"Not at all."

He strongly felt her aura, both sexual and spiritual, the energies mingled. But he tried to talk as though unaware of her as a woman, neutrally, quietly creating a small island of sound in the middle of the silence. Someone sitting a few rows away would not have understood.

"Events like this test a person's faith. Someone who professes indifference may be drawn back because the church makes the ceremonies of our lives and the ceremonies create memories."

It sounded recited to Julia, like a lesson learned, a speech rehearsed, from a man thinking of something else.

"Well, I think it is cheap and cowardly to come running to the church when something terrible happens to you, if you do not believe normally."

"God doesn't think that."

"How do you know what God thinks?"

Her directness startled him. She could see it. Something in his manner made her want to do that, to prick his assurance. Instead, it made him sound more positive.

"The church doesn't think that. The church knows human nature. It knows that people have nowhere else to turn. There is no other institution in their lives fitted as the church is to guide them in their spiritual yearning for meaning." He paused.

It did soothe her to sit there listening, conscious that he was saying the things clergymen said, annoyed yet comforted by the banalities. She listened less to the words than to the confident tone of his voice, musical, oddly intimate in this huge space, where no one ever talked conversationally.

"A loved one dies, dies too young, as your husband has—"

The direct words crashed into her again, causing a new clutch of fear.

"It is a violent affront to your sense of the world. It is only natural to ask, What does it mean? Where has the soul gone? The church is the only place organized to answer those questions."

Julia said quietly, "I do not believe in a life after death. His spirit exists because I remember him; his mother and father and Lucy remember him. That is where his spirit will live."

"If it gives you comfort to—"

"I didn't say it gives me comfort."

Peter detected the anger in her voice. "I would not presume to argue with you, Mrs. Robertson."

"My name is Julia."

"I know—but I felt it presumptuous to use it."

Julia did not answer but looked at him questioningly. She felt his eyes fixed like an eagle's, piercing.

"We don't know how he was killed. The prime minister told

my father-in-law Charles died a hero. I don't know how. I am still trying to believe that he is dead." She turned back.

He looked at her clear profile against the shadows. His body was telling him urgently to take her in his arms, to kiss the mouth that gave her face such a generous look. He had never known any physical desire so strong.

Julia gathered her muff from the seat. "I must be going. They'll be wondering what's happened to me. Thank you, Mr. Wentworth."

"My name is Peter."

PREPARING FOR BED, Margery noticed herself lingering, reluctant to undress. The house was chillier than her parents'. There, she had been able to wear a fine nightdress. Now she was looking for a heavy flannelette. She wanted to find it before she took her clothes off and got chilled. Peter was downstairs in his study. The children were finally asleep.

She found the nightgown and was beginning to undress when Peter came upstairs. She turned away, embarrassed at undressing in front of him. Peter said nothing, but took off his reversed collar and put the gold studs on his chest of drawers. In the mirror he saw Margery bent over, in her petticoat, naked above the waist. The bones of her spine stood out startlingly, as if sharp enough to pierce the skin. She was so thin that her ribs were too obvious, her small breasts hung pathetically. She was gaunt, unappetizingly thin. He continued undressing.

In bed, with the light off, they lay on their backs, apart from each other, silent.

Margery had crossed off the last day on her calendar. Tomorrow she was due. Tomorrow she would know. She considered it with the same clarity that had calmed her since she had decided what to do. The children noticed the difference and had stopped tiptoeing around her.

She was calm but frightened. She was due tomorrow but did not have the usual feeling when her period was imminent. Its absence was like a presence. She had first noticed it at the eleven o'clock service. She had gone with her parents and the children. She had actually braided Abigail's hair. Peter was at the altar, assisting. The thought came into her head that the usual premonitory sensation was absent. The congregation was large, and they were squeezed in their pew. She felt slightly dizzy, but it wasn't the usual feeling. She tried to remember what she had experienced just before she knew she was pregnant with Abigail and Michael. It was too blurred. Too many emotions behind too much pain, beyond a mountain range of pain and sadness. In each case she had missed two periods before going to Dr. Menzies. She couldn't remember, even with Michael, when she was more anxious. If she didn't develop that feeling it could mean she was late.

She couldn't eat lunch. The sight of the roast beef her father carved, the fat congealing around the roast potatoes, made her queasy. She had not been hungry for a week. It was all right. The future, for months so impenetrably dark and forbidding, had brightened. It was all right.

Peter noticed that Julia did not come to eleven o'clock communion. The Robertsons were there, with Lucy and her girls. All the Robertsons looked older in their grief. Elizabeth wore a black veil, which she lifted only for communion.

Dean Creighton had prayed for Charles, and his voice quavered slightly:

> Finally we commend to thy fatherly goodness all those who are in any ways afflicted in mind, body, or estate; especially thy servants Archibald and Elizabeth Robertson for the grievous loss of their son, Charles, upon the field of battle; that it may please thee to comfort and relieve them, according to their several necessities, giving them patience under their sufferings, and a happy issue out of their afflictions. And this we beg for Jesus Christ his sake. Amen.

The dean hurried out of his personal feelings into the comforting prayer for the forces of the king:

> O Lord of Hosts, stretch forth, we pray thee, thine Almighty arm to strengthen and protect the forces of our king in every peril of sea, and land, and air; shelter them in the day of battle, and in time of peace keep them safe from all evil; imbue them ever with loyalty and courage; and grant that in all things they may serve as seeing thee who art invisible, through Jesus Christ our Lord. Amen.

Peter calculated that she might come to evensong, when there were fewer people, the cathedral dimly lit. The boys in the choir fidgeted and whispered. People coughed. He could not see her in the gloom.

He thought of her luminous looks as the choir sang the Magnificat:

For he hath regarded the lowliness of his handmaiden.

And a setting full of high, vaulted notes for the treble voices in the Nunc Dimittis:

Lord, lettest now thy servant depart in peace: according to thy word.

The beauty of the words and music, the smell of the beeswax candles, the Gothic shadows, always created a climate of faith. Was that all his faith was, a climate of accumulated sounds and smells?

Rapidly Peter got to the east door to say good night to the departing worshipers, but Julia was not among them.

Lying on his back, staring into the darkness, he saw her again as he had the day before, sitting in the empty cathedral. Every detail was crisp in his vision, the outline of her thighs under her coat, the texture of her white skin under the black fur of her hat, her gray eyes shadowed in fatigue and sorrow.

He helped her out of her coat. She took off her hat. She fell against his shoulder and his arms were around her. His lips were against her neck. Her perfume was in his mind.

That fantasy had come again and again since yesterday. His imagination added a detail, subtracted one. The scene played itself in her front hallway or in the porch of the cathedral. This time he saw her pull off the black fur hat, dislodging the pins, and her blond hair tumbled down. He sighed.

"Are you sad, Peter?"

He was startled by Margery's voice. Her hand reached for him, touched his side, timidly felt for him.

"Do you love me?"

"Yes, of course."

Margery moved closer to him.

"Would you hold me? I'm frightened."

She could feel his exasperation as he turned and embraced her, dutifully. "There's nothing to be frightened of."

She moved against him and whispered, "Make love to me, Peter."

He was disconcerted. It sounded so forlorn. It was ages since Margery had said that to him. Before Michael was born. He couldn't be sure. He had forgotten that she used to say it.

Her words released a tiny electrical current of memory. It crossed and conflicted with another current, one of distaste, initiated by the sight of her naked, emaciated back.

She moved one hand down to find him.

The delicate touch started another, stronger current. The currents crossed and recrossed: he wanted her—he did not want her. He did not *want* to want her. It was ten days since they had hurriedly made love, she lifeless, exhausted with crying. He did not want to give in to this woman who caused him distress, whose backbones he had seen, gaunt and reproachful, her sad breasts, the stark ribs—all suggesting neglect, raising disgust. He did not want this woman. He wanted the woman whose perfume he could imagine, who held her fur hat at the length of her arm as her blond hair cascaded over his face.

Margery touched him and, against his will, desire became imperative. Impatiently he turned, rudely, urgently raising her nightdress. She moved eagerly to accommodate him. He felt her new thinness like a stranger as he found his way into her and gripped her hips.

Margery whimpered, "Oh, darling! Oh, darling!"

Dry, rough, quickly over: resentful in spite of the release, guilty for his indifference, angry at his need, Peter rolled away.

It is over for us, she thought. He loathes me. I have strained whatever love was there too far, and it has snapped. I wanted to be nice to him, for once.

"What has happened to us, Peter?"

"I don't know!"

There was silence.

She remembered the dream about Charles and that evening long ago, with Peter sitting alone, apart from her and Charles, gazing at her across the fire. She knew then, she thought: I am unimportant to him.

"I wanted to be a good wife to you, Peter."

The silence stretched longer and longer.

The silence was terror to her, blacker and blacker as it lengthened. If only he would say one kind thing to break it. But the black emptiness continued.

Peter knew it. The silence was intolerable. He should say something to break the silence that insisted like a nerve-tearing high note held unendurably. . . . The longer it continued, the more important would be any words that broke it. Anything might have released the tension in the first seconds. After a minute, two minutes, it had to be an apology; after three or four, it had to be a confession; after five or six minutes . . . At each moment the lighter words appropriate to a previous moment passed by. His indifference seemed to shout itself in the darkness.

He could think of nothing to say.

And it was then that Peter knew he had stopped praying.

STEWART SAT UP LATE, going over the Woodworth test results. They had revealed no discernible patterns. The shell-shock patients were all individuals, and their answers varied considerably. The ratio of "neurotic" to "normal" answers was within the normal range. He could find no obvious correlation of answers with individual symptoms or with the shell-shock syndrome overall. Only one man seemed to be sending a clear signal. That was Corporal Ransome, the man on crutches, athletic-looking in his upper body but dragging his paralyzed legs behind him.

Stewart had noticed him the first day at Camp Hill, the most remote of the seven. He was good-looking, with a big jaw, but under his dark eyebrows the eyes focused on nothing, or on the space between things. Looking at Ransome, Stewart felt that his personality had vacated the premises.

He had answered all 116 questions and finished well before any of the others. Then he had picked up his crutches and pulled himself back to his bed. His bed was by the window. He could sit on it and stare out at the bare winter elms. He never spoke.

Ransome had given the wrong or neurotic answers to thirteen of the questions, and to some he had added comments.

*Do you usually feel well and strong?* He had answered No, not now, and the same to *Do you usually sleep well?*

*Are you frightened in the middle of the night?* Yes.

*Are you troubled with dreams about your work?* Yes. The next question, *Do you have nightmares?* he had underlined heavily and added "terrible."

Stewart went over his other answers.

*Do ideas run through your head so that you cannot sleep?* Yes.

*Do you feel well rested in the morning?* No.

*Do you feel tired most of the time?* Yes.

*Have you ever fainted away?* Yes.

*Have you often fainted away?* No.

*Have you ever had an arm or a leg paralyzed?* Yes, legs still.

*Have you ever lost your memory for a time?* Yes.

*Do you ever have a queer feeling as if you were not your old self?* Yes.

*Are you ever bothered by a feeling that things are not real?* Yes.

*Do you feel sad or low-spirited most of the time?* Yes.

The emphasis on dreams and nightmares, being frightened in the night, cried out for exploration. Stewart decided that in the morning he would find Dr. Hart and pursue it.

NO ONE HAD EVER SEEN so many coffins together. They lay in rows on the frozen ground in the yard of Chebucto Road School, the unidentified, unclaimed dead, finally ready for mass burial. Standing outside the picket fence in the dense crowd, looking into the schoolyard, Peter had to turn his head to see both ends of the line of coffins.

The crowd was stunned, forced to understand the immensity of the disaster. Each of them had probably seen some persons dead or injured in the explosion; some had perhaps seen a carload of bodies. Many had seen the vastness of the damage in the North End. But the sight of nearly two hundred coffins left them silent with awe.

There were very small coffins among the large and medium-sized. A few were white. Most of them were mahogany-colored, gleaming with varnish and new brass handles. Their newness was startling to behold. Beside their shining surfaces, everything else was shabby, used, soiled: the winter schoolyard, with its residue of dingy snow, the undistinguished brick of the building, the somber winter clothes of the crowd. The coffins, reflecting all these objects, were on another plane of reality. They looked too perfect, too factory-shiny to be there. They looked there by mistake.

They had come from wherever coffins could be found—Amherst, Truro, New Glasgow—and the designs varied, some curved like ships at the head and foot, others square, angled at the shoulders and tapered to a smaller foot. On each was a small bunch of flowers, whatever the devastated city could find in mid-December. On each was a plaque, recording where the body had been found, age, sex, hair color, build, distinguishing marks and tattoos, clothing, contents of pockets, jewelry. Every effort had been made to document whatever might help a relative who turned up later. One mother had been found clasping a baby so closely they could not be separated: they were placed together in one coffin. The Mortuary Committee had kept the bodies as long as they could, hoping for identification. They had embalmed most of the bodies to prolong the time they could be kept. Today the city had decided they must be buried.

The multidenominational funeral service was held in front of the school. The dead filled the schoolyard, so the living congregation gathered outside the fence. There was no music. Occasionally, a ship's deep horn throbbed through the cold air from the harbor, interrupting the prayers. A siren sounded somewhere. The noon gun from the Citadel went off, its boom echoing through the dense, moist air. These extraneous sounds, like the occasional quiet cough from the standing crowd, made the silence only thicker. Anglican, Catholic, Presbyterian, Baptist, and Methodist clergymen and a rabbi prayed. Then soldiers began lifting the coffins onto open trucks, sliding them as respectfully as they could but still rasping loudly on the rough wood of the truck beds. It took a long time, while the people shivered, and stamped their feet, their shoulders raised to their ears, their arms tight against their sides for warmth.

Finally all the trucks were loaded, their tailgates locked, and the cars carrying officials and clergy were in line behind them. The silence was filled with the sound of electric starters and coughing engines, and the cavalcade moved off down Chebucto Road.

Peter wanted it to be over. He sat huddled in the back seat of an unheated touring car with a canvas top, his hands in his overcoat pockets, his right hand worrying the white feather, which, like Julia, would not leave his thoughts. He was chilled to the bone by the hours of standing. The cold had drained him of any emotion except impatience.

It was more than the cold. If he could get back to the South End early enough, it would be a reasonable time of day to call on Julia

Robertson, to offer whatever comfort he could. And conversation. A half-hour in her presence for any reason. Perhaps teatime.

As the senior clergyman, the Anglican bishop of Nova Scotia had been asked to lead the services, but the old gentleman could not stand the penetrating December damp. The dean substituted.

"The fact is," Dean Creighton told Peter in the slow procession to Fairview Cemetery, "the fact is, Margaret and I are very much afraid that our old friend may not be with us for much longer."

"I had no idea he was so ill," said Peter.

"He is not ill, specifically, with anything. Just a general weakening. You know what he looks like. The doctor told me that one bad chill—say, from coming out to this—would be pneumonia. And he'd be gone. Like that!" The dean snapped his fingers.

The file of cars and trucks stalled at some obstruction, then continued.

"I don't think he has been the same since his wife died. Something seemed to die in him too. It often happens."

"I presume it would entail considerable change for you if . . ." Peter did not want to finish the question.

"Yes, I suppose it would," the dean said, looking out the car window, then turning back. "Well, why not be honest? Of course I have thought about it a good deal."

"You are the next senior figure in this province."

"Nothing is automatic, Peter." It sounded like something the dean had cautioned himself or his wife. "There would have to be an election. The lay council, as well as the clergy."

"I meant that there is no other obvious candidate on the horizon."

"Perhaps," the dean said. "But it is not unknown for committees to look beyond the obvious horizon. They could find themselves a bishop in Ontario or British Columbia, if they wished. They could even go to the United States. Several quite distinguished members of our flock have gone to graze in those lusher pastures."

Peter knew whom the dean meant: an archdeacon who published frequent collections of muscular sermons and homilies. Despite his seemingly ineffectual manner, Dean Creighton had the calculating and political spirit as necessary in the church as in any career.

Now, if the dean were to be chosen bishop of Nova Scotia, as everyone expected, what would happen to Peter himself?

"How is Margery?" As if he knew what Peter was thinking.

"Oh, fine, sir."

"There will have to be a memorial service for the Robertson boy. I'm wondering whether the bishop will feel strong enough to officiate. It's the appropriate thing. He needn't take the whole service, but if possible, he should be there."

Clearly, Peter thought, Creighton would like to officiate himself, for friendship with the Robertsons and for the grandeur of the occasion.

"Everyone will be there. There hasn't been anything like it for a long time in Halifax. Son of a very prominent family killed. Everybody respects Archie Robertson. My heart aches for them."

Peter waited. Would the dean say it?

The older man sighed, took off his pince-nez, and rubbed his nose while Peter indifferently eyed the winter landscape and the strange faces watching the procession.

"God moves in mysterious ways, his wonders to perform."

Yes, he would say it.

"I had a talk with the wife," Peter said. It was wise to establish that. The dean was close to the Robertsons. "I mean Charles Robertson's wife. I found her in the cathedral on Saturday afternoon. Sitting alone, in some shock, I think. She had just heard the news."

"In the cathedral? You surprise me. She hardly ever comes. How was she?"

"She was quite composed."

"She wasn't with them at communion."

"I talked with her a long time, to say what I could to be helpful."

"Well, that's good work, Peter. Poor thing. Perhaps she'll find some need of us now. She's a remarkably good-looking young woman."

"Yes."

"Well." The dean sighed. "Life is for the living. I suppose she'll get married again eventually."

The idea surprised Peter. Julia marrying again had not occurred to him.

"Ashburn," the dean pointed out as they passed the golf club, the fairways covered with unmarked snow. "Four more months of this. Mid-April, if we're lucky. Poor old Archie!"

Peter knew it was where Creighton played with Archie Robertson.

"You should take up golf, Peter. It's very relaxing. You're such a natural athlete I'm told, you'd probably be very good at it. Walk away with all the prizes."

Dean Creighton was vain about his golf. A silver cigarette box he'd won years before as the president's prize at Ashburn was always polished and prominently displayed.

"I'd be happy to introduce you. Clubs like ours give the clergy a special rate, you know."

But beyond the fees, Peter knew, was a set of golf clubs, and the clothes, and shoes; and Margery wanted to join the Saraguay.

"I've got my hands full just at present."

"I understand," the dean said. "But the fresh air might do Margery some good too. The ladies have quite a jolly time out there."

Peter felt himself trapped. Years of deference to this self-satisfied man stretched ahead of him, with no spiritual reward. Years of poverty limiting all opportunities to live. Even if the dean became bishop soon, all that was in prospect for Peter was a minor rector's position and more scraping financially. If he had been older, as Creighton's trusted curate, an archdeacon, Peter might have had a shot at replacing him.

Chaplains serving overseas would be returning with decorations and the aura of glory about them, but the bishop had thwarted that ambition for Peter. The humiliating white feather was in his pocket. He was cold. They were driving away from Julia's house. He should not go to Julia's house. He would not go.

"Peter, we've been stopped for ages. Just go along and find out what's happening."

Glad to get out of the freezing car, Peter walked along the line of vehicles stalled in the lane leading into Fairview Cemetery. He found a cluster of people at the cemetery gate, which was closed with a chain and padlock. An army colonel was arguing with a civilian.

"Some colossal foul-up," said the colonel. "Apparently the Fairview people refuse to bury these people. They won't put unidentified people in consecrated ground."

"It's outrageous," a civilian said. "No one told us."

"No one told me!" the colonel said. "What am I going to do with two hundred coffins sitting there—full of bodies?"

Someone was shouting, "We've got to turn back!"

A young officer, breathless from running, saluted the colonel. "We've got to turn back, sir. The Relief Committee chairman just arrived. The grave was dug on some ground back along Bayers Road."

"Unconsecrated ground?" Peter asked.

"I don't know, sir," the officer said.

"To hell with that," said the colonel. "If the grave is dug there, that's where we go. Let's get this organized. We'll have to back every vehicle up, reform our convoy in the other direction." The colonel was happily pragmatic.

Peter walked back. What pettiness! Is this what had become of the Christian faith after nineteen centuries: tiny subdivisions bickering in a winter landscape, their own prideful differences more important than the disaster that had struck them? Is this what he had committed his life to?

Julia Robertson would understand. She had expressed similar feelings herself.

SUPERSTITIOUSLY Julia had dreaded telling her parents, as though that act would confirm that Charles was dead. Every time she made herself think those words for the telegram, they gripped her with a spasm more painful than the constant ache she now felt, that her heart was being held in two hands and permanently squeezed. At last, she had sent it and was now writing. Her mother would want her to come home to Montreal or, worse, to come herself to Halifax.

She put down her pen on the blank sheet of writing paper and went to the cupboard to look at the black dress, still unworn, bought on the last trip to Montreal. She held it against her and looked in the mirror. It was the new length, showing her ankles. It would not do for mourning in Halifax. From the back of the cupboard she pulled out an older black dress, seldom worn, less fashionable, but respectably long.

Her eyes felt dry in their sockets, her legs heavy from too little sleep; she was lightheaded from having eaten almost nothing on Sunday.

Julia hung up the black dress and looked around the bedroom.

The bed had to be made. Her stockings had to be washed. She had to bathe and do her hair and put clothes on, as if Charles were still alive. She would have to eat and sleep. Her period would come and go, month after month. These clothes would wear out and she would have to go shopping for new ones. She would have to go out and talk to people. She would probably go to teas, to the Saraguay, go swimming when the summer came, and play tennis. Her tennis racquet needed restringing. She would have to live. Her life continued.

She saw all this in a moment. The thought was so extraordinary that in her dressing gown she sat in the small armchair to think about it. She never sat there, and it gave her a strange perspective on the room and the things in it. Everything would continue as normal. The dressing table would stand there, the desk in the window, looking across Victoria Park to the cathedral; the bed, the rug, the curtains, all waited as though Charles had never been here. She felt disembodied, not in the room either, just looking in on it as a stranger, someone not aware that something was missing.

She dreaded the days and weeks ahead. She wished it were a year from now, everything taken care of properly: the newspapers, the friends of the family, the memorial service. None of it would make a difference. She thought of the cottage, how she would love to be there, to look at the sea and think.

She thought, I must *do* something!

Julia sprang up and ran downstairs to ask Mollie to heat some water on the stove. She would wash her hair.

Mollie said, "If you wait till tonight, you'll have running hot water. The man came by to say they're turning the gas back on later."

"No, I want to wash it now."

THE GAS COMPANY sent employees from door to door saying the gas was being turned back on. It was the only safe way to make sure that stoves and hot-water heaters were shut off and to inspect any pipes or joints shaken loose in the explosion. There was little such damage in the South End. The gas man told Margery, "Everything looks fine."

His words hung ironically in her mind. Everything looks fine.

Her period had not come. Anxiety about it had disturbed her all night. She had dreamed or half-dreamed so many possibilities that by morning she could not be sure whether she felt the signs or not. Now she knew that she was pregnant. She could not eat breakfast, and she avoided Peter. After what had happened the night before, she could not look at his eyes. When he left for the mass funeral, she sent the children out to play and sat down with a cup of tea but scarcely touched it. Even in a woollen pullover and dressing gown she felt cold. She shivered from the fears that would not leave her.

She had been sitting there when the gas man arrived.

"But when will the gas be on?" She stood watching him examine the pipe leading to the Ruud heater and the gas stove. He was whistling cheerfully. It was strange to her that he was whistling. She felt like a patient looking out a hospital window, amazed that other people are not sick.

"In this part of town, five o'clock today. Time to cook your dinner. You'll be glad to forget the wood stove, eh?"

"Yes."

"Better keep everything turned off till then. You can tell if it's on by putting a match to the pilot light, here."

"It always goes out," Margery said.

She closed the front door behind him, noticing in the hall mirror that she had let him see her in her dressing gown with her hair undone. That would have shocked her in the past, but not now.

She went back into the kitchen and looked at everything very carefully. There were four doors: to the scullery leading to the back door, to the pantry, to the dining room, and to the front hall. She looked around for something, finally going upstairs to the linen cupboard and bringing down a thick towel. She rolled it tightly and laid it against the space at the bottom of one door. The roll was too narrow, and she could feel a draft coming under the door. She unrolled the towel and rolled it again lengthwise. This time it stopped the draft. She removed it, folded it, and put it back in the linen closet. Tomorrow morning she would need four towels.

She was pleased with her careful planning. She went back into the kitchen and remembered the keyholes. She thought about cotton wool, then the children's modeling clay. A small ball would seal each keyhole. She was thinking very clearly today. She went up to Abigail's room and rummaged in the old toy chest. There was a lump of clay, all colors wadded together, at the bottom, one side matted into a doll's hair. She felt how malleable it was but left it there. Abigail noticed everything and would ask her why it was in the kitchen. There would be time in the morning.

The toy box had been hers as a child. It was covered with a pretty printed fabric, faded where it had faced the windows. The musty smell was familiar. She looked at the tangle of things inside. Abigail kept her things very differently. When told to tidy her room, she threw everything in the toy box, slammed the lid, and called out, "My room's tidy, Mummy. May I go out now?"

Margery had been much neater. It soothed her to make her room perfectly tidy, not a wrinkle in the bed, all her shoes pointing the same way in the cupboard. It made her feel good to take everything out of a drawer and put it back, carefully folding and placing each garment in neat piles. The symmetry made her happy.

Abigail was messy. She had no time for neatness. She tumbled toy animals and dolls in with books and crayons. Margery had rescued them many times, sat them in the chair or against the pillow on the bed, but her daughter lifted the covers to jump into bed and let them fall, or threw them at Michael like missiles. It hurt Margery to see them like this. Once again, Margery took all the dolls and animals and sat them up on the bed and on the chair, two on the little bookcase. She tidied the dolls' hair and straightened their dresses. It was a shame they did not have names as Margery's did, but Abigail couldn't be bothered. Perhaps when she came back and saw them so neatly arranged, she might find a new interest in them.

Margery was looking at the tidied arrangement when she heard the doorbell again. She was embarrassed to find Peter's mother at the door.

"Hello, dear. I saw you at church yesterday, but John wanted to go home quickly. Is everything all right?"

"Yes," Margery said dully. "I've been meaning to come over, but I haven't been feeling well."

"Oh, dear."

Dorothy Wentworth took off her coat. Her neat, sensible clothes, her gray hair combed back into a tight bun, made Margery feel untidy and undressed.

"Well, what's the matter?"

The same question from her own mother always carried an accusatory note, but Dorothy Wentworth asked in a way that made it natural for a woman with two small children not to feel well and to be in her nightdress and a sweater at eleven o'clock on Monday morning.

"I'm just feeling a bit washed out."

"Well, isn't that fortunate? I've brought some neatsfoot jelly. I thought you looked a little peaky yesterday. You know, I have really worried that on top of all the other dreadful things happening, there might be influenza or some pneumonia going around. Come and sit down, and I'll make us both a cup of tea. I just brought one or two other things."

As usual, Dorothy had a basketful of things she had baked or cooked. Her aura induced guilt in Margery. Peter's mother was so competent, she had managed to live nicely on so little, she was so persistently cheerful.

"I'll just go up and change," Margery said.

"Oh, heavens no. Don't worry about me. We're just two girls together." She said *gerruls*. She bustled around as though it were her own kitchen, asking about the children, and eventually put two cups of tea on the table and sat down opposite Margery.

"There we are! You know, to tell you the truth, after I saw you yesterday, I wondered whether you were expecting again." She never approached a subject indirectly.

It startled Margery. She answered like someone caught in a guilty act. "No!"

But Dorothy Wentworth smiled. "Well, that's probably for the best. You've got plenty to keep your hands full . . ." And she prepared to talk about something else.

It was like talking to a man, an impression strengthened by Dorothy's heavy eyebrows and faint mustache. This was more like talking to her father. He asked a question, you answered, he accepted it, and moved to another subject. There wasn't the trail of cobwebs that clung to her mother's words, forcing Margery to say things a dozen times before they were clear.

Her own mother would have said, sharply and archly, "Are you sure?" and the catechism would go on.

Dorothy Wentworth was obviously why Peter was so sure of himself in some ways and so driven in others.

"It was wonderful of your mother to put you all up like that after the explosion. How is she? I haven't seen her in ages."

"She's fine."

"Peter told us about your father's generosity over the church windows. That is a wonderful thing. The poor place looks so dark and strange now, but they couldn't leave it with the snow blowing in."

They looked at each other, and Margery turned away. If she had not been Peter's mother, Dorothy was someone to whom Margery might have told everything. She felt tempted. But she could not tell Peter's mother.

Margery's appearance worried Dorothy. The girl had never looked so untidy. The house was often a mess, but if anything normally showed care it was Margery's dress and hair. It was a good thing she had come today. She would have to do something. She kept talking while she observed her daughter-in-law.

"Isn't it wonderful how so many people are helping Halifax? Have you been reading about it? Ships arriving from Boston and New York full of supplies. Trains coming from all over. Governments around the world sending money. You'd think in the middle of this dreadful war, with thousands of soldiers being killed, no one would notice our trouble. Halifax is such a wee place. I think it's very touching that people care so much. The Australians and New Zealanders. Quite the other side of the earth." She said *airth*.

Usually her arrival put Margery into a small frenzy of apology about the state of the house, but today she seemed indifferent, partly absent.

"Isn't it a shame about Charles Robertson. So dreadful. You must remember him, Margery? A wee, towheaded laddie."

"At least his wife has no children," Margery said.

"Yes, it's a blessing, I suppose. But I feel so wretched for Elizabeth and Archie. Their only boy—their only child."

Dorothy paused and looked at the wan face opposite her.

"At least I was able to have Peter—after his brother died."

Dorothy surprised herself by saying that. She never talked about herself. But Margery appeared not to be listening. Her wide-set eyes, larger in her thinner face, were focused somewhere else.

"Well," Dorothy said cheerfully, "what are the children having for lunch?"

"Lunch? I hadn't thought about it yet. I don't know."

Lunch, Margery thought, and then supper and breakfast and lunch and breakfast and supper, and breakfast, lunch, and supper . . . With a small thrill, she remembered her plan. Everything would be solved. She wouldn't have to worry about any of this.

"Some soup, I think."

"Why don't you let me get it for them?" Dorothy said, getting up. "I expect they'll be in very soon."

Dorothy rolled up the sleeves of her dress and set to work. She had watched Margery for years, but had never interfered directly. She brought baskets of things. She took the children for walks in the Public Gardens or Point Pleasant Park. She took them to pick berries or wildflowers. In the beginning she had spoken to Peter, but he bristled so defensively about Margery that she held back. It was his bed and he must lie in it. Margery was a sweet girl, who had really had to struggle against the influence of her mother. Such a silly, snobbish woman.

"She'll do better when she gets used to it," Peter had said when they were first married.

But it didn't happen. Margery tried very hard. She was bright and willing but was too much the prisoner of her mother's vanity, Dorothy thought. Cynthia Tobin had ideas of a grander, richer catch for Margery and had groomed her only for that. Margery had scarcely been in a kitchen before she was married.

Now Peter didn't talk about it at all. Well, he would have to. His wife was in a very bad way. If she wasn't pregnant, she was obviously ill. Something had to be done for her.

Dorothy was glad she had come.

"Here, before the children come in, have a cup of this yourself."

"I'm really not hungry, thanks."

CORPORAL RANSOME refused a wheelchair with a shake of his head and manipulated himself on crutches down the long corridor of the asylum. The familiar sour smell enveloped them. Dr. Hattie had given Stewart an unused office, and Dr. Hart had agreed to let him interview the paralyzed soldier.

"If anyone asks, say it is psychological testing."

Ransome did not swing on the crutches but walked them forward one at a time, putting no weight on his legs. Two women patients with pudding-bowl haircuts and shapeless dresses stopped to gape at the handsome young man dragging his feet behind him, toes down.

Stewart had seen the medical history. Ransome had responded to nothing. They had tried cold and hot baths. At Queen's Square in London, they had applied electric current with the Faraday machine directly to the paralyzed legs. The muscles had contracted when stimulated, but had remained paralyzed. When needles were inserted, Ransome did not feel them, and the tissues did not bleed when punctured. Hypnosis had not worked, nor did he respond when his consciousness was lowered with chloroform. There was a note of exasperation in the comments of some doctors, who had scribbled, "Sullen . . . uncooperative . . . alienated . . . not interested in recovery." One had written, "Posture and expression of typical dement."

"Do you want to smoke?"

Ransome took one of the offered Craven "A"'s and lit it with Stewart's match.

His pale blue eyes were so vague, it was impossible to tell whether they were focused on Stewart. They betrayed no curiosity.

"John, look at me."

The use of his first name probably startled him, because he did look and, for a moment, focused.

"Do you know who I am?"

Ransome looked through him. Stewart could see no expression but felt contempt in the blank face.

"My name is Stewart MacPherson. I am not a doctor. I am a psychologist. Do you know the difference?"

Ransome blew smoke out but did not answer.

"Do you remember last Saturday, you filled in a questionnaire? A lot of questions? You remember, don't you?"

Silence. Stewart stubbed out his cigarette. He noticed Ransome's burning closer to his fingers.

"Don't burn your fingers."

Ransome looked down and stubbed out the cigarette. The response was an achievement.

"Well, in case you've forgotten, this is the list of questions that you completed." He turned it so that Ransome could read it. The patient glanced indifferently.

"These are your remarks, see? You wrote this. Do you usually feel well and strong? You wrote: No, not now. See that? Do you usually sleep well? You wrote: No, not now. Right?"

He looked up to find the pale eyes staring at him, not at the paper.

"I thought it might help you to talk about it."

"About what?"

A faded voice, too small for the man, unused to talking.

"We can talk about anything you like."

Stewart was sure that Ernest Jones would have a way of immediately pulling the thread that would bring this man out of himself. His own approach sounded stumbling, amateurish. But he had to remember to go slowly, be patient.

"Tell me how you feel today. Did you sleep last night?"

Ransome still had not sat down. He looked around the small room, at a dusty office bookcase holding a few old textbooks and files, at a fly-specked photograph of the asylum staff from the 1880s, grim Victorian faces against a grim building. Stewart waited.

"I'm not going back there."

"Back where?"

"You know—over there. The war."

"But you'd like to get better?"

"I'm all right."

"Do you think if you got better they'd send you back?"

"That's what they said."

"Where do you come from?"

"Chatham, New Brunswick."

"Is your family still there?"

"Yes."

"What members of your family?"

"My mum and dad and two sisters."

"Any brothers?"

"One died."

"Do they know where you are now, that you're back in Canada?"

"I don't know."

"Have you written to them?"

"No."

"Won't they be worried about you?"

"I don't know. I didn't feel like it."

"What would you like to do, John?"

"Get out of this place."

"Where do you want to go?"

"I don't know. Somewhere—I don't know."

Stewart waited, but nothing more came. "Tell me about when you first got paralyzed."

"I don't remember."

"You don't remember how it happened?"

"No."

"What's the first you do remember about not being able to use your legs?"

"In the hospital, the field hospital."

"Tell me about that."

"I've told them all a hundred times."

"But I'm not a doctor. Do you mind telling me?"

"I woke up there and my legs didn't work. They said I'd been brought in unconscious. I'd been unconscious for a long time."

"Do you know how long?"

"I don't know."

"Is that why you said in the questionnaire that you'd fainted away once?"

"I must've if they found me unconscious."

"What's the last thing you can remember before you were unconscious?"

"We were back at base camp for a week's rest."

"Then you went back to the front?"

"They found me unconscious. The company was all gone."

"They had left or . . . ?"

"They said they were all killed."

"But you don't remember going back to the front?"

"No."

Ransome was communicating orally but appeared to be using only part of his brain, his consciousness very little engaged, repeating answers he had given many times. His eyes remained opaque. They made Stewart think that the receptors functioned but the interpretative function of vision was shut down. Ransome was no more animated than at the beginning.

"You said in this paper that you were troubled with dreams and nightmares."

"Yes."

"Would you tell me about them?" It was the question Stewart had wanted to ask from the beginning.

"I don't remember them."

"Not at all?"

"No."

"Do they wake you up?"

"Sometimes."

"Do they frighten you?"

"Yup."

"And you don't remember them at all?"

"No."

"Did you have a dream last night?"

"I don't know."

"Did you wake up frightened in the middle of the night?"

"I woke up because Macaulay was screaming blue murder."

"John, the next time you know you've had a dream, the minute you wake up, try to remember it. Then you can tell me about it when I come to talk to you again."

He couldn't tell whether Ransome had heard.

"Would you like these cigarettes?"

"It's nearly a full packet."

"Keep them. And try to remember a dream."

Stewart held the door open and watched Ransome work his way up the gloomy corridor. His shoulders and arms must be very strong to move that painful way. And he had never sat down.

This was difficult. Reading case histories by Freud or Jones made it sound easy. How handy it would be to have an Ernest Jones around, always so confident in his intuitive leaps. Perhaps too confident, too pat, but it made for quicker notes and better papers.

Stewart wasn't even sure he would like Ransome's personality, if what was hidden ever came out. But he was determined to continue.

ALL DAY PEOPLE CALLED, as word spread about Charles. Calling cards and small envelopes with condolence notes began to accumulate on the silver tray in the hall. The doorbell rang so often that Mollie let Betty answer it.

Julia stayed upstairs while her hair dried, tidying her room with special care. She washed underclothes and sorted stockings that were confused in her drawer. She took all the shoes and boots out of the floor of the cupboard and mopped out the woolly dust. She felt a compulsion to put everything in order.

Her hair was very thick and took hours to dry. Impatient that it was still wet, she went down and lit the fire in the small sitting room and finished the drying on her knees, brushing it out in front of the fireplace.

. . . .

During the morning Peter's impatience built up. He kept telling himself he would not go to Julia, yet continually looked at his watch as though he had an appointment with her. He felt that he was swimming against a strong tide of time that pushed him backward while a stronger current was pushing him toward the house on South Park Street.

The burial was interminable. The clergy could not leave until all rites and ceremonies had been performed in the small dignity the city was granting its anonymous dead.

Soldiers carried the mismatched coffins into the large raw trench other soldiers had dug. The freshly opened earth was like a brown wound staining the white snow. They laid the coffins side by side from one end of the trench, then laid another row at the feet of the first. The clergymen, the officers, the few civilian officials shivered, trying not to stamp their feet lest the gesture seem disrespectful.

Peter again wrapped his scarf under his chin, turned his overcoat collar up as tight as he could, and dug his hands deep into his pockets, burrowing in his mind toward the thought that warmed him.

Watching the coffins, he found himself thinking about his brother, James, who had died at fourteen. His mother had mentioned him only when Peter asked. He could see the wistfulness come into her eyes. She would answer, her eyes and her voice full of tears. James was with the angels. When very young, Peter believed that James had become an angel himself. Whenever he did anything to be scolded for, Peter, not his mother or father, said, "James wouldn't do that." It was never possible to be as good as James, because James was with the angels. It was odd to realize now, but he had never told himself James was with God.

He knew where the grave was. In a melancholy mood he would go there and look at the stone.

IN LOVING MEMORY
OF OUR BELOVED SON
JAMES WENTWORTH
Born March 10, 1874
Taken to God, August 7, 1888
He is with the angels

The inscription had different meanings as Peter grew older. During his divinity studies, the line "He is with the angels," seemed out of character for an Anglican churchman as austere as his father. It had a Low Church, almost evangelical ring to it, at the very least sentimental.

He puzzled over the fact that James had drowned less than a year before he was born. To Peter's questions when he was little, his mother had said, "We dearly longed for another child, and God was kind to us."

Slowly the dates meant more to him. As a husband and father, he understood how their grief must have thrown his parents passionately together. They had conceived him scarcely two months after James's death. Was it accidental, or did they intend to replace James? He never dared ask his mother.

James had been visiting a friend at a cottage in Hubbards. One morning before anyone else was up, the two boys found a dory on the beach and launched it into the surf. The friend told what happened. They rowed out, each holding one of the heavy oars against the wooden thole pin. A wave slapped the pointed bow, and James lost his oar. They tried with the other oar to fish it back, but the waves carried it out of reach. Leaning too far with the heavy oar, James fell in, and the waves pushed him away. Like many boys at the time, he couldn't swim. The Wentworths made sure Peter learned very early.

Peter looked around miserably, his chin low in his collar. The Catholic monsignor and a younger priest were standing nearby. The monsignor wore his overcoat outside his surplice.

The feeling of emptiness returned, the feeling of nothing at the bottom to stand on, nothing but an accumulation of remembered ceremony.

He imagined an intellectual Catholic, a scholar, perhaps a Jesuit, not like the proletarian monsignor and the parish priest shivering here at the gaping gravesite, but a learned and sympathetic man, in a dark, book-lined study with a fire, where he could sip a sherry in a worldly way and discuss matters of belief and doubt. If only Stewart MacPherson were not so facetious, so determined to score debating points. But there were things he would never discuss with Stewart. He should have known better with the diary. Now Stewart knew that Peter still had it. He had carefully put it away, but suppose Margery came across it? She had a habit of wrenching open drawers and snatching a piece of expensive writing paper for a note to the milkman. Margery. Peter shivered inwardly. White and withdrawn this morning, she had not met his eyes when he left. Sometimes he had just had enough, and it hardened his heart.

Yet later, standing on Julia's doorstep, he worried that Margery might pass by and see him.

The door was opened by Betty, who stared with her one eye.

"Is Mrs. Robertson at home?"

"Yes, Father," Betty said obediently, opening the door wider. She too thought he was a Catholic priest, and led him directly into the small sitting room.

"The priest is here!"

Peter saw Julia's shoulders bent toward the fire, tapering to a small waist in her dressing gown. Her golden hair hung forward from the naked nape of her neck. She was brushing it down, but suddenly threw it back to turn and look.

"Oh!"

Her hair tumbled again as she scrambled to her feet.

The scent of the clean hair fell about him. The room was warm with the flowery odor. Peter's nostrils were full of it as he retreated, and Julia, clutching her robe together with a towel and brush, hurried past him to run up the stairs.

"Excuse me, I'm terribly sorry."

The child stared at them both.

"I beg your pardon," Peter said.

"Please make yourself comfortable." She called from the stairs, "Mollie!"

From farther up: "I'll just be a few minutes!"

Mollie came bustling from the kitchen. "Betty! You tell me when someone is at the door. You don't just let anyone right in."

"But it's the priest! Mama said you always let the priest in."

"I'm very sorry, sir," Mollie said. "Would you like to sit in the drawing room?"

"If you don't mind, I'll stay where it's warm. It's very raw out today."

Peter wanted to linger in the climate she had left behind. The little room was informal, a small sofa and two armchairs grouped by the fireplace, a bookcase and a framed picture of a partly nude woman, to Peter's eye garishly modern. If Julia, who knew about art, had bought it and hung it, it must mean something. Her experience was disturbingly wide. But the painting did not look like Halifax.

She came downstairs, her black dress reminding him that he was visiting a woman just widowed.

"I'm afraid you caught me a little unawares." She sat, very straight, in the chair opposite him, her feet drawn back under her dress, her hands in her lap. She had done her hair quickly in a loose braid tied with a black ribbon. Her eyebrows were so pale that he had to look hard to see them. Perhaps previously she had darkened them. The paleness of her skin made her lips rosier.

Each time she encountered Peter, Julia felt the physical current between them intensifying, alternating rapidly between attraction and aversion. She was very conscious of him physically—his muscled face, his large hands. She looked at him expectantly.

"It must be difficult for you at a time like this to have your family so far away, in Montreal."

She wondered how he knew that. He seemed so knowing about her.

"Yes . . . you know I've just sent the telegram. All weekend I couldn't bring myself to . . ." Her voice trailed off as though she had begun thinking of something else. "It was part of believing it myself. Actually I may have to go to Montreal. Or they'll come here . . ."

Peter knew she was thinking aloud.

"Anyway, the Robertsons have become like my own family. Lucy dropped by this morning. They are very kind to me."

"I saw them in church yesterday."

"Yes, they always go."

"I thought you might—in the circumstances. In fact, I looked for you at evensong."

"Did you?" How strange he was. The intensity had returned to his eyes, steel arrows pinning her like a mounted butterfly. He made her uncomfortable.

"The circumstances have not changed me—if you mean Charles's death. If I had the faith of his mother, if I could draw some meaning from all this, but there is no meaning I can see—and there is no point pretending." She smiled sadly, and the small laugh creases around her lips deepened. "It's not very polite of me to be so blunt."

There was silence and he wondered what to say. He noticed

several pipes in a rack on a table behind her. He remembered what Dean Creighton had said: she'll find someone else and remarry.

Peter said, "I've just been to the funeral of all the dead they couldn't identify from the explosion."

"How terrible. I'm afraid I haven't been paying attention. How many were there in the end?"

"Nearly two hundred—out of two thousand dead."

"Oh, my goodness! Two hundred. But how did they—manage?"

Peter told her, and she was quiet for a moment, thinking about the scene.

"Did it make it easier for you to be there, being a man of God, I mean, having your faith, believing? Did that make it bearable"— her eyes were moist—"to see those children buried?"

Peter felt his whole future hovering over his answer. The facile phrases came rapidly: *We cannot know what God's will is . . . Those who believed will have everlasting life . . . The Lord giveth, the Lord taketh away.*

Instead, he heard himself saying, "As I watched, I thought of my mother and father. They had a child before me, a boy. He lived to be fourteen and was drowned in an accident."

"Oh, how terrible!" She lifted her hands to her lips. Part of his attention registered the perfection of her fingernails against the perfection of her lips, each the same natural tint of pale rose.

"As I watched the little coffins being carried into the grave, I wondered how my parents must have felt, seeing their son buried after all those years of cherishing him."

"Did you know your brother?"

"No. I was born a year later. I've taken his place."

She thought that this stiff man with the piercing eyes had suddenly become human and likable.

"Did you go into the church, did you find your calling, because of that?" she asked.

He looked at her, astonished. He had never thought of it that way.

"You see, my father is a minister. He's a canon at the cathedral —not active in parish duties—he's a scholar."

"It must have been very hard for you to know that you replaced another person." How would she know that? "But you haven't said how your own faith helps you through something like today. Would you tell me? I want to know."

Peter laughed in embarrassment. "That's not an easy question to answer." What had helped him through today was the knowledge that he could hurry to see her.

"But you are the man of God. You are the one with the answers. You come to comfort me. Can you comfort yourself when you need to?"

Her challenging manner thrilled him, reminding him of the bold spirit in the diary. It rushed into his mind to say, *I have no faith.* She made him want to drop his guard, to act impulsively, but he pulled back from the edge.

"I suppose, if you believe, the fundamental, metaphysical questions that torment man—why are we here, what is the purpose of life, who made life—are put aside. They are dealt with. When faith is a habit, it reduces the chaos of life. It removes the terror of thinking that everything is meaningless."

"Isn't it meaningless when things happen like the explosion that kills so many innocent people . . . the children you saw buried today? Isn't that meaningless? Isn't the war meaningless, with thousands and thousands of people killed? Where is the meaning of God in that? How does believing comfort you? Please, tell me."

Color was rising in her cheeks. He did not want to argue with her. He wanted to hold her close to him and smell the hair whose fresh odor still hovered in the warm air of the sitting room. He wanted to stop her questions.

"Isn't God supposed to be behind everything, guiding and willing this?"

"Man turned away from God in disobedience by exercising his own will. He must live with the consequences." He felt she was forcing him to say these tired things.

"Oh, disobedience! Fiddlesticks, Mr. Wentworth! Look at Charles's mother. Mrs. Robertson is a devout woman. Why should she be punished? Mollie's daughter and her husband, very faithful Roman Catholics. They went to mass, they went to confession. How did they deserve what happened to them? The awful story you told me of the woman trapped in the burning house. I've thought about that again and again."

"The church says—"

"Not the church. What do *you* believe, Mr. Wentworth?" She

did not use Peter. "When you see the little girl who let you in? Did you look at her good eye, that special Irish hyacinth dark blue. She has lost one of them; behind the bandage is an empty socket. And worse. The doctors say there are injuries in her brain that I can't bear to think about. What do you believe when you see that, Mr. Wentworth?"

He had not been so vehemently catechized since the arguments at King's, the constant badgering by Stewart. Peter wanted to be brilliant with her, but to stop her questions. His body was aching with the awareness of her body. If only he could take one of the slim hands, now flicking into a gesture, now lying demurely in her lap.

"Where is the comfort—or is there no comfort—in being a believing Christian when things like this happen?" She pressed her hands urgently together to emphasize the question.

"You have to believe to know the answer."

"Oh!" She looked disappointed that he had taken refuge in such sophistry.

"You have to believe to believe."

"But when evil wins, as it seems to be winning now?"

"Surely that's what we're fighting in France—the forces of evil?"

"Don't you think the Germans believe the same? They are Christians, too. Aren't their priests and ministers telling them that God is on their side?"

"Presumably," said Peter.

"Did you see in the paper what the bishop of Birmingham said? It made me so upset. He said that when men were killed and went to heaven, Christ would say to them, Good job, well done!"

"Well—it's a way of comforting people."

"But how does the bishop of Birmingham know that?"

"It's really just a metaphor, to tell people that their sacrifice has not been in vain."

"But he's pretending he knows, isn't he?"

"When a priest is ordained, something passes from the bishop's hands that goes unbroken back to the Apostles and Jesus Christ himself. The line through saints, martyrs, bishops is unbroken. That is his authority."

"But aren't the Catholic bishops and Lutheran pastors in German cities telling their people the same thing? They believe in

Jesus Christ. It made me angry—this was weeks before I knew about Charles—angry to think of that man gaily sending all those young men off with the idea that they're on their way to heaven. Instead of being appalled by the war, doing everything it can to stop the killing, there is the Church of England cheering on the sidelines. And I suppose in Germany there is the Lutheran Church cheering, like two sides in a school rugby match."

She was surprised at her own vehemence. It was as though she wanted to punish Peter Wentworth for being a healthy, live, intact man, who both annoyed her and drew her interest. If he were not a minister, she would never talk so freely, so intimately to him.

"Well, churches represent nations. They grow out of societies. It's hard for them not to express their national feelings in wartime."

"But why is a German Christian who says God is on his side wrong and an Englishman is right?"

"It's human nature to think so, or hope so. Just as it is to believe in a higher power. The idea is inborn."

"What makes you think that?"

"All the authorities down the centuries have concluded that. People may not call it God, but it is their thirst for perfection, for the Platonic ideal, for an escape from death, from the prison of our flesh."

She was so intelligent, so vibrant, and so sensual a woman. He pushed on, reaching back to his divinity school training.

"God is an abstraction that has been humanized to make him more credible, imaginable to the simple people. God is not a bearded man in the sky. Those are ways of allegorizing the human yearning for perfection, for the spiritual part of man, which can be immortal, to triumph over the physical, which must die and decay, the unconditional over all that is conditional in man."

Peter heard himself saying something he had learned but had never accepted personally, never believed, because his own concept of God had remained anthropomorphic.

"Then whom do *you* pray to? Do you pray to a person you imagine?"

He avoided the question.

"Everyone has his personal conception of God."

"Well, I do not." She turned and looked at the fire. She had said it quietly, modestly, not arrogantly. This beautiful woman simply denied God, without affectation. He felt himself letting go, all the years of self-discipline falling away.

She left her chair and picked up the brass fire tongs to put a lump of coal on the fire. It fell back into the bucket. Impatiently, she reached for it with her fingers, but he stopped her.

"Please, let me." He took the tongs. Her wrist felt his fingers brush. He could feel his heart beating. If she stayed beside him, kneeling, he felt it was inevitable that they would embrace.

She had a momentary impression, an absurd conviction, that Peter Wentworth was going to turn and kiss her. She looked at him, felt the electricity between them, then got up and sat back in the chair. She could think of nothing to say.

He was still on one knee, the tongs in his strong hands. She could not read his expression. He had turned back to the fire.

"Grandma says do you want tea?" Betty was standing in the door. Mollie had made her put on her best dress.

"Thank you, sweetheart." Julia put her hand on Betty's black curls. "The nice way to say it is: Would you like some tea? I'll go and tell Mollie."

Afterward she thought about her feeling that he was going to kiss her, and his strange behavior when Archie Robertson came in just then. His face was flushed from the cold, and he was so eager to talk that he had left on his overcoat and scarf. His expression was pained and jubilant. He was a little short of breath.

"Julia, my dear!" He kissed her cheek and squeezed her hand. "Oh, hello. Peter Wentworth, isn't it?"

"Yes, sir." Peter got up to shake hands. "How do you do? I was dreadfully sorry to hear about Charles."

"Well, yes—thank you. It's good of you come and comfort Julia. But I must tell you the news. I've had a telegram from Ottawa. From the prime minister." His eyes filled with tears. "The king has awarded Charles the Victoria Cross! For extraordinary valor." He tried to stop his unmanly weeping but could not.

Julia, weeping too, went to her father-in-law and hugged him. They wept together.

Mr. Robertson collected himself and blew his nose. "What do you think of that, Peter?"

"Well, sir. It is a great honor. It would feel strange to congratulate you. It doesn't compensate for your loss. But it is a great honor. It is the greatest honor."

Archie Robertson had recovered. "I can tell you, it makes me very proud, to be—to have been his father."

"We were just going to have tea," Julia said. "Won't you join us?"

"Yes, my dear." Archie removed his coat, took it into the hall, and sat with them.

"It's the first Halifax VC. It may be the first Nova Scotia VC."

The news of the medal was emotionally neutral to her. It gave her a moment's pleasure to see Archie's spirits lifted, but she imagined it would mean little to Elizabeth. Medals were men's tokens. She knew right away what she would do with the medal. A posthumous medal was given to the widow. She had seen it often enough in the papers. When they gave her the Victoria Cross, she would give it to Archie. Her tears began again as she thought of the pleasure it would give him. Elizabeth Robertson would understand why she was doing it. Yes, she would give the VC to Archie.

Archie Robertson said to Peter, "I told the dean yesterday that my wife and I wished to give a window for the cathedral in Charles's memory. I think now it is even more fitting. He belongs not just to us but to Halifax, to Nova Scotia, to Canada."

"He is a symbol of the nation's sacrifice, sir. Our faith is built upon sacrifice."

The professional clergyman had risen so fulsomely in Peter's voice that Julia looked to see whether he was speaking ironically. She could see no sign, but he was too sure of himself and it annoyed her.

"You put it very well, Peter. And I'm grateful for the sentiment."

"Thank you, sir."

She heard the doorbell.

Then the afternoon grew very confused. People kept arriving. At the door was a messenger from the editor of the *Halifax Herald,* with a note asking for a good photograph of Charles. They wanted to run a large picture tomorrow morning. They were just taking the portrait of Charles in uniform from its frame in the drawing room when the bell rang again, and it was Stewart MacPherson. Julia greeted him warmly, holding his hand in both of hers for a moment, a gesture that Peter noticed.

"Please be absolutely sure that they send this photograph back," she said to the messenger.

"Yes, lady."

"It was done at Gauvin and Gentzel. They'll probably have the negative, Julia," Archie said.

"But this is the one I have lived with," Julia said quietly to him and then turned to Stewart. "Please come in. I'm sorry. You know Archibald Robertson and Peter Wentworth."

Stewart saw that Peter gave him an odd look as they shook hands. Of course—now Peter must know the diary was Julia's.

Julia noticed that Stewart's tweed suit needed pressing. She noticed how feelingly he spoke to Mr. Robertson, drawing him aside to talk about Charles. She heard him say quietly, "I regret that I didn't know him well. He was a few years younger, but I always felt what a fine, manly fellow he looked. I used to see him playing tennis but more often sailing, I think. It is a terrible loss for you."

"Thank you, Stewart. I've just been telling the others that they're going to"—he swallowed and was again on the verge of weeping—"they're going to award him the Victoria Cross!"

"Oh, that is wonderful, deeply moving. The Victoria Cross. You must be tremendously proud."

"I am, actually." Robertson was wiping his eyes with his handkerchief.

Julia saw Stewart notice Betty half-hiding behind the doorframe and give her black curls a friendly pat, as she had just done herself. His affection for the little girl touched her.

Stewart's arrival irritated Peter, making him sit on, wanting to make an excuse, but powerless to leave.

Julia led them into the sitting room but, looking around, said, "I think we'll move the tea things into the drawing room. It's too small in here. Betty, would you ask your granny for another cup and some more hot water? Thank you."

Stewart was looking at the picture in the sitting room.

"It looks like Matisse."

"It is!" Julia smiled, surprised. "I bought it in Paris. I was studying there. Jim Morrice—do you know the Montreal painter? He's a friend of Matisse. He helped me, so I got it very reasonably. I sold a bracelet my parents had given me. I've had it put away. So many people don't like it." She nodded toward Archie Robertson across the hall, and whispered, "He thinks it's awful."

"Well, didn't someone call him a monster, or something like that?"

"A wild beast, *un fauve.*"

"Oh, yes. Here, let me help you." Stewart picked up the tea tray.

Peter heard Stewart's remark and saw the conspiratorial whisper. He felt a stab of jealousy. Of course Stewart knew things like that, with his money and all those summers running around Europe before the war.

They settled in the drawing room and had tea. When she saw that Betty was out of the room, Julia said to Stewart, "Do you have any more news?"

"I've talked to Lewis Watson, the neurosurgeon at Dal. He thinks the case is so unusual that we should consult a man named Cushing in Boston. Cushing has done the most advanced work."

"In Boston? Would Betty have to go there?"

"For now, Watson can send a report to Cushing. It might not be necessary for her to go. It's not something that can be reversed, he says. It's just a question of the best predictions of how it will affect her development."

Julia turned to her father-in-law. "I've told you that Mr. MacPherson has been wonderful about Mollie's granddaughter. So generous with his time"—she turned, smiling—"with your time."

"Would you mind if I went and told Mollie?" Stewart asked.

"Of course not," Julia said. "She's been waiting to hear."

"He's an odd fellow, that MacPherson," Archie Robertson said when Stewart had left. "You knew him well, Peter, didn't you? I recall you two were chums."

Peter said, "Yes, we were at school and college together."

"He may be a little unconventional, Father," Julia said, "but you can't imagine how kind he's been to Betty. He has almost adopted her."

"I didn't get a good look at the little thing," Archie Robertson said. "Can we have her in and have a look?"

But that was interrupted by Lucy arriving with her two little girls, and Betty came out to see them. Elizabeth and Sarah shook hands gravely with Julia and then escaped to the kitchen with Betty and Mollie. Another cup was brought and the circle grew larger. Stewart returned.

Stewart thought that Lucy looked more haggard than Julia from the news about Charles. Her jolly tomboyish manner was subdued. She kissed her father and Julia and shook hands with the two younger men. When she sat down, she took her father's hand and held it. Her eyes looked red. She immediately noticed the missing picture.

"Oh, you haven't taken his picture away?"

Julia explained about the newspaper.

Lucy said quietly, "The girls are very upset. They keep asking, if Uncle Charles can die, what about Daddy. They've never known closely anyone who died." She started to weep and turned away.

Julia saw Charles's familiar gesture of turning his head. All the ways in which Lucy resembled her brother were suddenly apparent. With a rush of affection, Julia got up and embraced Lucy. The blank picture frame affected her too. She should have given the newspaper another photograph. She felt there were too many emotional forces in the room pulling at her.

"I think we need the fire on in here. It's a little chilly after the study. Would you mind?" She handed the matches to Archie, who was glad of something to do.

Peter sat quietly, trying to look at the others and follow the conversation with his eyes, but against his will they were drawn back to Julia. Every detail: her graceful thumbnail pressed on the china handle of her teacup. She kept giving him quick, inquisitive glances. He felt that he knew her better than he knew Margery. In turning to the others, his glance passed the empty silver frame. Charles was gone.

Beside it was the wedding photograph, almost identical with the one of Peter and Margery. Looking at it now, and looking away, not wanting to stare, but looking again at Julia's face with the veil thrown back, Peter recalled her description of her wedding night. He glanced at the real Julia, talking earnestly to Lucy, and back at the photograph of the wedding.

The diary had told him how sensual this woman was, how she liked to make love, got hot with the thought of it, perspired in her dresses, was impetuous, took risks, could laugh at herself, hated her mother, liked her mother-in-law, had traveled, liked music, had studied art; a woman rich in the life of the body and of the spirit. He swallowed dryly at the intensity of his desire for her.

"Mr. Wentworth had to go to the mass funeral today for the victims of the explosion," Julia said. She would not use his first name. "He said there were nearly two hundred coffins. I suppose it is important to remember that for a moment. It puts our loss in a different light."

Stewart also watched Julia, sitting demurely, appealing in her black dress. The diary made it impossible not to think of her sexually, but her physical presence made the diary irrelevant. That was interesting; the woman was far more exciting than her diary, however candid it was. The diary was like a medical abstract, highlighting some symptoms; the real woman gave infinitely more complex signals.

He intercepted the intense light of Peter's gaze fixed on Julia. Stewart recognized that intensity. He had seen it over the years. It used to be directed at Margery. But Stewart had never seen Peter look so fixedly, so hungrily, at anybody as he did at Julia.

As the afternoon closed in, they talked about Charles.

Lucy said, "It's so hard for me to imagine my little brother a hero. You think of a hero as someone in the books, devil-may-care. Charles was very careful—I don't mean afraid—he just wanted to think something out before he did it, like going into a tricky place in the boat. He could be like an old woman, fussing and checking, sounding again—"

"But he never cracked her up," said his father. "He may have bumped a rock here and there, we all do, but he never ran her aground."

"He could feel his way into the cove in a fog," said Lucy, "as though he could smell it. He'd terrify me. There's almost never any wind on those days, scarcely enough to move the boat, and he'd come drifting in. He'd listen to the noises on the shore, the rout they call it, the different sound the waves make in different places. Sometimes it felt close enough to touch. You could hear people talking, yet you couldn't see a thing. Every minute I'd swear we were going to hit something. And he loved to say absolutely nothing until, at the very last minute, he'd say, 'We should be there now.' He'd swing her around and the mooring would miraculously appear out of the fog . . ."

Julia, Peter, and Stewart listened. When they turned, the empty picture frame stared at them like Betty's bandaged eye.

Archie Robertson said, "You can't predict who's going to be a hero. Look at Nelson, a tiny little man physically, probably the weakest man on board any of his ships, quite a feminine man, you'd have to say in some ways, yet with the heart of a lion and a way about him that inspired everyone around him. Look at that RN chap you danced with at Government House, Julia, the dark-haired lieutenant with the DSO—what was his name?"

Peter looked at Julia, then rapidly at Stewart, each realizing the other knew, as they turned back to Julia, who flushed, but raised her chin, determined to be honest. "Lieutenant Boiscoyne."

"Boiscoyne, that's it. Who would have thought to look at him? A sort of drawing room dandy, a real ladies' man he looked. But he'd won a DSO."

Julia kept her eyes lowered. She felt they were all staring at her. When she looked up, Peter Wentworth had the peculiarly intense, almost impertinently intimate look she now recognized.

She said to Stewart, "You're the psychologist, Mr. MacPherson. What makes one man a hero?"

"Well, I don't know. In *The Master of Ballantrae,* Robert Louis Stevenson says, 'Not every man is so great a coward as he thinks he is' "—Stewart turned to Peter with a laugh—" 'nor yet so good a Christian.' I wrote it down years ago when I was a boy and felt very much a coward myself. Peter was a hero to me then, absolutely fearless physically. I was a miserable fellow, afraid of every-thing."

Lucy laughed. "Even I could beat you running, Stewart, or climbing fences."

Stewart said, "Probably still could." Everyone laughed. He pulled out his cigarette case. "Do you mind if I smoke?"

Julia shook her head. Clearly Peter had mixed feelings about being praised by Stewart. She could see how uncomfortable Peter was, the corners of his mouth drawn back, with Stewart perfectly at his ease announcing his own weaknesses. How different they looked to her.

She looked at her father-in-law, who had taken an offered ciga-rette. She could imagine him thinking that the awkward man had been spared because he was short-sighted, and the clergyman, who looked athletic and strong, had been protected by his clerical collar. What parent would not be resentful? Others never even saw the battle.

Archibald Robertson was talking about the city's recovery. The quantities of supplies arriving, the amounts of money promised by many countries meant that replacing the devastation would make a better city than before.

Julia said, "It needs to be. The conditions in the North End were awful—where Mollie's daughter lived. And the rates of disease were appalling. Much worse than Montreal, which is a bigger city."

"First they have to build temporary housing for the homeless people," Archie said. "Fifteen thousand of them, so it won't be until next summer or fall that they can start planning new neighborhoods."

Stewart said, "It may take a lot longer to repair some of the psychic trauma in this city."

"What is trauma?" Julia asked.

"Trauma is a wound. Medically, any kind of wound. Psychology borrowed the same Latin word for an emotional wound."

"Trauma is a Greek word," Peter said, irritated that Stewart held her rapt attention.

"Well, you're right, of course. Greek, then Latin, but, interestingly, the word *Traum* is also the German for dream, and terrible dreams may be one of the obvious symptoms. The war has created a great many examples of traumatic neurosis, like shell shock. I've been working with some of them."

Archie Robertson snorted. "You can't help wondering whether some of those supposed shell-shock cases we read about aren't just cowards finding a way to save their skins."

"Well, with respect, Mr. Robertson, it is fear, but their illness means they can't overcome their fear, as other men do. They become powerless to act, and they're ashamed of themselves for letting the other soldiers down."

"Can they be cured?" Julia said.

"Some very quickly. A little rest, a sharp talking to, and they snap out of it and go back to the front. Other cases, about a third of them, are much more difficult. In extreme cases there's a real breakdown of personality."

"But if it doesn't cure itself, how do you heal a psychic wound?"

Stewart laughed. "Well, to be honest, not much better now than all the things mankind has tried—witchcraft, sorcery, magic, religious exercises, exorcism, drugs, hypnosis, isolation in madhouses, imprisonment, cold baths, electric shocks. I'm prejudiced in favor of a fairly new technique called psychoanalysis."

Julia asked, "And have you found many people hurt—mentally affected by the explosion?"

He described the zeppelin man's hallucination and the woman who mistook the wrong body for her brother, and several still in hospital.

"That sounds fascinating," Julia said.

"I suppose we're all affected in some way," Stewart said.

"Oh, it sounds morbid to me." Lucy got up. "The woman in the morgue gives me the shivers. Sorry to interrupt, but I've left the girls too long, and I promised to go and see Mother."

Her father got up too. "Come with me, old girl. We'll go together." He turned to Julia. "Why don't you come home and have supper with us?"

"I think I'll just stay quiet tonight. It is wonderful about the VC." Julia went into the hall to help with their coats.

Stewart said quietly to Peter, "What are you going to do about the diary?"

Peter looked at him coldly. "It's of no importance now."

"Did you burn it?"

"I haven't decided yet."

"It's not very fair to her just to sit on it. I think you should destroy it or give it back."

Peter turned and went into the hall. He seemed in a hurry to leave, finding his coat, pushing past Archie and Lucy, saying a quick good night from the door.

"Oh. Good night, Mr. Wentworth." Julia turned to Stewart. "Thank you for coming. I think your work sounds important and interesting. I'd love to know more about it."

"Really?"

"Yes, I mean it," she said. "Good night."

Stewart left so filled with her presence that he walked several yards down South Park Street before remembering he had come in the Paige. As he got in, he thought, She is the most attractive woman I have ever met.

Every step took Peter away from what he desired toward what he dreaded, the barely controlled hysteria he always found in his home at suppertime.

His hand immediately found the frayed white feather in his coat pocket. Angrily, in the dark, he dropped it to the sidewalk and ground it into the slush with his heel. Mention of the diary had angered him. Of course he should have burned it immediately or returned it to her anonymously. That Stewart knew made it worse.

He had never felt this way. Women had never been a matter of curiosity to him. Now this woman devoured him. Or he wanted to devour her. He wanted to possess her. He could not think clearly when he was with her. Her insistent questions about faith were like the thunderous cracking when you ventured too far on new ice. And she still called him Mr. Wentworth.

It was Stewart who was poised, gracious, seeing the small thing to do, picking up the tea tray at the helpful moment. He saw the look Julia gave Stewart when he arrived and saw again her two hands clasped for a second on his. It was typical that Stewart recognized the painting, those garish daubs, and typical that he liked it.

It was an old hurt, the wound of other people's wealth. The assurance it gave Stewart to be able to say, "It looks like . . ." (Peter couldn't remember the artist's name), implying that he and Julia had been everywhere and seen everything. Humiliating to be so hard-up. He needed to go to the tailor to pick up the suit. Margery would disapprove, but a suit for four dollars? Now her father was going to pay for a maid. Even more humiliating, more dependent. And no end to it.

The Victoria Cross. Both men in Julia's life, Charles and Lieutenant Boiscoyne, were war heroes. People would be talking about nothing but Charles Robertson, VC, for months. The memorial service would be almost a state occasion. The dean, a friend of the Robertsons, would make sure of that for political reasons, too.

Boiscoyne. She blushed when her father-in-law came out with the name. Peter thought he might have blushed. But she recovered swiftly, asking Stewart what a psychologist thought a hero was.

He arrived home to find that, tonight, Margery had arranged everything with obsessive care. The house was unusually peaceful; Abigail and Michael had been bathed and were happily eating boiled eggs, dipping toast fingers in the yolks.

"Mine are toast soldiers," Michael said. He had yolk around his lips.

"Mummy's upstairs—getting dressed," Abby said importantly. "Granny was here today. She's going to take us to her house tomorrow morning."

His mother's visits always made Margery a more conscientious housekeeper—for a day or two.

When he opened the bedroom door, he found her dressed, staring into the dressing table mirror, as if at someone she did not know. She looked at him in the same way, a person she did not recognize. She could find no words.

He had his hand on the doorknob. "Would you like a glass of sherry?" He couldn't remember when he had last asked her that.

She hesitated, looking puzzled. "Yes."

Peter was glad for her quiet mood. He didn't want to talk. He poured two sherries and left hers on the sideboard in the little dining room. He took his into his study and sat down at his desk. In the bottom drawer on the right-hand side was Julia's diary, but it was not locked. He must have forgotten. Careless.

His house felt mean and dark compared with Julia's; cramped, full of shadowy corners that neither the sun nor electric light often reached. The colors were drab and somber. Julia's rooms were filled with light, even on a gray winter afternoon.

She had asked how his faith helped him deal with the pain of his life. Until now, it had been like an anesthetic. It made all the humiliations, the disappointments, if not a joy, at least tolerable. His burden for Christ. Poverty humbled pride. But the anesthetic had worn off.

He wanted to open the drawer quickly and look at a few pages of the diary, to renew his contact with her. No, he must resist. In the bookshelves he spotted Augustine's *Confessions*. He rose and pulled it down. He had not opened it since the examination at King's.

Verily Thou enjoinest me continency from the lust of the flesh, the lust of the eyes, and the ambition of the world. Thou enjoinest continency from concubinage . . .

Margery put the children to bed and came quietly downstairs. He heard her distantly in the kitchen. The sounds mingled with his reading.

And since Thou gavest it, it was done even before I became a dispenser of Thy Sacrament. But there yet live in my memory (whereof I have much spoken) the images of such things, as my ill custom there fixed; which haunt me, strengthless when I am awake: but in sleep, not only so as to give pleasure, but even to attain assent, and what is very like reality.

Margery had made more effort than usual for supper: finnan haddie—smoked haddock, poached in milk with white sauce and boiled potatoes, rings of hard-boiled egg sliced on top. His mother had given her the recipe, but Margery's sauce was lumpy, and there wasn't enough salt.

She served it without speaking and sat opposite him. When she looked up, her eyes focused over his shoulder. She seemed unnaturally calm.

"Are you going to talk to some of the maids your mother has in mind?"

Her eyes connected with his for a moment. He could not read her expression: opaque, a closed look, not inviting penetration.

"Your mother stopped by this morning."

"Abigail told me."

"She said she hoped she'd see you tomorrow morning. She's coming to have the children for the morning. Do you have to go out early?"

"I have to take morning service."

"You'll miss her. She's not coming till nine."

Margery wasn't hungry. The white sauce was congealed and unappetizing. She had been very ill with her two other pregnancies.

She watched Peter eat. The precision of his table manners irritated her. He held his knife and fork almost at their tips, his elbows close to his sides. Her father had much rougher table manners, as her mother often remarked. Peter's were too correct. There was something self-conscious and prissy about them. Canon Wentworth and Peter's mother didn't eat like that. It was something Peter had adopted for himself, like his half-English enunciation, too correct, intended to impress someone.

It was the first fault in Peter she had permitted herself to acknowledge for a long time. All the faults in their married life had been hers. Her failures. Things she observed as negatives about Peter, she had pushed aside. What did they matter, compared with her gross failures? She watched him eat in his precise, too careful way. What did it matter if his table manners irritated her? He did what he had to do. People admired him for everything he did. They told him how handsome he was for a minister. The old ladies loved to hear his speaking voice in the services. The dean admired him, and Mrs. Creighton.

How lucky you are, Margery, they all said.

Her father respected his mind and his discipline. Her mother thought him wonderful; such an asset to have a good-looking son-in-law who can talk gracefully at the dinner table. No one ever had a negative word to say about him. Some of the other girls thought he was too deep. Margery didn't try to fathom how deep he was now; she knew he was not as kind as he had been. His impatience with her was showing. The way he drew back the corners of his lips when she spoke; the way he was clearly thinking of something else when he was with her.

"You can have mine if you're still hungry. I don't feel like it."

"You're sure?"

She watched him eat her entire plate, too, silently.

"I have some reading to do."

That curtness was different. He usually helped her clear the table, wash or dry the dishes, before going to his study.

Margery went up to bed. Everything seemed simple to her. In the bathroom cabinet were the narcotic drops she used to soothe the children when they were teething or had upset tummies. For them she put ten drops in a glass of water, and to make herself sleepy a few times she had used fifteen drops. Tonight, to be sure, she counted thirty drops, or, rather, she counted twenty-one, lost count, started again, and counted ten more. She drank it quickly. She did not want to lie awake. She wanted everything to be solved. She wanted to sink into the comfortable blackness of sleep. She wanted to push aside, hide behind, the black curtains of sleep, the knowledge that something had broken in Peter's feeling for her. Something had broken . . . Since the explosion something had broken . . . not as nice . . . Something broken . . . something . . .

> . . . the higher part of our nature aspires after eternal bliss while our lower self is held back by the love of temporal pleasure. It is the same soul that wills both, but wills neither of them with the full force of the will.

St. Augustine was too intellectual for Peter tonight.

> I was held back by . . . all my old attachments. They plucked at my garment of flesh and whispered, "Are you going to dismiss us?"

The ascetic thrill of denying the flesh, of reaching for something higher, that Peter had felt reading the saint in college had gone.

The *Confessions* and Julia's diary lay side by side on his desk. The house was quiet. He was impatient with Augustine. The chapter that had thrilled him as a student was cold to him now. The concupiscent power Augustine described, so strong that it invaded his dreams, forcing him against his will to be incontinent in sleep, had electrified Peter then. It was his own life. It greatly reinforced his sense of vocation that fifteen hundred years earlier a man had lived whose psychology was real to a young priest struggling in the twentieth century.

The young Augustine had denied himself no sensual pleasure, had never curbed his sexual curiosity. It was stretching human nature to believe that the repentant sinner did not harbor a residue of satisfaction. It was all there in his mind as he developed the idea of original sin.

Was it more saintly to turn continent after such unbridled indulgence, or to be continent as Peter had been? Whom does God favor: the prodigal son or the brother who does not stray? The reformed sinner or the man without sin? Augustine had it both ways. Peter was annoyed with him, as though the great saint had changed since college and let him down.

Margery was the only woman Peter had ever known, the only woman who had ever piqued his sexual curiosity. He had pursued God before desire, not after becoming the slave of desire like Augustine.

The image of Julia kept insinuating itself, and the fantasy of taking her in his arms, of feeling her hair fall over his face. What did he desire beyond that? Could he even imagine her legs opening?

He opened the diary. He knew just where to turn for the lines that inflamed him.

I want him to kiss the nipples and put them in his mouth. I once tried to put myself in a position where they would be near his lips, but he did not do it.

He turned to the day of the picnic at Herring Cove.

Bunching my skirts up, I sat on the granite with my feet in the sea. After a few seconds, the water was numbingly cold, but

I left them in to see how long I could stand it. There was something exciting about the pain of testing myself, as though it gave me physical contact with C. The numbness crept up to my thighs before I finally got up.

Her pleasure seemed so innocent that it made Peter's arousal by it seem innocent too. She said her knee tasted of salt. He had never tasted the skin of a woman's knee. He had never kissed any part of Margery except her face and her hands.

He turned to another place that was dark to him and sinful, her night on the train.

Then I imagined him in this bed with me on the train until the excitement was unbearable . . . thinking about it had raised me to such a pitch that I shook all over and found myself perspiring and shivering.

It had disturbed him that she could think of three different men; now it drew him, giving him license to think of her physically. She was not a chaste virgin, remote and unattainable, despite her angelic looks. Her woman's senses were full of desire for male contact. It was nearly two years since she had slept with a man, and now, when her mourning wore off, she would know that more than ever, the emptiness, the loneliness.

He wanted her physically and fully. He wanted to see her out of her black dress. He wanted to kiss her nipples.

DEAN CREIGHTON sat with the bishop. Even close to the fire, wearing a cardigan and a woollen dressing gown, the old man felt chilled. The skin on his hands was almost transparent. His housekeeper was out, and the dean had made them each a brandy with hot water. The little visits now took place almost daily, as the bishop felt too frail to risk the penetrating December damp.

The dean related the events of the morning at the mass funeral. Both men shook their heads over the unseemliness.

"I have never heard of anything like this," the bishop said weakly. "How dreadful!"

"Well, we helped to bury the *Titanic* victims. Remember, 1912?"

"Ah, yes, we did."

"But it wasn't ghastly like this, or cold like today. I put on two pairs of Stanfields and I was still frozen to the marrow."

"Two pairs of Stanfields!" The bishop chuckled and sipped his brandy. His bony hand trembled as he raised the glass, and he steadied it with the other.

He smiled as the dean described some delicate maneuvering. Did he, as surrogate for the Anglican bishop, or the monsignor, for the Catholic archbishop, take precedence in the giving the blessings?

"We are almost the established church, whereas they are, what, a cofounding religion? That might give the edge to us, but, then, does the Catholic archbishop's surrogate outrank the Anglican bishop's? I thought it best to have no scenes, so I simply deferred. Monsignor gave me a look under his biretta as though he suspected some trick of condescension. I had a wicked temptation to whisper, 'Virgins first!' "

"Oh, Donald!" The bishop chortled. He loved slightly risqué jokes, particularly about the clergy, and in his time had been a prodigious teller of them. "I wonder what he would have said if you had?"

"I wonder whether he would have gone first!"

The poor old bishop spluttered in his drink and laughed so hard he coughed, and Donald Creighton had to take the glass out of his hand for a moment.

When he recovered, the dean pulled out the preliminary list of damage estimates for all the churches in Halifax and Dartmouth and the cost of repairing them. Most of the damaged churches were not Anglican, evidence that their writ did not run far in poor areas of the city.

"But the most important news is that Charles Robertson, Archie's boy, has been awarded a VC."

"The Victoria Cross? How extraordinary! Archie must be very pleased. What an honor for Halifax!"

"But it's very sad. You remember, we heard on Saturday that the boy died from his wounds."

"Oh, dear, yes. I had forgotten."

"Do you remember we talked about a memorial service?"

"So it's a posthumous VC?"

"That's right."

"Well, well—how very sad."

"It will mean a rather different memorial service. There has never been a local VC. And the son of a very prominent old Halifax family—friends of the prime minister. I would expect a huge turnout. Almost a state occasion."

Dean Creighton feared he was making it sound too enticing.

"Can we manage with the cathedral in such a damaged condition?"

Obviously his memory was still intact when the news had time to sink in.

"Oh, we can manage. It's really just a matter of some windows blocked up. It might stimulate people to donate a window here and there. It is a bit dark. A daytime service feels like evensong."

"I always liked the coziness of evensong," the bishop said wistfully.

"The question is, sir, whether you will feel up to leading the memorial service yourself."

"Oh, I don't know—"

"Well, don't worry. There's time to consider. It would certainly be most fitting for the bishop of Nova Scotia to officiate. If you didn't—"

"We could always call in another bishop, couldn't we?"

"Oh, I don't think that would be necessary."

"Quebec could probably get down here in time. It's only an overnight train. He'd probably like to be asked."

"Why don't we see how you feel in the next few days, Bishop? It's really your place. If, at the last minute, you didn't feel up to the long service—"

"Then it would be too late to ask another bishop, wouldn't it? He'd need some notice."

Disconcertingly to Dean Creighton, the discussion or the brandy had perked up His Grace noticeably.

"Well, you could always take my place, Donald." The old man looked at him knowingly. "I dare say it won't be long before you are doing that in any case."

"Oh, no—"

"No. I feel a little tireder each day. I wouldn't be surprised if the Good Lord asks me to join him quite soon."

The dean murmured comfortingly.

"In fact," the bishop went on, "I had been thinking of it before you came. Not about *my* death, particularly—the prospect doesn't perturb me—but about all these young men cut off in their twenties. I did remember Charles Robertson's death. It just slipped my mind for a moment. I cannot find any comforting way to explain his death, and all the others. It's thousands and thousands now, isn't it?"

"I tell myself they are fighting willingly for king and empire," Dean Creighton said.

"But, Donald, they are still dying thousands at a time! There has never been anything like this in history. Last year, I'm not sure when, I had a letter from a friend in Newfoundland. I knew him in a mission in Labrador years ago. We spent a summer there. He told me of a one action a soldier wrote him about. They sent a Newfoundland battalion into action. A thousand went in and in one attack half of them were killed. These are civilized times. We are all Christian people. The Germans are a civilized nation. So are the French. I do not see any explanation that justifies slaughter on this dimension. I see no glory in it for anyone. I pray as earnestly as I know how for comfort and guidance. I am quite perplexed—very perplexed."

The old man is losing his grip on reality, Dean Creighton thought. Better not encourage him to do the memorial. Even if he were physically able, he might come out with sentiments like these.

"I am not sure I would be able to give much spiritual comfort to Archibald Robertson if I saw him," the bishop continued. "What a waste of a young man!"

"But the VC?"

"The VC is nice for us. It makes us feel proud. Perhaps it lessens the pain for the family. It doesn't do much for the boy, does it?"

"Shouldn't we think that it sends him to paradise sooner?"

"I wonder whether he would think that was a good bargain."

The bishop had always been politically canny, a statesman in church politics, a diplomat in civil politics, never dogmatic about doctrine or ideology. In short, a model Anglican bishop in Canada, civilized, dignified but compassionate, deferential to custom and authority, with a twinkling way of asserting himself firmly. But since his wife died, he had changed. Donald Creighton had never heard him so bleak, so empty.

"They're having much more difficulty recruiting them now. Conscription or not."

"I'm not surprised," said the bishop. "If I were a young man, I wouldn't be eager to go."

"I respectfully disagree, sir. If you were young, if we were both young, we would both probably have wanted to go with the first wave. The call thrilled young Canada when it came. Look how badly Peter Wentworth still wants to go."

"I wonder whether Peter's desire to go overseas isn't a wish to get away from his troubles at home," the bishop mused. "That occurred to me after you told me about his wife. War is a wonderful excuse to run away from responsibilities."

"Well, I had never thought of that," the dean said.

"I think you should find more for Peter to do. Send him around the province. Keep him busy."

"I do, I do."

"Find more errands for him. Use him as an archdeacon. Let the rectors get to know him and depend on him: listen to their complaints and carry their messages. You know what I mean. He'll be very useful to you when I move on."

The dean murmured his consoling murmur.

"But—I haven't moved on yet! So, how about the other half before you face the awful winter night?"

With an energetic thrust and no tremble, the old bishop held out his glass. His cheeks glowed and his eyes sparkled.

## HALIFAX HERO AWARDED
## POSTHUMOUS VC

### MAJOR CHARLES ROBERTSON

### CITED FOR ACTS OF HIGHEST

### VALOR IN FRANCE

The picture from Julia's living room, as large as in the frame, appeared with a double black border.

Stewart read all the details. Charles Robertson had obviously shown the kind of bravery that does not know it is bravery. Now it would be embalmed in all the ghastly purple writing and the tawdry sentiments wartime patriotism creates—this awful mixture of jingoism and near exultation in death. The writing smacked of competition to be marked for patriotism, to be graded for war enthusiasm.

The *Chronicle* was blazoning its own series, UNSUNG HEROES OF THE EXPLOSION, a $25 prize for each story printed. Stewart turned it aside to look at Charles Robertson's picture.

What point could possibly be served by continuing to sacrifice young men like him? He was probably not an exceptional fellow; not much imagination, to judge by Julia's diary; emotionally some-what repressed, but kindly and decent and quite able, like Archie, to run an important business. Sooner or later it had to stop. Nei-ther Britain nor Germany could feed men into the war machine forever. There would have to be a cease-fire sooner or later and a political settlement of some kind.

It was interesting that Canadians fought so well. So many VCs for the small CEF. What made Canadians such devils at war? Canadians were very quiet people, normally, most unwarlike. Shy and laconic was the average fellow on the farm, in the fishing boat, the worker in the city; not much bravado.

London couldn't have made Canadians go. But that's irrelevant, because many were thrilled to go. At one point so many people got themselves made officers and sent to England that they almost outnumbered the men: thousands of officers milling around Lon-don with no one to give orders to. Major Coleman had told Stew-art that.

From Julia's diary it was clear that Charles was one of the first to be fired up to go. Now he was a dead hero and she was a widow.

What would it do to her to be the widow of such a hero? They would want to use her for recruitment, for the election. She would lose her anonymity. She would become a chattel of the awful industry of patriotism. They would try to parade her at war bond rallies. Again Stewart felt, as he had with Peter and the diary, a desire to protect her.

It would be a difficult day for her, more difficult than yesterday. People would call, sincere in their good wishes but, in reality, wishing to share the thrill of the Victoria Cross. He suspected that Julia would shrink from that. For a moment, Stewart thought of inviting her to come with him as he continued to interview his cases. He looked at the telephone and decided it was intruding too much.

. . . .

Julia could not read the newspaper. The familiar picture staring at her from the front page looked unreal, the black type was meaningless, like a foreign language with one recognizable proper name leaping out. People began telephoning. She had just been downstairs for the third time when it rang again. It would be like this all day. She called down, "Mollie, would you say I can't talk just now?"

She still felt confused. Last night their presence had comforted her, but she wanted them gone. Yet when they left, she felt forlorn and weepy. Everything her eyes touched reminded her so poignantly of Charles that her sense of aloneness grew in every dimension. There was no comfort now in fingering something of his— his pipes in the sitting room. They were no longer tokens of his return but stabbing reminders that he would not return. Each object drove the reality further into her heart.

The stimulus of talking had driven that reality back; when the others left, it crept in like fog coming into a room after the fire gets low. The night stretching ahead of her seemed an endless prospect —far emptier than all the nights of the two years since Charles had left.

When everyone had gone, she sat and poked the fire. With a start, she remembered her certainty that Peter intended to kiss her. She blushed, and jammed the poker savagely into the coals. There was a quality about him that both attracted and irritated her. He was too sure of himself, with his handsome face and knowing stare. Yet his presence excited her. Again she felt that thread of terror, the conviction that the primitive woman in her would not be tamed; that she was the prisoner of her body; that it would drive her into impulsive behavior. Archie Robertson's reference to Neville Boiscoyne was disturbing too. He had spoken with no malice but had touched a nerve. Lucy had shown a knowing look. But Peter Wentworth had blushed as though he knew.

It was stimulating to argue with him, yet he angered her for a reason she could not identify.

After tonight there would be tomorrow night and Wednesday and Thursday and all the nights of her life. The procession of empty evenings marched ahead, furnished like this one, in this house, the same furniture. She saw herself sitting in the same chair wearing the same, slightly outdated black dress—a Miss Havisham, in black.

Now, in the light of day, she smiled and noticed that she was smiling. She glanced up at the Matisse and felt her spirits lift. It always gave her instant reassurance: the painting was like a dream that said life is beautiful.

She heard the telephone ring again and the doorbell. Mollie answered the telephone, so Julia went to the door and found the postman. Only old men seemed to be postmen now.

He handed her several letters and said, "Mrs. Robertson, I am very sorry to hear the tragic news about your husband." He had tears in his eyes.

"That is very kind of you."

"Still you must be a very proud woman, too. It's the greatest honor there is, the Victoria Cross."

"Yes."

"He's made us all proud of the effort Halifax is making for king and country." He stood straighter as he said it, then went down the steps.

Julia's own tears blurred the writing on the envelopes in her hand until, with a shudder, she saw they were from Charles. Five of them. The wave of fresh grief that seized her was different from any before. Mollie heard her crying and came out.

"What's the matter, dear?"

Julia lifted her hand with the letters.

"Oh, dear God. They're from him?" And Mollie too began to weep. "It's more than a heart can bear, isn't it?"

Julia usually read Charles's letters sitting on their bed. She retreated there now and leaned against the pillows but left the letters unopened in her lap. She thought of dates and time passing. This was probably the last she would ever hear from the man she had given her life to, but who had needed only a small part of it.

At last she opened them all and arranged them by date. The words "My dearest Julia" started her tears again. The handwriting, slanted, still boyish, brought his personality vividly into the room and her heart. She had to put the letters down until her sobbing stopped. Then she read:

My dearest Julia,

You must have heard about Passchendaele by now. It was very costly. Very big losses. But it did something for our spirits. It's funny, but each battle we get through we feel more Canadian. We really feel we are carving out a piece of the world's regard. No, I don't mean that exactly. Sounds too pompous. Maybe it's our own self-regard we are trying to earn. Correction: we have earned. The rest of the world isn't watching. But the Brits are watching. Even Haig, that hellish incompetent, is watching. Haig came trotting by on his horse to look at us the day after Passchendaele ended. We were lined up along the road, pretty casually, literally back from hell and a lot of us not back. Half the men there could have happily shot him off his horse. You can't imagine the contempt for that man among the officers—I mean senior officers as well as my level. I don't know about the men. I dare not raise the subject with them. Don't want any mutinies like the French. They had to shoot hundreds of their own soldiers to get control of their army. But among those of us privy to scraps of gossip that the staff officers bring back from the briefings, the reaction to his arrogant stupidity is murderous. I can't imagine Genghis Khan or Zulu chiefs throwing away thousands of lives as casually as Haig spends British lives—and ours. It is one thing to swallow your own terror, put on a good face for your comrades and for your officers, if you think the generals sending you into battle have a good plan and want to lose as few men as possible. But to go knowing that you and your company, your battalion and a dozen others are being sent because the General Staff can't think of anything else to do!

Months ago, when we were stalled, Haig was like a boxer, half dead on his feet, punching, getting punched, punching, getting punched, because he couldn't stop and couldn't think of a ruse or feint; but each punch here meant throwing in several thousand men, and hundreds of them fell. Then the Germans threw a punch and we killed hundreds of them. And we threw another punch: hundreds more dead. We gained nothing; they gained nothing. Or we gained a hundred yards of godforsaken terrain, mud hills, and water-filled craters, held it for a day, then lost it back to them.

But I suppose Haig in his way is as numb to the big losses as we've become to the small losses. It's amazing to see what your mind gets used to. It's not only inhuman but pushed to the last extremes of inhumanity.

Where was I? Haig. The other day he came by. We had mustered the men along the road. We all stood there, muddy, exhausted, staring like dumb animals. This natty little figure, with his scarlet cap band and general officer's tabs, trots up and says casually, "Well done, chaps!" as though we'd won the under-fifteen soccer match at school.

They told us Currie (our general) had to fight with him to let him use our troops *our* way. Tactics. No more suicide waves.

The Aussies are watching. Good troops and fighting for the same thing we are, I guess, some recognition from the Brits that we exist!

The poor British don't know any longer what they are fighting for. We wonder about it among ourselves. To keep the class system going? The French, at least, are fighting for their own land.

In the next letter, Charles wrote:

I wish I had studied politics instead of so much engineering. I know all about stresses and vectors and mechanical advantage, and I don't know a damn about the kind of people who govern us or what it's all for. I know Dad likes Borden. From here Borden looks like all the politicians in black frock coats and silk hats, lying like fakirs to keep their heads from the guillotine.

I'm now acting major. Smitty bought it, poor chap. I don't want to talk about that. I had to write to his wife.

I'm really beginning to understand that smart tactics pay off. For months I thought it was all hopeless. One lot of idiots and ruthless commanders on our side send thousands of men to certain destruction, lining them up like the redcoats against the French in the 1700s, so that a few survivors can take a hill, so that the German commanders can order just as pointless a counterattack against the hill with losses just as heavy. A victory for home consumption on both sides. Then it takes two days to clear all the bodies off the field. Some of them don't get taken away. Artillery shells come in and blow them into small pieces— feet, arms, heads flying through the air in a storm of earth. Or the wounded are buried by the earth thrown about, or they drown when the rain comes and fills the new craters. I know for a fact that hundreds of our men drowned at Passchendaele, just slipped under the mud.

Our trenches got so slimy at the bottom, you couldn't know what you were standing on, mud or rotting men. The smell was indescribable, but if they were shelling, you couldn't escape it. Haig sent thousands at a time to wallow through the slippery, sucking, oozing mud under withering fire, and he expected the men to do it, not once but again and again. It is amazing to me that there weren't more deserters.

But now I'm acting bttn 2 i/c, I can see there are cleverer and stupider ways through it. Currie is finding the cleverer ways. Got to stop now.

In another letter:

It has taken me two years of this madness to discover what makes me tick. I must have been half-asleep before all this. I had never heard of the Bolsheviks, who have now taken over in Russia.

A very bright fellow has joined the bttn. He won a Rhodes Scholarship and studied political economy at Oxford. He says what really caused this war was Britain's fear of being eclipsed by Germany economically. For ten years the Brits watched with mounting alarm as Germany's scientific and industrial might and merchant tonnage surpassed their own and Germany began edging Britain out in overseas markets. He says some British leaders talked privately years ago of having to go to war with Germany to stop it. It helped that Germany has a madman as kaiser, but there would have had to be some other pretext to stop Germany if he hadn't given one by invading Belgium. So what we Canadians are doing here is saving Britain's bacon and export markets, because the Germans were beating them at their own game, fair and square.

I never paid the slightest attention to political arguments at McGill. Engineers didn't debate much anyway; spent far too much time getting drunk and playing bridge. I didn't have a position about Lloyd George and the terrible things he was supposed to be doing that had everyone so excited. And I had no clear idea of Canada as something on its own, a nation in itself; never thought of it that way. I got on the troopship in

Halifax that day thinking I was going to serve Britain and the king. I didn't even think *empire*—just *Britain*.

We came over here as all sorts of different things, but I think we'll go back more Canadian.

Another letter:

I'm getting quite good at this stuff and am enjoying the skills. We've have been through so much that I've almost outgrown being afraid. Almost—bad luck to boast about anything like that. It's useful, because when you're terrified, you can't use your imagination to consider anything but saving your own skin. And you're more likely to do that and save some other skins around you if you can use your imagination.

It is stupid, though, because the purpose of being here cannot possibly be worth all this slaughter. Fine young fellows by the hundreds and thousands being led up—sent up—pushed up—bullied up—frightened up—like steers to a slaughterhouse. And they go. Company after company of them docilely go! Not docilely. That's wrong. They go, we all go, convinced the purpose is fine. There is a crazy new spirit buoying up our chaps because the Canadians have made a real difference. After Vimy and right through Passchendaele there's been a weird elation. Our chaps know we're the ones they send in when it's impossible. You want to break an unbreakable German line? Send the Canadians!

The odd thing is that kind of spirit breeds more confidence, and more confidence drives you forward. You don't feel tired, you don't feel as frightened, you think you can take the hill and you do—probably with fewer losses. You even hear our fellows bursting with pride because "we lost more than that British regiment next door." In fact, I think half of what has driven the Canadians is the wish to show the miserable blank-blank Englishman how to fight this war. The British attitude of superiority may be the fuel that drives our people like devils. There are fewer British-born soldiers in our ranks than in the first wave of volunteers. But I think "showing the Brits" is more important to our men than showing the Germans or the French or the Yanks (well, we haven't seen much of them). You could never say this to anyone, but I'm sure I'm right about this: we're here to show the supercilious Brits that the dumb colonials know how to fight. And we're showing them. Our colonel was joking yesterday, after a briefing at GHQ, that they ought to put Canadians in the front line now as a ruse, to make the Germans think a big attack is coming, when they mean to launch an offensive somewhere else. Perhaps we're getting a little big for our britches, as Mother used to say.

Fortunately, we now have some brighter chaps like Currie in command. They have become a lot smarter than the Brits in making gains on the Huns without sacrificing a thousand men for every foot. So I have an attitude I can't explain. I am exhilarated to find I can do this quite well. And nothing is more important than doing this well. Nothing is more important than the war. I have never known anything where the purpose was so clear. It makes me think of the welder's torch in the shipyard, so bright you cannot look at anything else, you cannot think of anything else. The war makes everything as clear and bright and singular as the welder's arc light.

The men do willingly what I suggest. Suggesting is much more effective than bellowing orders at them, or shrieking, as I've heard some do when the men are sullen and uncooperative. But not many officers seem to have discovered the art of suggestion.

We've had some more successes—at least by the way success is measured here. And, I repeat, not being afraid restores the game! At the same time I witness it almost as if I were the spirit of a dead soldier myself (with no body to care about anymore). I look down and witness the grinding, awful stupidity. The glory is stupid. The sacrifice is wanton, immoral, and stupid. The blindness and inhumanity are criminal.

If Canadians weren't part of the British Empire, we wouldn't be here, but being here is the most exciting thing I can imagine.

She had not been wrong about him. This was the Charles she knew was there: full of good sense, a practical mind, the boy who could see that the emperor had no clothes. The independent boy who was very quiet but who thought things out for himself. That was the other side of the silent, distant boy. She knew his feelings about the British. He hated being patronized. And he thought one person as good as another, no matter what his background. No snobbishness. And educable when his interest was caught.

Reading these letters was like discovering that the man she had thought was inside the man she had married was really there after all. She was falling in love all over again with the spirit of a dead man.

No one talked with that kind of plainness about the war. It must be the secret men over there kept. Now and then one of the wounded at Cogswell Street or Camp Hill, in pain or deep anxiety about the reception he would get at home, would say something like, "No one back here knows anything about what it's like."

Julia picked up the *Herald* and forced herself to read the story about Charles: "With steely resolve . . . total unconcern for his own safety . . . the dauntless courage of Canadian manhood . . . the spirit of noble sacrifice young Canadians have gladly brought to the service of their king . . . The hearts of Haligonians swell with justifiable pride at this noble act . . . To paraphrase President Lincoln, this son of Nova Scotia has given that last full measure of devotion."

She hated the enthusiastic tone, the cynical effort to wring every last drop of patriotic fervor out of Charles's exploit and death. A surge of anger went through her. She thought for a moment, then jumped up.

In the bathroom she washed her face and tidied her hair, collected Charles's letters, and went downstairs to get her coat and hat. She felt carried along by her determination.

A brisk walk of fifteen minutes brought her to the offices of the *Halifax Herald*. When she said she was the widow of the officer on their front page that day, they conducted her rapidly to the editor.

In the scruffy newsroom of old desks and battered typewriters, heads turned to watch the beautiful woman sweeping through in her black fur hat and collar.

She had conjured up an image of someone repellent; anyone who could produce such sickening prose day after day must be a white slug of a man. In fact the editor, Mr. Finlay, was thin and tired, with receding reddish hair and a mouth that suggested loose dentures. He received her in his waistcoat and shirtsleeves, but hastily put his jacket on.

"It is an honor to meet you, Mrs. Robertson, although I am deeply sorry for the reason, and to thank you for lending us that very good picture. I hope you are pleased with it."

"Yes," Julia said.

"If you like, I can get them to give you back the original right now. I know you were anxious about it."

He got up and spoke to someone outside his office.

"I came for another reason. I brought some letters I have just received from my husband. I think they give a very vivid picture of what it is like there and what he felt—shortly before he was killed."

"You would let us publish your husband's letters?" He looked very interested. Letters from the city's only VC, letters from a dead hero? A newspaper's dream.

"That's why I brought them." Julia pulled them from her bag.

His reddish eyebrows lowered cannily. "What, ah—what would you expect us to pay for them?"

Julia was indignant. "I didn't expect anything. I don't want to be paid."

He smiled. "In that case the *Herald* will be proud to publish them. It will be an honor for our newspaper and a privilege for our readers to hear the thoughts of a man as valiant as your husband. And I will take great care when we have set them that you get them back."

Surprised at how easy it had been, Julia collected her photograph and was shown out with elaborate courtesy. She walked home with angry pride.

Wait until the public reads the truth instead of the sickening rubbish the papers always write. Wait until the Reverend Peter Wentworth reads that.

WHEN DOROTHY WENTWORTH brought the children back, Margery did not answer the doorbell. It was not until she had rung a third time that Dorothy noticed a note pinned to the inside door. She opened the outer porch door and read it.

*Don't let the children come in first.*

It was in Margery's hasty scribble, on a piece of torn writing paper folded once over. It filled Dorothy with dread.

"What does it say, Granny?" Abigail reached for it.

"Wait here, dear. Both of you. Wait here. Granny will go round and let you in."

There was no alley between these houses. Very alarmed, Dorothy ran around the corner and down the lane behind the fenced gardens. She let herself in the garden gate and climbed the wooden steps to the back door. In the scullery she smelled gas. When she opened the kitchen door, it choked her. Dorothy darted outside for a deep breath of fresh air and went back in. Margery was lying on the floor, her head and shoulders on the open oven door. There was a rushing noise from all the open gas burners. Quickly Dorothy turned them off. Another breath outside, then back into the kitchen.

The doors to the kitchen had rolled-up towels blocking the space at the bottom. She kicked them away and opened the doors. The towels had been wetted. She opened all the doors to the kitchen, then ran back outside for another gasp of air. Then she struggled to open the kitchen windows, but the storm windows meant that only three small ventilation holes could be opened.

Her nursing habits came back. She lifted Margery's limp wrist and felt for the pulse. The skin was cold. Her face was blue. She had placed a pillow on the oven door and laid her face on it.

How terrible! How awful for you, you poor lassie!

There were tears in Dorothy's eyes. At last she could feel a faint slow pulse.

Thank God!

"Granny! Granny, let us in!" Abigail was calling faintly from the front door.

"Wait a moment, children!"

Coughing in the gas, Dorothy held Margery under the arms and dragged her away. Her head lolled like a dead person's. She noticed how carefully Margery was dressed, as though ready for a smart luncheon.

She pulled the body out onto the back porch, gasping for fresh air. She rolled Margery over face down and pushed on her back as she had been taught with drowning victims. A small quantity of vomit came out of Margery's mouth. After a full minute of artificial respiration, Dorothy was out of breath, and could not tell whether Margery was actually breathing. Her color did not improve. The children were pounding on the front door.

Dorothy left Margery to find the telephone. She asked the operator to send an ambulance urgently and tell it to come down the back lane. She ran upstairs and pulled blankets off the bed, noticing that it was neatly made. Downstairs on the back porch she wrapped them around the limp body. She tried to pull Margery into a sitting position and hold up her arms to open the lungs, but it was too much for her. Propping the body against the porch railing, she lifted the young woman's arms and brought them down.

Dorothy took the pulse again. Still there but very feeble. She was barely alive.

She pushed Margery down, rolled the body over again, and knelt beside it, pushing down on the back of the chest, holding down, then releasing for a few seconds. It was very tiring, but she kept on.

I'll have to find Peter. And what about the children? They mustn't see her like this.

She covered Margery's shoulders and hurried through the house to the front door.

"Can we come in now? You were an awfully long time."

"Abigail, I have something very important to ask you. And you, Michael. Now listen to me. I want you to go back to my house and see Granddaddy. You stay there and and I'll come back very quickly."

"But why? We've just been there." Abigail said.

"Never mind, dear. Go along like good children. You can have a special Scottish toffee from the tin with Bonnie Prince Charlie on it."

"Can I too?" said Michael.

"It smells like gas," Abigail said, wrinkling her nose.

"Run along now."

"I need to go to the bathroom," Michael said.

"You'll just have to hold it until you get there."

"Perhaps he'll wet his pants!" Abigail said, gleefully.

"I won't!" said Michael.

"You will!"

"I won't!"

They ran off. Dorothy rushed back through the house. The strong gas smell lingered, but she could breathe.

Margery was still unconscious and her pulse just as feeble. What else could she do? Keep Margery warm. Hot-water bottles. In the kitchen Dorothy filled the kettle, hesitating a moment and sniffing the air before striking the wooden match.

The ambulance men came.

"Coal-gas poisoning," one of them said immediately. "Accidental?"

"Yes, of course." Dorothy said.

"We've seen a lot of it. When did you find her?"

"About ten minutes ago."

"I think you got here just in time. She's pretty far gone."

"But she's going to recover?"

"It's a close call. The doctors can tell you at the VG."

She watched them put the stretcher into the back of the boxy ambulance and then telephoned her husband.

"Are the children back there already? I can't tell you more now. There's been an accident here. Don't alarm the children; they don't know."

"What sort of accident?"

"John, for pity's sake, don't say that. They'll hear you! Listen to me! I came in and found the gas on in the kitchen. Margery was unconscious. But she's still alive and they've taken her to the VG."

"Oh, dear God. Did she—"

"Don't say any more. Be kind to the children, John. Read them a story—a children's story. And I promised them each a toffee."

The kettle whistled, and with a shaky hand she took the teapot she had used yesterday and made tea, then sat down for a moment to recover.

*I should have spoken to Peter last night. I ought to have rung him up. She looked dreadful yesterday—and no wonder! But how could she be so unhappy as to do this! The poor, poor lamb! I'll have to find Peter, and he must tell the Tobins. They'll be frantic.*

Before she left, Dorothy closed the oven door and took the pillow out of the kitchen. She unrolled the wet towels and hung them to dry. Details no one needed to see.

Dorothy Wentworth was never flustered, but in the back of her mind was an uncomfortable thought: as Peter's mother she was somehow responsible for this.

Peter was visiting St. Paul's when the Royal Navy chaplain came to invite the rector to lunch on board H.M.S. *Knight Templar* and warmly pressed Peter to join them. He remembered the name from Julia's diary and accepted.

The three clergymen walked down to the dockyard. The ship was alongside for repairs to funnels damaged in the explosion. Rubble from damaged dockyard buildings was still being cleared away, but the docks were working, with warships being loaded and fueled.

By the time wardroom etiquette had been punctiliously observed, Peter had drunk several glasses of wine, his sips replenished so smoothly by the steward that he drank without noticing.

All the talk was of Robertson's VC. Everyone had read the newspapers. Peter listened to Julia's husband's name being uttered with quiet respect on all sides by young officers, some of whom looked like schoolboys but sounded already war-hardened.

When the toast was made to "absent friends" Peter realized through a haze that he was lifting his glass to her husband. He said little. He wanted to be inconspicuous.

On deck he sucked in the freezing air, but his head still felt thick as he and the rector were piped ashore and walked up to St. Paul's. There, he found a message to call his home.

"Peter. I've been desperate to get in touch with you." The urgency in his mother's voice frightened him before he heard her message.

"It's Margery. I found her with the gas on in the kitchen. She's alive but she's very ill. Peter, she had closed all the doors and put a pillow on the oven door. It was very deliberate. But she's alive. They took her in an ambulance. You'd better go straight to the VG."

"What about the children?"

"They didn't see. They're with your father. I'm going there now. Don't worry about them. Just go to Margery."

After a numbing instant to consider, Peter ran up the hilly streets, until he had to slow down to a rapid walk to catch his breath.

Why did you have to do that?

Why did you have to do that?

Oh, please, why did you have to do that?

That he had been drinking at lunchtime—he almost never did and could feel the wine in his head—made it worse.

How did he not notice that she had gone so far?

But why did she do *that?* Why didn't she talk to me? Oh, God, Oh, heavenly Father. Peter didn't notice that he was praying.

He hurried along Spring Garden Road, past the boarded-up shop windows, finding without thinking the prayers for the sick:

We beseech thee to hear our prayers for this thy servant, for whom we implore thy mercy . . .

Oh, God, if she should die . . . She must not die.

But behind everything, repeating itself like the unstoppable pulse of blood in his head: Why did you have to do it?

The first glance made him think she was dead. She was deathly white. There was no sign of breathing. Under the skin of Margery's forehead was a black mark, like a scribble with a heavy pencil. Her hand was cold. She looked and felt dead.

The hospital was still crowded with explosion victims, but she had been put in a small room, alone.

"She hasn't recovered consciousness," the nurse said.

"But she is going to?"

"It isn't certain yet. You can sit with her. The doctor will be in presently."

Peter sat in the chair by the high bed.

Her dark curls were matted against her face. He took her hand and squeezed as if to force his own warmth into the cold fingers. Merely asleep, she would have awakened to the pressure, would have looked at him shyly, childlike, frowning, then smiling. No response. Her eyes were glued shut. Wherever her consciousness was, it was far from knowing that anyone had touched her. Her hand was clammy.

A young doctor came in, and Peter introduced himself.

"I didn't expect a clergyman. This must be a shock to you."

"Yes. It is."

"She was nearly dead when they brought her in. Probably only a few minutes from death if she hadn't been found. She's breathing, her heart is strong, the vital life signs are good. But we don't know what will happen."

The doctor was talking so loudly that Peter thought it would waken Margery, but there was no sign that she could hear.

"When will she wake up?"

"I can't say. I'm afraid you have to face the reality that she may not. It's possible she'll come round. If she does, we won't know for a time whether there will be any lasting effects."

"Lasting effects?"

"Gas-poisoning cases can recover physically and mentally.

Sometimes for a short period a large memory loss, sometimes permanent loss of some brain function."

"Do you mean she will recover but not be quite well?"

"I did not say she will recover. That's uncertain. She's had very severe oxygen deprivation. Just how severe, how total, how prolonged, we don't know. The outcome can't be predicted. It depends how strong she was physically."

The doctor talked as though it were a matter of complete indifference to him. Peter heard it as hostility, implying that if he had looked after his wife better, she wouldn't have tried to gas herself.

The doctor lifted Margery's limp arm and pinched the skin above the elbow. "Looks a little undernourished. Has she been eating properly?"

"Not much. She's lost her taste for food."

"For how long?"

"I've noticed it for several weeks."

The doctor let the arm fall back on the bed as though it were dead.

"Since it is your profession, I would advise you to pray for a good result. Only God can help her now, and her own instinct to live"—he looked at Peter—"if she has any."

Despite the doctor's scorn, Peter knew a sense of relief. Margery was their responsibility now, not just his.

"You can stay here if you wish. Or go home and we'll call you if there's any change. It may be many hours before we know. You understand that we'll have to report this to the police."

"No. Why?"

"It's the law. All cases of attempted suicide must be reported."

"But this must have been an accident!"

"In any case, it's a formality. They'll ask you some questions. They don't prosecute."

The doctor went back to the bed, felt Margery's pulse, and lifted one of her eyelids. "Nothing to be done now but wait," he said. "I'll look in later."

Left alone, Peter sat down. She lay as still as death. She may be dying. She actually might die. *She might die.* He could not believe this. It was not real. There had been times, to his shame, flashes of his imagining her dead. But he'd never actually wished her dead. It had come into his mind, a possibility, but he'd never welcomed the thought. Now it might happen! He could be looking at her a minute from now and see nothing different, and she could be dead. The soul would have departed. The children would have to be told. Everyone would have to be told. Even if she lived, everyone would have to be told. The Tobins would have to be told right away. He would have to do that. He would have to tell them now. Oh, God!

He looked at her face.

Why did you have to do such an extreme thing, such an awful thing? Could it have been just an accident? The gas had just come back on. Did you forget one of the burners?

No. The oven door, the pillow, towels against the doors. It was terrible to think of the loneliness in a soul that could face that ghastly way out. He shuddered. To be so calculating. When had she decided, this woman—once warm and laughing—now so corpselike? What tortures of the mind, what dreadful thoughts did she have? How could her agony have been that great? The pillow on the oven door made him want to cry, to bury his face in his wife's breasts and beg her forgiveness, to tell her that she had never been as alone as that. Life was never so devoid of hope. Nothing could have been so awful as to send her into that blackness, her head on a pillow on the oven door.

He got up, took a deep breath, and walked around the bed. Margery's clothes were hanging on a hook. The dress puzzled him. She wore it only on special occasions. The shoes on the floor were her newest. She had dressed for this. He looked back at her comatose form.

He went back to the bed and took Margery's hand. It was still cold, and a sense of dread made him put it carefully down.

What if she died? Bad enough if she recovered, but if she died? How could a person think that another would be better off dead? Monstrous to think it, yet the thought flickered across his other thoughts. If Margery were dead, then Julia—

None of these quick thoughts were words in his mind; they weren't even pictures, but they were thoughts, and they came with incredible swiftness, faint flickers of lightning, leaving him shocked by the dark landscape they momentarily revealed. Yet they did not fundamentally shock him. The thought—if Margery died, then Julia—kept recurring. He was ashamed; he wanted to turn the page, close the book, leave the room.

But in all that he was trying to feel something. In reality he did not feel very much—just a low background dread and some excitement.

Peter looked at his marble wife. How could he be honest with himself about what he felt, when the habit was so strong of feeling what he thought he ought to feel?

CORPORAL RANSOME told Stewart he still could not remember any dreams. It was their third meeting in the dusty office at the asylum.

"Did you dream last night?"

"I don't know."

"Did you wake up, or did you sleep through the night?"

"I always wake up."

"What were you thinking about when you woke up?"

"I can't remember." The pale, unfocused eyes seemed to say, I don't want to remember. I won't remember.

"Have you tried to remember?"

"How can I try to remember? You remember or you don't remember. You can't try." The little flash of anger gave him the most animation Stewart had seen.

Ransome arranged his crutches and pulled himself up. Since the arms did all the work, Stewart could see the strain in the tendons in Ransome's hands.

"Don't you want to talk today?"

"I don't want to sit down."

"Why not? It must be very uncomfortable standing when you can't use your legs."

"I don't like sitting."

"It must hurt your arms."

"They're used to it."

"When you think about your legs, can you remember what it felt like to move them?"

"Sure."

"If you imagine with your eyes closed that you're lifting your leg, can your mind feel the sensation of moving?"

"Sometimes."

"Does it feel that if you opened your eyes you would see your leg moving?"

"I dreamed once I was playing hockey."

"When was that?"

"I don't know. Some time ago."

"Since you came back to Canada?"

"I guess so."

"Did you play a lot?"

"Yup."

"Where?"

"In Chatham." The day before, Stewart had tried to learn more about the family in Chatham, but Ransome had told him nothing.

"Tell me what it was like playing hockey."

"I don't want to."

"Why not?"

"It makes me feel bad to think about it."

"Feel bad how? Tell me the feeling."

"I don't know. It makes me feel like—sick to my stomach."

"Thinking about hockey?"

"Yup."

"Do you have any idea why that is?"

"It goes away if I think of something else."

"Well, think about hockey right now."

"I don't want to."

"No, just for a moment. Imagine you're playing hockey. What position do you play?"

"Defense. I don't want to think about it."

"Does it make you feel sick now?"

"Maybe."

"What else does it make you think of?"

"Nothing."

"What happened in your dream about playing hockey?"

"I don't know. I don't remember."

The slight animation in Ransome's face had vanished. His spirit had closed in again. But it was something. Thinking about playing hockey made him feel sick.

The soldier shifted uncomfortably to ease the crutch pad in one armpit. That was another thing: sitting made him uneasy.

"Are you tired? Want to sit down?"

"I'm all right."

"Why do you dislike sitting down?"

"I don't know. I told you, I don't know."

"Does it hurt your legs when you're sitting down?"

"I don't feel nothing in my legs."

"Would you like a cigarette?"

Perhaps he would sit down to smoke. But Ransome took the cigarette, strained forward to Stewart's match, then leaned against the wall.

"When you told me you get frightened in the middle of the night, is it thinking about hockey that's frightening?"

"I can't remember."

"Did you ever have an accident playing hockey?"

"No."

"Did you get hurt?"

"Nothing much."

"Do you get into fights?"

"Sure."

"Did you really enjoy the game, or did you hate it?"

"I don't want to talk about it!"

"Did the violence in the game frighten you?"

"Me?" For a second there was almost a smile, a flicker of personality.

"You weren't frightened when you played?"

"For Christ's sake, stop talking about hockey!" Stewart could feel the violence of the game in the outburst.

"Are you feeling sick?"

"Yes!"

Ransome did look like a man who might throw up. But why?

"Can you tell what you're thinking?"

"Nothing."

"Here." Stewart held out the ashtray for Ransome's cigarette end. "I'll tell you something, John. When you get upset like this, when you feel sick about something like hockey and you don't know why, that may be telling you something very important."

"What?"

"If we could find that out, perhaps you could use your legs again. The doctors can't find anything wrong with them. What's wrong with them is in your head. Perhaps by talking like this we can find what that is. But you have to help."

"I don't want to talk about hockey."

"All right. But the next time the idea of hockey comes into your head and you feel sick, try to see what other things it makes you think of."

.   .   .   .

BY WEDNESDAY MORNING, Margery was still unconscious, and Peter had lived since Tuesday afternoon believing she might die or recover with an impaired mind. He had thought that telling the Tobins would be the worst, dreaded facing his parents and children, agonized about telling Dean Creighton, but it had come out easily and to great sympathy.

The worst was being alone all night in his own house. To be near the telephone in the hall, he had spent Tuesday night on the living room sofa. The cushions were too soft, and even in two blankets he was cold. He never fell completely asleep but spent the night in a fever of semiconsciousness, dreaming, knowing he was dreaming about Margery dead or Margery committed to a madhouse.

The smell of gas was still oppressive. He had opened doors and windows, but that did not get rid of the smell, only made the house too cold to bear. The cushions and the blankets he slept on smelled of gas.

He saw the signs of her last terrible moments—the keyholes in the kitchen plugged with the children's modeling clay.

Shaken, Peter sat down to consider that. Such meticulous detail. She was never that careful in planning anything. The lump from which she had pulled the small stoppers was on the kitchen table. It showed where her fingers had gouged out the pieces, her anguish frozen as in a sculpture.

Even more awful to him was the note she had tacked to the front door. His mother had taken it down and left it on the table.

*Don't let the children come in first.*

It overwhelmed Peter with horror and tenderness. To stop at that moment, everything else ready, about to commit herself to the oven and the pillow . . . She had left no note for him, only for his mother, knowing she would be back with the children. It was a last gesture of motherhood, her legacy to them: don't see what I am doing. It made him shudder. He looked at the edge of the paper, torn in the same desperation as the finger gouges in the clay.

He took the note into the study. The piece it was torn from was on his desk. The drawer holding the writing paper was still open. But on top of the desk—the hairs on his neck rose at the sight— was Julia's diary. It lay beside *The Confessions of St. Augustine,* where he had left it the night before. His heart was beating rapidly.

He stared at the two books. Something in their positions suggested that they were not as he would have left them. But he couldn't remember. No. In that state she would never have been curious about the books on his desk. Gripped by sudden disgust, he seized the diary and went into the cellar. He opened the furnace door and threw the diary onto the glowing red coals, pushing it with the long poker until he saw it begin to burn. He banged the door shut. Its clang made him think he heard the telephone. He ran upstairs, but the telephone was silent. Near sleep, he thought again that he heard it ring but was mistaken once more.

Partly asleep he relived the conversations with everyone.

Cynthia Tobin had been slightly hysterical. "How sordid and awful. I am so embarrassed that your mother should have found her like that." But at the hospital she melted at the sight of her inert daughter. She kissed Margery and smoothed her hair from her forehead.

She asked a nurse, "Will that terrible black mark on her forehead go away?"

George Tobin looked at Margery gravely, went out to find the doctor, and came back to Peter.

"Same as you said. Nothing to do but wait." George put a fatherly arm around Peter's shoulders.

"You can't blame yourself, Peter. You wish you'd done things different. God knows, I wish I had. But there's been a strange streak in that girl from when she was young."

Through the night the note came back again and again.

*Don't let the children come in first.*

Twisting and perspiring, he awoke anxiously at three o'clock in the morning. When he telephoned a nurse said, "No change. We'll let you know."

At eight o'clock Wednesday morning, they said Margery was still unconscious. To revive himself, Peter started to draw a hot bath, then reconsidered, pulled out the plug, and filled the bath with cold water. It took his breath away to plunge in, but he needed to discipline himself.

When he got to the hospital, the day nurse told him excitedly that Margery had awakened, taken a sip of water, and drifted off again.

"It's a very good sign."

Peter waited by the bed. They asked him to leave while they bathed her and changed the sheets. When he returned, she looked as unconscious as before but her hand felt warmer.

An hour had passed when he was startled to hear her whisper clearly, "Peter."

Again. "Peter!" Her eyes were open. A transformation like witchcraft. Her entire face was younger, her eyes soft and luminous, her smile that of a young girl. She stretched as she did after a long sleep, as though a spell had been lifted.

His heart swelled with gratitude. All the assumptions of the wretched night evaporated with her smile.

"Come closer! I have a secret to tell you."

He leaned close and she whispered, "I'm really not pregnant!"

Astonished, he stepped back to look at her. She smiled happily. And then he remembered.

*If I am pregnant again, I will kill myself.*

"Aren't you happy about it?" she asked.

"Yes."

"You didn't want a child, did you?"

"No."

"So it can be just the two of us."

The odd inflection, a statement not a question, gave Peter the disturbing notion that she was talking about years ago—about not being pregnant before Abigail and Michael.

"Listen!" She pulled his head down as Abigail did, to whisper, "They said I started my period. They brought me some napkins."

She had never talked openly about it. She said it a little coquettishly: their secret.

"So now it can be the two of us." And with that smile he had not seen for years, she drifted off again into unconsciousness.

She left Peter stranded in unreality.

Margery did that all afternoon, waking for a few moments to smile, hold his hand, say a few words, then drift off.

The doctor said, "You're very lucky. She's making excellent progress."

She never asked for the children. She appeared to have awakened in 1912 or 1913. She made no mention of the gas nor asked why she was in hospital but acted as though she knew why or didn't care.

He told his mother, "I don't think it's a good idea to bring the children yet."

Also disturbing: when he told her something, she asked the same question a few minutes later.

"What day is this?"

"It's Wednesday."

"Oh, yes."

And three minutes later: "Peter, I don't know what day it is."

"It's Wednesday."

"Oh, it feels like something else."

Her parents came, overjoyed. Cynthia said, "Darling, look, I brought the bed jacket with the broderie anglaise."

"Oh, it's lovely!" She touched it with a weak hand. "Where did you find it?"

"In your cupboard at home, dear."

"But I don't have one like that."

The doctor said, "It's not uncommon to have some memory loss. Those close to her will notice it more than we will."

"Does the memory comes back?"

"It may. I haven't seen that many cases. You'll need a psychologist who studies that sort of thing."

Of course. He could ask Stewart to come. Margery was fond of him. And now Peter could tell him with a clear conscience: he had burned the diary.

He was frantically busy—at the hospital, walking two blocks to consult Dean Creighton about the memorial service, calling on the Tobins, going to his parents' house to see the children.

Walking on these errands, Peter caught himself praying fervently, with an open heart, offering his thanks for God's mercy on them. It was as if he became a younger, more innocent self.

He had another bad night. The future looked awful. Margery, semi-invalid, less competent than before, his own prospects blighted, at best an insignificant parish somewhere, a mean rectory —a future of mediocrity and resignation.

And then on Thursday morning the most extraordinary thing happened.

Peter was sitting at Margery's bedside when the scornful young doctor appeared. He looked at Peter with a generous smile and held out a newspaper.

"Have you seen this?"

"No, what is it?"

"You'd better look."

Margery's nurse and others crowded into the doorway.

Peter opened the *Chronicle* and saw his photograph on the front page.

"I don't understand."

"Read it!" they all said.

## HERO COMPETITION
## WINNER ANNOUNCED!

## HALIFAX CLERGYMAN
## IS GREATEST UNSUNG
## HERO OF DISASTER

## RISKS LIFE IN
## BURNING HOUSE FOR
## TRAPPED AND DYING
## WOMAN

### Others have to drag
### him to safety

Beside the type was Peter's photograph, made when he had been appointed a curate.

"Congratulations!" said the doctor, and reached out to shake Peter's hand.

"Congratulations!" the nurses said and began clapping.

"I don't understand," said Peter.

"You're a hero. You've been keeping it under your hat. Read it."

Peter was as amazed by the transformation in the doctor's manner as by seeing his picture. He sat down and read the story.

> For a week *Chronicle* readers have thrilled to stories of heroism in the disaster that devastated our city but could not destroy our pride—stories discovered through the *Chronicle*'s exclusive

competition: "Unsung Heroes of the Disaster."

The *Chronicle* offered $25 for each story printed, plus a Grand Prize of $100 for the story our editors considered the best.

Today the *Chronicle* announces the winner. He is Sergeant Richard Spenser of the Halifax Rifles, recently posted home after two years in France, where he was twice wounded.

On hearing of the *Chronicle* competition, Sgt. Spenser came forward with the story the *Chronicle* is proud to publish today.

### SGT. SPENSER'S STORY

On the morning of the explosion, I was with No. 2 Company, 1st Battalion, marching to Wellington Barracks.

When the explosion happened, we were immediately ordered into the disaster zone to render assistance.

Our search party was joined by an Anglican minister. Laying aside the dignities of his cloth, without any thought for his own safety, this gentleman threw himself wholeheartedly into the rescue effort.

We worked all out to save men, women, and children from burning and collapsing buildings. Often we found only dead bodies. Other times, the flames drove us back.

In one wrecked home, we found a woman pinned down by a huge beam. Not twenty men could have lifted it. We were only half a dozen, and the house was on fire. The bit of wall left was crackling and blazing.

I said, "Get out, men, the wall's coming in." Bits of it had commenced falling down.

But this parson was cool as anything. He said, "We can't let her die like that!"

"Get back, sir," I shouted. "You'll never save her. You'll just lose your own life."

"My life isn't worth living," he said, "if I save it by ignoring her suffering."

"Don't be a fool, Padre," I said. But there was no stopping him. He threw off our grip and ran back through the flames.

I shouted, "Come back, sir! Come back. The wall's going to fall." Then there was nothing to do but go after him. We did, and I saw a sight that broke my heart. I'll never forget as long as I live.

There was this young minister, down on his knees on the broken glass and plaster, giving that lady the last rites. He was Anglican and she was Catholic, but he didn't care. There were flames and smoke all around. The heat was terrible. But he stayed there, cool and quiet, making a cross on her forehead and saying—I'm a Catholic and I know the words: *Ego te absolvo . . . In nomine patris, et filii, et spiritus sancti.*

He said them. The lady smiled a blissful smile, like she could see Jesus or the Blessed Virgin.

We dragged him out a second before the wall crashed in. We heard the woman scream—and then she was quiet. All you could hear was the crackling of the flames, and the searing heat made us shield our faces.

It made me cry, even after all I've seen in France. As long as I live, I'll never forget what he did for that woman. He ought to get a medal. He's as brave as any soldier.

----

The *Chronicle* has identified the clergyman as the Reverend Peter Wentworth, 29, Curate at All Saints Cathedral, Tower Road, son of Canon and Mrs. John Wentworth of 238 Tower Rd.

The *Chronicle* is proud to bring this heroic deed to light. It demonstrates that Canadians on the home front are showing the same spirit of selflessness and self-sacrifice as the gallant men who have brought such glory to our country's name in France.

It shows that but one heart beats in all our breasts in these troubled times, soldiers at the front, men and women in the factories and farms and homes of Canada . . .

Peter stopped reading. The memory of that incident was paralyzing in its embarrassment.

"Aren't you proud of yourself?"

"Well, it didn't happen quite like that."

"I think you're just being modest. I think it's a damned good piece of work. I'm proud to know you."

The nurses clapped again.

Margery said, "What's happening?"

Her nurse bent over, speaking as if to a child: "The newspaper says your husband did a very brave thing in the explosion. He's a hero."

"What's the explosion?" Margery asked.

Peter, the doctor, and the nurses looked at one another. The doctor said, "I think she needs to be quiet again."

Her nurse smoothed the covers on the bed, adjusted Margery's pillow, and went out, shooing the others ahead of her.

"Why were they clapping?"

"Why don't you rest, and I'll explain later."

"I am very tired." And she had gone again.

The chief nurse came back in and spoke quietly: "There's a telephone message: please call the dean's office at the cathedral. I'll keep an eye on your wife."

"Peter!" Dean Creighton bellowed over the telephone. "Why didn't you tell us about this? It's marvelous."

"I'm afraid they've blown it out of all proportion," Peter said.

"Don't be so modest, Peter! There are times to take credit when credit is due. I am just tickled pink that someone had the good sense to come forward and tell the story."

"I think he did it for the money. That sergeant was anything but friendly to me when it happened."

"Never you mind! I've had the *Star* on the line wanting to know more about you. They want you to tell the story in your own words. Can you come over to lunch? This couldn't have come at a better time, Peter. Can you do that?"

"Well, yes, I think so."

"Good. I'm just going to call the bishop. I don't think he gets the *Chronicle*."

It was quite absurd, the way the sergeant had told the story. Clearly the man had done it for the money and, presumably, a joke. One hundred dollars was a huge amount of money.

He's probably sitting somewhere with a large supply of liquor, laughing his head off.

Peter walked on.

Or did I judge him too quickly, blinded by my distaste for his manners?

Over lunch, Peter protested to the Creightons that he had not been so heroic, and Margaret said, "Oh, Peter, it's so typical of you to efface yourself like this!"

The bishop sent his congratulations.

"But," the dean said dramatically, "and this is the big news: Monsignor Murphy called. He has not called me for years except on the strictest business. He told me he is sending a letter to the newspaper and read it to me, praising your act of interfaith generosity. He said—I quote him—your example flies like an angelic spirit over the pettiness that often keeps our churches apart."

"In fact," said Peter, "I didn't feel that way at the time." He remembered his squeamishness, the initial reluctance, his remorse afterward.

The *Chronicle* and *Star* sent two reporters and a photographer. Messages began accumulating. The dean came back from the telephone. "Arthur Halliwell wants you to come and be presented tomorrow. The governor general will be here to inspect the disaster."

"Oh, Peter, what an honor!" Margaret Creighton said.

"I think you'll have to go, Peter," her husband said. "And we're still hoping they'll come to the memorial service for Charles Robertson. Halliwell is going to try. My goodness, things are turning out well, aren't they!"

"I'd better get back to the hospital. Margery is still very shaky—when she's awake."

"We should thank God for our many blessings, Peter," his superior said, with particular intensity. "Give her our love."

And when Peter had left, the dean said to his wife, "This has saved our bacon—and his. Can't have a clergyman's wife attempting suicide. It happens, but it is very bad for everyone."

"What if she had succeeded, Donald? I heard Dorothy got there just in the nick of time."

"I dread to think, my dear. As it is, things couldn't have turned out better. Now we have two heroes to celebrate."

THE *Herald* refused Charles's letters, and the editor telephoned Archie Robertson about them. Julia found out when the Robertsons came to pick her up for the governor general's reception.

Suddenly flooded with anger, she flared up. "How dare he call you about it. They were my letters. They were written to me."

"Julia, the poor man Finlay was terribly upset," Archie said. "He could go to prison. It's against the law to publish material that has evaded the censorship. He said the letters are almost treasonous."

"Then he is a coward!" Julia said. She stood very straight, shaking with indignation. She had never had cross words with Charles's parents.

"Come now, my dear. He's doing his job."

"Have you read the letters?" Julia asked.

"I felt I had to when he brought them to me."

"Don't you feel they should be published, that ordinary people deserve to know the truth—when the newspapers and the politicians won't tell them?"

"I wish you'd sit down quietly, my dear," Elizabeth said. "You're making me terribly nervous like that. I know you're upset—"

"I am very upset. These letters are written by your son. They're all making a great fuss over Charles and calling him a hero, but you don't want people to know what he thought about the war. I'm sorry to be making a scene, but I hate this. You seem to be taking their side. Don't you think that's a betrayal of Charles?"

Her tears began to flow.

"The last words we'll ever hear from him. He can't stand all the false heroics the newspapers and officials put out and he wants us to know the truth."

"But he didn't expect you to give them to the newspaper. He said keep it to yourself. He knew this information wasn't official."

"But why does it have to be official? People are sending their sons and husbands over there thinking it's a glorious thing to do—" She was sobbing and talking, holding a handkerchief to her mouth. "They think the sacrifice is in a great cause, and look what he says! The cause isn't worth so much life. The generals like Haig are throwing lives away!"

"Opinions like that will give aid and comfort to the enemy." Archie took her firmly by the shoulders.

"But it's your son who's saying it!"

"Julia, you're becoming hysterical, my dear."

"Archie, it's time we were going if we're not going to be late," Elizabeth said. She put her arm around Julia. "Why don't you take a moment to powder your nose and settle yourself? We'll wait for you."

Still angry, Julia said, "May I have the letters, please?"

Archie Robertson held them out, but Elizabeth said, "May I ask a favor, dear? Archie read them quickly but I haven't. Would you let me read them?"

Her voice was so touching and her expression so sweet that Julia whispered, "Yes," and held them out. Then, remembering that Elizabeth's loss was as great as hers, she embraced her mother-in-law and went quickly upstairs.

"I never knew she was that headstrong," said Archie. "That was a very bold thing to do."

"I like her for it," said his wife.

"But that temper! Did you know she could flare up like that?"

"Darling, she is very upset. People can't always keep their feelings bottled up just to be polite. And she makes a very good argument."

"But the law is the law. What would Borden think? What would happen to the morale of the country, and the people's will to carry on with this, if the papers published all the pessimistic stuff people think about the war?"

"Perhaps then it would end sooner."

"More likely we'd lose it because we'd become a nation of crybabies, like the Americans."

"Archie, that isn't like you!"

"Well, dammit, I've lost a son, too!" His voice broke.

Elizabeth patted his shoulder. "Then we should all go and stand up for him and be proud of him. Here's Julia. Come along. We've just time to pick up Lucy."

Julia was composed but angrily quiet in the corner of the back seat. When Lucy got in, Julia pecked her cheek but had nothing to say, as annoyed at herself for her outburst as at the editor, Finlay, for his cowardly behavior. He could have called her directly instead of going behind her back. But of course he wouldn't call her: she was a woman, and he would have had an emotional scene to deal with.

And why shouldn't civilians know the truth about the war? Civilians were paying for it. Civilians were sending the men to fight it. Two thousand civilians in Halifax had just been killed because of the war.

*It will give aid and comfort to the enemy.* She shuddered with fresh anger.

Lucy said, "Have you heard about Peter Wentworth's wife? Susan Gastonguy told me Margery was found in their kitchen with the gas on and all the doors closed."

"Oh, how ghastly!" Elizabeth said. "Is she all right?"

"Apparently just all right. Susan was finally allowed to see her last night, and Margery can't remember a lot of things."

"How strange, on top of the marvelous story of Peter's behavior in the explosion. Everyone's talking about that."

"She did it before the story came out, on Tuesday morning, Susan said. Dorothy Wentworth found her and they rushed her to the VG."

"Poor thing." said Elizabeth, "I'm so glad it's not worse."

"Lucy said, "Susan has been pretty chummy with her. She says Margery's been miserable ever since her first child."

"Yes, I've heard that, too, but it's not nice to gossip about it, Lucy," her mother said.

"Tuesday morning?" Julia said. "We saw Peter Wentworth the night before, do you remember? He and Stewart MacPherson were with us all at my house."

"That's right!" Lucy said. "And Peter was very quiet that evening. I wonder if they'd had a row or something."

Julia remembered that Peter was prickly in Stewart's presence and then went home. Had he unleashed all that pent-up intensity on his wife? It was hard to imagine a clergyman fighting with his wife.

Lucy said, "Peter has always seemed so bound up with himself."

"Well, he certainly did a brave and generous thing," Archie said. "And imagine keeping quiet about it all this time."

"He told me the story," Julia said, "when he first came to the house, just after we heard—about Charles. He told me the story, but he didn't say he had risked his life."

"There's obviously a lot more to young Wentworth than we knew about," Archie said.

As chairman of the Relief Committee, Arthur Halliwell had arranged that certain Haligonians be presented to the governor general in his own stockbroking offices. If that provided inadvertent advertising, he had the good excuse that City Hall was now as crowded and smelly as a railway station. All those to be presented to the Duke and Duchess of Devonshire assembled on Friday morning in front of the blackboards showing chalked figures from Thursday's stock trading in New York and Toronto. There were the members of the Relief Committee, leaders of the Voluntary Aid Detachment, St. John's Ambulance, Red Cross, and the Robertsons and a few others to be honored individually.

Halliwell went in person to the station to greet the governor general in his private railway car. He had been awake during the night, fretting about the correct way to address a duke who was also governor general. In the morning he fussed over his tie and left the house early to let his barbershop give his mustache and his boots some professional attention. He emerged, powdered, scented, and polished, but was not prepared for the devastating nattiness of the aide-de-camp, Lord Smithson, an elderly general in the Coldstream Guards. Without appearing studied or contrived, Lord Smithson's toilet—uniform, gleaming buttons and leather, pink skin, sideburns and mustache—made Halliwell feel ill dressed and badly groomed. And Smithson's speech was as clipped and polished as his appearance, making Halliwell's Halifax accent sound provincial.

Above all that was His Lordship's manner, silkily correct, both condescending and unpretentious, a most disconcerting combination. It made Halliwell spiritually retreat a few steps before finding the courage to press his interests.

He knew the feeling well. The assumption of authority bred into these Englishmen was the secret force of empire. It emanated from the king, whose personal envoy was now close by in the same ornate railway car, like a lump of radium, emitting rays of influence, invisible but powerfully felt.

"Should I address him as Your Grace because he is a duke or Your Excellency because he is governor general?"

"I think you'll find he answers to both." It was said dryly, easily, with a little laugh of condescension.

"I wanted to have a moment, if possible, to acquaint him with the few people we've assembled to be presented."

"Quite right. If you'll tell me, I'll brief him."

Halliwell described them, ending with the Robertsons, "the family of our just announced winner of the Victoria Cross, Major Robertson."

"Ah, yes, the Robertson VC. We were informed about that."

Lord Smithson did not say that the piqued Colonial Office in London had instantly complained of the way the prime minister had maneuvered around the governor general directly to Downing Street, politician to politician, skipping the niceties of royal protocol.

"Archibald Robertson, very prominent Halifax family, major shipbuilding and repair, vital in the war effort, personal longtime friend and supporter of Sir Robert Borden . . ."

"Aha." That was why Borden had done such a quick end run around Rideau Hall.

". . . and the two Mrs. Robertsons, the major's mother and his widow. I thought if His Grace were gracious enough to say a few words, it would be very comforting to them."

"Quite appropriate," murmured the general, taking notes. His voice came thin and pinched from the back of his nose. "He'll be delighted, of course."

Halliwell said, "We don't wish to presume, but I've been asked by the dean of All Saints Cathedral, on behalf of the bishop of Nova Scotia, to inquire whether there would be any chance of

Their Graces attending a memorial service tomorrow afternoon for the Robertson boy."

"Out of the question, I'm afraid." The aide consulted the slimmest diary Halliwell had ever seen. "We must be in Fredericton by tomorrow afternoon."

"I see, but may I raise one other matter? Have you by any chance seen this?" He held out a newspaper cutting. "An editorial in the local paper. You won't have heard of this young clergyman, but his extraordinary act of heroism has just come to light."

The aide-de-camp read the short editorial extolling Peter Wentworth.

"Went into a burning building to give this woman the last rites? Church of England minister?"

"Yes, and apparently just got away himself. Everyone is talking about it. It seems to stand for the spirit of the city and the thousand acts of generosity and unselfishness the disaster has inspired in people. I took the liberty of inviting him to be present."

"Quite right, Mr. Halliwell! Good judgment. What an extraordinary thing! I shall just slip in and have a few words with His Grace. Shan't be long."

The governor general was less formidable than his aide. The duke looked a little foolish, small staring eyes in the fleshy face and drooping mustache of a music hall Englishman. But Hallwiwell knew that the duke was a shrewd politician, who had served in several British cabinets and had cleverly navigated the treacherous waters between Ottawa and London. He also had the easy manner of the aristocrat. In the car he said to Halliwell, "Extraordinary thing, this clergyman of yours, Mr. Halliwell. I've never heard of a Church of England minister risking his life to give a Catholic the last rites. Have you, Harry?"

"No, Your Grace."

"There ought to be some kind of recognition for conduct like that, some civilian award. I shall have to take advice. Harry, make a note for me."

"Yes, Your Grace."

Yes, thought the governor general, looking at the grim streets passing by, a rather neat way of matching Borden's trick with the Robertson VC. A noble gesture from His Majesty to this miserably unlucky city. Its morale is very important to the war effort. All the convoys assemble here. The servicemen involved would be decorated anyway. But a civilian, a clergyman: the people of Halifax would think it a very fitting gesture, almost an award to the entire city.

"Now, you're going to show us everything, Mr. Halliwell. I want to see it all myself so that I can give His Majesty a first-hand account."

It thrilled Arthur Halliwell to have so direct a connection to the king.

The procession drove up Barrington Street, through the cleared streets of the Richmond district, to Fort Needham. The duke and duchess alighted, and Halliwell pointed out the Narrows, where the *Mont Blanc* and the *Imo* had collided.

"You can see the hulk of the *Imo* lying over there on the Dartmouth shore. The main force of the blast came directly up here. Sadly, many people went to their windows to watch the fire. Hundreds of them were lacerated by shards of window glass—those who survived."

"Appalling sight. Simply appalling. Reading about it doesn't convey the magnitude."

A warm feeling of gratitude filled Halliwell at the duke's perspicacity.

"There was, of course, no way for a small city to prepare for such a disaster. But somehow we have managed."

"But you've managed magnificently, from all I hear."

The governor general turned to the landscape of crushed and obliterated buildings behind him.

"And what is going to happen to all this?"

"A complete rebuilding of this end of the city. We've just begun planning. All this rubble will have to be cleared away, the sites for new streets and neighborhoods laid out. It will allow us to make a far better place than it was, probably improved sewage and paving, playgrounds for children, and decent houses."

"But all the people who lived here?" the duchess asked. "Where are they now?"

"Temporarily housed all over the city, Your Grace." Halliwell found that he slipped quite easily into using *Your Grace*. The more often he said it, the more pleasant it sounded to say it. Your Excellency would have sounded pompous and slightly foreign. Saying Your Grace made him feel at one with the Devonshires, the royal family, all the manifestations of Britishness that were so warming.

"Some have moved to other towns in the province. Many hundreds are still in hospital. We've made all sorts of places, like schools, into temporary hospitals. We'll be seeing one this afternoon. We have plans to erect temporary housing on the Exhibition Grounds to get many of the people out of the makeshift places they're in now. And, I'm afraid, there are still bodies we have not found."

The duchess looked down and shuddered. "Under all this?"

"There are still many people missing. Now, Your Grace, it's very raw and cold up here. Perhaps we should return to the motors. The people we've gathered to be presented are next."

That evening Julia resumed the diary improvised from sheets of writing paper:

I was astonished to see Peter Wentworth. He turned up while we were waiting for the GG, looking ghastly—haggard and gray —as though he'd had no sleep for days. Wouldn't be surprising, considering what he must be going through with his wife. He looked at me and the Robertsons as though he didn't know us, then came over apologetically and shook hands. That fanatical gleam in his eye was gone. We all spoke warmly to him of the act the papers were praising, and he murmured that it was greatly exaggerated. Yet when he was presented to their Exes, he stood up very straight after his bow and, while blushing a little, had no hesitation in answering questions.

They talked to him for several minutes, and I wondered how he could so easily divide his mind and feelings between the awful business with his wife and this bit of show, which did not embarrass him. We gave him a lift back, but of course none of us spoke a word about his wife. I found myself overflowing with sympathy for them both and with questions I felt it tactless to ask. But I confess that my principal curiosity was for him: how can he live with what she did—and with whatever drove her to do it. Mingled with curiosity is a sense of horror. I've never known anyone who tried that. In my nights of greatest despair and loneliness, the idea of killing myself has never entered my head.

Our own presentation was perfunctory enough. Elizabeth and then I curtsied deeply—and unsteadily. I worried about getting caught in my skirts, since it was chilly enough to keep our long coats on and I haven't practiced since I was presented years ago to the old GG, the Duke of Connaught. The Devonshires both said comforting, practiced things about sacrifice for a greater good. With his droopy mustache, he looks like Lord Kitchener gone to seed. He looked at me indifferently and gave me a limp handshake. But the duchess seemed sincerely affected and held both my hand and Mrs. Robertson's together for a moment with a tear in her eye.

Archie stood up so proudly, he might have been receiving a medal himself. I see more clearly how conventional he is. I had scarcely quieted my rage from an hour earlier. All the time we waited, I had a mad impulse to say something loud and provocative in public. There were newspaper reporters there and photographers. But all such thoughts evaporated with the entrance of the Devonshires. However ordinary they look, they have that glow of importance about them that made all the girls of the Volunteer Aid Detachment look pop-eyed with wonder, and Arthur Halliwell burst his buttons with self-importance. I'm not pretending that I wasn't thrilled myself. I was. Gratitude—or pride or whatever it was—came over me and quite dispelled any rebellious thought I had. These two people stand for the king and empire that all the sacrifices are being made for. It shouldn't have been the wretched newspaper editor or the Robertsons I was angry at but these lordly beings. Yet I felt nothing of the sort. I was suffused with God-Save-the-King feelings. I got quite warm, almost perspiring, a certain sign I was excited.

My storm over the letters this morning was quite unpremeditated. I wish I could talk to someone sympathetic, like Stewart MacPherson. He is sensible about things. And a psychologist.

I must compose myself for tomorrow's ordeal: the memorial service for C.

The afternoon paper has a letter from the Roman Catholic monsignor praising Peter Wentworth's act of Christian generosity, "in the spirit that reminds of the early days of our church." I suppose he will be assisting at the service.

I feel much older tonight, full of experience—and exhausted. But I have to wait up because Lucy is coming by with a black veil she has fixed up for me.

. . . .

SINCE CORPORAL RANSOME could not remember his dreams, Stewart thought word associations might offer a glimpse into his unconscious. He spent an evening making a list of innocuous words with stimulus words like *hockey* and *sitting* distributed among them.

"I'm going to play a little game with you, John. I'll say a word and you tell me the first word that comes to mind. If I say tree, you might say . . . ?"

"Woods?" Ransome said.

"Exactly. There is no right or wrong word. It's any word you think of."

It was becoming apparent that Ransome was quite bright. Stewart got his list out.

"Dinner?"

"Eat."

"Food?"

"Drink."

"Cigarette?"

"Yup."

"I meant the word *cigarette*. What word does it make you think of?"

"Smoke."

"Spoon?"

"Fork."

"Cup?"

"Tea."

"King?"

"Empire."

"War?"

"Guns."

"Soldier?"

"Dead."

Interesting but not surprising.

"Winter?"

"Cold."

"Ice?"

"Snow."

"Hockey?"

"Skate."

"Girl?"

"Boy."

"Baby?"

"Mother."

"Walk?"

"Run."

"Sit?"

"Stand."

"Chair?"

"Shot."

That was very odd, but Stewart continued.

"Climb?"

"Stairs."

"Bed?"

"Sleep."

"Legs?"

"Hurt."

"Hospital?"

"Sick."

"Shell?"

"Shock."

"Trench?"

"Mud."

"When I said *chair,* you said *shot.* What did that mean?"

"I said *sit. Chair, sit.*"

"I am sure you said *shot.*"

"I said *sit.*"

"When I said *soldier,* you said *dead.*"

"Well, it makes sense, eh?"

"But *chair* and *shot* don't make sense?"

"Not to me."

It was very frustrating. It made Stewart realize how untrained he was for what he was doing. He was sure Ransome had made a revealing connection. But he didn't immediately know how to bring it out into the open.

Freud, Jones, and the others seemed to find the truth right away. They made the cases neat and tidy, reducing all the complexity to a few deft lines, like the Matisse painting in Julia's sitting room. Utterly simple, utterly persuasive, with its arbitrary color and clear outlines. "A wild beast," critics called Matisse, and the world thought worse of Freud. The quick intuitions of modern art resembled the intuitive leaps of the psychoanalytic school across the synapses of the old thinking. Matisse the artist, Freud the psychoanalyst overlapped.

Stewart felt excluded and discouraged.

IT AMAZED PETER how rapidly his fame spread. The Saturday newspapers printed pictures of him, along with the Robertsons, being congratulated by the governor general. The *Herald* and *Mail* had been forced to acknowledge the story created by their rivals, the *Chronicle* and *Star*.

When Peter arrived at the vestry, members of the choir shook hands and congratulated him. The dean came in to show Peter a telegram from the bishop of Ontario saying an account had appeared in the newspaper there.

Peter was aware of a subtle shift: the part of him that was embarrassed by the exaggeration and ashamed of the fame it brought gradually made way for another part, which welcomed the adulation and believed he deserved it. The first part had a sneaking anxiety that the foul-mouthed sergeant would suddenly turn up, saying it was all an invention. But the other part dismissed that anxiety. The two forces in him disputed the history of that moment, but the world wanted the revised version, and Peter found it easier to believe that the world was right.

All the sourness of his situation with Margery rose in his throat when he opened his cupboard and saw no surplice. There was his cassock, academic hood, and tippet. Just then, Mrs. Grenville, the plump woman who laundered the choir surplices, came up, carrying his surplice proudly aloft like a banner, beautifully ironed.

"Mr. Wentworth, I knew you had far too much on your mind to think of this. So I thought I would just do it for you. There you are!"

She gave him the hanger with a look of pride and affection Peter had not seen before.

"Mrs. Grenville, I can't thank you enough. It was extremely thoughtful of you."

She beamed and whispered, "You're a very special person to all of us, Mr. Wentworth. We're very proud of you. If there's anything I can do for you, don't hesitate a moment to ask me."

"Well, thank you. God bless you."

This busty woman in her fifties, with her graying hair and red hands, looked at him like a young girl in love.

"Just remember. Nothing is too much trouble." And she went away.

Peter felt a moment of sweet well-being as he buttoned the many small buttons of the cassock.

When the doctors said that Margery could leave the hospital, her parents insisted that she go to their house, where she could be nursed. Peter was relieved. The children could be cared for there too, although Margery had yet to ask for them. She behaved as though she had forgotten they existed. She was recovering well physically. The black mark on her forehead was fading, and her cheeks had some color. But all recent years were absent from her memory. She behaved as she had when they were first married, and her eyes echoed some of the dancing light of their honeymoon months. If Peter mentioned the children, she acted as though she hadn't heard.

Most distressing was her loss of memory for immediate things: a question just asked, something just told her. She laughed and reached for a little pad to write it down. Her hospital table and bed were covered with the reminders she had written, three or four notes saying the same thing: *Doctor says go home Sunday* or *Peter coming three o'clock*. The doctors could not predict when her memory might return.

The other change was her physical demonstrativeness to Peter. When they were alone in the hospital room, she reached for him, put her arms around his neck, and pulled him down to kiss her. He was very aware of her in the bed but nervous that a nurse or doctor would come in. Margery had lost such inhibitions. She kissed him greedily, possessively. It made him uneasy, aroused by her, but faintly repelled.

He could hear the muttering hum of the large congregation through the vestry door. He knew that Julia would be sitting in the front row on the left with the Robertsons; the lieutenant governor, and other dignitaries on the right. At the governor general's reception, her fine pale face, the blond hair almost hidden by her black fur hat, was so beautiful, it took his breath away. When it was his turn to be presented, he felt her watching. In the Robertsons' car their hips had touched, and her perfume was now familiar. She looked at him with such sweet anxiety that he was touched. No one mentioned Margery. Perhaps they did not know. When he went out now with the procession, Julia would be watching.

The vestry woodwork trembled with the bass pipes as the great organ played a Bach prelude. Dean Creighton came back from his house, escorting his two old friends, the bishop and Peter's father, Canon Wentworth. As a courtesy he had invited both to lunch before the special service. Each was there to lend dignity; the bishop to give his blessing, Canon Wentworth to read a lesson. The dean and Peter would carry the rest.

His father took Peter aside. "Your mother and I would like you to come to supper with us after the Robertsons' reception. She particularly wants you to—as I do."

"Yes, Father, I'll come." Peter had been putting off the talk he knew he must have.

Stewart MacPherson had arrived early and found the cathedral empty, strangely dark, with many windows covered. He had not been there in years and strolled about as one did when sightseeing cathedrals in Europe, reading the few memorial plaques.

He took a seat near the rear, watching other people arrive. He had come at Julia's invitation and planned to go to the Robertsons' afterward. It was unlike him to accept such invitations, but Julia was different. With her independent mind, she was not society; she was not Susan Gastonguy.

Arthur Halliwell and his wife and pretty daughters took their places, as did many naval and army officers, British and Canadian.

Stewart had no patience for those who rushed to put themselves in authority, the boys who made committees at school and college, who loved being secretaries or presidents of clubs. The war was their great chance in Canada: people with a bit of money or connections who got themselves made colonels; people seeking to draw credit to themselves who loved to strut this imperial stuff, falling over themselves to be better daughters or sons of the empire.

Stewart saw Dorothy Wentworth arrive, leading Peter's two children, but not Margery. Then the Robertsons came in with Lucy and Julia. He could see, beneath her hat and from the rear of her veil, her shining hair and neck.

. . . .

Julia, dressing for the service, had caught herself trying to arrange her hair becomingly and stared at herself in the mirror. A woman does not stop making herself attractive because she is dressing for her husband's funeral. An odd thought. How often the totally irreverent thought came to her when convention supposed a heart full of piety.

She got up from the dressing table and went to the cupboard of Charles's clothes. She took out the suit she most liked him in and turned it inside out. But as hard as she sniffed, she could smell nothing of him. His smell had gone with his soul, gone long before, in fact. She smelled the two military brushes on the chest of drawers and detected a faint suggestion of lavender. In the bedside table she found the oval tin of Yardley's brilliantine. Yes, the old odor. She closed her eyes, imagining Charles, conjuring him from the smell, but opened them again and saw herself in the mirror, standing in her petticoat, sniffing a tin of brilliantine. It looked so pathetic, so sterile a thing to do. The brilliantine was not Charles. If she went downtown, she could buy another tin that Charles had never seen or touched, and it would smell the same. The emptiness and futility of what she was doing made her impatient. She held the Yardley's tin over the wastepaper basket, hesitated a moment, then dropped it resolutely.

"He is dead," she said to her reflection, "and I cannot cry anymore."

She was wrong. The hymn "Abide with Me" and the sound of a sob from Mrs. Robertson brought copious tears. The familiar phrases in the prayers for the dead brought more. But it was the bagpipes that made her, in common with everyone in the Cathedral, sob openly, her shoulders shaking. Elizabeth Robertson on one side and Lucy on the other held Julia's arms.

Only the bagpipes made Stewart feel anything. Toward the end of the long service, there was silence, then a lone piper, hidden in the cathedral transept, began playing a lament. Involuntarily, Stewart shivered.

The rude, primitive snarl of sound ascended the clustered columns into the vaulted roof, seeking escape into the open air, where the notes could evaporate conventionally into the mists, into the heather, into the Highlands of the Scottish imagination. But trapped in this Gothic space, this metaphor for northern forests, there was no escape. Above the drones, the half-human voice of the chanters, the glottal, liquid notes collided with stone and wood; reverberated, echoed, and re-echoed, reminded and insisted, twisting the wounds in their hearts.

The pipes awakened feelings about the death of Charles Robertson greater than those evoked by the prayers or the eulogy, or the psalms and anthems the choir had sung. Those well-tempered dignities vanished at the first notes of a sound that far predated the organ in antiquity; preceded the chromatic setting of the anthems and hymns; a sound older than the seventeenth-century English prayers; far older than the English language, more ancient than the Bible itself.

Most of the people in that packed congregation had some Celtic blood in their veins. Even those who did not find in themselves a sympathetic yearning, as though something spoke across thousands of years, across all history of wars and brave men dying; a sound from the very cradle of humanity, where the bagpipes were born before Jews or Christians or Muslims; a sound none could hear in this setting without shivering in his skin. It made them all grieve for Charles, for other young men, or for love of the abstract Britishness it was their sweet duty to fight and die for.

It was a cheap trick, Stewart thought, wiping his eyes. They were all vulnerable. The sentimental Scottish imagination had become part of Canadian patriotism. Men who had no Scottish blood could be stirred by it, sent to war in its trappings, and made to weep at the sound of the pipes chilling the heart in an Anglican cathedral.

The Robertsons had invited many people to their large house on Young Avenue after the service. Sliding doors had been parted between the rooms opening off the wide front hall. A maid in black with a white apron and cap helped with the coats. There were fires burning in each room, candles in silver candelabra as well as the electric chandeliers. In the dining room was tea with sandwiches and biscuits. In the library were drinks for men who went looking for them.

Julia stood with Lucy and her parents in the front hall, greeting the lieutenant governor and military aide, the mayor, Arthur Halliwell and the Relief Committee, the clergy, various senior officers, including a colonel in Highland dress uniform from Charles's regiment in Montreal, and the piper who had played in the cathedral.

After paying their respects to the Robertsons, many guests stopped to congratulate Peter. Archie Robertson looked into the sitting room and muttered to his wife, "You'd think we'd given the reception for Peter Wentworth! Look at that."

Elizabeth hushed him, but then the dean came out to collect them and to raise his resonant churchman's voice. "My friends, pray silence for a moment. May I have your attention just a moment?"

Conversation subsided, and people crowded into the doorways opening into the hall.

"Dear friends, I wanted to add a word that I deemed too personal for the solemn service in the cathedral. Our hearts are full of pride and sadness. The enormous congregation that filled our cathedral is testimony to the pride of this city in one of its great and heroic sons, who will live in the annals of valor, Charles Robertson, VC. My poor words cannot add a jot to, nor would I want them to subtract a jot from, the moving and eloquent words we have heard from His Excellency, His Grace the bishop, from General Montague.

"To many of us, Charles Robertson was like our own son. To Margaret and me, unblessed by our own children, he was almost a son. But the outpouring today demonstrates that this fine young man represents something beyond his human clay. He represents the spirit of this city and this old province by the sea, and this Dominion, united now as never before in our determination to see good triumph and evil crushed, whatever the cost . . ."

The words *whatever the cost* seared Julia as wanton and cruel; her eyes met Stewart's and she knew he agreed.

"Charles Robertson has given his life for that cause, as have many other Nova Scotians. The Robertsons have given their only son. Because they are my dear friends, as well as my parishoners, I feel their loss acutely and personally. But my purpose is not to wring your hearts, or theirs, or Lucy's, or Julia Robertson's any further, but to make an announcement."

It went quickly through Peter's mind that the dean was going to talk about him.

"As you all know, our beloved cathedral has suffered grievously in the disaster. We were more fortunate than some churches, but

still the losses are severe. It is my honor to tell you that, to commemorate their heroic son, the Robertsons are to give a large
memorial window, in memory of all who have given their lives in
this great conflict."

There was a murmur of approval.

"Ours is the cathedral church of this ancient province of the
Anglican communion. Their gift will memorialize all from Nova
Scotia who fell. Thus will their names and their glory live, as they
themselves will live in heaven, forevermore. Dear friends, all of us
thank you."

Archie Robertson, red in the face, mopped his eyes with his
handkerchief, blew his nose, and straightend his back.

"Thank you, Donald. I am not going to make a speech. Elizabeth and I, and I am sure Lucy and Julia, are deeply touched that
all of you cared enough to come today. It is hard for me to say
which feeling moves me most, pride in our son, grief for his loss,
gratitude to all our friends for your friendship, and"—his voice
wavered a little, so he raised it to a low shout—"and an even
stronger desire to get this damned war won!"

"Here, here!" an officer shouted, and the cry was loudly echoed
with a burst of applause. Men clustered around Archie, shaking
hands and slapping him on the back. Women encircled Elizabeth,
and other small groups formed.

With two cups of tea, Dorothy Wentworth approached Stewart,
offering him one. He had the warmest feelings about this woman,
whom he had admired more than his own mother, and who now
looked so small beside him with her neat gray bun and wrinkled
face.

The drawing room was large, and they found a quiet corner to
sit in.

"It is stunning about Peter," Stewart said.

"I hope it doesn't go to his head—all the things they are saying
about him," Dorothy Wentworth said. They both looked toward
Peter, who was talking to several men including the British admiral.

She turned back. "Stewart, have you heard about Margery?"

"No. Heard what? I haven't seen her today."

"She is very ill. I tell you this as a good friend and because I
know you have tried to help in the past. Last Tuesday, I found her
with the gas on in the kitchen . . ."

How rapidly the mind worked. Instantly, still listening to her, he could picture it, knew he had been expecting it for years, see Margery infinitely desirable at dances before the war, remember his own desire and her indifference, see her wan face on the street—all without missing a syllable of Dorothy Wentworth's urgent words.

". . . she had asked me to take the children for the morning, which was unusual. When I came back, that is what I found."

"Oh, how awful! Is she all right?"

"She is gradually recovering."

"It wasn't an accident?"

"For your ears, Stewart, it was clearly not an accident. Her preparations were very serious."

"Is she really all right?"

"She is recovering—slowly. She has been in the VG. I wondered whether Peter had told you."

"No, I haven't seen much of him recently."

Dorothy looked at him significantly. "I thought you should know."

"Do you mean you'd like me to speak to Peter?"

"I thought you should know." Dorothy smiled and patted Stewart's hand in the friendly, unsentimental way she used to pat him as a small boy.

He was about to ask more when Susan Gastonguy sat down. "I'm sorry, Mrs. Wentworth, am I interrupting?"

Stewart smiled and Dorothy got up, saying she wanted another cup of tea.

"Stewart, I haven't seen you in ages. What have you been doing with yourself?"

"Well, the usual."

"Did Mrs. Wentworth tell you about finding Margery?"

"Yes."

"I was devastated to hear it. I suppose I've been her closest friend for years, and I had no idea she was so—what is it?—so despairing."

Stewart, half-listening to her repeat the details, glanced at Peter talking animatedly to a group that now included Julia Robertson. How could Peter be here? And why was he turning his arrowhead profile so intensely to Julia Robertson? But, then, the Tobins were there as well.

Colonel Gastonguy, Susan's father, came up, holding a glass of whiskey. "Hello, Stewart. Haven't seen you in donkey's years."

Stewart rose out of respect for the older man, whom he knew as a bore.

"Someone was just telling me you're doing a study of shell shock—and so on."

"Well, yes."

"I think it's a lot of nonsense myself."

Stewart saw Susan sigh in annoyance and look away. He heard someone talking about "Unionist Government."

"In other wars, in my war, they didn't have such notions. If a fellow was a coward or afraid to fight, they simply shot him, as an example to the others."

"Well, we've done some of that in this war," said Stewart. "Is that a whiskey you have, Colonel?"

"Yes, I found it through there."

"I think I'll just do that, if you'll excuse me—" and Stewart left them.

"Oh, Daddy!" Susan said irritably. "You chased him away!"

Julia, listening in the group near Peter, had turned to see Susan Gastonguy approach Stewart warmly and noticed his quick departure. She observed how unexpectedly distinguished Stewart looked in his black morning coat. She had seen him only in rumpled tweeds. She wanted to talk to him.

Elizabeth Robertson touched her sleeve and beckoned her to follow. "Come upstairs with me. I thought you might welcome a quiet moment. It's so noisy, with everyone chattering."

In her bedroom, they could faintly hear the hubbub of the large party below. Elizabeth opened a drawer and took out Charles's letters.

"I wanted to give you these back. Sit down for a moment. You were sweet to let me have them. I know how upset you were yesterday, and until I read them I didn't quite understand why." She put her hand on Julia's. "And now I do."

Julia felt tears coming and took a deep breath to control herself.

"I told Archie yesterday that I admired what you did. I made him read them again last night. He still doesn't see it as you and I do—in fact, as Sandy did. Such a waste." Mrs. Robertson sighed. "So little point. When you hear that point of view, it usually comes from people we're inclined to disregard."

Julia said, "I thought if people heard it from Charles—no one could accuse him of being unpatriotic. Especially now. I suppose the editor was bound to know your husband."

Elizabeth said, "Halifax is a very small place and people don't like to rock the boat. But Archie doesn't know any editors in Montreal. Montreal may be different."

Julia looked at her mother-in-law, who was smiling in a way that made her smile too.

"Perhaps I will," Julia said.

"I've told you before, I am very fond of you, my dear. I had hoped you'd be part of the family forever, that you and Charles would bring us grandchildren. Now—"

She looked away and sighed, and in the gesture Julia recognized the way Charles had so often turned his head away, the gesture she had mistaken for a wish to be far away on his own—some impatience with the present. Elizabeth turned back.

"Now you'll probably find someone else and set up a new life."

"I can't imagine that," Julia said.

"Don't stop yourself from imagining it. No—just listen to me for a moment. I'll tell you this very directly. I thought of it last night after reading these letters. You are a beautiful young woman with an entire life ahead of you. You don't owe us any more loyalty than you've given us already."

Julia embraced her.

"I wish my own mother saw things as clearly as you do, and as generously."

"One's own mother never quite seems to. Would you like to powder your nose before we go down again?"

Cynthia Tobin had insisted that she and George accept.

"It isn't often we get invited there."

"But I don't know them well, and with Margery—"

"George, our not going won't help Margery."

In fact, George was privately pleased that Peter's connection brought him into a circle that included the lieutenant governor, the mayor, and Arthur Halliwell, who might be very helpful in the huge construction projects ahead.

"Hello, George, haven't seen you in ages," Halliwell said. "The dean tells me you've been extraordinarily generous with the cathedral."

"Well, if I hadn't done it, they might still have the snow blowing in."

"Quite right. It was hard for us to know where to turn, the first few days. Everything needed doing at once. You know the mayor, of course. George Tobin, Tobin's Construction. George has done all the smashed windows in the cathedral without charge."

"Well, the temporary covering, at any rate."

"Ah, Dean," Halliwell said. "I thought the service was magnificent. Sorry the duke and duchess couldn't manage it; they had to go on to Fredericton. But for all the melancholy occasion, it was magnificent. You know George Tobin, I believe."

"No, I haven't had the pleasure of thanking you in person, Mr. Tobin. You've been a paragon of generosity and efficiency."

Halliwell said, "I think it's magnificent how the whole city has pulled together in this. His Grace told me just yesterday that the whole empire should be proud of the way Halifax has borne its war crisis. I thought it very penetrating of him. It's as though our city had suddenly been thrown into the front lines—worse, really, because we weren't trained for this sort of thing."

"Well, the empire may be proud," George Tobin said, "but it's a good thing the Americans were quick off the mark with all their help. I think we'd still be sitting around twiddling our thumbs for want of supplies."

The lieutenant governor had overheard. "Oh, has it really been that decisive, the American help? They've been very generous, granted. But what about the trainloads of supplies from Ontario, for example—nails, glass, putty, beaverboard."

Tobin persisted. "Well, sir, as someone in the business, knowing exactly what building supplies there are at any one time in the city and where they come from, I'd just repeat what I said: it's a good thing the Americans were so quick."

Colonel Gastonguy heard this. "The Americans? It's just money, isn't it, and they've got plenty of it."

"George, why don't you come and see me?" Arthur Halliwell said. "We've got an enormous planning and construction job ahead of us. We could use some professional advice."

"I'd be happy to," said George.

•  •  •  •

When Stewart found Peter alone for a moment, he said quietly, "Your mother's just told me about Margery. I'm very sorry to hear it."

"She's getting better."

"But what are they going to do for her now?"

"The doctors say rest is the thing. A complete rest cure. No responsibilities. No anxieties."

"I see. Do they think that will help any more than it did in the past? These things progress."

Peter glanced away, obviously eager to end the conversation.

"Would you like me to come and see her?"

Peter turned back. "Perhaps when she's feeling a little stronger. I'll let you know."

After Julia came downstairs, every time she looked up from a conversation, she met Peter's eye. The look she associated with him, the inquisitive stare, had returned. When he left with his parents, she thought he pressed her hand as though he had a right to.

She found Stewart alone and sat near him.

"Forgive me collapsing, but I am so tired from being nice to everyone. Well, that's not very charitable. People have been as sweet as they could be. It's just a great strain."

A maid passed through the library with a tray of glasses. It felt like the end of a long party, shreds of more relaxed conversations from different rooms. Halliwell's orotund voice; the dean's cathedral voice.

"You've known Peter Wentworth a long time, haven't you? Lucy told me."

"We were very close when we were children, and we were away at school together, then college."

"I have the feeling you're not as close friends now. Is that right?"

Stewart laughed. "Yes, that's right. Why do you ask?"

"I think he's a strange man, even for a clergyman." She turned to him abruptly. "Do you know his wife? Margery? Is that her name?"

"Yes. I've known her for a long time."

"So you know about—what's happened?"

"As a matter of fact, I've only just heard. Peter's mother told me."

"Lucy told us yesterday. I've had a sick feeling about it ever since."

She sat with her hands in the praying position, fingertips to her lips, that he had noticed several times. The frown between her eyebrows was unfamiliar.

"Is she—is Margery—what you would call mentally disturbed? I'm so ignorant about these things, I don't know what to ask."

He looked at her, wondering how discreet to be, but his impatience with Peter swept that aside. "She suffers from neurasthenia. It became manifest after the birth of their first child, about five years ago. You understand that I am not a doctor, not a psychiatrist. I am a behavioral psychologist. But I think it's accurate to call her condition a form of neurasthenia—the spirits are depressed; all the energy and joy of life disappear."

Lucy came in. "Oh, here you are! What a good idea! I'm so tired." She sat down beside Julia.

"We've been talking about Peter Wentworth's wife," Julia said, but Stewart felt the intimacy destroyed.

"Do you know any more?" Lucy leaned toward them. "I just couldn't bring myself to ask Peter about it. He seemed so keyed up."

Stewart said, "He told me just now that she's getting better."

"Is that all?" Julia asked. Her face betrayed curiosity about Peter. And the idea struck him that this lovely woman, newly widowed, might be falling in love with a man who had secretly read her private diary. No, he was imagining it.

She opened her eyes. "Is neurasthenia something that can be cured?"

"Sometimes, but not with any certainty."

"What happens to someone who can't be cured?"

"They go on living as best they can, if they have families who will look after them. Or they go to nursing homes. If they're a danger to themselves, they may have to be confined."

"You mean the insane asylum?"

"Yes."

"How terrible." Julia shuddered. "It makes me depressed to think of it."

She was silent and lovely in her black dress, looking away into the room. In the sitting room someone began playing the piano, and a few voices began, "There's a long, long trail a-winding into the land of my dreams." Julia turned to Stewart. Her eyes were brimming with tears, and the sight made his stomach seem to change location in his abdomen.

She smiled and said, "Would you mind taking me home?"

They collected their coats and said their goodbyes.

Elizabeth Robertson said, "But I thought you'd stay and have a little supper with us. Are you sure? You'll be all alone in that house."

"Mollie will be there."

The Robertsons kissed and hugged Julia and shook hands with Stewart, and they went out into the cold night. When the front door closed they could still faintly hear the piano. Someone was playing, "Keep the home fires burning, while our hearts are yearning . . ."

As he helped her over the snowbank into the car, he was conscious of the grip of her gloved hand, the warmth through the thin leather.

In the car Julia was quiet and then said, "They all seem to think the war is still right, as the dean said, whatever the cost. What do you think about it?"

"I think they should consider an armistice. Negotiate an end." Stewart realized he had never said this to anyone.

"You know, in the last few months, just before he was killed, Charles was appalled by the war. He'd decided to stop pretending to me. His last letters were absolutely frank. I took them down to the editor of the *Herald*. He said he'd publish them, but when he read them he called Archie Robertson, not me. He said they could get him sent to jail. They were treasonous. So I actually had a row with the Robertsons. I just felt I had to do something."

"That was very brave of you."

"Or foolish." She laughed.

"No, brave, I think."

He felt her turn to look at him, then look to the front again. She was quiet. To his regret they had reached her house on South Park Street.

"Are you going to go on living here?"

"You mean move to another house?"

"I mean you would be free to go anywhere you liked, wouldn't you?"

That startled her. "You know, I haven't thought of that. I suppose you're right."

Again he helped her over the rough snow.

"Thank you for bringing me home." She turned to go in, then turned back to him impulsively. "Would like to read his letters?"

"Well, if you're sure. Yes, I would."

"I don't know anyone else who is saying what he says."

She opened her bag and handed him the envelopes.

"Good night."

"Good night. May I call you?" Stewart said. "We have some unfinished business with Betty's eye."

"Yes. Please call. And thank you again." She shook hands and ran up the steps.

Mollie came out of the kitchen and looked at her.

"Well, it was some beautiful service, dear. I cried my eyes out. And the people that came. Everyone in the world was there." She gestured to the hall table but withdrew her hand superstitiously. "Those came." Two telegrams lay on the silver tray. "I hope it's not more bad news."

Could it yet be all a mistake? They had the wrong person? Charles is alive?

She tore one telegram open. It was from her father.

AFTER MEMORIAL SERVICE MOTHER AND I DEARLY HOPE YOU WILL
COME BACK HERE FOR CHRISTMAS AND REST. LOVINGLY DADDY

"I'd forgotten about Christmas."

"With everything else, there's been no time to think of it, or feeling for it. There's not going to be much of a Christmas for many in Halifax."

Julia opened the other telegram; it took her a few moments to understand it.

MD OTTAWA ONT DECEMBER 22
MRS JULIA ROBERTSON
HALIFAX N S
7091 SINCERELY REGRET INFORM YOU EIGHT NINE SEVEN SIX EIGHT
FOUR ACTING MAJOR CHARLES ARCHIBALD ROBERTSON 42 BATTALION

OFFICIALLY REPORTED DIED OF WOUNDS DECEMBER FIFTEEN. DIRECTOR
OF RECORDS. 10:15 AM.

"It's from Ottawa. They say that Charles is dead."

"But we've known that for ages!"

"Only because Mr. Robertson knew someone important to
call." Saying this made her feel older, like a parent. She was standing there with her coat on, the telegram in her hand.

"Think of all the families who don't know for weeks. There are
families right now probably who don't know their son or husband
is dead. There will be people celebrating Christmas when the man
is already dead."

"Oh, you shouldn't say that, dear! It's bad luck. Never call
anyone dead that isn't."

Julia read her father's telegram again.

"If I went to Montreal to my parents' for Christmas, would you
and Betty be all right?"

"I imagine. It's likely we'd go down to Alice's. She's asked us."

"Mollie, you didn't tell me!"

"I didn't want yous to be here alone. I thought if you're over
here, I'd stay over here."

Julia kissed her. "You're very kind, Mollie, but I think I will go,
if I can get a ticket."

"If you go alls the way to Montreal, will you be coming back?"

"Why, of course."

"Well, I was just wondering whether you'd be needing me?"

"Mollie, if I live in Halifax, I'll always need you."

In her room, for the first time she felt truly alone. The telegram
said he had died on December 15. He had sailed on December 15,
1915. Two years to the day.

In the lost diary she had written how she felt about him on
particular days. Already that was vague in her mind. The loss of the
diary presaged the loss of Charles himself. What good would it do
her now to remember how badly she had missed him when she
was sure he was coming back?

She did not really want to go to Montreal, yet the idea was
childishly comforting. Certainly she did not want to go back there
to live. Much better Halifax than that. But if not either, where?
Stewart said she could live anywhere. But where? Stewart was
thinking like a man. He meant *he* could live anywhere. Lucy said

he was quite well off, and a bachelor, with no ties. He had spent a lot of time in Europe. He could go back there if he wished. And the notion strayed past these thoughts that Stewart was such a comforting person to be with. But a woman by herself could not very easily go off—she could hear her mother say "go traipsing off"—and live abroad—"not something a nice woman would do."

Charles had spoken of going back to Europe with her after the war. That memory for a second intensified the ache she felt. That was her grief now, a quiet sadness, like a noise in the distance, that suddenly grew louder and more painful when she remembered one particular, then faded again into the background.

Stewart probably would go off after the war. He looked unsettled here. He couldn't rattle around in that big house by himself. She imagined him on a walking tour in the Alps. On escorted school hikes into the mountains, the girls had met such men. She remembered finding one in hiking gear, sitting on a rock and having his lunch of chocolate and fresh bread and cheese. He was English, an Oxford student on a walking trip, with a cap and stick and a small haversack. She thought about him afterward. How free he had looked to the regimented schoolgirl—going where he liked; getting on trains and boats; lodging in whatever hotel he chose; staying for as long as he wished; eating in little restaurants.

She imagined Stewart going to galleries, to libraries to study, to conferences with European psychologists. What an interesting life and what a pleasant companion!

Peter Wentworth by comparison appeared trapped. A clergyman made very little money. Even if his father-in-law was well off— coining it, Lucy said—Peter had children and the extra burden of a sick wife. Learning about Margery had added a color to the palette of her feelings about Peter. Pity was now mixed with the irritation and excitement she felt with him: irritation with his being oversure of himself; excitement at the magnetism of his presence, his urgent good looks, his impertinent stare. It still startled her to remember that downstairs, in this house, she had been sure he was about to kiss her. He was strange, not a comfortable companion, but perhaps that is what drew her to him.

When she removed her clothes, before pulling on her night-dress, Julia looked at herself in the long mirror. Her body: still young-looking, with slim hips, small waist, and high breasts. The body she had thought of mostly as her body *for him*. No longer that. She put her hands on her breasts. It was her body, and it was two years since he had touched it.

She quickly put on her nightdress and got into bed, continuing to shiver until she had warmed a place under the covers.

Stewart read Charles's letters. He had heard the same antiwar sentiments from soldiers he dealt with, but offered with shame and embarrassment: never from a successful officer on active service who reveled in the tactics as much as he despised the strategy.

Why had she asked him to read them? Out of anger at his death, certainly, anger at the leaders who caused it. But was it not also a sign about her feelings? She was no longer Charles's exclusive confidante; she no longer belonged to him.

Women had always looked at Peter first, but this was absurd. Peter, the great moralizer, was acting like a man in a trance. He did not see reality. He had a crisis on his hands with his wife, and he was not only denying it but was openly making advances to Julia.

Stewart sat at his desk and pulled the upright telephone toward him. He hated initiating calls on the instrument. It was a little phobia he intended sometime to analyze. He would much prefer to write a note or see someone in person. He got up and poured himself a whiskey. He sat down again and looked at the telephone. It was not the way he did things.

He took a piece of writing paper and with his fountain pen wrote:

Dear Julia,

I read Charles's letters and found them very moving. I would like to return them. There is also something I greatly desire to discuss with you. Could you spare me a few minutes? It is very urgent to me.

Yours,
Stewart

He found an envelope and stamp and, without putting on his coat, walked to the postbox on the corner of Victoria Road. He came back invigorated from the cold and sat down to finish his whiskey and ruminate.

She was an extraordinary woman, in every way likable, desirable, companionable. It gave him a warm feeling just to think of her. She pushed all the other women he had known into the shadows. Two unanswered letters from Christine Soames lay on his desk, accusingly. Julia was dazzling look at, intellectually alert and curious, honest and open, skeptical and funny. Her eyes filling up at the sound of "There's a long, long trail a-winding" had melted his heart. It was how her eyes had looked the day he first met her, bringing Betty back to Mollie.

It was much too soon. She was only now going to bed on the day of her husband's funeral. The thought of her going to bed alone stirred him. But if asked, she could only say, "No," or "It's too soon," or "Will you give me some time?" At least she would know how he felt. His intentions would be clear. He had never felt like this before: never with this purity and certainty, never with such a gladdening of the heart. Why shouldn't he telephone her after all? No, it was late. Too startling and too crude. She would get his note by early afternoon tomorrow.

Stewart went to bed a happier man than he could remember being, in his range of adult emotions, and he slept well.

It was not until he had bathed and shaved, made himself breakfast and walked out to his office at Dalhousie for the exercise and to kill some time, that he realized it was Sunday. There would be no postal delivery until tomorrow! He decided to go in person and started for Julia's house, then thought he should have a note to leave in case she was out, and walked rapidly home. With the new note, he got out the car to drive up South Park Street.

He found Mollie and Betty with their coats on and learned that Julia had gone to Montreal.

"Her father sent her a telegram, and she said she'd be gone a few weeks. She called first thing this morning and all the seats was booked tomorrow. The only seat was on the early train. They didn't have a sleeper. Just day coach. She has to sit up all the way to Montreal. So she went. She hardly packed no clothes. But that's the way she is. She makes up her mind and she's off. One minute she's got a face as long as a wet Sunday, and the next she's all excited and away. I don't blame her. She needs a change of scenery, poor thing. Betty and me are off for the train down to my sister's for Christmas."

"Well, I have the car. I'll give you a lift to the station."

At the station, Stewart carried Mollie's suitcase to the train.

"Betty, I'm going to give you your present after Christmas. But I can tell you what it is."

"What?"

"We're going to get you a new eye."

The child looked troubled, and on the train platform he squatted down to her level.

"It won't be an eye you can see with. We can't do that. But it will be a beautiful blue eye that will look just like this eye. Just the same color. Then everyone will think that you have two eyes. And you won't have to wear this bandage anymore. So most people won't even know. Will you like that?"

"Will it hurt?"

"No, it won't hurt. You'll be able to put it in and take it out whenever you like. You think about that, and when you come back to Halifax, I'll take you to get it."

Mollie said, "Thank you. That's the best Christmas present she could have."

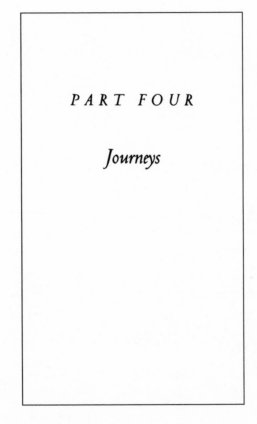

*PART FOUR*

*Journeys*

JULIA HAD NEVER TRAVELED in the day coach on a long journey. She found a corner by the window but was soon jammed in by a large woman with three small children and many bags and baskets. Wartime and the Christmas holiday filled every inch of space. Soldiers on leave, a few already drunk, others playing cards, arguing, singing, asleep against their kitbags, some with girlfriends in their best clothes, eating chocolates. There was continuous movement in the aisles by conductors, ticket takers, men with large baskets of sandwiches, drinks, chocolates, and oranges. The car smelled of the orange peels that littered the floor, along with sandwich wrappers and chocolate papers. Every man who came through, for that matter every woman passing, had a long glance for the elegant woman in black with her blond chignon, reading or gazing wistfully out the window at the deep winter landscape, such a contrast to the woman beside her, bursting out of a print dress, wiping a child's nose, doling out graham wafers and milk. She had a red face and unruly blond hair inappropriately curled into ringlets. Every time she leaned over to reach into her basket or to give something to a child, she sighed deeply, because the movement forced her to compress her large stomach.

Her name was Mildred; her husband, Bill, a stoker in the navy, was off at sea. She was taking the children to her mother's at Bathurst, New Brunswick.

"It's the first Christmas Bill's been away. I didn't get a tree. The idea of decorating it meself made me so lonely, I couldn't face it. Are you married?"

"Yes." Julia didn't want to tell the whole story, but it came out. "My husband was killed in France. He was wounded and then later died of his wounds."

"Oh, dear now! How long ago was it?"

"Just over a week. He died on the fifteenth."

"Only a week? You poor thing!" She was looking at Julia's clothes. "An officer, I suppose?"

"Yes, he was a major. He went out on a patrol at night and was very badly wounded. They took him to a hospital in England, but he died."

"Oh, you poor thing." She put her big hand on Julia's arm and patted her. "I am very sorry." The woman's prominent blue eyes filled with tears. "I don't know what I'd do if anything happened to Billy. He got torpedoed once. I nearly died when I heard it. But they put him right back in another ship. Do you have any children?"

"No. My husband went overseas soon after we were married."

"That's a blessing, isn't it? And a major's pension must be pretty nice to live on. Can you imagine where I'd be with these three if anything happened to Billy? What would a stoker's widow get, even stoker first class? It's hard enough trying to feed us and buy clothes and pay the rent with him alive. I've heard of sailors' widows"—she leaned over to whisper—"going on the streets to make enough to live. And there's plenty of that going on. I know it sounds cruel, but you've got to think on the best side, don't you? How long was he gone overseas?"

"Two years."

"Two years? You haven't seen him in two years?" She looked very closely at Julia, who knew what she was thinking.

"At least a sailor gets to his home port once in a while. Now they've started the convoys, it's regular, every six weeks or so. I couldn't stand it if it was longer."

To change the subject, Julia asked about the explosion. Mildred had been lucky: the apartment was shaken but not badly damaged.

Long after it was obvious from the smell from the baby, she sighed and said, "I suppose I better change him." She heaved the smelly infant onto her shoulder and lurched down the car to the washroom.

Julia went to lunch in the dining car, then walked back through the Pullman and parlor cars and opened the heavy door to the observation platform. She leaned against the railing for as long as she could bear the cold, taking deep lungfuls of the frosty air scented with engine smoke. Her spirits fell into tune with the rhythmic statement of the wheels, and she watched the landscape rush away. The air currents created by the huge movement sent small whirlwinds of snow twirling away on the embankments. The movement suggested that her past was rushing away, rushing away with the tracks and telegraph poles left behind, big, then small, then tiny, then invisible.

When she climbed the stairs in the Westmount house, she felt a stranger in the familiar room, with its candlewick bedspread and Habitant hooked rug.

Grief had altered her perspective, and she found unexpectedly generous feelings toward her mother. She was met with the same darting, peppery inquisition that was Heather Montgomery's manner:

"How are you, dear? How are you really? Do you feel all right? What a tragedy, what a tragedy! We feel so terrible for you. Are you eating? Do you eat enough? Can you sleep? You look awfully tired!"

"I had to sit up all night in the day coach, Mother."

But Julia now saw it not as an annoyance, a probing for weakness, an intrusive prying, but as her mother's form of affection. It was, if a little pesky, also comforting. She made the odd discovery that she loved her mother and that her mother loved her.

Her father, Norman Montgomery, was as always calm and sympathetic, if a little shy with Julia.

"Just take it easy, dear. Take it easy for a little. It must have been a very great shock to you."

"You can do whatever you like, dear," her mother rattled on. "Whatever you like. You can stay in bed and rest. You can just read. Do you still like to read so much? Well, we can get you lots of books and you can read. You can go for walks. You don't have to go and see anyone."

Her mother did have a way of making all this rest sound exhausting, but this time Julia did not let herself become annoyed. Instead, she leaned over and kissed her mother, something she hadn't done she since she was a child. Mrs. Montgomery started to speak, but her voice was choked, so she patted her daughter's cheek and wiped her moist eyes.

ON MONDAY, Dr. Hart called Stewart to say that Corporal Ransome wanted to see him. It was the afternoon of Christmas Eve, and the asylum felt more forlorn than usual. The staff had put up decorations, but they looked pathetic in the cheerless winter light falling through barred and uncurtained windows. In the main corridor he passed relatives nervously bringing presents to inmates who might not know why.

Corporal Ransome was dressed but lying on the his bed. The other men had been taken out for a walk.

Stewart sat on the next bed and gave Ransome a new package of Craven "A"s. "A little Christmas present."

Ransome opened the package and lit one. He appeared more at ease, less suspicious of Stewart.

"I guess I remembered something." It was mumbled, half-embarrassed. "About hockey."

"Tell me about it."

"See, I used to play hockey a lot. In Bathurst. Me and a friend were the best defensemen. I hadn't thought about him for a long time. Since he got killed."

"What was his name?"

Ransome's mouth worked for a moment until the name came out hoarsely: "Paul Sullivan."

Stewart waited.

"We were in school together; we played hockey. We joined up together. I talked him into it. He always hung back a bit, and I was the one that took the risks. His mother didn't want him to join— she's French Canadian—but his dad is Irish, and he agreed with my dad. They both work at the paper mill. Paul and me were going to work there soon as we got out of school. But everyone was so charged up then. There was parades all the time, with flags and bands. They had war bond parades, with decorated floats, and flags all over the cars and trucks, and people marching with the bands. Paul had a sister named Yvette, and I think I did it to show off to her, and he did it because of me, and because it was more fun to go off to be a soldier than go into the mill where our dads worked."

Ransome, who was twenty-one, sounded like a man of sixty recalling the foolishness of his youth.

"We went up there, you know, to Valcartier in Quebec to train, and it was pretty stupid, not enough equipment, living in tents. No one was really sure what they were supposed to be doing. But it was a lot of fun, like getting away from home and going off to see the world.

"It was worse when we got over to England. Real confusion

and rain all the time, coming in under the tents—and cold. There wasn't enough barracks space.

"But that was all roses compared to France. On the bad days it was sheer hell. You can't really describe it. The shelling makes such a noise hour after hour that its makes your head ring and it does something to your balance. It was hard to stand up, like you were drunk. And scared. You grow up thinking you're not sup-posed to get scared, or supposed to pretend you're not scared. We were scared, all right, and when it stopped and it was quiet, you felt like crying. The danger was you'd get braver in the lulls be-cause you felt a lot safer, you know.

"When it was on, you got huddled down, digging holes in the sides of the trenches and crawling into them like groundhogs. The shells kept coming, screeching in. When they got the range, they kept 'em coming. Each one seemed closer. The whole earth shook like an earthquake. Each shell sent up showers of earth and mud that all came down again in the trenches. Sometimes you could get half-buried in it. It had stuff mixed up with the earth, bits of wood from the duckboards and trees, pieces of helmets, shell casings. And pieces of bodies. It could sicken you. You'd brush the earth and mud off and see a man's finger fall down. Turned your stomach. Made you want to puke. But I'd feel such relief that it wasn't my finger that I'd more likely start laughing."

Ransome turned and looked out the window, as if he could hear the noise of the trenches.

"Paul took it a lot harder than I did, right from the start. He'd go dead white a couple of minutes after we heard the first shell. He put his hands over his ears and curl up in the bottom of the trench or one of the side dugouts, as far away as he could get from the noise. Sometimes he'd scream to drown it out. If it stopped for a minute, you'd hear Paul screaming alone. He'd be shaking and trembling all over. He was a brave enough fellow in normal life, but he told me several times he couldn't stand it.

"In the middle of one bombardment, he shouted at me. I couldn't hear anything. He tried to shout in my ear, but I couldn't make it out. I thought from his lips he was saying, I'm going. I'm going. I couldn't really understand what he meant, but he went back down the trench and disappeared where it turned a corner. As a corporal I couldn't leave to go after him. I guess I thought he was going to find some dugout that was quieter. Hours later, when the shelling stopped, word came back that he had run away. They had seen him going back behind the lines. An officer ordered him back but he just kept going. He'd even left his rifle . . ."

The door opened and Ransome's six fellow patients came in from their walk, their noses red from the cold, but the same lost expressions on their faces. Ransome turned away from them. Stewart got up from the bed. Its owner said to him, "Did my friend come back while I was out?"

"No, I don't think so."

The red-haired man had immediately curled up and put his hands over his ears. The twitching man was still jerking his hands out and back, and the mumbler was still conversing silently with himself. Each was locked in his symptoms.

Stewart walked around Ransome's bed to catch his eye, but he could see, before asking, that the man had sealed himself off.

"John, would you like to go down the hall and go on talking?"

Ransome's eyes were again as opaque as in their first meeting.

"We were making a lot of progress. Keep thinking, and I'll be back in a day or so."

As he closed the door, a nurse said, "Dr. Hattie would like to see you, if you have a moment."

There was holly on the pictures in Hattie's office, and the old doctor held up a bottle of brandy.

"I thought I'd offer you a spot of Christmas cheer before you're off."

"Well, that's good of you. Thank you. Merry Christmas!"

"Merry Christmas!"

"I must say, all the efforts of your staff to make it Christmassy are extraordinarily poignant. I don't know why it should be, but I found myself wanting to weep when I saw the streamers and tinsel outside."

Dr. Hattie laughed, two red spots on the points of his cheeks. "As a good Freudian, you should probably work at that feeling. Some sadness about Christmas in your childhood, perhaps."

"I've never thought so," Stewart said. "I was very indulged that way. Big Christmases. Lots of presents."

"Then perhaps you felt sorry for others whose Christmas couldn't be as full as yours. Anyway, I didn't mean to . . . The professional habit becomes too strong."

There was an urgent knock and a nurse looked in. She was out of breath from running.

"Can you come? One of the soldiers in Ward Twelve has gone wild. We're short-handed because of Christmas Eve."

They hurried after her and could hear a man shouting long before they reached the room. Ransome was sitting at the end of his bed, his face twisted in fury. He held a crutch by one tip and was swinging it violently at the other men, who shrank back from him. He was screaming, in a demented voice, "Take it away! Take the goddamned chair away! The bastards! The bastards!"

He crashed the heavy end of the crutch into a wooden chair that had been moved from the table. The chair was nearly destroyed. His other crutch lay splintered and broken on the floor.

"Take it away! I'll kill them! The bastards! I'll kill them!" Ransome screamed.

Dr. Hattie pushed forward and tried to grab the crutch, saying soothingly, "Now, now, young man. It's quite all right."

But Ransome's powerful arm snatched the crutch away and swung it back, hitting the old doctor in the shoulder and knocking him down.

The nurse and Stewart grabbed Ransome's arms and pinned them down as a male attendant came in with a straitjacket. Before they got him in it and tied the arms, Ransome had stopped fighting.

Stewart helped Dr. Hattie off the floor.

"I should learn to let the younger staff do that. I'm all right, but I think we should find somewhere quiet for this fellow. What's his name?"

"John Ransome. Corporal. I've been talking with him. Haven't I, John? We're making good progress."

Hattie told the nurse and attendant to find a room in which Ransome could cool off and let his wardmates settle down. He was lifted into a wicker wheelchair and taken out.

In the corridor, Hattie said, "Come back to my office. We deserve that Christmas drink now."

But Stewart said, "If you'll excuse me, I think I should go and talk with him now. While he's still feeling it so strongly."

"I'd let him reflect on it a bit. Nothing very helpful happens in a storm of anger. It's like having a small fit. Too much adrenaline in the system for any rational behavior."

"But I think he's stopped. He was talking very freely for the first time until we were interrupted."

"All right. I admire your dedication. I'll be here for a while. Let me know what happens."

The nurse and attendant were putting Ransome on a cot, the only furniture in a small room that had heavy wire mesh over the window. The straitjacket forced him to lie on his side.

"Aren't you going to take that off?" Stewart asked.

"It's always better to leave them for a while to cool off," the nurse said. "It puts them in a calmer frame of mind."

"Is there a chair I can sit on?"

"You going to stay here with him?"

"I want to talk to him."

"Does Dr. Hattie know?" She was suspicious, a plain woman with heavy eyebrows.

"Yes, he knows."

She returned with a chair, and Stewart sat down.

"Do you want me to stay with you—in case?" she asked.

"No, I'll be all right."

Alone with the trussed-up man, Stewart felt uncomfortable. He pulled the chair closer to the bed. "Do you want to go on with our talk?"

Ransome's pale eyes showed no light of communication.

"We were having an important talk when the other fellows came in. Do you remember, John?"

There was no flicker of response.

"You were telling me about Paul Sullivan and how terrified the shelling made him. How terrified you were, but he felt it worse. And then he left. Told you he was going. Isn't that right?"

The color in Ransome's irises was as flat as a cat's. His mouth was set. One could read anything in that blank face: murderous anger, indifference, a mind lost in deep meditation.

"I thought you wanted to tell me the whole story, John. If you did tell me, I think it would make you feel better. Perhaps you're worried that I'll tell somebody else. I promise you I won't. It will be a story you tell only to me. I give you my word on that. You can trust me."

John Ransome gave no sign that he heard. Stewart looked at him. The strength of the shoulders and arms was apparent even through the straitjacket. But the legs lay limp and useless.

"I'll make you a bargain, John. You trust me, and I'll trust you. I don't think you want to be violent anymore, so I'll take you out of that jacket. You don't want to talk trussed up like that. Right?"

Feeling apprehensive, Stewart bent over and untied the long arms of the straitjacket. He pulled Ransome up into the sitting position, unwrapped the arms, and slipped the garment off. Ransome rubbed his forearms as though the circulation had been cut off.

"Would you like a cigarette?"

Ransome didn't speak but took one and accepted the match. It was the ritual that had begun several of their conversations. Stewart sat back and smoked his own cigarette. He was tempted to ask Ransome the reason for his violence but didn't.

"Do you want to go on with the story? It's very interesting."

Ransome used one hand to push his legs over the side of the bed, giving Stewart a moment of anxiety. But Ransome said in a reasonable voice, "There's no place to put the ashes."

Stewart laughed. "Then we'll have to use the floor. Throw it. I'll step on it."

He put his shoe on Ransome's cigarette end, then on his own. Ransome lay back on the bare mattress and looked at the ceiling.

"Paul and me used to go catching salmon in the Miramichi, up the river. We'd clean a big salmon and cook it right there. I'd forgotten about that too. When I think about it, I can smell the salmon cooking on the fire and taste it. Oh, Jesus. Oh, Jesus. Oh, Jesus." Ransome covered his face and began shaking.

"They caught him miles away and we heard he was being court-martialed for desertion. I tried to go and see him, but they refused permission. Our sergeant said, 'I wouldn't get my name mixed up with his.' We waited but no word came back about what happened to Paul.

"About a month later, we'd been moved back to a regroupment area for a week. A proper sort of camp. We slept in huts. We had hot showers and we got some of the lice out, got shaved, had haircuts, clean clothes. There were regular hot meals and a quiet place to sit and write a letter. I kept telling myself I had to write to Paul's mum and dad and Yvette, but I didn't have the heart to and thought maybe I'd wait anyway till I knew how bad it was for him.

"The bugles got us up about four, well before dawn. It was a cold, raw morning. There was frost over all the trees and earth. We fell in on parade but were told to stack our rifles. We thought that was odd, but we were more concerned about being marched off into the dark and cold on empty stomachs.

"They marched us at a fast pace along country roads about half an hour to some old buildings. It was getting light. There were several other battalions already formed up in a big courtyard. You could hear the officers' orders echo off the buildings. They formed us up with the other units; we still didn't know the point of the exercise. There was a sort of hut made of two-by-fours with burlap tacked on the sides, about the size of a privy.

"A senior officer came out of the buildings, a colonel I didn't know. They brought us to attention and he read from a piece of paper. King's regulations. I didn't listen until I heard him say, 'Penalty for desertion in the face of the enemy is death.' An awful feeling came over me, like I wanted to be sick.

"Then I heard boots marching on the cobblestones, but I couldn't look around. They passed us. An escort of four soldiers with rifles and fixed bayonets. Between them two more soldiers, and they were holding Paul. His hands were tied behind his back and they were holding him up because his legs were so weak he couldn't hardly walk. I saw his eyes for a second. They looked like they didn't see anything. He was as white as when the guns were firing. My legs began to shake so's I couldn't control them. I was scared. I was shaking all over. I wanted to shout out but I was too scared.

"They marched or half-dragged him into the burlap hut. We couldn't see anything that happened inside. I heard the firing party given orders to load, aim, and fire. The volley echoed off those buildings in the damp air. It practically made me vomit. I was shaking all over, sweating and shivering at the same time.

"They turned us to the left in column of threes, then quick-march. As each platoon passed the hut, they ordered eyes right.

"I saw him. His body was tied to a kitchen chair, slumped over. I saw his face clearly. I took about two more steps and my stomach came up and everything turned gray and I thought I was going to pass out but I didn't. I kept marching in a daze. I kept thinking it was me that had persuaded him to join. I remembered his mother crying. I remembered Yvette crying when we left. And they had shot him sitting down. The goddamned bastards had shot him sitting down, just because he was scared of the shells."

Ransome's voice had changed. When Stewart glanced at him, he was looking at the ceiling, tears running down the side of his face. He yawned, and when he started talking again he sounded half-asleep.

"They marched us straight back to the front . . . sent up our rifles and kitbags up by truck. I stayed in that daze. There was a big battle, but I didn't hardly notice it. I was lying there shooting and ducking . . . big shells landing . . . machine gun fire . . . the Germans coming . . . Germans going back . . . the stink of cordite in the air. And all I was thinking was: They shot him sitting down. The bastards shot him. I couldn't believe our own side would do something like that. I couldn't believe it. In the battle I must have passed out from concussion. They found me there. All the others were killed or gone. The Germans had gone by and retreated past me again and must have taken me for dead both times. But when the stretcher bearers picked me up, I couldn't move my legs. I didn't remember anything about Paul. It was like . . ."

There was a long pause. When Stewart looked, Ransome had fallen into a deep sleep. Stewart watched for a minute, then tiptoed out. He closed the door quietly and met the nurse halfway down the corridor.

"I left Ransome sleeping quietly."

"Well, that's a blessing. It's busy enough around here tonight."

"Oh, I took the straitjacket off him so that he could talk."

"You shouldn't have done that! He could have attacked you or harmed himself."

"I think he'll be quiet."

"I'll keep an eye on him. Dr. Hattie had to leave. He asked me to tell you Merry Christmas."

"Thank you. Merry Christmas to you."

"Merry Christmas." Her severe face broke into a smile, then she rustled down the dim corridor in her long starched apron under the loops of twisted red and green crepe paper.

Outside it was clear and cold. Stewart lit a cigarette and looked at the stars beyond the bare trees. Christmas Eve. Peace on earth, good will toward men.

"MUMMY FORGETS EVERYTHING!" Abigail said petulantly. She was leaning sulkily against Peter's chair in the Tobins' study, picking at threads in the slipcover. Peter was reading. Margery was resting in her room upstairs. Michael was out with his grandparents.

"She said I could have the special dress for my dollie, and then she didn't remember. Daddy? But she wrote it down and she still didn't remember. And she *said* it! She really did!"

Abigail was trying to push herself toward actual tears.

Peter said, "When Mummy finishes her rest, I'll talk to her about it. All right?"

"But when *will* she finish?"

"Soon. When the others come back."

"Well, when are they coming back?"

"Hmm?"

"Daddy?"

"What?"

"When are they coming back?"

Peter put down his book, feeling the familiar mixture of annoyance and compassion. He picked the little girl up, plopped her on his lap, and put his arm around her.

"You have lots of other dresses for your dollie. Didn't Nana give you three dresses for Christmas?"

"Yes."

"Well, why don't you go and put one of those on the dollie?"

"Because they're not the special dress Mummy has! And she doesn't remember."

"Well, she will." He gave Abigail a kiss, meaning to set her down and pick up his book, but she said, "I don't think she ever will!" and began to sob.

Peter pulled her against him and held her tight, soothing her back with one hand. She was tired. Her hair had fallen out of its clasps. It was better to let her cry a little. But he felt just as the child did—desolate.

There were scraps of paper all over the house, a little trail of dementia and insecurity, pinned to pillows, dresses, left on sideboards, as Margery attempted to orient herself in her bewilderment. She treated it like a game, an amusing game of scatterbrain. She seemed to remember just what she wanted to. It was the world she didn't want to remember that baffled her, and she dismissed it as amusing inconsequentia. The notes were a show that she was trying. Peter didn't think she was trying.

Abigail said, "You're prickly!" and pulled her face away from his tweed jacket. She got down from his lap, her spirits restored.

"I'm going to ask Cook for a biscuit."

"All right."

Margery behaved as though she and Peter were on their honeymoon and no children had come into existence. She talked to Abigail and Michael like an aunt or their mother's friend. The doctor had ordered a complete rest, and she had no responsibility for looking after them. Cynthia Tobin had found a nursemaid to help the other servants. The nursemaid was off because it was the Sunday after Christmas.

To Peter, Margery was more demanding, disconcertingly greedy for sex. He slept at the house on Tower Road but came to visit and have many meals. The Tobins asked him to move in, but he said Margery should have her room to herself. The first time he came into her room, she pulled him onto the bed. Some inhibiting mechanism had been broken. She started making love to him with the door of her bedroom half open. He was nervous that someone would come in—one of the children—and the nervousness made him want to stop. Then he became aroused and broke away to shut the door and lock it. They made love rapidly, almost violently, in a tumble of the stuffed animals she kept clustered around her. He had his clothes back on before his heart had slowed down.

She found him at home at Tower road in the daytime, because he had suggested he might be there, and they came together so hungrily that she pulled him down on the chesterfield in the living room. All the physicality Peter had denied himself, or she had denied him in the years of their marriage, all the hungers she had suppressed, were suddenly indulged in a burst of mutual desire that would not be satisfied.

Margery began to recover her looks. Her black curls shone again, and her eyes glowed, like those of a young woman in the dawn of her sensuality. She put on a little weight, although, when Peter's sexual desire was spent, she still looked unappetizingly bony. Her pelvic bones protruded and her upper thighs were too thin.

She never referred, even obliquely, to the day she had turned on the gas. Dr. Menzies found a doctor who specialized in nervous disorders. He suggested it would be better to wait until Margery brought it up herself. Her mind might be in a delicate balance; it would be wise not to strain it by bringing up the most painful moments in her life. She was recovering physically, and he was pleased with her progress. Her long-term memory seemed to be deepening every day. Suddenly she would remember something, perhaps from a year or two before they were married.

Her cure was total rest, a healthy physical regimen, brisk walks for exercise, but nothing too tiring. No domestic responsibilities and no strain. It suited Margery perfectly. She was fully absorbed in herself: her baths, her clothing, keeping her room tidy, sewing, mending, arranging her drawers. Occasionally she would start a book but put it down after a few pages.

The Tobins were pleased with her returning health. Cynthia acted as though Margery had had some physical malady like measles and was making a fine recovery. George talked to the doctors very carefully, and he was even more cordial to Peter.

"I'll tell you straight, Peter, I'm very proud of you as a son-in-law. Everybody in town is talking about you. Not just in Halifax but around the country, I hear."

It was true. The cathedral was receiving letters from all over the Dominion, from other clergymen, from Catholic priests and ordinary people. Some sent cuttings from their local newspapers.

They were in the study after dinner. George had loosened the dinner jacket Cynthia made him wear and was sipping the glass of port he had brought from the table. Margery had gone upstairs. Peter wondered if she was getting into bed. He could slip into bed with her quickly before he left the house.

"But it's not just having a famous son-in-law. Of course that's nice. But I have a personal reason for caring about what you did. And you'd probably never guess it."

He drank and smiled shrewdly at Peter.

"No, I can't."

"I was a Catholic when I was a kid. You didn't know that, did you?"

"No, I didn't."

"I dropped it completely when I married Cynthia. I had enough strikes against me socially in her eyes without dragging a poor Catholic background into it as well. And the truth was I'd stopped going much. Fell off from confession around the time I began having something to confess"—he laughed—"and never got in the way of it again. But one of the reasons I turned into something, and so did my brothers, is that my mother chased us off to mass every Sunday, got us clean in that rotten kitchen, no real bathroom in that house, put clean clothes on us, gave us a penny for collection, and pushed us off. The priests did the rest, and the sisters in school. Saint Joseph's, the place that got destroyed in the explosion. Anyway"—he took a drink—"I don't want to bore you, but I'll tell you one thing. I got tears in my eyes when I read that story in the paper about you. Because that old lady you helped could have been my mother. It wasn't, of course. She died years ago. But it could have been. And the fact that you sent her off into heaven feeling saved, with the proper rites, moved me very much." Tobin pulled the handkerchief from his breast pocket and gave his nose a loud blow.

Peter's sensitivity to praise for the incident had dulled now. His facial gestures and modest words had become automatic. But George Tobin's confession stirred his sense of shame. He was tempted to say, But you have me wrong; I had to be pushed into it. He might actually have said something, but Tobin wasn't finished.

"I've always liked you, Peter, but I always thought were a bit of a cold fish, to tell you the truth. Now I know you have a lot bigger heart than I suspected. You probably can't imagine what it does to thousands of ordinary Catholic people in this city to see someone in the high and mighty Church of England making that kind of gesture. If you ran for alderman in the North End now, you'd probably get elected. Catholics feel really despised. Do you know that? It's not just that it's posh to be C of E. Everyone knows that. It's that the Anglicans lord it over others so much, the damned women on the committee for this and that, women like Cynthia, so hoity-toity, as though Catholics were something dirty and less than human. Are you listening to what I'm saying?"

"Yes, of course. I've felt it myself."

"Well, I've kept you long enough. You probably want to say good night to Margery before you toddle off home."

"Thanks." Peter climbed the stairs two at a time and opened Margery's door. She grinned at him, like a girl with a secret from her parents.

She whispered, "I thought you weren't coming!"

"They think I'm just saying good night."

"Quickly, quickly. I've been waiting."

She sat up in bed and pulled her nightdress over her head. Her breasts looked depleted, but that did not lessen his quick desire for her.

"I want to touch you."

"Just a moment."

"Quickly. Come here. Here. There. There. Oh! Oh! Oh!"

"Not too loud."

He was walking home five minutes later, his overheated body impervious to the cold night, the snow squeaking under his boots. But his spirits were utterly deflated.

On an impulse he continued up South Park Street. He knew from the dean that Julia had gone to Montreal. He stopped opposite her house and stared at it. No lights on. Mollie and the little child with one eye must be away. He remembered from the diary that Mollie had a sister in Chester. Now he regretted having burned the book. He had no contact with Julia, and his soul yearned for her. Margery quieted his body's clamor, but that was almost fornication. There was a doctrine that concupiscence within marriage was fornication. There was no meeting of souls. Like two dogs pumping away in the street. What devil had loosed that desire in her?

Margery was floating happily into sleep. Her mind had wandered into the beach scene years ago with Charles. It was startlingly clear, even to the little clutch of fear she remembered as the shadows of the falling night turned the fir trees at the water's edge into menacing symbols. Peter was younger. He was shy, and she had to encourage him. If she encouraged him enough to make the steps, he could be hers forever.

ON CHRISTMAS AFTERNOON Stewart made the journey back across the harbor to the asylum. Ransome had returned to the ward with the others. There were new crutches by his bed, but he did not want to use them. He was alert but listless. He let Stewart push him to the office in a wheelchair and remained sitting in it while they talked. Telling his story had not released him from its emotional bonds but had left him confronting stronger feelings of guilt.

"Why should you feel it was your fault, John?"

"It was me that talked him into joining up."

"But you didn't force him to join. He made his own decision, didn't he?"

"But I was always joking with him and pushing him to do it, trying to shame him into it."

"Suppose you had just said, Paul, I'm joining up, and left it at that. What would Paul have done?"

"I don't know."

"If you were such close friends, hockey teammates, the best pair of defensemen, would Paul have said, 'Fine, John. I'll see you after the war'?"

"No."

"Why not?"

"Because he would have wanted to come too."

"Well, think about that for a moment. You said he would have *wanted* to."

"Yes."

"If he had wanted to, you wouldn't have had to force him."

"But his mum was getting at him all the time. She was crying and carrying on. She didn't see any good in the war. She listened to all her French people, the church and things, saying it wasn't a war for Canadian boys to fight. It's Britain's war, and stuff like that. She said that to Paul all the time. She said it to me when I'd go over to their place."

"Well, if you'd left him alone, would Paul have listened to her —and stayed home?"

Ransome thought about that. "No. I don't know."

"Tell me what it was like, when you talked about it. What you said, what Paul said, and his mother. And Yvette. You haven't mentioned her today."

Ransome looked at it him. "I don't want to talk about her."

"Why not?"

"I don't know. I just don't"

"Because it makes you feel bad?"

It came out with a sob. "Because she made me promise I'd look after him."

Stewart watched him cry and wipe his eyes on his shirt cuff.

"She said Maman will die if anything happens to Paul. You won't let anything happen to him, will you, John? I said no, I won't. What did I know what it would be like? And I wanted her to think I was so Jesus strong and brave myself, I'd have said anything she asked."

"Was Yvette your girlfriend? I mean not just Paul's sister?"

"Sort of. I wrote her letters from France. Before."

"Does the family know what happened to Paul?"

"I don't know."

"You told me several weeks ago that you didn't want to write to them. Do you still feel that way?"

"Yes."

"Why?"

"I can't. I know they're going to blame me for what happened."

"What if you wrote and told them the story just as you told it to me yesterday?"

"I couldn't tell them."

"You know, I listened to it yesterday, and I didn't feel you deserved any blame. Not at all. I felt sorry for you."

"What about Paul?" Ransome flared up. "Paul's the one you should feel sorry for. They shot him!"

"But you're the one who's alive. We can't help Paul now. His suffering is over. Yours isn't. His family's pain isn't over. You're the one who's so full of sorrow and guilt that your mind is telling your legs not to work."

"But I deserve it. It was my fault that he got shot."

They talked for days like that. Stewart could demonstrate to him, logically, why he should feel no guilt, but Ransome could not believe it. The conversations kept circling the core of guilt.

It was wearying. The exhilaration Stewart had felt on Christmas Eve when Ransome finally blurted out his terrible story had worn off. As he left for the drive back to the ferry each day, he wondered whether it wasn't a waste of time. At night he reread notes from cases of hysteria reported by Jones and Freud and felt discouraged, dismayed again by their apparent simplicity.

Discouragement added to Stewart's feeling at loose ends. There were houses where he would have been welcome over the Christmas holiday, but he didn't feel like inviting himself. When Susan Gastonguy asked him to a party, he made an excuse. Being alone was nothing new; what was new was being alone and aimless but with Julia constantly in his thoughts.

She wrote from Montreal, apologizing for not following up with Betty as she had promised, saying she felt compelled to get away from the sad memories for a few weeks. She would be in touch when she was coming back. Her Christmas and New Year's greetings ended, "Love, Julia Robertson." The three words tripped up his heart for a beat and stayed with him.

The letter prompted him to think about Betty, and he went again to see Lewis Watson, the neurosurgeon at Dalhousie. After examining Betty, Watson had written to Dr. Harvey Cushing at Harvard. The outlook for the child was hard to predict. Some functions of the pituitary were mysterious; others simply unknown. In rare cases, adjacent parts of the brain had been damaged as well. Cushing was now studying the results of British and French battle injuries—there were no American casualties—but most of the field hospital examinations had been too hasty, and the follow-up too unsystematic to be useful.

Cushing was pursuing a hypothesis that some functions of the hypothalamus and pituitary occurred independently of the actual organs. He suspected that surrounding tissues and blood vessels might be imbued with whatever substances the glands secreted. Extremely interesting, Watson said. He would not have heard about it except for Betty's case.

"However, it makes the prognosis for your patient only more uncertain."

"She is not my patient. I'm a psychologist in the philosophy department. I'm not a doctor."

"I see, yes. Well, you obviously know more about these matters than the general practitioners of my acquaintance. I'd like to sit down with Cushing and go through what might or might not happen. But I can't get away. The explosion has given us more neurological emergencies than we could ever have imagined. We've doubled, even tripled, our schedule of surgery, and I have all my classes at the medical school. Going to Boston is out of the question."

"But I could go," Stewart said. "I could go with further advice from you and talk to Cushing. It wouldn't be neurology we'd be talking anyway, but how to manage her and what to expect."

"That's right. As I wrote to Cushing, from my examination of her, there's nothing a neurosurgeon can do for her. I could write him again."

"Or telegraph?"

"If you're in a hurry."

Stewart was pleased. It would be good to get away from the Ransome case for a few days. He could go to Boston and talk to Cushing, then go to Montreal with the new information and call on Julia. The plan pleased him by being both casual and direct. He would turn up and surprise her.

He called Lucy Traverse for Julia's address and thought he detected the raised interest in her voice when he said he wanted to call in Montreal.

He explained to Ransome and reported to Dr. Hattie, who said, "It may help him a little to have to think it through himself."

Cushing replied to Watson's telegram agreeing to a meeting, and Stewart bought a ticket to Boston. Julia so dominated his thoughts that he was in the taxi going to the station before he remembered Christine Soames, who lived in Boston. Had his unconscious been guiding him to her? No, the moment it occurred to him, he easily put her aside. The woman he wanted more than any in his life was Julia Robertson.

He paid the taxi and carried his bags into the station. The words OCEAN LIMITED—MONTREAL sprang at him from the board showing arrivals and departures. For a moment he imagined walking up to the ticket window and changing his reservation to Montreal. But he had an appointment with Cushing.

He could not cast off the Ransome case. The fascination and the frustration both rode with him to Boston. Perhaps Ransome's family and Sullivan's could convince John that they did not blame him —if they didn't. Perhaps Yvette Sullivan could convince him. It should be possible to find them. Chatham was not a large town.

JULIA'S PARENTS waited for several days before telling her about her cousin Jeffrey, and they told it very reluctantly, with great embarrassment.

"You'll have to know sooner or later, Julia. We'd much rather not tell you. He was sent back as a coward."

"Well, that's putting it a bit crudely, Heather," her father protested. Jeffrey was his dead brother's son.

"I never thought he was soldier material anyway," Heather said. "He got to the front, and there was a battle, and he ran away. He was frightened, and he ran away. The men he left were killed. They caught him and tried him—"

"Court-martialed," her father said.

"Court-martialed him, and he was sentenced to be shot for desertion!"

"Oh, my God!" Julia cried. "I can't believe it. It's too terrible!"

"There was an appeal; they changed it to imprisonment and sent him back."

Her father said, "It is really rather horrible. I've gone to talk to the authorities. I think we have to face the fact that Jeffrey is in prison for ten years."

"And branded for life as a coward and a deserter!" Heather said. "How is that young man—you know I never liked him that well —how is he going to pick up his life after this?"

"Can I go to see him?" Julia asked.

"Oh, no, dear, you don't want to go down there, not in your present state."

"But of course I must see him."

"But it's a foul place, your father says. Not a nice place at all, dear."

"If you want to go, I'll go with you, Julia."

"Thank you, Father."

They went on the one day a week the military detention center permitted visitors. Jeffrey was led out to the visiting room wearing prison coveralls. He was gaunt and shaking. When he saw Julia, he began to cry. The room was cold and smelled of unwashed bodies. A military policeman barked out, "Prisoner, sit down, hands on the table! Visiting time fifteen minutes!" He marched to the door and took up a position stiffly at ease.

Jeffrey looked a miserable shell of himself. His eyes and cheeks were sunken. His hair was shaved above the ears. His hands would not stop shaking.

"I heard about Charles." His voice was a hoarse whisper. "I'm very sorry. I'm glad about the VC, but I'm very sorry." He began to cry silently, as though he had learned to do it that way, without making a sound. His saliva made a bubble.

Julia offered him her small handkerchief, but the policeman shouted, "Visitors are not permitted to pass objects to prisoners."

"It's only a handkerchief," Julia said furiously.

"No objects," the policeman said, more reasonably.

Jeffrey's appearance filled her with pity. A sour smell came from his clothing. And this shrunken, trembling man was the person she had once lived for. She shuddered now look at him.

Jeffrey couldn't talk coherently, and they left, Julia saying she would come back.

On the way home her father said, "It's not fair, the way they're treating him. It's not just confinement; it's humiliation. It's more punishment than a man would get for many crimes. But there's no sympathy, especially here in Quebec. The conscription battle has drawn very hard lines. Pacifists, conscientious objectors, deserters, criminals are all the same. Human scum. There are probably lots of French Canadians in that prison who just object to the war."

"But we must do something about it!" Julia said. She remembered the conversation in her drawing room about shell shock, men who could not control their fear. "I'm going to write to Stewart MacPherson."

IN THE NEW YEAR'S HONORS LIST, the Albert Medal for "heroic action during the Halifax Explosion" was awarded posthumously to Lieutenant Commander T. K. Triggs, RN, Acting Boatswain Albert Charles Mattison, RCN, and Stoker Petty Officer Edward S. Beard, RCNVR, who died trying to put a towline on the S.S. *Mont Blanc,* and to the survivor, Able Seaman William Becker, RN. The medal was also awarded to two sailors who helped put out a fire on the nearby tug *Musquash.*

One civilian was on the Honors List. For "risking his own life to bring relief to a woman trapped in a burning building," the Albert Medal was awarded to the Reverend Peter Wentworth, Curate of All Saints Cathedral. Like the medal to Lieutenant Commander Triggs, Peter's Albert Medal was in gold.

The telephones began ringing the moment the newspapers were out. On the same day, an engraved card with a ducal crest arrived from Ottawa, commanding Peter to appear at a special investiture at Rideau Hall. In the envelope was a personal note from the ADC, General Smithson, saying the governor general particularly hoped Peter would come, as there was something of a private nature he wished to discuss.

"I can't imagine what that is," Peter said to Dean Creighton.

"It must be something very important for him to have written like that."

"Well, I don't see how I can go."

"Of course you must go. You've become a national figure with this, Peter. Of course you must go."

Peter could not bring himself to tell his superior that he simply did not have the money for a return train ticket and the cabs, hotels, and meals that would be necessary. Virtually every penny was budgeted.

But he did not agonize long before approaching George Tobin, whose admiration had been so clearly expressed. When he bluntly explained his poverty, Tobin's reaction was the same as Dean Creighton's. Cynthia's was even more vehement.

"Not go to Government House for the investiture? Why, Peter, that is the silliest thing I have ever heard."

"I would only need to take the day coach," he said apologetically to George.

"Don't be stupid, Peter. The trains are jammed with troops these days. The railways can't keep up with the need. Here's a hundred dollars. Travel decently; get yourself a Pullman. Look," he said, confidentially. "You and I know what it is to be hard up. We both know. We don't have to prove anything. Play your luck, Peter. You never know when it's going to change. Go and get your medal, and good luck to you."

Peter's parents were pleased, but his mother was more concerned about Margery. How was she doing? What plans did they have for her? What were the doctors saying?

Canon Wentworth looked at Peter over his thick reading spectacles and pulled his pipe from a cardigan pocket.

"The Albert Medal, Peter? That's the civilian award. It has such a Victorian ring to it. We scarcely hear Albert's name mentioned anymore, except for things she named after him—Albert Hall, Albert Bridge, Albert Embankment, not to mention the Albert Memorial. Well, think of that, Dorothy!"

His mother spoke with her eyes on her knitting. "And what is this mysterious private matter they want to talk to you about, do you suppose? What on earth would it be? Well, it's quite an adventure for you, dear, isn't it?"

She finished a row, her free needle poised to begin another. "Now, don't forget with all these exciting things, laddie, that you have a very sick wife who needs your attention."

He left in some anger. His parents were deflating when the Tobins were enthusiastic.

Margery had to be told several times that he was going on a trip and why.

She said, "I must write it down," and did, but an hour later she had forgotten.

She came into their house unexpectedly and arrived in the bedroom a little breathless to find him packing a suitcase.

"But where are you going? Are you leaving?" She said it with genuine surprise.

"I told you this morning. I'm going to Ottawa."

"But why to Ottawa?"

"Margery, I explained. I showed you the newspapers. The New Year's Honors List. They're giving me a medal. The Albert Medal."

"How long will you be gone?" Aggrieved, she plumped on the bed beside the suitcase.

"Just two or three days."

"Will you miss me?"

"Of course I will!" He was turning back from his chest of drawers with starched collars he had hastily collected from the Chinese laundry on Inglis Street.

She stopped his hand playfully as he put the collars in the suitcase and pulled him gently.

"Margery, I haven't much time."

"Yes, you have!" And she pulled his hand more firmly, setting him slightly off balance.

That made her giggle and put her other arm around his neck to pull him down.

"Kiss me. Please, Peter."

He gave her a peck and straightened up.

"No, kiss me really."

"There isn't time. I've got to leave."

"Don't you want to . . . ?" She pulled her skirt up on one silk stocking, and he felt an immediate tremor of response, both instant desire and instant repugnance at how blatant she had become.

"I've got to finish packing."

Lying back, her eyes wide open, the pupils large, she pulled the skirt farther up. She began undoing a stocking suspender. His determination began to melt, but he closed the suitcase and started buckling the straps.

"I said I must go. The train's at two."

He swung the suitcase off the bed. Margery stood up quickly and twitched her skirt down. What she said made him freeze. In her normal voice she said curiously, "Why were you reading that woman's diary?"

The words crashed into his head. He could do nothing but stare at her. She had read Julia's diary! And she had remembered! Through the fog in her head that shrouded everything else, she remembered! Peter was numb.

"Did you like her because she liked making love so much—more than I did? Is that why you were reading it?"

"It was something that came into my hands—because of the church—because of the church, I was asked to read it."

Margery still looked at him with her wide-set eyes, very puzzled, a child awakened from a dream, who might fall asleep again any moment.

"I'll explain it when I come back. It's too late now. I have to rush."

"Why are you suddenly going to Ottawa?"

She was enclosed again in the fog.

Peter could think of little else in the long train ride to Montreal for the connection to Ottawa. He was tormented by thoughts of Margery and Julia. Had finding the diary driven Margery to turn on the gas? Oh, God! It made him sick to think it. How much had she read? And when? He had always locked it in the bottom drawer—except that once. He was certain. Or, no, once he had left it on the bedside table and, full of anxiety, found it that evening. When Margery was at her parents' just after the explosion. Had she come to the house and seen it then?

*That woman,* she said. Did she know whose diary it was? Had she told anyone else? He turned over and over in the top berth until the sheets twisted around him. But when he switched on the reading light, it was only 3:10 A.M. The steam-heated train was stifling. In his hasty departure he had brought nothing to read and had to lie with his torturing thoughts.

Things had turned worse and worse. Margery was not only seriously ill; his mother—he resented it—was right. But still worse: Margery knew about the diary that had twisted his emotions and desires for weeks. He had pushed it out of his thoughts. The motions and noises of the train made him think of Julia, on this same route, perhaps right at this point, somewhere in northern New Brunswick or eastern Quebec, racked by her desires. It aroused

Peter to think of that. The sudden frequency of intercourse with Margery had made his own body more demanding. He recalled refusing Margery the previous afternoon, remembering her provocative pose with a margin of exposed flesh above her stocking. If she were here now, he would not refuse. If Julia were here now . . . It was Julia he was going toward . . . She was somewhere in Montreal, but he didn't know where. He realized that he did not know her family name. Stupid. He could have inquired quite innocently. He could have telephoned while changing trains to Ottawa. He could have heard the sound of her voice. How stupid not to have thought of it.

IN BOSTON, Stewart felt the excitement of America gearing up for war as Americans did everything, loudly, self-importantly, as though they had just invented it. Flags and red, white, and blue bunting outshone the Christmas decorations. The streets were aswarm with soldiers, exhibiting high spirits Canadians had not felt since 1914. Trucks festooned with flags of the Allied nations chugged through the crowded streets, Klaxons hooting, soldiers shouting through megaphones, pedestrians turning to cheer and applaud them.

The bustle, the cocky young conscripts, the glowing eyes of the girls on their arms, the swagger of newly minted sailors bursting out of bars arm in arm, the noisy joy of New Year's Eve in his hotel facing the Common, the shouts and singing and horns and booming fireworks, all told Stewart how low spirits at home had fallen in three grinding years of war shortages, blackouts, and daily lists of the dead.

Canada had lost tens of thousands of men. He had not noticed how grim and melancholy Halifax had become, even before the explosion, until he felt the hustling enthusiasm of Americans hurling themselves into this great adventure. Even the recruiting posters were less grim and shame-directed. The Americans had a jaunty, sexy poster of a cute blonde in a sailor's uniform, saying provocatively, "If I were a man . . ."

Canada had long exhausted that spirit. Superpatriots were now using the meanest propaganda to shame the laggards into enlisting. The newspapers carried lurid appeals from men in the trenches. One of them suggested sending pacifists to the front, in cages, to make them sniff for poison gas. Posters told women to remember how the Germans had treated women in Belgium, and goaded them to shame their men into going. The war had brought the Canadian sense of decency very low.

Stewart thought, The public should hear more views like Charles Robertson's, and John Ransome's account of the execution of Paul Sullivan.

Waiting until the holiday was over for his appointment with Cushing, he enjoyed the amenities of the bigger city: restaurants, the theater, the many bookstores.

Christine Soames lurked in his thoughts. Because he was in her city, he half-expected to run into her. He really did not want to see her but was tempted by the certainty that she would want to see him, a certainty he could not extend to Julia.

On an impulse, he asked the hotel to put in a trunk call to David Hart, the army psychiatrist in Halifax.

"I'm sorry to bother you on a holiday. I wonder if your records include Corporal Ransome's home address. He told me he comes from Chatham, New Brunswick. I think it might be helpful to write to his family. Would you have any objection to that?"

"I don't suppose so. I've already notified them that he's in hospital here for observation."

"Oh, you have? You see, I thought it might help to tell them how guilty he feels about a friend who was killed and that he's sure, back home, they're all blaming him too. If they wrote saying they don't blame him, it might make a difference. I don't know what else to try."

"I can't see what harm it can do."

Stewart wrote to the Ransomes that night, enclosing separate letters for Paul Sullivan's parents and his sister, Yvette. He wrote that John had a heartbreaking story to tell but was burdened with paralyzing guilt for events that were not his fault.

Dr. Harvey Cushing was gaunt and vital-looking, socially prominent—he had been painted by Sargent—already famous for his discoveries about overstimulated adrenal glands. Indeed, the disease now carried his name.

He was fascinated by Betty's case and had intended to ask Watson for careful observations on how she developed.

"We are only beginning to discover how much we have yet to

learn about the inter-relation of the glands. When we come to that stage in science—knowing what the questions are—we are on the verge of important things."

It would be useful, Cushing said, to have accurate records of Betty's height, weight, fat distribution, temperature, blood pressure, analysis of urine, dental development, appearance of secondary sex characteristics, and onset of menses.

"Although I have great doubt that this child will go through puberty at all. Conversely, there may be abnormal secretion of breast milk, even if the breasts are immature."

The scientist in Stewart understood, but his spirit quailed at this detached account which neglected all of Betty's humanity and personality.

Cushing would pause to think, then rattle on. "She may lose her appetite control and be insatiable for food. Any sign of that?"

"I don't believe so. I haven't heard it mentioned."

"How long since the injury?"

"December sixth, the Halifax explosion."

"Of course, what am I thinking of? Incredible. Watson says the neurogological cases are very heavy. Let me see, I made a few notes on his report. She could well be a case of *diabetes insipidus,* an inability to retain water."

"What effect would that have?" Stewart was taking notes.

"It can mean a need to drink water all the time—many quarts a day—and to urinate frequently." The elegant man shuddered. "An awful way to live, if she lives very long. And that is the big mystery here. None of what I'm saying is watertight, you know."

"What's the principal threat?"

"Probably adrenal insufficiency. Inability to survive the sorts of stress that are common—an accident, an injury, some big infection. Her system may not respond. Could be a drop in blood pressure instead of an increase. She may be lethargic, easily tired. She may feel cold even when it's warm enough for everyone else—although when that is in Halifax, I don't know."

They went on to discuss the related topic of shock, the imperfectly understood reaction mechanisms. Cushing was curious, as he was just leaving Harvard to lend his skills to the military. He questioned Stewart about the cases he had observed; asked whether the Canadians had any success in curing the war neurosis, and what proportion recovered spontaneously.

Stewart described the sixty-five percent "quick cure" rate at British hospitals. "But there's no doubt that it's somewhat coercive, and the figures don't tell us how many break down again. For the other thirty-five percent, the outlook is bleak."

He described the cases he had seen, how even the Ransome case showed no improvement in the paralysis.

Finally, Stewart asked whether anything could be done for Betty.

"Nothing. Watson's asked me that. He can't think of anything, and neither can I. We can't reconnect the gland. We don't know what substances the pituitary generates, how many there are, and we haven't the slightest idea of their chemistry, so any medical activity to repair the damage or replace the effect of the gland is out of the question. As long as she can manage it, I would treat her normally. Send her to school. Ah, that reminds me: her mental development. It's possible that her cognitive faculties may not develop much further. Is she an intelligent and articulate nine-year-old?"

"Very," said Stewart.

"Impossible to know, but in the range of possibilities. What she has now may be the summit of her intellectual ability. She may continue to develop, or she may deteriorate, become prematurely aged in the brain, and senile. One could hypothesize a woman of thirty, in stature and physical development a prepubertal child of nine, but with aged features, lines, gray hair, and a failing memory. It's also possible the worst case will never happen; there can't be any explicit prognosis. I wish I could examine the child myself. It is a most unusual case."

"Perhaps one day there may be an opportunity to bring her to Boston," Stewart said.

OTTAWA WAS DAZZLING in the January cold. An achingly bright sun in a cloudless sky reflected off deep drifts of freshly fallen snow, with large dollops still plump on the evergreen trees. The taxi driving Peter to Rideau Hall passed sleighs jingling along with people wrapped in furs. The governor general's grounds were a large wooded estate, the long drive winding between steep banks of snow, with vistas of tall spruce and fir.

Footmen and military aides showed Peter his place near the end of a long line of men to be decorated. Many were officers in dress uniform and, toward the end, a few women officers in the Canadian Army Medical Corps, and other civilians. Peter was the only Albert Medal to attend.

The Duke of Devonshire, resplendent in the blue sash of the Garter and two other orders of knighthood, recognized Peter when he stepped into place, and bowed.

"My warmest congratulations, Mr. Wentworth. Good to see you again," and pinned a gold medal with a ribbon of blue and white stripes to his jacket.

Discreetly, General Smithson asked Peter to lunch in a private dining room. Peter had never eaten anywhere quite as elegant. The surroundings and the purring manner of the older Englishman made him conscious of his clothes and table manners.

Lord Smithson led the conversation easily through many things until dessert, when he said, "Well, if it wouldn't be too pushy of me, a little business?"

"Fine," said Peter.

"His Grace was very taken with you in Halifax and by what he heard about you. The duke is an astute judge of character. His years in politics and all that. He was impressed with the story of your—deed—before he met you in Halifax and doubly impressed when he did."

"Well, thank you."

"Not at all. Now, it happens that the duke has never appointed a private chaplain, as some of his predecessors did. His Grace did consider bringing over a clergyman who was a friend from Chatsworth House, his estate in England. But the gentleman became a military chaplain and had the bad luck to be killed at the Somme."

"Oh, I'm terribly sorry."

"His Grace, and particularly the duchess, were very cut up about it and let matters slide until, quite out of the blue, it occurred to him to appoint a *Canadian* chaplain. It came to him after they'd met you. So the purpose of our little chat is to ask, Would you would be interested? If so, a formal invitation could be made. We have confidence that your name would be greeted with wide approval, Mr. Wentworth."

Peter was thrilled. He could not have imagined a more exciting appointment. Chaplain to the governor general!

"I'm a bit overwhelmed by the suggestion."

Lord Smithson rose, flicking an imaginary crumb from his trousers. "Naturally, you'll need a little time. While you're here and collecting your thoughts, why don't we stroll about the place a little? His Grace is out and the duchess is resting. We can look round."

He gave Peter a tour of Rideau Hall, the state rooms, the more personal living rooms, in which he noticed silver-framed photographs of the royal family, including the late King Edward and King George, personally autographed to the duke and duchess. He was shown the large library, with long windows opening onto wooded grounds deep in new snow. They looked at the small chapel, in which Peter could imagine holding intimate services for the Devonshires and their guests.

To know and speak to people of such exalted rank, people next to the royal family, to be their spiritual adviser, was a stunning prospect.

Lord Smithson paused in the chapel. "Let me raise the religious aspect. While your brave conduct in the explosion is what first commended you, we have inquired about you as a clergyman. It was very gratifying to His Grace to discover that your theological credentials are equally impressive. You served, we understand, on the Commission to Revise the Book of Common Prayer."

"I was the secretary to its prolocutor in one phase, then the assistant in another. Yes."

"So, you see, Mr. Wentworth, we do not think of you as a common or garden parson."

They continued the tour. He was shown a small apartment where the chaplain could live, but was told that he could live outside if he preferred.

"I'm afraid I have to ask you a practical question. What is the stipend?"

"Well, actually, there is no stipend, you see. It is anticipated that the chaplain will find what's necessary from his own resources. It is not expensive living. The quarters are quite pleasant, actually, and you'd have most of your meals here, when you're in residence, on duty, so to speak, like the rest of us."

"I see." The prospect was delectable to Peter. A dream. Time to himself, time to study. A semimonastic life. But a very good library; he had seen that. A charming chapel, distinguished and interesting companions for meals. The apartment was elegant. And without having to be put into words, but strongly felt, it was escape from all his problems in Halifax.

"If there are questions I can help you with . . ."

Could he tell this elegant Englishman, to whom anxiety about money looked as foreign as lint on his uniform, how poor he was?

The general said, "On the stipend question, some arrangement might be made with your bishop to continue your remuneration whilst you undertook these duties. They would not involve the entire year. The duke and duchess are often absent from Ottawa."

Perhaps, Peter thought. It was certainly tempting. He struggled to sound dignified. "I'm quite bowled over by the suggestion. I would need a little time to consult the dean at least and my family."

Yet even as he gave himself time, Peter knew he should not consider it. He couldn't leave Margery in Halifax—unless, unless it would be better for Margery to be apart from him for a while.

"Indeed. Take a few weeks. When you've thought it over, drop me a word here. I'll give you my card."

As he left Peter with a footman to show him out, General Smithson said confidentially, "It certainly wouldn't harm a fellow's career to be chaplain here for a year or so."

"Oh, no. I understand that very well."

A car took him back to his hotel. He wanted to do nothing but go to his room and think. It was like winning the Governor General's Medal at Rothesay, the sweetest feeling; nectar flowed in his veins; something no one could take away, no matter what else happened. The name Peter Wentworth would always be there in gold on the varnished plaque in the dining hall. Now he would always be the clergyman who won the Albert Medal. He would always be the Canadian clergyman the Duke of Devonshire had chosen as private chaplain. Of course, people would know that only if he accepted.

Peter took off his jacket and looked closely at the Albert Medal, First Class, in gold, for extremely heroic acts. He hung the jacket on a chair and lay on the bed with his head propped up on pillows where he could see the medal. The blue and white stripes would be very conspicuous on his black tippet. But on top of that, imagine being be asked to be the private chaplain!

His mind had skipped once over the possibilities of taking the offer and produced an instant negative. He lay back to reconsider: there had to be a way, because he felt he could do anything.

Anything could happen to him. He had been lifted involuntarily, as on the Lord's wings, ever since he had gone to the aid of that poor woman. And if the public version was a little overblown, it was undeniable that he had been there, his instinct to help the woman. Each time he remembered, the gloss thickened, like a painter's varnish, over his hesitations, moments of antipathy, his squeamishness. He was there. How many men who won medals in France, like Charles Robertson, did precisely what the citations said? Someone had to witness an act under extreme conditions of fear and danger—explosions, poison gas, shellbursts, utter terror.

What mattered in the world was having the marks placed beside your name, your efforts credited. The world exaggerated; the world ignored. Some men were overpraised; some praised less than they deserved. You saw it at school, and it continued through life. Some men had a knack of being noticed when it mattered; others tried to be noticed and made fools of themselves; most went unnoticed.

He was clearly being noticed, lifted, intended for higher things.

JULIA AND HER MOTHER went shopping. Julia needed presents for the people in Halifax she had neglected at Christmas. In Morgan's, where they found two charming dresses for Betty, her mother said, "You know, these days you don't need to wear black forever."

Julia feigned a questioning look, but she had understood perfectly.

"We could just look at some things; it's only one floor up."

"Mother, I don't feel like buying clothes."

"It doesn't hurt to look."

They looked at spring and summer dresses. When the saleswoman held one against her black dress, the color was so startling that Julia protested, "Oh, I couldn't wear that. It's much too bright!"

Heather Montgomery said, loudly enough to include the saleswoman as an ally, "You're not going to stay in widow's weeds forever? We're still in Victorian times. Things are changing. Look at the skirts those girls are wearing, and shoes, not boots. The war is changing things. You don't have to lock yourself up like a nun. You have to look ahead."

"But I don't feel like buying things now. And if I did want to wear something brighter, I have lots of things at home."

"Now, look at that, Julia! Isn't it lovely? Isn't it?" Her mother pointed to a gown on a mannequin, a white organdy that Julia could imagine herself wearing at a garden party.

"Well," her mother said in resignation, "then we should look at another black dress, if that's all you'll wear. You can't wear the same one all the time."

"No, Mother."

"At least look at some underclothes. No one's going to see that!"

She continued to resist, but the sight of the clothes and her automatic no to a new black dress told her that her mother was right.

Buying the gifts turned her thoughts to Halifax but not as forcefully as a second visit to Jeffrey.

It was too soon for a reply from Stewart MacPherson but her father said, "If some of these men are classified as shell-shocked and given medical treatment, the army must have a procedure. Let me talk to a barrister I know, a KC, who does some work with the federal government."

The KC referred Mr. Montgomery to a young solicitor who worked with families trying to get their sons exempted from conscription.

The solicitor was pessimistic. "The whole subject's terribly volatile just now. Everyone is afraid to coddle these men for fear it will open up the door to thousands of pacifists or conscientious objectors. Especially here in Quebec. The situation's very tense. They won't say say so, but conscription isn't working. Even in Ontario parents are using every exemption the law gives them, or helping their sons to run away and hide. But it's harder to have them exempted on medical grounds once they're in the army—almost impossible."

"But if Jeffrey is ill, he shouldn't be in that awful place. He should be in hospital."

"Someone has to rule that he's legally ill. Normally that's done overseas. There's a procedure."

"Who can do that here?"

"A judge, perhaps. But someone has to bring evidence and petition for a hearing. You say there was an appeal against the court-martial verdict? There would have to be another appeal."

"How could we do that?"

"I think you would need doctors or experts in the field to present evidence that he fitted the definition, to argue that a mistake was made in France."

"Then Stewart MacPherson is the person to tell us. He's a psychologist in Halifax who has been working with cases there."

The solicitor said Halifax was important, because it was the main port for returning casualties, where they were first classified on arrival back in Canada.

"They've been challenging the more conservative military view and I think they succeeded in getting some disciplinary cases redefined. If we could secure the arguments they used, the medical papers and the legal briefs, it might give us a place to start. Since they've set the precedent, the army may listen here."

"Then I should go back to Halifax and ask Stewart for whatever we need," Julia said.

"You could write to him," suggested her father.

"But, Daddy, look at Jeffrey! We've got to do something quickly." She knew she sounded like a little girl. "I think I should go right away."

"Julia, dear!" her mother said. "You were going to stay weeks and weeks."

"I know, but seeing Stewart MacPherson quickly is the way to help Jeffrey."

"I think Jeffrey's a lost soul," Mrs. Montgomery said.

Impatient to leave, Julia made a final visit to Jeffrey. She found him more in control but still looking at her with eyes that haunted her long afterward.

"I'll see what I can do for you, Jeffrey." She reached out and squeezed his hand warmly.

"Visitors may not touch the prisoners!" the guard said.

Julia turned, furious. She was about to say, Oh, go spit!, something she hadn't said since she was a little girl. The silly phrase made her laugh at the guard. She blew a kiss to Jeffrey and marched out.

Her parents took her to Bonaventure Station.

"If she insists on going, Norman, at least pay for a drawing room," her mother said. "She came up day coach."

"Thank you, Mother. That's sweet." Julia kissed her, realizing that she had kissed her mother more spontaneously and often on this trip than she had in years.

Even settling her in the drawing room aboard the Ocean Limited, her mother was still protesting: "It's too soon, dear. It's too soon. You needed more time away. We could have gone to the Laurentians for a few days. Why didn't I think of that? Norman, why didn't we think of that?"

But Julia's thoughts had jumped ahead to Halifax.

Stewart MacPherson left Boston for Montreal satisfied. Cushing's opinions gave no new grounds for hope, but they didn't extinguish hope altogether. It was very useful information.

He looked forward with excitement and anxiety to meeting Julia. His train would arrive late, so he would stay at the Ritz and call her first thing in the morning.

He watched the winter landscape of the Berkshires and the Adirondacks as the train headed north.

What is the new morality for those of us trying to live rational lives in a scientific age? What makes an act moral when we have dismissed Christian morality? I am an emancipated man, free of religious superstition, yet my conscience was shaped by it.

What would become of that morality if women were as free to choose as men? I surprised Julia by saying she could live where she liked. She hadn't considered that, nor I. It put the idea in my head that she could live with me. But never for a moment have I thought that we should just have an affair, she at my house or I at hers, as I've had with other women. Why is it different with Julia? Why does she awaken the conventional morality in me; why does she seem pure and make me feel pure, when neither of us is so in any literal sense?

Suppose I knew Julia had exactly paralleled my sexual and romantic episodes, with as many men as I have known women, would I think her as pure as I think myself? To be honest, no. Old thinking is too hard to erase. Will Freud's ideas become so commonplace in a few years that they will change the whole climate of opinion?

It is simple for us to see the patterns of behavior when men like

Frazer study primitive cultures, but those people would have killed Frazer if he had demystified their sexual taboos to them, the way many people would be happy to kill Freud now.

Stewart could feel the germ of a lecture: the psychology of resistance to new ideas. Ideas that threaten established thinking terrify societies as they do individuals. People are more afraid of new ideas from a Matisse, or a Freud, a Stravinsky, a Diaghilev than they are afraid of sending their sons off to war. Ideas frighten them more than organized killing. Going to war is an old idea, usually made to sound reasonable or honorable or unavoidable. Defending the king and empire is an old idea, hallowed by time. Even a thrilling idea, proof of manhood. They called Matisse a wild beast for using color in a new way, but his pictures did not kill anyone. People who didn't like them didn't have to buy them or look at them.

They don't call our political leaders wild beasts for continuing this slaughter. No one calls our generals wild beasts for executing shell-shock cases as deserters or cowards. Any barbarity may be committed in the name of the conventional idea, firmly entrenched.

Yet in the last analysis—that's funny—I can't intellectualize what I feel about Julia Robertson. It makes me primitive and irrational.

Peter Wentworth's train from Ottawa left him stranded for the afternoon in Montreal.

"Change of service," said the man at the ticket window. "No day train today. Ocean Limited leaves at six-forty now. Orders of the War Board. Too much war freight and soldiers on this route, so they're cutting back passenger service."

He ended hours of walking and sightseeing outside Notre Dame Cathedral, admiring the façade with its statues of the saints, and was drawn in. He felt foreign yet comforted in the dark, ornate interior, rich with the smell of incense and candles lighted near the effigy of the Virgin.

He passed a confession booth and could hear from the murmur that it was in use. The priest's name was on a card in the slot outside. There was another booth, with a penitent waiting her turn. The desire to confess himself came over him like a desire for physical release, a longing for spiritual detumescence. For an instant he was seriously tempted to slip into one of the booths, but shrank from explaining his clerical collar. He left the incense-rich air for the horse smells in the frosty, darkening afternoon.

As he walked back to the station, three companies of soldiers marched by, carrying heavy packs and rifles. They preceded him down the station platform to board cars at the head of the train. Peter found his seat in a Pullman car named Rivière du Loup. This time he had been fortunate to get a lower berth.

When the train was under way and the first sitting for dinner announced, Peter walked forward two Pullman cars to the dining car. Sitting alone, in the black dress he recognized, with her back to one of the etched glass partitions, was Julia.

His heart lurched. She was reading a menu and had not seen him.

"Julia? How nice to meet you here. It's Peter Wentworth."

She looked up, dazed for a moment. "Mr. Wentworth?" She blushed. "Are you going to Halifax, too?"

"Yes. What good luck," Peter said. "Would it be all right with you if we ate dinner together? I don't want to intrude."

She smiled. "You're not intruding. It'll be much nicer to have someone to eat with."

He sat down. The waiter came up and said, "Will it be dinner for two, then?"

"Yes."

"Excuse me, Reverend, on one bill or two?"

"On one."

"No, no. Please, Mr. Wentworth. On two!" Julia said firmly to the waiter.

Peter had lost his exhausted appearance; his gray eyes had recovered their glitter. His presence across the table—she had never sat with him quite so near—aroused the familiar mixture of excitement and dread.

"Dean Creighton told me you had gone to Montreal for Christmas," he said. "Did you enjoy your visit?"

"Oh, yes. But what were you doing in Montreal?"

"Actually, Ottawa," and he told her about the Albert Medal. His words were modest, but his demeanor expressed satisfaction. He took the medal from his pocket to show her.

Julia admired it carefully and gave it back.

"You must be very proud, Mr. Wentworth, and you should be."

He could not stop. Over the soup he told her about the invitation to become the governor general's chaplain.

"But how thrilling!" She clasped her hands together. Her eyes were shining with pleasure for him.

"I'm not at all certain it would be possible. There are a number of factors. I need to think about it."

He did not mention his sick wife; she must certainly be the crucial factor.

"The dean has leaned on me very heavily for the last two years. I have asked him and the bishop many times if I could go overseas as an army chaplain, but they've always refused."

"I didn't know that. That was very fine of you to try. Not many men are going now who don't have to."

"But to be asked is very gratifying," Peter said.

"Oh! You mean the position in Ottawa? Yes. It's a great honor to be asked."

Peter noticed how exquisitely her slender neck rose from the black lace of her collar. Her hat, with a black veil drawn back, had a flat brim that cast her eyes into shade when she lowered her head.

Listening to his resonant voice, she remembered its soothing effect on her the evening she went alone to the cathedral—the voice that created a little pool of intimacy around them in that vast dark space.

The waiter reappeared, balancing dinner plates and vegetable dishes on one arm. "One roast lamb and another roast lamb. Brussels sprouts, roast potatoes, and turnips. Mint sauce. There you are. Enjoy your dinner. Sorry we can no longer offer you any wine with your meal. The law has spoken."

"He sounds English," Julia said. "Like a steward on one of the liners."

"Oh, yes." Peter laughed.

One of those references that gnawed at his self-esteem. He couldn't have made such a remark.

Julia raised the napkin to her lips and he again noticed the delicacy of their shape and color. He was not hungry for food. His sexual hunger was rising.

"I had a terribly sad experience in Montreal," she said, putting down her knife and fork. "I have a cousin named Jeffrey Montgomery.

So that's his name, Peter thought. J is Jeffrey.

"My father's brother and his wife died many years ago, leaving Jeffrey an orphan. Montgomery is my maiden name. Jeffrey and I were very close growing up . . ."

He listened, forming pictures as she talked, pictures of a girl jumping from a beam into the hay, her skirt flying, and of her doing things with Jeffrey she had not done with Charles.

Her eyes moistened as she described the detention center and Jeffrey's defeated, haunted look.

"He looks like a scarecrow, so thin and wasted, awfully frightened. I thought I would ask Stewart MacPherson to help. Do you remember, he told us that day about working with the shell-shock cases?"

Peter's mind flicked aside the mention of Stewart.

"I wrote him from Montreal. I think he's a very good and thoughtful person, don't you?"

"Stewart and I go back many years together," said Peter.

She laughed. "That sounds like a way of dodging the question."

"Oh, of course he's a good person. He's just taken some odd twists and turns."

"With women? Lucy Robertson said he'd become something of a Don Juan."

"Well, if it were true, it would be indelicate of me to say so, wouldn't it?"

"But if it were not true, it would be indelicate not to, wouldn't it?" she teased. As always when she got engaged in an interesting conversation, a little color came into her cheeks.

"Years ago, I had reason to think he was seeing a very—unusual kind of woman, when we were in college."

"And since then—has he followed your advice and walked the straight and narrow path of virtue?" She was clearly mocking him.

"I don't think that would be altogether true."

"It all makes him sound quite wicked, and he certainly doesn't seem wicked. He seems rather comfortable and honest."

Talking about Stewart had turned on the gay spirits he had perceived in her diary but never witnessed. Her teasing laugh made her even more delicious.

"Now, your worship and m'lady." The Cockney-sounding waiter was back. "For sweets, I can offer you tinned peaches and whipped cream, apple pie, baked custard—the mince pie is finished."

The conductor passed, saying loudly, "Next stop. Rivière du Loup! Rivière du Loup in five minutes!"

"Oh, that's the name of the car I'm in," Julia said.

"So am I!" and their eyes met as the information registered with each of them.

"We're running late," the waiter said. "We're part troop train tonight. They put three extra cars up front with a battalion of soldiers. That's their officers over there."

Behind Julia they saw the officers, all young, laughing excitedly. As she turned, Peter noticed the slender waist and the fullness of her breasts. At the back of her neck were wisps of loose blond hair too short to be pinned up under her hat.

"I don't envy the poor blighters where they're going," the waiter said.

"They look so young." Julia's face had lost its animation.

The waiter said, "Better them than me. I'm lucky. I got a bad lung. What's your pleasure for dessert?"

"Just some coffee, please," Julia said.

"Coffee," Peter added.

Julia was silent; her hat brim shaded her face. When she raised her head, the table lamp showed tears in her eyes.

"If you asked to go overseas, you must have believed that this war is right."

"Well, yes, I do."

"But as a man of God, you'd have to explain all the killing to yourself and believe it justified, wouldn't you? Or you would not have wanted to go."

"I could have wanted to go for other reasons."

"What reasons?" She looked surprised.

"Because everyone was going. It was the thing to do. It was doing the right thing because our country was at war."

"That's why Charles went. Of course he knew nothing about it then. They all thought it would be over before they got there. They would miss the fun! But, you know"—she lowered her voice—"Charles did not think it was right—at the end. His last letters turned very bitter. It was odd. He actually liked what he was doing. It exhilarated him, I suppose, when they had successes. But he was disgusted at the way they used young lives. He called it wanton. He thought General Haig was a criminal."

She described taking the letters to the newspaper and the editor's refusal to print them.

"Can you imagine that? He said he could go to jail for printing them. I brought them to Montreal, thinking I might try the *Montreal Gazette*. Then I got so involved with Jeffrey that I lost heart and didn't do it. Do you think I was wrong? Do you think I should keep trying until someone prints them?"

"You'd probably have a hard time with any newspaper. Antiwar views are very unpopular."

"But don't you find that terrible, Mr. Wentworth? We live in a country where people are supposed to think for themselves. How can they do that if they're fed nothing but cheery news and lies?"

"Because it would stop the war. The mothers and wives of those young men"—Peter nodded up the dining car—"wouldn't let them go to fight."

"Wouldn't that be a good thing? If we've fought for three years, slaughtered thousands and thousands of men, I don't know how many thousands, and wounded so many more? In Montreal, you're beginning to see them everywhere on the streets, men on crutches, men with one leg. If neither side can win after three years, why shouldn't we just stop it and call it a stalemate? Stewart MacPherson thinks they should negotiate an armistice."

Peter was enthralled. The physical ache to embrace her returned. He could scarcely think of coherent replies and did not want to compete; he just wanted to to go where she went, listen, and drink her in.

Behind her quiet but emphatic voice, the paneling in the dining car creaked with the movement of the train; the cruets, water decanters, cream pitchers, and glasses tinkled as they moved.

"Doesn't the church have any doubts about it? I know the church supports the war. Anglican ministers were preaching sermons saying vote for the Union Government, so your bishops and people must still think it's the right thing?"

He didn't want to talk about this. "Yes, they do. They believe that the harder we try, the sooner we'll end it. To give up now would mean that all those who died have given their lives in vain. It's a very strong argument. In my parish visiting, I've had to talk to many families who have lost men."

"The way you talked to me?"

"Well—yes. The deaths of their loved ones have to mean something."

"Even if they don't mean anything?"

"They don't think that."

She paused to think. "No, I suppose they don't. Archie and Elizabeth Robertson don't think that. And they've seen Charles's letters. Perhaps his mother does. Oh"—she sighed deeply—"I don't know."

Peter wanted to reach across the table and take one of her hands.

"But still, if all those killed *have* died in vain, sending more will just mean more die in vain! Isn't that true?"

"You don't really believe that your husband gave his life for nothing?"

She lowered her head. "Sometimes I do. Sometimes I do." In a few moments she appeared to shake off these thoughts, because she smiled.

"Do you remember when we were talking at my house, you said no one believes in nothing because the idea of God is born in us. Do you remember that?"

"Yes, I remember." The afternoon when he was so strongly tempted to kiss her.

"I've thought about it since. And I simply don't believe it!" She laughed a little self-consciously. "I remember some of what you said about the human thirst for perfection, the escape from death . . ." She particularly remembered he had continued "and the prison of the flesh," but she skipped that. "Why does that that automatically become something you have to worship?"

"Sorry, Bishop," the waiter said. "I shall have to ask you and her ladyship to settle up. We have to close the dining car to make everything shipshape for breakfast and get a little shut-eye."

When they looked around, the dining car was empty. The waiters were stripping tables and setting them with fresh linen.

"I had no idea it was so late," Julia said. She paid from her purse. Peter paid, aware to the cent how much of George Tobin's hundred dollars he still had.

"I don't feel sleepy yet. Would you like to talk some more?" Julia asked as they got up.

"I would."

He followed her through the dining car, watching her body sway to the train's movements, the delicate way she put a few fingers out here and there to keep her balance. He opened the heavy door and they walked through the cold, squeaking vestibule between the cars, with its powder of blown snow. In the next sleeping car all the berths had been made up, so that they walked between two walls of curtains. Their car, Rivière du Loup, was in the same condition. They passed the open door of the men's washroom, where several officers were sitting on the bench, with the porter, laughing, passing a silver flask. The laughter followed them into the muffled corridor of curtains.

"I don't know where we can sit," Peter said.

Julia whispered, "I have a compartment; it has chairs. If that doesn't embarrass you."

"Not at all."

Julia opened a door in the paneled corridor and he entered the private room. Her bed had been made up across the window but there was still floor space for two armchairs. Peter noted her black coat with its fur collar on a hanger, the polished washbasin, and immediately smelled her perfume. The space was so small that they had to move self-consciously around each other to sit down. Before she sat, Julia turned on another shaded lamp. She removed her hat and hung it on a hook.

"There! Isn't this cozy?"

She tried to sound brisk and social, but her heart was beating more quickly. What had seemed so casual a suggestion now appeared a very big step as she sat in her chair, turning her knees to one side so as not to be near Peter's legs.

She had actually brought this man, who gave her such odd feelings, into her room on the train, alone, and had closed the door. Their eyes met, strangely, for a moment. Her cheeks felt warm. Her whole body felt warm. He sat self-consciously in his chair, his large hands on his knees, as if waiting to spring up. But of course he was a clergyman. His clerical collar stood out with particular vividness. It was all right to be with a clergyman.

"What were we talking about?" Julia raised her hands together in the familiar gesture. "Oh, yes! Is the idea of God born in us?" She felt she was chattering like a nervous hostess. "Oh, I'm sure that ideas like goodness and perfection are there. We think of them. Or someone teaches us about them. But moving from that to making a mighty, invisible being who has to be obeyed, to be worshiped, who supposedly hands down rules, the whole structure of the church, all the churches . . . I just can't grasp the logic of an all-wise, all-powerful something up there running everything."

"I didn't mean logic. I meant the intuitive sense of God's presence that most people have."

"And I don't have." Julia smiled.

Peter would have said anything not to break the mood.

"Of course, there are logical proofs, if you like. The most famous were devised by Thomas Aquinas."

"What are they?" she asked. Any real curiosity she had was rapidly ebbing across another tide rising from her awareness that he was the first man she had been alone with since Charles.

"Well, it's not something one gets asked every day . . ."

"On a train, in the middle of the night." She was smiling.

The atmosphere was charged. In the silence Peter felt the train moving under the chairs and heard the clinking of the glass in its nickel-plated holder against the water carafe over the basin.

"What were these logical proofs?"

Peter talked to keep talking, aware of the absurdity of trying to remember Aquinas, aware that it did not matter.

"This train is moving. We know what started it. But what started the first motion—the earth, the stars? Something that did not move itself must have started them moving. That's one proof."

"What are the others?" The pupils of her eyes had grown large.

"Everything in nature serves some purpose, so what is the ultimate purpose?"

"I know something that serves no purpose." Looking at her, he could see the teasing schoolgirl she had been.

"What is it?"

"No, I take it back." She made it a game.

"What is it?"

"I'd rather not say. It's silly."

"All right. As Thomas Aquinas said, everything in nature serves some purpose."

That forced her to say it. "They told us in art school, the nipples on a man's body serve no purpose!"

"Well, I concede you that."

"Does Thomas Aquinas?" The gleam of challenge had come back to her eyes.

"Another of his proofs: we know that there are degrees of perfection in the world. This rose is perfect; that rose isn't fully out; that rose is past its best; that rose has a flaw. One rose is more perfect than another. If there are degrees of perfection, logic demands there must be something that is more perfect than anything else.''

She watched his hands as he kept track of the items on his fingers.

"There are others, but you understand the approach."

She was smiling. "It sounds very arid to me. Something you had to learn for an examination."

"That's just what it was—and I haven't thought about it since."

It sounded like a rare moment of candor, and the charm of it moved her. She found him looking at her very intently and instantly detected the different tone when he said, "Julia, I really don't want to talk about this."

It might have had a hundred meanings, but she heard only one. The words electrified her. She couldn't take her eyes from his, and she found breathing difficult. Everything turned gray in her sight except around his face and eyes. She felt practically unable to breathe. Finally she said quietly, "What do you want to talk about?"

Then he was kneeling beside her on the floor. He seemed uncertain for a moment, then grasped her thighs through her dress and was pressing his face against them. The shock of his touch went through her body.

Her hands fell automatically to his hair, and she caressed it. He lifted his face and found her lips and they clasped each other, mouth devouring mouth, their hearts beating wildly, tearing their lips apart for a gulp of breath, like drowning swimmers before submerging again.

She felt her whole body responding. She stroked his back, his arms. He kissed her throat. He pressed his face against her breasts, and, with a sigh, she clasped his head there with her hands while kissing his hair.

The power of her desire was frightening to her. It was sovereign and terrible; it was too burning-delicious to stop. Too parched to stop drinking the hard sweetness of his mouth. Eating his lips. Yet she wanted not to. She wanted to fight him off. He was presumptuous. But her heart was beating wildly. She hated him for doing this. Her nipples ached to be touched. She was angry with him, and she wanted to have him in her.

No one would know. No one would know. They were alone on a train in the middle of nowhere, in the middle of the night.

She started to wrench away but reached behind her and turned off the small lamp. They embraced anew, hungrier still. In the dimmer light, she tore away again. She slid over the bed and lay across it to extinguish the other lamp.

They were in near darkness with pale shadows from the window and the winter night racing by. He found her on the bed and lay alongside her. She felt him and she knew she would let him have her and she hated him for making her want him.

She wanted his mouth. She wanted his hands on her. His hands were pulling at her dress. Her fingers were unbuttoning his vest and pulling at his shirt. She moved over the warm skin of his back and she felt his hand wrenching at her petticoats, moving along her thighs. She was delirious with desire. He tore off his jacket. She sat up to unhook her dress at the back.

Seeing her reach upward, Peter whispered, "Will you undo your hair?"

"What?" She scarcely had breath to talk.

"Will you let your hair down?"

She sat on the edge of the bed, reaching up, and rapidly pulled the pins out. Now he was kneeling on the floor, his head against her breast. Her hair tumbled about his face, bathing him in its perfume. Peter groaned.

"Oh, Julia, I am not worthy of you."

"Don't be silly."

"I am not a real hero."

"Don't stop." She kissed him, whispering, "Don't stop."

But he pulled away.

"It's all a story . . . what everyone is making the great fuss about."

She couldn't understand why he had stopped. Hadn't she made it clear that she desperately wanted to go on?

"The reason the governor general gave me the medal. The reason he wants me to be his chaplain. The reason for all the newspaper stories."

It had the rhythm of the litany.

"Come," she whispered, pulling at him. "Come." But he held back.

"First, I have to tell you. It's the reason for all the editorials, and the letters of congratulation, and people stopping me in the street. It's all a story."

Julia listened impatiently, resentfully. Her aroused body ached to go on. He sounded like a character in a play, speaking not to her but to someone else.

"The sergeant made it up for the money. For the newspaper competition. He was a sneering, brutal fellow. He mocked and scorned me all morning when we were pulling bodies out. Making fun of my profession and the Church of England."

"Tell me later," she said. "Peter, tell me later." She held his head in her hands and put her lips on his, but he turned his mouth away.

"When we found the woman trapped in that house and she said, 'Father, give me the last rites, absolve me,' I recoiled from her. I'm ashamed of it now, but something in me was revolted at the idea. I shrank from her Catholicism. She pleaded with me, and I said, 'But I'm not a Catholic; I don't know how do it.' What I really felt was, I don't want to soil my hands with this. And she was dying, with this terrible weight crushing her body and the building on fire all around us. In the end he made me do it. The sergeant. He swore at me. 'Absolve her or I'll kill you." He forced me down on my knees in the broken glass and dust until I did it. And when she thanked me with that beatific expression on her face, the sergeant snatched me out of the fire just in time as the wall fell on her and we heard her scream. I was terrified and I was ashamed of myself."

She raised a hand to his cheek and felt hot tears, which she smoothed away. If she could calm him down. . . .

"I wanted everyone to think me a hero, to think me brave. I wanted to go overseas, but privately I wondered if I would be a coward. Would I be so frightened that I ran away like your cousin? Now because of this fake, everyone thinks I'm a brave man, a hero. For the rest of my life I'll be known as a hero. When it first came out, I really tried to protest. I said, 'That's exaggerated. It didn't happen that way.' But my vanity loved the idea of the story, and little by little I didn't protest anymore and I almost came to believe the story myself. I wanted to believe it, because I wanted you to think of me as a brave man. The moment I saw you, I was overcome with desire for you. I couldn't take my eyes off you. You were the most beautiful woman I had ever seen. I wanted you and I knew I couldn't have you. It was shameful even to want you.

It was a sin. It was the most shameful thing I have ever wanted. But when they called me a hero and everyone applauded, the day the governor general congratulated me and I knew you were watching, something changed. My false story had become a real story, deceiving me into thinking I was worthy of you, when you've been in love with two men who were real heroes, and I—"

A flutter of uneasiness went through Julia. "What do you mean?"

Peter was a disembodied voice, expressionless, compulsive, the voice of confession. "Your husband won the Victoria Cross, the ultimate recognition for valor, the most extreme sacrifice. And Lieutenant Boiscoyne won the DSO for courage—"

Julia suddenly felt cold, prickles of cold, all over her skin and scalp. She took her hands from his head.

"What do you mean? Lieutenant Boiscoyne?"

"The British officer you fell in love with—" Peter understood where he had gone and stopped, transfixed.

Even before he had the words out, she knew. It was instantly clear. All the odd little things that had puzzled her about Peter collided in the knowledge. He knew it all. The diary! She couldn't believe it. The diary!

"My diary!" She moved herself away from him.

He said nothing.

"You have my diary!"

Still no answer.

"Tell me!"

His voice had faded to a whisper. "I found it the day after the explosion. I was collecting clothes for the homeless. It must have fallen out of some clothing Mollie gave me."

"And you read it?"

"Yes."

"You've read everything in it?" Her voice was breaking.

"At first I didn't read it. I was just looking to see if I could tell whose it was. I couldn't tell. All the names were initials. But as I read, I fell more and more under your spell. I kept trying to find out who were were. I wanted the lovely woman in the diary. Julia, listen to me. I confess it to you, fully and contritely. I dreamed about it. Then I discovered who you were. It was in the newspaper that your husband was wounded. Mrs. Creighton said your name and pointed out the house. I came straight to see you. I'm telling you the absolute truth. I am deeply ashamed, but I must tell you."

"Don't tell me!"

"I have to tell you."

"No, I don't want to hear."

"But I must tell you. I know what I did was reprehensible. I am deeply and heartily sorry. I crept back at night and read you."

"Where is it now?" Her voice was distant and cold.

"I burned it after—I burned it."

"Oooh!" She wailed like a small child and threw herself down with her face in the pillow. He felt excluded from her crying and waited helplessly. The train racketed on.

Then she raised her head. He could not see her face in the dim light, but her voice destroyed all intimacy between them.

"Go away!" It was full of contempt. "Get out of here!"

He scrambled awkwardly around the woman's body, warm and giving a moment before, now rigidly hostile.

"I must find my jacket."

"Find it and go. Go! Go!"

Abject and ridiculous in the darkness of the swaying train, he could find nothing.

"I'm afraid I'll have to turn on a light."

This time her voice was almost a scream. "Do whatever you have to do and go!"

He found the light. She had curled up, her face hidden by the pillow and the disordered golden hair. In the mirror he saw a clergyman with his collar crooked and hair wild. He straightened the collar and smoothed the hair with his fingers, snatched up his coat, opened the door, and stepped out.

Immediately, Julia got up and locked the door. She ran water in the basin and washed her face and hands to get the feeling of him off her skin. Despite the washing, she felt unclean, violated.

The lace around the collar of the black dress had been partly ripped off in the frantic struggle. How could she face Stewart Mac-Pherson and the others like this? She felt a compulsion to mend it immediately. She got out of the dress, found a needle and black thread, and carefully attached the lace. She then dressed herself neatly, did her hair, and prepared to sit up for the rest of the night. She could not get into the snarled bed where he had been.

She had distrusted Peter. He had made her uneasy. Now she

remembered all the little signs that made him seem too knowing. That was the meaning of the look when Archie Robertson mentioned Neville Boiscoyne. How terrible to have his name thrown at her by this wretch! By this charlatan! All the shame she had felt at being aroused by Neville; how she had fought against it, and succeeded, had torn herself away in time. To have his name used by this despicable man! That it would be Peter she gave herself to —almost gave herself to! What would Stewart think if he knew?

Peter Wentworth was unspeakable. He had been spying on her through her diary, like a peeping Tom. He knew all her secrets. He knew all the things she had done out of loneliness. He knew before he approached her how lonely, how vulnerable she was, how she longed for her husband. Her face burned with indignation and shame. He was like a jackal sniffing around, waiting to pounce and tear—and he had pounced. She had not led him on. But she had. Of course she had! The diary had led him on. He was sure what he would find. She had no secrets left.

Peter crept into in his lower berth, not turning on the light and not undressing. He raised the blind, and the luminosity of the winter night made a pale glow.

His stomach felt sick and in his testicles and groin was the burning of sexual excitement not satisfied. But they were faint sensations compared with the shame, the humiliation—and the relief of having told her. His spirit withered again in the memory of her scorn, her disgust, the sickening tone of her contempt.

She had been passionate in her response, a woman like a whirlwind, and his hunger for her had been uncontrollable until—suddenly—a stronger thought possessed him, and his desire shriveled. To tell her first, to cleanse his conscience, until that had run as out of control as his physical desire, overflowing, a dam bursting.

Before that, the conversation about God, a mock conversation, an excuse to keep talking to her. But her curiosity had forced him to confront the very questions he had been avoiding himself.

And now there came to Peter an instant of understanding.

There is no God for me.

There is no God in any sense I have understood all my life. There is only Man. I stopped praying because there is no one to pray to. We are only praying to another part of ourselves.

There was no deeper religious meaning. No oneness with God.

No flash of light. The self-denial he had practiced all his life to deepen his religious feeling; all the effort of self-denial; all the winter mornings he had felt more spiritual because the chapel was freezing before breakfast. There never was a God there.

Whom do you pray to, she asked that afternoon. He had known then and pushed the thought away. He had been praying to what he had thought from childhood lay just beyond his belief and discipline. He had prayed, believing that if he lived with enough discipline and obedience, ultimately he would see God. The more he curbed himself, the more he believed.

To whom do you confess? This had bothered him for so long. In the Anglican Church everyone confessed to God. The Catholics confess to men.

The idea of love, forgiveness, generosity, compassion, resistance to temptation, disdain for material things, that was all in us. Christ was an example—if his life was anything like the gospels—but a human being. At bottom there was no God.

Peter felt terror and joy mingled. He was short of breath, and his heartbeat was loud in his ears. It was as though he had just run a race or scaled a frightful sheer mountain cliff. This negative epiphany moved him as he had always expected to be moved by the actual sight of God.

He was shivering. He pulled off his clothes and crawled under the blankets, trembling.

And if there was no God, no supernatural being, only the best and worst in human nature, the divisions in the churches were all products of human vanity. They became even more ridiculous, millions of people spending their lives, punishing themselves and other people, sacrificing people, torturing people, flailing them with guilt and sin, to believe this is the right way, to worship what is just a part of ourselves. There is no punisher, only the feeling that we should be punished. I was the punisher of myself because I thought I could never be like James.

Peter Wentworth trembled under the blankets, his hands against his lips, aware vaguely that Julia's perfume was on him. The train tore through the frozen forests and he shivered—ashamed, humiliated, and yet elated.

Julia did not go to the dining car for breakfast and was too sick in spirit to feel hunger. When the porter came to make up the bed, she remained in the compartment, saying she did not feel well. He offered to get her some coffee, and she accepted. He came at lunchtime but she was not hungry. In the afternoon he brought her a tray with tea. She did not leave the compartment.

She tried to read, but her agitation would not let her concentrate. Over and over again: How could she have permitted herself to let it happen? She knew and she did not know. She knew that she had desired and disliked him simultaneously.

She had led him on. She had brought him into the compartment. She had known what she was doing, known somewhere below her mind. It made her skin prickly with heat to think of it. She had not been able to stop herself.

No wonder he had driven his wife demented. What a duplicitous, sneaking man! He was right about one thing. His heroism was a fraud. And he reveled in his confession. He wallowed in his own disgrace. He wanted to confess. He wanted to tell her every detail.

Now she could see that he had never been interested in what she said. The way he dismissed what she said about Jeffrey. The way he smiled knowingly. He had looked at her sexually. He had consumed the diary and thought that she was starved for a man. That was what the diary would have told him. Hiding it under his minister's dress. He thought her a woman who was desperate for love. She would take any man who was there. Wasn't that just the fear she had noticed in herself? He had treated her like a prostitute. He had had that glint of certainty in his eyes from the moment she first saw him—the day he came to her house to console her about Charles. He had read all of the diary then. He had that look of insinuation that made her so angry. She was right to be angry. Her instincts were correct. He was too sure of himself. And she had let herself go with him. She had invited him in here.

Better to have succumbed to Neville Boiscoyne, who would have sailed away forever, than to Peter Wentworth. How could she live in a small city like Halifax and avoid seeing him? Yet why should she creep away and hide because Peter had taken advantage of her? No, they had taken advantage of each other.

What if, in his weird confession, Peter had not blurted out Neville Boiscoyne's name? The fact of his having read the diary might never have come out. Then she would have slept with him. Would they have parted sweetly, as lovers? No. She had hated him even as she wanted him physically. Julia did not want to remember the emotion of those few tempestuous moments that had been washed away by his confession.

As the train speeded on, she would suddenly remember something else she had written, and shudder to think that Peter had read it and would remember it. In all her anxiety that someone might read the diary, she had never imagined someone like Peter, someone she knew, an outsider whose prurient mind would be obsessed by it. Someone who would be aroused by it as if it were pornography.

She shuddered and took a long breath. There were hours to fill with thinking.

"Hello, may I speak to Julia Robertson, please?"

"I'm sorry, she's not here. Who's calling, please?"

"My name is Stewart MacPherson. I'm a friend of hers from Halifax."

"Oh, yes, Mr. MacPherson. I'm Julia's mother. She told us about you. She'll be so sorry to have missed you. But she took the train back to Halifax last night."

"Oh, I see." He said it with such falling spirits that Heather Montgomery said, "I'm so sorry to disappoint you!"

"Thank you."

For a moment Stewart was crushed. He had not expected that. He was not accustomed to moving rapidly. He had been able to plan things deliberately. Now he found himself running down two flights of stairs to the desk in the Ritz, ordering a reservation on the next train, sending a telegram to Julia saying he was returning and needed urgently to talk to her.

By lunchtime he found himself on the train to Halifax, on a brilliant winter's day, following the route Julia had taken the night before. The Maritime Express made more stops than the Ocean Limited, taking thirty hours instead of twenty-four to make the run. All afternoon Stewart fretted through the station waits, at Levis . . . Rivière du Loup . . . Rimouski . . . Mont Joli . . . Matapedia.

He tried to lose himself in the books he had bought so eagerly in Boston. He had been impatiently waiting for A. A. Brill's translation of Freud's study of wit. As much as Freud's lucid and elegant argument captivated him, Stewart's eyes kept straying from the book to the revolving vistas of fir trees and snow, the lonely farms and snowbound villages of eastern Quebec, to think of the woman he was hastening to see.

Now he was nervous about how she would receive him. She had spoken about him to her parents—well, she had mentioned him. That was a good sign.

Impatiently, Stewart got up and walked back to the men's room. After going to the toilet he went into the large washroom with the row of steel washbasins. The Negro sleeping car porter was dozing in one corner. Looking at himself in the mirror, Stewart saw tousled brown hair in need of cutting, a face inclined to flesh under the chin, a body heavier than might appeal to her. He opened the waistcoat of his tweed suit and tucked his errant shirttails into his trousers, then buttoned the waistcoat, holding his stomach in. When he tried, it was almost flat, certainly an improvement on his schooldays.

"You want me to shine up them shoes a little for you, sir?"

Stewart looked down, embarrassed, knowing his shoes were a mess, weeks without polish. He still let things go too long. He would have to do better.

"Thank you, yes."

The porter brought out a shoebox with a folding lid, on which he placed one of Stewart's feet.

"A fine gentleman like you want to look his best from head to toe," the porter said, applying a cleaning solution. "You don't put your best foot forward in this world, people going to get the wrong impression."

"I suppose you're right." Evidently the shine came with a sermon.

"You have yourself a real pair of shoes there. Fit for the king. It's a pity you don't keep 'em shined up real good."

They were English, purchased where his father had bought shoes. They were slightly cracked across the instep, because he neglected to put trees in them. The porter, more gently, was echoing Stewart's father, reviving the sour emotions those memories always evoked.

He was too relaxed about some things. If he was going to change his life, he would have to quicken his pace.

He went to sleep concluding that he had been exaggerating his potential with Julia, and slept badly, all the negatives surfacing.

•   •   •   •

GEORGE TOBIN took Abigail and Michael to the station to meet Peter. That morning he told his wife, "Maybe it'd be good for Margery to come down too. It would get her out of the house for an hour—maybe get her out of herself a little."

Margery got as excited as the children. She bathed and dressed herself carefully and asked her mother for some rouge to brighten her cheeks. The nurse dressed the children.

The awed children saw two giant steam engines, coupled together, grind in, panting as though exhausted. They waved excitedly to the lordly engine drivers and raced to meet their father down the platform. Margery ran after them and greeted him radiantly, with a big hug and a warm kiss. George Tobin came up, and they insisted that Peter pull out his medal to show them. He did so reluctantly.

Margery clapped her hands. "I'm so proud of you!" She kissed him again. Peter glanced around nervously.

Julia saw the scene from the corridor window of the sleeping car. A redcap had already carried her luggage to the platform, but she retreated to her compartment and sat down firmly. She had glimpsed Peter's nervousness and his haggard face. She did not want to see that again. She had also seen his wife looking pretty and happy, not ill, which added to her anger at Peter. Only when she was sure they had left the platform did she leave the train, find the redcap, and ask for a taxi.

Margery had changed again. To Peter she was noticeably more knowing. She remembered why he had gone to Ottawa. Some of the little stitches she had dropped in conversation now stayed knitted.

The moment they were alone in her room, she embraced Peter passionately. She wanted to make love right then. That had not changed. He did not want her. He whispered, "Later, later. It's too soon." Abigail was calling him to say good night. Smiling in complicity, Margery let him go.

The children said their prayers, and he tucked them both in. Michael said, "Daddy, what's a hero?"

Abigail imitated her grandmother's sound of irritation and and said, "Everybody knows what a hero is. A hero is a man who kills Germans! Stupid!"

"I'm not stupid."

"Yes, you are, a stupid boy!"

Peter closed the bedroom door to compose himself for a moment. A hero is a man who kills Germans.

The few moments with Margery had reawakened the sexual ache left from those frantic devouring moments on the train, Julia as ravenous as he; then her withering contempt. He stood listening to the murmur of voices coming upstairs with delicious cooking smells. The world was quite normal around him. He went downstairs to the dinner Cynthia had mounted to celebrate his medal.

They drank a toast to Peter and made him describe the tiniest detail of the investiture. Reluctantly, uneasily, he did so, and they took his diffidence for modesty. He omitted only his private lunch at Rideau Hall and the invitation to become the governor general's chaplain.

After dessert, George tapped his glass with a knife and said, "I have an announcement to make. We are all very proud of Peter. He has brought great honor to this family. And he has brought honor to this city. And he has brought honor to his church. And I would like to pay my personal respects to that in a way I can do best. Peter, as you and I know very well, I made a gift to the cathedral of the window coverings that were necessary right after the explosion, to keep the weather out."

"Yes. It was a splendid gesture."

"Well, now I'm going to go one better. To commemorate your act of generosity, an act the whole town is proud of, I will replace, for free, all the glass in the cathedral: stained glass for stained glass, plain glass for plain glass—except for the memorial window the Robertsons are donating."

"Why, George, you didn't tell me you were going to do that. Darling, that is a magnificent thing to do!"

Peter, rapidly calculating, added, "It is magnificent. It is extremely generous. I am sure the dean and the bishop, everyone, will be very grateful."

There was a moment of quiet, and Margery said in her charmingly absent-minded way, "Tell me again why the windows in the cathedral need replacing?"

Peter and her parents all looked at her horrified. Cynthia got up and kissed her.

But Margery disarmed them by saying with her new positiveness, "I'd like to walk Peter home!" Cynthia and George exchanged indulgent glances with Peter.

Outside Margery took his arm and held it tightly against her breast.

"I missed you so much, so much, so much, darling. I can't bear to have you away."

Her manner made Peter afraid, although he could not define the fear. Immediately the front door closed, she fastened her body to his.

"Let me come upstairs—for a minute. Just for a minute. It feels like such a long time. Just for a minute." She was whispering hotly in his ear.

She undressed rapidly, as though she had planned every move, and slid into bed before Peter. Her eyes had the enlarged pupils that seemed new to him. Embarrassed, he turned off the lamp. He thought of the lamp in the train. In the darkness he got into bed as though with a stranger, echoes of Julia in all his senses conflicting with the messages from Margery's body. She came to him immediately, demanding. He did not want her, but the ache in his body commanded a response to hers until he was as urgent as she.

Soon afterward, Margery got up and dressed.

"Mother will be expecting me." She sounded happy.

With coat, hat, and gloves on, she came back and tucked the covers lovingly around him. She knelt beside the bed and whispered, "I'm going to be a better wife to you, Peter. I've made up my mind to make a whole new start. And I'm so happy. I'll see you tomorrow."

She touched his cheek with her gloved fingers and kissed him on the lips.

That was the difference, or part of it. She was wearing a new perfume. It created an aura: elated, harder, and more determined.

"Good night!" she sang from the stairs, and he heard the front door shut.

The thing he had dreaded most had not happened. She had not mentioned the diary. Exhausted, he fell asleep.

STEWART AWOKE to watch snowbound New Brunswick reeling by. The day passed slowly and the train was running late. There was a long wait at Debert Army Camp outside Truro, as though the authorities could not decide whether to put troops on the train or take them off. Soldiers lounged on the platform, smoking, dozing against their kitbags. They had full field equipment and were probably headed for Halifax to be shipped overseas. Their boredom and the future that awaited them filled Stewart with sadness.

It was well into the evening before they reached Halifax. Stewart was tired and his exhilaration had ebbed away. It was after nine; too late to call Julia. And it was better like this. It was foolish to think of approaching her now. He would appear too unfeeling and insensitive. He would know better in a few weeks. The whole idea was a fantasy, a foolish fantasy.

He collected his much-traveled leather suitcases, heavy with new books. He was looking down when he reached the end of the platform and did not see her until she said, "Stewart?"

He couldn't believe it. Julia's face framed by the black fur hat and collar was ethereally beautiful to him.

She smiled tentatively. "Do you mind this?"

"Of course not. I'm thrilled."

"You telegraphed. You said you wanted to see me urgently. I am dying to know why. And I need to see you. I can't wait till tomorrow. But why were you in Montreal?"

"I went to see you."

"Why?" She smiled searchingly.

He ignored her question. "Did you get the newspaper to publish the letters? Charles's letters?"

"Oh, no! But that's why I want to see you. I meant to, but, you see, something awful has happened—"

He couldn't hear her in the echoing station. Around them people met and embraced, kissed passionately, shook hands heartily. They were being bumped by soldiers' kitbags and the suitcases of civilians pressing forward. Stewart picked up his bags and said, "Come over here."

She took his arm and clung to it as he shouldered through the crowd. He found a space on a bench a few feet from a sleeping soldier. He had to lean close to hear her.

"Something terrible has happened, Stewart. My first thought was to tell you. Because you might be able to help."

"What?"

"I have a cousin, Jeffrey Montgomery. He is the son of my father's brother. His parents died long ago—when he was nine.

They were climbing in Switzerland and were buried in an avalanche. Jeffrey and I practically grew up together."

Stewart felt discovered, dishonest. He knew about her cousin, and he should not know. But he listened to Julia's account of Jeffrey's quick battlefield court-martial, death sentence, the wait for execution by firing squad, the last-minute commutation to long imprisonment, the broken man in detention. She was crying when she finished.

"Yes, I can help. There are ways, as your solicitor said; there are ways we've used here. I don't know all the ins and outs in military-legal terms, but I'll find out tomorrow. I'll see the doctor who runs the unit here. He knows how it's done, how you get the right army medical people to talk with the right army legal people to release him for treatment. Part of the argument is deterrence. You might convince some of the military brass that studying these people could prevent more cases."

He was saying too much, but she was listening.

"Do you think there's a chance we could get him out of that place?"

"I think so. You know, these people aren't all sadists. I don't think they enjoy ordering men shot or locked up. They've just convinced themselves it's the right thing. It's a kind of mass hypnosis. The trick is to dehypnotize and make them see that the right thing is something else."

"Oh, thank you!" She put her gloved hand out to touch his. "You make me feel so much better. I can't tell you."

She was still looking at him curiously. "But why did you say you came to Montreal?'

"Julia, I've been thinking about this conversation ever since the moment I left you the last time. The minute I got home I knew what I wanted to say to you. I wrote you that night and posted the letter. But stupidly. I'd forgotten it was Sunday. I went round to your house, and Mollie told me you'd gone to Montreal. I was in despair. You don't really know much about me—"

She smiled. "You might be surprised. Lucy Robertson is a fund of information."

"Whatever you've heard—and I'll deny it all—I'm familiar enough with the proprieties to know that what I want to say may be hideously out of place—not just this place—"

Looking around at the swarming station, the soldier next to him, he laughed but was quickly serious again.

"That too. But I mean too soon, too precipitous, not the way things are done. I know I am presuming. I'll understand if you tell me, flatly. As bluntly as you wish. But, Julia, I have to to say this to you. I have fallen helplessly in love with you and I want to ask you to marry me—when the time is appropriate—if it ever is appropriate. That's what I came to Montreal to say."

Again those gray eyes magnified by tears. But she was smiling.

"Helplessly?"

"I cannot help myself. All the things I want to say sound trite— but I feel them. And you're the only woman I have felt this way about."

Her eyes darted back and forth between his, as if searching for a true reading of him.

"I have been arguing with myself every minute of the trip from Montreal. I had made up my mind not to tell you."

"Why?" Julia was pulling a handkerchief from her muff.

"I thought it was too soon. Too sudden. That you'd need more time."

Still she looked at him most searchingly.

He laughed a little nervously. "What should I take it to mean that you've been sitting here listening to me? Should I be pleased that you haven't jumped up and rushed away?"

"I can't explain what it means. I'm not sure why I came here to meet you. I just had a strong feeling that I should."

They were looking at each other very carefully. He took a deep breath.

"Before you say anything more to me, there's something else I have to tell you. If I tell you, you may despise me, but if I don't tell you, it would be a fundamental dishonesty."

"What is it?"

"Do you remember in *Anna Karenina,* when Kitty accepts Levin, he insists that she read his diary so that he'll have no secrets from her?"

"Yes?" She looked up very puzzled. The word *diary* resonated ominously.

"I know you were reading *Anna Karenina,* Julia."

"I don't understand."

"Someone found your diary the day after the explosion. The

person showed it to me, thinking I might be able to identify the owner.

"And you read it?"

"Yes."

"Oh, no!" She turned away and covered her face with her gloved hands.

"I read it, as I might have read a paper in psychology, a case history. I read it because I was asked to, and I gave it back to the person."

"You've read it, too!"

"Yes. And I can't go on pretending I have not. When you mentioned Jeffrey—"

"Oh!"

"I know about Jeffrey."

"I can't stand this!" Her face was flushed.

"Do you understand why I had to tell you?"

Julia got up, very distressed. "Please. I can't listen anymore. I must go home." She ran out of the waiting room. Stewart followed her.

"I can take you home."

"No, thank you."

"Let me get you a taxi."

"No. I can manage!"

A taxi was pulling up to the curb. She ran to it and got in. All Stewart could do was say "Good night" and close the door.

Julia did not smile or respond. The woman who had been so open to him, so eager to listen, had turned her head coldly away. The warm current of feeling was cut. He walked back to his suitcases and sat on the bench to smoke a cigarette.

He had leaped and missed his footing and fallen into the chasm.

The soldier said, "Ran out on you, did she? Can you spare a smoke?"

THE DEAN STOPPED PETER for a whispered conference outside his office. "I want to keep something private, just for now. Come with me."

The senior clergyman led Peter through the side door into the cathedral transept.

"I'm afraid our old friend is very ill."

"The bishop?"

"He has pneumonia. He's very weak. The doctor tells me it could go quickly, or he could fight it and be with us for a while."

"That's very sad news," Peter said, his mind racing with speculation.

"I'd just like to say this, Peter. If God takes our dear bishop, there will, of course, be an election. If it were God's will that I win that election, which is not wildly improbable, being realistic, it would fall to me to appoint the new dean of the cathedral."

"Yes."

"It would be my intention, Peter, to appoint you."

"But—well, sir—I am truly astonished!"

"You are still quite young and inexperienced, it's true. But in wartime, younger men are advanced more quickly. Battlefield promotions. We are in such a situation. Many men are away. Many English clergymen who might normally be among us are not. You are head and shoulders the most able of those serving here. You know the workings of the diocese and our cathedral intimately. Your judgment is sound. And we have the wonderful fact that you are now widely known and admired."

"Are you sure the older and deserving men would tolerate someone my age being appointed?"

"They would have to tolerate it if I make the selection. Besides, that is life, Peter. Even in the church, mediocrity is passed over. Think about it but keep it under your hat."

Why on earth would the dean tell him something so important, when the bishop had not died and might even recover? He got his answer almost immediately.

"I gather your trip to Ottawa was a great success, although it must have been very tiring. You look exhausted."

"I was on my way in to tell you."

"It so happens that I had a telephone call which suggests that it may have been a much greater success than you anticipated?" The dean looked sly.

"Who telephoned?"

"I was quite impressed. I'm not in the habit of receiving expensive trunk calls from Ottawa, at home, in the evening. The aide-de-camp, General Smithson. He told me he had offered you a post as private chaplain."

"I'm sorry you heard it from him. I was just coming to tell you."

"Well, I don't need to tell you that it is a wonderful chance. Wonderful. It could lead anywhere." Dean Creighton looked dreamily at the undamaged transept window. "It could lead back to England . . . the Mother Church." He paused and looked significantly at Peter. "But if you were to accept, Peter, it would obviously not be possible for me to make the appointment I have just described . . . if the need, God forbid, should arise."

"Yes, I see."

"I do not tell you this to put any pressure on you. Merely to point out the alternatives."

"Of course. I'm deeply grateful for the confidence, sir. Very grateful. I'll try to be worthy of it. I will think over what you said."

The dean rose.

"Let us pray that God's grace renders all our speculations pointless, and erases any traces of base ambition from our hearts."

"Amen," said Peter.

Holding the end of a pew for support, the older man lowered his gaitered knees to the floor, and Peter knelt beside him to pray.

Peter thought rapidly. You did not need to believe to advance in the church, only conform. The less he believed, the more they wanted to promote him.

Essentially Dean Creighton was telling him, Say no to the chaplaincy now if you want to be offered the deanship. But if he refused the governor general, and the bishop recovered, there would be no deanship to be offered. Or if the bishop did die, Creighton might not be elected. He was popular through the province but not loved, Peter knew, not loved as the bishop was. Some provincial rectors considered Creighton high-handed and socially condescending. They sensed his ambition.

The dean rose with cracking knees and left. Peter crossed to the center aisle and looked around at the great church that could be his. He did not genuflect before the high altar.

With the deanship went the huge deanery next door at no cost and double or triple—Peter was not quite sure—his present income. In George Tobin's surge of good will and anxiety for Margery, he now wanted to pay for two maids, the nursemaid already hired and a housemaid. The deanery would have plenty of room for them all. And the new Margery could preside over a handsome establishment.

·  ·  ·  ·

The new Margery excited Peter and dismayed him. She improved each day, discovering some zest for life. She made fewer notes, somehow finding ways to use her memory. She behaved correctly to the children, though she never mentioned them when they were not present and sometimes ignored them when they were.

"Mummy," Abigail said. "Mummy?"

Everyone else looked at Margery, who was bent over a collar she was sewing with tiny, elegant stitches.

"Mummy!"

"Margery, she's talking to you," Cynthia said.

"What?" Margery looked up with her charmingly bewildered smile. "Oh, I'm sorry. What is it, dear?"

She acted as though somewhere in the house she had a married sister who was the mother of Abigail and Michael. She had redefined motherhood on her own terms.

When the nursemaid asked, "What do you want Abigail to wear today?" Peter saw Margery look genuinely perplexed, as though she needed a moment to remember who Abigail was.

"I like the sweet little blue dress."

"It's in the wash. She wore it Saturday."

"Oh, then, anything that's clean."

She never asked the maid or her mother or Peter any questions about the children.

She was different. She shocked them by smoking a cigarette after dinner.

She was increasingly attentive to Peter, clever at finding moments alone with him, very demanding moments. She never raised her fear of becoming pregnant. It was Peter who began worrying about the safe time of the month.

"Shouldn't we be careful . . ."

Which Margery impetuously dismissed: "Oh, never mind that!"

The sudden quirks of her memory gave Peter real moments of fright; it was as though her mind had popped open and a strange bird had fluttered out.

A few days after his return Margery walked with him to the cathedral, holding his arm possessively. Out of nowhere she said, "I know who wrote the diary, Peter." She said it with a little laugh, like a thirteen-year-old with a secret. If she had turned her head, she would have been looking directly at Julia's house. As it was, their positions forced Peter to face it. He avoided doing so, with great strain. Did Margery know the house?

"Poor thing. She's been through so much. I might invite her to tea. Just for a chat."

It made him perspire and then shiver. She didn't mention it again, but remembering the remark later made Peter cold.

Margery must have read the diary very carefully. She never interrogated him directly about it, never launched into the recriminations he feared. But every now and then, some detail would fly out. She once whispered in the dark, "We could have a honeymoon. Daddy would send us to Bermuda. We could swim in the sea and walk on the beaches . . ."

Was she deliberately mocking him? He was sure she was not. Apparently her waking mind slipped momentarily into a dream, and in the dream she quoted the diary, without knowing that she did.

Each reference made his soul shrivel a little, but also excited him. In the years of their marriage he had secretly longed for a wife as passionate as this. Now he had such a wife, and her erratic memory found constant ways to remind him of the woman who had dismissed him with withering contempt.

"I'd love to take a cottage by the sea. We've never done that, darling. I love the perfume when the bayberry leaves brush my skirt. I love the sound of the foghorns at night."

In their lovemaking she moved her breast close to his lips. In the dark he put the nipple in his mouth.

STEWART had been collecting materials to send to Julia. In his neat academic handwriting—as meticulous as his other habits were not—he had conscientiously reported all of Cushing's information about Betty. And with Dr. Hart he had put together the records that could help to support a legal appeal for her cousin.

But the closing had given him trouble, and he had not sealed the bulky envelope. His letter was businesslike but his heart rebelled at signing it, indifferently, "Yours sincerely," or some conventional variation.

He did not want to be curt nor maudlin nor self-pitying. What could he say that left him some dignity?

On a separate piece of paper, in the same italic hand, he wrote:

On the very personal matter I raised—doubtless inappropriately —at the station, my feelings have not changed. If it should come about that you feel differently, please do not be too shy to tell me. It would make my life to hear it.

Yours,
Stewart

It increased his heart rate to write it, fold it with the other sheets, and seal it in the envelope. It was a big step. It answered his need to make one more gesture. If she did not respond, it would be final. He addressed the envelope.

Not since adolescence had he known anguish so concentrated and persistent.

In one mood it galled him that, with all his experience and all his supposed understanding of psychology, he could be tortured like this, put on the rack. In another mood he cursed himself for blurting everything out at the station, wrecking his chances. In another he forced himself to dismiss the pain of Julia by consigning her to a category: women with whom he had been unsuccessful. One lived and learned. There were more women to be met.

However desirable, Julia was just another woman. She was governed by the same biology and the same psychology tied to that biology. She ate, drank, slept, used the toilet, menstruated, bathed, dressed, undressed, brushed her hair like other women, and, no doubt, in the essentials made love like other women. Her body made new cells and sloughed off old ones. She consumed oxygen and expelled carbon dioxide. She trimmed her hair when it got too long and filed her fingernails. She had to cut her toenails. But there he paused—he could not visualize Julia sitting naked, like Anne-Lise, one foot on the other knee to cut her nails. Julia's aura demanded that he imagine a pose more refined.

Another letter had arrived from Christine Soames, excited and passionate. Her father had relented. With her mother's help he had been persuaded to let her return to Dalhousie when it reopened. She was overjoyed.

"Not seeing you is driving me crazy. I can't wait to be with you again. I know we'll have to be extra careful, but with your lovely big empty house, that should be easy."

A gust of Christine's uninhibited sensuality blew in with the letter and stirred him as if she had rung the doorbell and said, as she characteristically did, holding her arms wide open, "Here I am!"

If all he wanted was a beautiful and accommodating body, it was right there in the package called Christine. Hadn't he been telling himself for years it wasn't necessary to marry to possess a body? Julia's uniqueness was in the qualities of spirit and personality that caused this yearning—entirely new to him—and caused more pain than he had ever felt.

"I have fallen helplessly in love with you."

"Helplessly?" He tried to remember her smile as she said that: sweet? ironic? tenderly amused?

It was strange how things happened. If there had been no explosion, the diary would never have fallen into Peter's hands. And with no explosion, Stewart would not have met her. So the explosion threw them together and tore them apart. It created and it killed.

Knowing that he knew about the diary was too much for her to bear. He agreed with her. It was too much, a violation of trust before there was any trust.

Even if she had been nursing some affection for him, as he thought she had, it couldn't weather that discovery, not after the other shocks she had received. Why was he deceiving himself? It was hopeless to pursue it.

He tore open the envelope, removed the sheet with the personal note, and read it over. It would only cause her more pain and him more humiliation. Stewart tore up the note and was about to address a fresh envelope when the telephone rang.

It was the gruff nurse from the Nova Scotia Hospital. "Dr. Hattie thinks you should come over, if you can."

"What's happened?"

"He's moving his legs. Corporal Ransome is."

"No!"

Within a few minutes Stewart was driving to the Dartmouth ferry. Approaching the asylum, he felt none of the usual dread. Even the long corridor where he met Dr. Hattie seemed less grim.

"A young woman came yesterday to see him. From his home town. And this morning he's moving his legs. Just a little, mind you. The muscles are badly wasted, but he's moving them."

Stewart did not have to look at Ransome's spindly legs; the young soldier's broad face had come alive, as though the current had been turned back on. The other shell-shocked men glanced up incuriously and returned to their private torments.

Even Ransome's voice sounded stronger. "When I woke up this morning, I didn't think what I was doing. I just put my legs over and started to stand up but they wouldn't hold me. But I'd moved them without thinking about it."

"Let me see you do it," Stewart said.

Sitting on the edge of his bed, Ransome lifted each leg slowly onto the bed then back to the floor without using his hands. The nurse clapped, her plain face radiant. Ransome looked proud and shy. He reached to the floor for his crutches and hoisted himself up with his muscular arms. But instead of dragging his feet lifelessly as before, he swung his legs forward and put his weight on them for a second before leaning again on the crutches.

"If you can do that," Dr. Hattie said, "you can walk again. It will take a while to build up the muscles but there is no reason you can't walk."

"Or skate?" Stewart asked.

Ransome turned on the crutches to look hard at Stewart. "Can I talk to you for a minute?"

In the corridor Ransome swung his legs and crutches rhythmically to the empty office. This time he sat gratefully and accepted a cigarette.

"I wanted to tell you something."

"All right."

"Yvette Sullivan came to see me. Paul's sister from Chatham."

"I'm glad to hear it."

"She said you wrote to them."

"Yes, I did."

"She made me tell her everything about Paul."

There was a long silence in which Stewart could hear again Ransome describing Sullivan's execution and felt the horror return. Ransome drew on the cigarette, as usual holding it with thumb and forefinger, flicking the ash with the nail of the next finger. He appeared undecided whether to say more. He dragged on the cigarette again and exhaled. Then with the back of his other hand he wiped away the tears that had formed in his eyes.

"She wants us to get married." He covered his face with one hand and sobbed. Emotion gripped Stewart—relief, pleasure, confidence.

"That's wonderful, John. I am very glad. Congratulations."

Leaving the hospital, Stewart felt as he had after reuniting Betty with Mollie, the day he met Julia. He wanted to take deep breaths of fresh air, to feed his exhilarated blood.

He had left home after tearing up his note to Julia, resigned and pessimistic. He did not want to go back now; he wanted to celebrate. His hunch had been right. For the first time he had made someone better, and the feeling was dazzling. He had despaired of ever seeing the psychoanalytic approach work for him, assuming that he lacked the gifts to make it work, aware of how little he really knew. As he left, Dr. Hattie had said, "Obviously you have a talent for this. The young woman was the catalyst, but this is your success. You really should think seriously about psychoanalysis as a career."

Nothing in teaching or in academic psychology had ever given Stewart this thrill of accomplishment.

On South Park Street he passed the Tobins' house and thought of Margery. He had promised Dorothy Wentworth many weeks ago to go to see her. He drove around to Tower Road and stopped at Peter's house.

The pretty and confident woman who received him was in total contrast to the apathetic and wasted figure he had last seen on the street. She looked like the Margery who had fascinated Stewart as an adolescent, but with a new, polished glitter. Her eyelashes were mascaraed, her cheeks slightly rouged, and she was stylishly dressed.

"Stewart, how lovely to see you! Do come in. Will you have some sherry?" Her assurance reminded him of her mother. Margery offered him a cigarette and smoked one herself. How could this be the woman who had tried to kill herself less than two months ago?

"I've been meaning to come by for weeks to see how—"

"It's a shame Peter isn't home, but he may come."

"I haven't seen him since he went to Ottawa to get his medal." Margery smiled blankly.

"The Albert Medal for his bravery in the explosion."

"The explosion. Yes, I know." She laughed happily like a child who has remembered a lesson.

Stewart looked for signs of vulnerability, and felt a license to be direct.

"How are you really feeling, Margery?"

She smiled brightly, her dark eyes luminous again.

"Oh, I'm fine. I think I must have been worn out with everything." She put out her cigarette awkwardly, and, in the gesture, she became pathetic to him. He felt a sudden conviction that the person he was seeing—the woman, her clothes, the flesh inside them, her glossy dark hair, her perfect teeth—was instantly disposable. Weeks ago she had been a few seconds away from being thrown on the trash heap, like a doll whose stuffing had come out. Now she seemed to be two women at once: one pleased with herself, the other deeply anxious; the woman who has got what she wants, the other desolate about losing it all. He could see both in consecutive gestures. She lit a cigarette with stylish confidence; she put it out with clumsy notions.

"How are Abigail and Michael?"

She darted him a questioning look, glancing from the smoldering cigarette end she was pushing ineffectually around the ashtray. For a moment he thought she was going to ask, "Who?"

But she smiled. "We have a nursemaid now," as if that settled everything. She settled back into the sofa and raised the small sherry glass.

"Stewart, do you know Julia Robertson?"

The startling question hung in the air as they heard the front door open and shut. Peter came into the room. Margery jumped up enthusiastically and kissed him warmly on the cheek. She made a humming sound and smacked her lips. It was so intimate, Stewart felt uncomfortable and Peter blushed as he disengaged himself to shake hands, not cordially, with Stewart.

All his life Peter had known envy, and the need to repress it, often directed toward Stewart's wealth. But he had never felt sexual jealousy. However, at the sight of Margery sitting provocatively, even flirtatiously, with Stewart, the emotion washed over him. Images of Margery's new sexual appetite collided with memories of Stewart's adventures and made him furious.

Stewart realized it was Peter whom Margery had expected and had prettied up for. She plumped happily beside him on the sofa, saying, "Isn't it lovely to see Stewart after so long, darling? We're having a glass of sherry."

Peter glanced at the mantel clock. "But it's almost teatime."

"We can have some tea."

"No, I have to go back to my visiting. I just stopped for a moment."

"Who have you been visiting?"

Both Margery and Peter seemed to Stewart to be talking in code. Without waiting for an answer, she said, "Would you like some tea?"

Peter said impatiently, "No, I can't stay."

"Oh, you have time for a cup." She had her mother's urgent, seductive way of offering things.

"No, don't bother."

"It'll only take a minute." She sounded like a child. "I can get the girl to do it."

"Margery, I really meant no!"

She sat back hurt, as though she, not the tea, had been rejected.

Without curiosity, Peter asked Stewart, "How are things?"

Stewart said, "Well, as a matter of fact, I've just had a very happy development with one of the shell-shock victims. He's been paralyzed in the legs for more than a year—"

Margery interrupted in her newly forceful way. "I was asking Stewart whether he knows Julia Robertson."

The remark was like a gun going off in the room. Peter started and looked at Margery, then at Stewart.

"Well, you ought to know her. She's a very beautiful woman, isn't she, Peter? And now, poor thing, she's a widow."

"I will have a cup of tea," Peter said hastily, getting to his feet.

"There, you see?" Margery jumped up happily and went out.

The mention of Julia's name fed Peter's anger and terrified him. What if Margery blurted out something because she had no control of her tongue?

"Who's treating her now?" Stewart asked.

"What do you mean?"

"What doctor is looking after Margery?"

"A nerve specialist. A man Dr. Menzies works with."

"What kind of treatment?"

"Basically a rest cure to build her up. She'd lost a lot of weight."

"I really think you should do something more. To me she sounds disturbed. I think we should find someone who can help her."

"I don't want to talk about it. Her doctors and the Tobins think she's making very good progress."

"But they don't live with her. What do you think?"

"Every day she is a little more like her old self. Cheerful. Happy."

"That's hard to believe. How is she with the children?"

"Stewart, you are not a doctor. I don't want you meddling in this."

Margery came in with the tea tray. "What are you arguing about? Your voices were so loud it sounded like a fight. Stewart, milk or lemon?"

"Milk, please."

Margery presided at the tea table deftly and elegantly, but her thin fingers gripped the delicate china of her saucer and cup handle so tightly, Stewart thought that the porcelain or Margery herself might shatter at any second. The more sprightly her conversation sounded, the more fragile, the more disposable she seemed. Holding their anger, both men stared at her as at a performer who might fall. To cover the silence, Stewart said, "I was going to tell you about the case I've been working on. A man who witnessed the execution of his closest friend, a man shot for desertion, and the shock of seeing that . . ."

Margery wasn't listening. She was looking at Peter, occasionally glancing politely at Stewart. When she put her cup down, her hand strayed to Peter's.

When Stewart finished Ransome's story, Peter and Margery murmured sympathetically, but Margery again touched Peter's hand and said to Stewart, "Peter has been working so hard I would love to see him go on a trip. We could go to Bermuda. My parents took me there once. I'd love to walk barefoot on the sand and feel the water so warm . . ."

Peter and Stewart exchanged a look, each knowing the other recognized the quotation. Horror rose in Stewart.

"No matter how hard you try, there's always a little sand in the foot of the bed . . ."

"Margery, shut up!" Peter exploded.

She fell back at the violence of his voice.

He shouted, "Don't talk such nonsense!"

She quailed against the back of the sofa.

"Peter, leave her alone!" Stewart commanded. "Leave her alone!"

Peter got up. "What do you mean, telling me what to do in my own house?"

Stewart stood, conspicuously taller and larger than Peter.

"You can't treat her like that. It's inhumane. She's disturbed."

"This is none of your business."

Margery shrank back further at the sight of the two men, who appeared about to come to blows.

"Don't! Don't!" she cried.

"Margery, go upstairs!" Peter barked.

"No. You'll hurt each other," she whimpered.

"Go upstairs!"

"Leave her alone, Peter."

Peter pushed Stewart's shoulder roughly to move him back. For the first time in his life Stewart felt an overwhelming desire to hit Peter and a similarly strong urge to put his arms around the whimpering Margery. He stopped, breathing heavily, looking at Peter's glittering eyes and compressed lips.

"Margery, I hope to see you soon." Stewart leaned over and patted her trembling shoulder. At the door he turned to Peter. "I'll write you what I think. If you won't listen to me, perhaps others will, like the Tobins or the dean. Goodbye, Margery."

He walked out carrying his coat. In the car he sat for a moment, feeling the anger pulsing in him. It took a few minutes to drive home and go straight to his desk to write the letter. But there was his unmailed letter to Julia. He could feel his heart still beating rapidly. He reached into the wastepaper basket and found the note he had torn up. He pieced it together and read it again, this time full of confidence, not pessimism.

On the very personal matter I raised—doubtless inappropriately —at the station, my feelings have not changed. If it should come about that you feel differently, please do not be too shy to tell me. It would make my life to hear it.

He took a fresh sheet of paper, uncapped his pen, and wrote it out afresh. Then he folded it, sealed the envelope, and walked to the postbox on the corner.

Writing so boldly to Julia felt like a victory over Peter.

In the middle of the night Peter awoke from a deep sleep with a feeling of spiritual ease, like someone coming out of a fever.

Then he remembered the afternoon scene, the squalid brawl with Stewart; the evening spent calming Margery's hysteria, his own anger finally dissolving in her passionate embrace.

It could not go on like this. Stewart was right, and Peter knew he had been resisting the truth. Margery needed something different from the traditional rest cure. He would have to go back to Stewart, re-establish their old friendship, admit that he, not Stewart, was now the one in need.

His mind was clear. Since the first shivering moments on the train, he had noticed a growing sense of relief. The need to earn God's notice was gone.

The very disciplines he had practiced to be worthy of God's attention had created an object for his own attention. The more he tried to please God, the more he assumed God was there to be pleased. The effort to find God *was* God. What he had been praying to was his own effort.

Peter had always known what he meant. In his life, as in the catechism, the questions came with certain answers. He was not used to analytical thinking; normally it confused and upset him; but on this night of clear thinking the revelations unfolded effortlessly.

He had misled many people.

He had behaved cruelly to Margery.

He had behaved stupidly to Stewart.

He had behaved unconscionably to Julia.

Of course she had invited him into her compartment and she could not control herself. But that didn't excuse him.

Reading her diary had cast a spell on him, as on a character in a fairy story, broken only when the right magic happened, when he humiliated himself and confessed his faults; moments when his own will was paralyzed or another will governed him.

*It is the same soul that wills both and wills neither,* Augustine said.

He also saw Augustine more clearly, the garment of flesh he put off with such agony. To become closer to God, many had tried literally and hideously to remove it, flagellating, mortifying their flesh. Others had simply renounced it—the Roman Church still demanded it—as Peter himself had done before marriage. Naïvely. It had neither purified him nor brought him closer to God, only deceived him.

How medieval that was; how unnatural; how unnecessary. The

garment of flesh is the garment Man cannot put off, and attempting to do so does not banish lust, pride, envy, or anything else.

Why should Margery's new appetites disturb him when they were no different from his own? Allowing himself to admit that allowed him to admit that it thrilled him too.

Sooner or later he would meet Julia. Although she would never come to the cathedral, he might run into her on the street. But the spell had been broken. It was Margery he loved, and pitied, and wanted. Feeling her warmth and hearing her contented breathing beside him filled his heart with sweetness.

There were others he should be truthful with, like the dean. He had tried when the sergeant's story first appeared, but his protestations had been brushed aside as excessive modesty. The dean was so worldly that the truth might interfere with his plans for Peter. Those plans required that he be the winner of the Albert Medal, widely admired and above reproach.

But he could not accept a major promotion in the church on such false pretences. By accepting the dean's plan or the governor general's, he would be founding the rest of his life on a lie.

It was strange, but now he could see it quite clearly: having been released from the burden of behaving for God, he saw all moral choices more plainly.

He had to tell someone in authority in the church. If the dean's motives disqualified him, he should see the bishop. The old gentleman had asked him to call, and the dean said the bishop's health had improved. That was it: in the morning he would call on the bishop.

Was the church still a profession for him? Perhaps not. But this new way of seeing things might make him a better priest than before, so preoccupied had he been in reaching for his own glimpse of God, his own epiphany. There were many things to think about in that light: the sermons he would have to compose, all the public prayers, the passages from the prayer book, the basic matters of faith, the promise of life everlasting, the question of sin. But he was filled with confidence that he could deal honestly with himself, as he could deal honestly with Margery.

Peter drifted back to sleep.

He was awakened in daylight by the telephone ringing downstairs. Dean Creighton spoke in his churchman's voice well-tuned with grief. "Peter, the Lord has taken our good friend to his bosom. The bishop died peacefully during the night. His housekeeper found him this morning."

When he hung up, Peter found himself weeping.

JULIA WANTED TO HIDE. Across Victoria Park, through her front windows, the Cathedral of All Saints menaced her. To shut it out, she drew the yellow curtains over the newly glazed panes.

Her wedding photograph and Charles's portrait restored to its frame reproached her. She could not cover them or remove them, but she avoided looking at them.

She was appalled and humiliated by her own behavior, feeling sullied and angry at once, violated and disgusted with herself. She felt sickened by the knowledge that would not leave her. She bathed and changed her clothes frequently, but her mood did not change.

Her clothes carried accusing associations from events where they had been worn. The black dress offended her because of the train and Peter. She tried to push that memory out of her thoughts but it sidled back in, arousing disgust and shame. She could see where the lace at the neck had been torn away and sewn back that night. Her stitches, neat but different from the original sewing, forced her to remember why it had been torn, how she had thrown herself at him, begged him to go on when he began his sickening confession. She hid the black dress at the back of her cupboard, out of sight. In reaching back she saw the taffeta evening dress and buried that too. The act of hiding the clothes made her even more conscious of the messages they gave her. She was tempted to take them to the furnace and burn them, but said crossly to herself, "Now you are really becoming foolish!"

She telephoned Lucy and Mrs. Robertson to say that she did not feel like calling.

After five days, Mollie returned, having left Betty with her sister. She found Julia pale and thin, living on cups of tea.

"I know you're sad, dear, but it won't get better making yourself sick, too." She went shopping for groceries and made Julia eat.

Still she huddled at home, hiding in her bedroom, afraid if she went out she would run into Peter or Stewart.

About a week later, Stewart's letter arrived with its renewed declaration, provoking a surge of new feelings. He had gone to enormous trouble, collecting all the material for Jeffrey and the information about Betty. She felt guilty that he had been put to such effort.

She knew now how much she had invested in Stewart. The idea had been building unconsciously that he would bring her relief and comfort. He was taking care of Betty. He would take care of Jeffrey. Back in Halifax with him, everything would be all right.

It was such a strange, bewildering night, waiting in the station after getting his telegram. She had gone there telling herself it was something to do with Betty. Perhaps she had actually gone to purify herself, although that sounded odd. She had to see his face after the incident with Peter. One of the first things she had thought on the train was how she would face Stewart MacPherson.

She hadn't wanted to leave the station. Her feet were cold from the drafts on the floor and her back was numb from the hard bench, but she didn't want to suggest they go. Sitting beside him, she remembered how she felt when he first came to the house to bring Betty; the comfort of being with him, of wanting to curl up at the end of a deep sofa on a rainy afternoon and talk with him.

The last thing in the world she expected was to be told he loved her and wanted to marry her. That unnerved her, but the shock that followed—his knowledge of the diary—was more than she could stand. All the nice feelings about Stewart were blown away. She felt as though she might be sick right there.

He knew all that she had written about Jeffrey. Julia's mind pictured the scenes she had described—she could not remember how explicitly—in the diary.

Perhaps this was making her unbalanced. She couldn't cower in this house like a madwoman. But she had to think.

It had started with Jeffrey. She had known it when she saw him in that sour-smelling room, thin and trembling—and weeping. She couldn't look at him without thinking that she had once held him close, and now the idea revolted her. Yet when he had come here to stay on his way overseas she remembered enough to have a little thrill that he might come creeping into her room—even though she didn't want him to. She had written that in the diary, and now Stewart knew. And Peter Wentworth knew! But that was some-thing else. Julia didn't care what he knew now. But it really hurt her that Stewart knew. He must think that she was awful, a woman with gross appetites. It is what she had often asked herself.

Did she have that in her from birth, from childhood? Is that why she had been willing to let Jeffrey touch her? She could have said no, I don't want to. But she did want to. She wanted to leap off the beam, and that started it.

And Charles. That was a leap into the unknown. It was hot and boring in Montreal that fall. Anything would have been boring after Paris, but there was nothing for her to do but come back. The men she had been friendly with there all made her uneasy, wary of becoming too involved. That was why they stayed in a large group, always in the cafés together, buying coffees for the interesting, talented men who never had any money. When she came back, she felt suffocated. No one to talk to. And the things she wanted to say all sounded affected even to her ears—when I was in Paris; when I was studying art in Paris—so she stopped.

I wanted to do something interesting with my life, she thought, and then, there was Charles!

Julia got up from the bed and went downstairs to the drawing room. She had been trying not to look at Charles's picture. She carried it and the wedding picture up to the bedroom and put them in the daylight by the window. Then she sat and stared at them both.

He looked young in both photographs. She remembered precisely the quality that had attracted her. It was just what had later given her so much anxiety: the idea that he was holding so much of himself back. It had made her sure that there were fascinating things to discover about him. She talked about Paris and he talked about sailing and they fascinated each other by listening—but by listening to each other or to themselves? Each had wanted to share the other's life.

It was impetuous to fall in love with him so quickly, but it was not a mistake. Neville Boiscoyne and Peter Wentworth were mistakes—men who exerted that magnetic pull on her body, and whom she did not really like. How could that be? Why had she been willing to abandon herself physically to men whose personalities she disliked? Or was that part of the attraction? No, she disliked them because they made her feel powerless to control herself, weak in their presence.

That was not how she felt about Stewart MacPherson. He was attractive; his hair was rich and his eyes were extraordinarily kind. But she did not think just about his body. He made her think of comfort, of pleasant conversations that would go on and on. Like the conversations in Paris, from one idea to another, with a lot of laughter.

She got up and went downstairs again, to the small sitting room where the Matisse was. Of all the people who had seen it, only Stewart liked it. It was deeply personal to Julia. The strange magenta and cool greens lifted her spirits. The painting had exuberance and humor and a sense of the sadness and sweetness of life; yet it was bold and racy, and spoke of absolute sureness.

Of course now Stewart knew all about her physical yearnings. And he could not be indifferent. Lucy had said with a nervous laugh that he had known some very "unsuitable" women. If he was so—well—experienced, would her diary have shocked him? What he thought mattered more to her than what Peter Wentworth thought, yet in an odd way Stewart's reaction gave her more anxiety and less.

The doorbell had not rung for weeks, and its sound startled her.

"Special delivery. Will you sign for it, please?"

Julia knew what the package was from its size. She had been expecting it. An official had called to offer a little ceremony of presentation, but she had asked that it be sent to her. There were many layers of wrapping. Finally there was a flat, velvet-covered box and, inside, the Victoria Cross.

It was curiously ugly, not a glittering star or a dazzling medallion, but a blunt Maltese cross in dull bronze, suspended from a plain crimson ribbon. Awkwardly, in the middle of the cross, a lion stood on a crown above the words "For Valour." You could even call it homely.

She stared at it a long time, expecting it to cause a rush of emotions. But no waves of grief broke over her. The sight of the medal prompted only a faint revulsion, then generosity. She wanted to give it to Archie Robertson—and quickly. She did not want to touch it and held it only by the case. She wanted to give it to Archie untouched by her. She would walk down to the Robertsons'. The decision made her feel energetic. It would do her good to get out. And it would give Archie a lot of pleasure. She closed the velvet box.

A sense of something not completed took her back into the sitting room where she had been looking at the Matisse, as though it held the secret to her happiness. She wanted her life to reflect the understanding the painting showed.

Stewart fitted into the mood of the painting; that was what she had been telling herself. He had that kind of understanding of life, not that he was an artist, but he looked at life with Matisse's tolerance and intelligence—and affection.

She thought about Stewart while she was dressing to go out. As always, actually doing something made her happier.

There was another difference between Stewart's knowing about the diary and Peter's knowing. Peter had not meant to tell her. It had slipped out. He would have gone on pretending with her. Stewart had come out with it himself. Right away. He had talked about Kitty and Levin's diary so as to be completely honest. She had to admit there was something admirable in that. He had not been forced to tell her; he could have kept quiet. But his conscience made him honest.

To be as honest as he had been with her, she would have to tell him about Peter. And that was out of the question: to admit she had permitted herself to be seduced on a train by a clergyman, or nearly seduced, by his close friend, or former friend, or whatever he was? Not only permitted herself but, to be honest, had actively encouraged him. She would die of shame to tell him that. She was ashamed enough to have him know what he already knew from the diary.

No, she had just been thinking that through again. She was not sure she was ashamed that he knew. He probably understood. And it was honest. It was presenting herself at her most honest. And that is what he had wanted to do at the station, to present himself most honestly. Of course it was not his own deeds he was confessing, only that he knew about hers.

She put on the hat that went with her navy blue dress. She couldn't wear black anymore, even to take Charles's medal to his parents.

Downstairs she hesitated before putting on her coat. A new thought almost took her breath away. How obvious it was, and yet she had not seen it! By telling her he was in love with her and asking her to marry him and then saying he had read the diary, Stewart was letting her know that there was nothing in the diary for her to be ashamed of. He had read it all, all the things she thought embarrassing, and they didn't disturb him. But she would not have known that if he had not forced himself to be honest.

It made her want to sit down in the chair facing the Matisse. She had been stupid not to understand what he meant; to go on agonizing over the embarrassment when, in effect, he had said, Don't worry about it. I love you. I want to marry you.

Her pulse quickened. What had he been thinking since that last meeting at the station? She had rushed out rudely, angrily. Yet quite patiently he had fulfilled what he promised, had painstakingly gathered the legal information for Jeffrey. Then, after all those professorial pages, his short, intense note:

*My feelings have not changed . . .*

What had it cost him to make the declaration and be brutally rejected? He said he had decided not to, because it was too soon. Well, it was too soon. But could she have the courage to be as honest with him? At the very least she owed him an apology.

*If it should come about that you feel differently . . .*

Julia looked at the Matisse. She thought she could see all the years ahead of her.

I want to do something interesting with my life.

*Please do not be too shy to tell me . . .*

She got up and took off her hat. She was trembling. She took a deep breath to calm herself, then picked up the telephone receiver.

"Operator, I don't know the number for MacPherson on Victoria Road. Stewart MacPherson. Can you connect me?"

# A Note on Fact and Fiction

Although this is a work of fiction, the description of the Halifax explosion is historically accurate, or as accurate as I could make it.

My original sources were my mother, Peggy Oxner, her brother, Breck, and my grandparents, Warren and Daisy Oxner, who lived through the explosion and told me about it when I was a child in Halifax. My interest was quickened by Hugh McLennan's *Barometer Rising,* the first Canadian novel I remember reading.

For factual accounts, I have used Michael Bird's *The Town That Died* (McGraw-Hill Ryerson, 1962); *The Halifax Explosion, December 6, 1917,* edited by Graham Metson (McGraw-Hill Ryerson, 1978); Samuel Henry Prince's *Catastrophe and Social Change* (Columbia University, 1920); and Mary Ann Monnon's *Miracles and Mysteries* (Lancelot Press, 1977). Alan Ruffman's three broadcasts on CBHT, Halifax, *The Halifax Explosion: Realities and Myths,* provided interesting new information.

For further research in specific areas, I have had invaluable assistance from the National Archives of Canada; the Public Archives of Nova Scotia; the Public Relations Office of Dalhousie University; the University of King's College Library; the Clarke Institute of Psychiatry in Toronto; the University of Toronto Medical Library; the National Institute of Diabetes and Digestive and Kidney Diseases, Bethesda, Maryland; Columbia University Library; the Oskar Diethelm Historical Library of Cornell University Medical College; and the New York Public Library.

Several real people are mentioned in my story: the Prime Minister, Sir Robert L. Borden; the Governor General, the Duke of Devonshire, and the Duchess; the Canadian Minister in London, Sir George Perley; the Commander in Chief, British forces, Field Marshal Sir Douglas Haig; the psychiatrist Dr. Ernest Jones; the neurosurgeon Dr. Harvey Cushing; and the painter James Wilson Morrice. However, everything they say or think in this novel is imagined, as are all the other characters.

## About the Author

Robert MacNeil is the co-anchor of the award-winning "Mac-Neil/Lehrer NewsHour," broadcast nightly on PBS. Born in Montreal, Mr. MacNeil began his journalism career with Reuters in London and subsequently worked for NBC News and the British Broadcasting Corporation. He is the author or co-author of five previous books, including, with Robert McCrum and William Cran, *The Story of English,* the companion volume to the PBS series of which Mr. MacNeil was host; and two volumes of memoirs, *The Right Place at the Right Time* and *Wordstruck.* With *Burden of Desire* Mr. MacNeil makes his debut as a novelist. He is currently at work on a nonfiction book about the Canadian people.

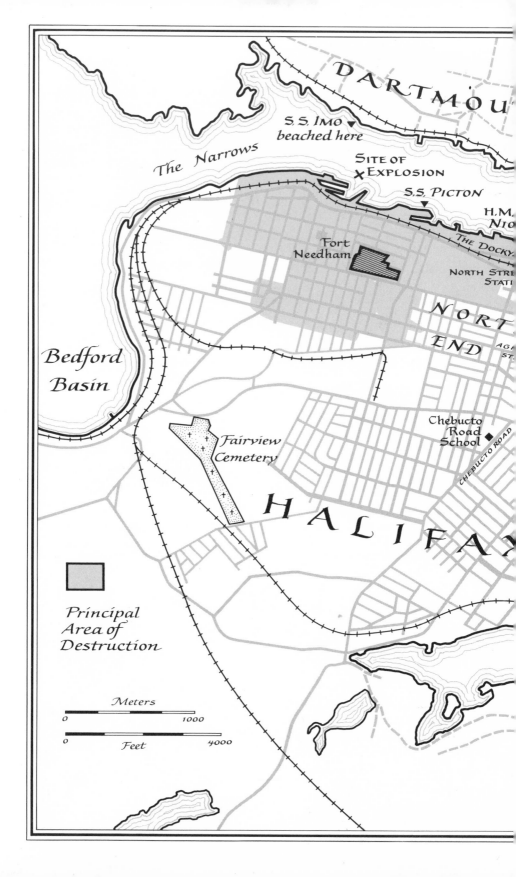

DARTMOU...

S. S. IMO ▼
*beached here*

SITE OF
✗ EXPLOSION

S.S. PICTON ▼

H.M.
NIO

*The Narrows*

THE DOCKY...

Fort
Needham

NORTH STRE
STATI

NOR...

END

AG...
ST...

*Bedford
Basin*

Chebucto
Road
School ◆

CHEBUCTO ROAD

Fairview
Cemetery

HALIFA...

■

Principal
Area of
Destruction

Meters

0          1000

0          4000

Feet